"There's a feisty new amateur sleuth in town and her name is Jenna Hart. With a bodacious cast of characters, a wrenching murder, and a collection of cookbooks to die for, Daryl Wood Gerber's *Final Sentence* was a page-turning puzzler of a mystery that I could not put down."

—Jenn McKinlay, *New York Times* bestselling author of the Cupcake Bakery Mysteries

A crime hiding in the sand . . .

When I neared within a few feet, I gasped. It was the figure of a naked woman—no, a mermaid—face turned sideways, a sandy hook coming out of her mouth, a clump of seaweed for her hair, and a drizzling of sand for her fingers. Care had been taken, each curve honed.

I started to giggle nervously. The mermaid reminded me of the painted woman in the movie *Goldfinger*. She looked so beautiful . . . so serene . . . so still.

I glanced around. Was the artist nearby, recording on video how people reacted as they passed? Would the treasure-seeking couple rat me out if I touched the mermaid's tail fin with my toe? Tough. I had to. Curiosity bubbled to boiling point.

I stretched out my foot and tapped the far end of the sculpture. It didn't crumble as expected. It resisted. Sand fell away and a flesh-colored toe emerged. Human.

A shriek gushed out of my mouth.

Final Sentence

Sentence

DARYL WOOD GERBER

BERKLEY PRIME CRIME, NEW YORK

THE BERKLEY PUBLISHING GROUP
Published by the Penguin Group
Penguin Group (USA) Inc.
375 Hudson Street, New York, New York 10014, USA

USA | Canada | UK | Ireland | Australia | New Zealand | India | South Africa | China

Penguin Books Ltd., Registered Offices: 80 Strand, London WC2R 0RL, England
For more information about the Penguin Group, visit penguin.com.

FINAL SENTENCE

A Berkley Prime Crime Book / published by arrangement with the author

Berkley Prime Crime Books are published by The Berkley Publishing Group.
BERKLEY® PRIME CRIME and the PRIME CRIME logo are
trademarks of Penguin Group (USA) Inc.

For information, address: The Berkley Publishing Group,
a division of Penguin Group (USA) Inc.,
375 Hudson Street, New York, New York 10014.

ISBN: 978-0-425-25804-0

PUBLISHING HISTORY
Berkley Prime Crime mass-market edition / July 2013

PRINTED IN THE UNITED STATES OF AMERICA

10 9 8 7 6 5 4 3 2 1

Cover illustration by Teresa Fasolino.
Cover design by Jason Gill.
Interior text design by Kelly Lipovich.

ALWAYS LEARNING   PEARSON

To my husband, the love of my life.
You make every day a delicious adventure.

Acknowledgments

Seek the lofty by reading, hearing, and seeing great work at some moment every day.

—Thornton Wilder

There are so many who have helped me along the way—family, friends, teachers, librarians, and more.

First and foremost, thank you to my family for loving me and not twirling your finger alongside your head when you think I'm nuts. That would be so embarrassing. Thank you to my dearest friend, Jori Mangers, for being there for me for so many years. Thank you to my first readers. Thank you to author pals Krista Davis, Janet Bolin, Kate Carlisle, and Hannah Dennison. I know you struggle through the same author's angst that I do; your feedback is invaluable. Thanks to my brainstormers at Plothatchers. Thanks to my blog mates on Mystery Lovers Kitchen and Killer Characters. And thanks to the Sisters in Crime Guppies, a superb online group.

Thanks to those who have helped make the Cookbook Nook Mysteries a reality: my fabulous editor, Kate Seaver; Katherine Pelz; Joan Matthews; and Kayleigh Clark. I appreciate all your insight and enthusiasm. To my artist, Teresa Fasolino, wow. Once again, you have amazed me. Thank you to my publisher, Berkley Prime Crime, for granting me the opportunity to write about this whole new world of characters. I am so blessed.

Thank you, librarians, teachers, fans, and/or readers for sharing the world of a cookbook shop owner with your friends. Thank you to my business team. You know who you are!

And last but not least, thanks to my cookbook shop consultant, a cookbook store owner herself, Christine Myskowski. I will never forget that first moment I walked into Salt and Pepper in Occoquan, Virginia, and felt like I was *home*.

Chapter 1

"**A**UNT VERA, STOP twirling me," I yelled.
   But she didn't. She continued to spin me in a circle.
My eyes pinballed in my head. My braids whipped my
cheeks—right, left, right, left. I didn't ordinarily wear
braids, but cleaning up a shop that closed thirty years ago,
over a year before my birth, was almost as dirty a business
as having a garage sale. I had dressed for the occasion:
cutoffs and T-shirt, so I wasn't worried about my clothes.

   "Stop," I repeated.

   My aunt cackled with glee. "Jenna Starrett Hart, I am so
excited."

   Because I had established myself in the advertising world
as Jenna Hart, I had used my maiden name even after my
husband and I got married. I decided not to change it to his,
which was Harris. Hart . . . Harris. They were too close to
mess with.

   "So excited," she repeated.

   No kidding. The striped walls of the bookshop blurred
together; I felt trapped in a kaleidoscope. Chipped walls
painted baby blue, olive green, and a weird fleshy pink color

flashed around me. Normally, I liked twirling and dancing. I adored music—rock and roll, country, and big Hollywood musical classics. My mother used to play the radio full blast when she drove me to art classes, and we would sing and car-dance to our hearts' content. But I had returned to my childhood town of Crystal Cove less than an hour ago, and I hadn't found my sea legs yet. Warmer than normal August temperatures weren't helping my equilibrium.

"Too-ra-loo," my aunt sang merrily. Her turban flopped to and fro. Copious strands of beads clacked against her phoenix amulet. Her royal blue caftan flared out around her large frame. "I have such a good feeling about our new venture. Sing with me. Too-ra-loo."

"Too-ra-loo," I croaked as I tried to slow her down by skidding on my heels. Three-dollar flip-flops didn't win the prize for gaining traction. Why couldn't I be a tennis shoe person? Except when exercising, I never wore them. "I'm feeling seasick." The breakfast burrito that I had wolfed down on the short drive south from San Francisco was rebelling.

"Oh, my, you do look a little pookie." Without warning, Aunt Vera released me.

Like a top, I gyrated out of control and landed chest-first against the shop's ancient oak sales counter. Air spewed out of me. My butter yellow T-shirt inched up over my low-slung cutoffs. I wriggled the T-shirt down and checked my body for broken bones—none as far as I could tell, but my abdominals would ache for days.

Aunt Vera clapped. She wasn't a sadist; she was ecstatic. "I'm so glad you said yes."

Yes, to moving back to Crystal Cove. Yes, to moving into the cottage beside her seaside home. Yes, to helping her revitalize the aging cookbook shop that resided in the quaint Crystal Cove Fisherman's Village.

"Now"—she pushed a plate of oatmeal caramel cookies that sat on the counter toward me, nabbing one for herself—"let's discuss you." Aunt Vera had no children; she had *adopted* me, by default. She nibbled and assessed all five feet, eight inches of me. "Cookie?"

How could I resist? My aunt excelled as a baker. She had perhaps the largest collection of cookie cookbooks I had ever seen. A favorite I loved to browse was *One Girl Cookies*. The history of the beloved Brooklyn bakery enthralled me, and the pictures were luscious. I popped a bite-sized cookie into my mouth—the caramel chips added just the right amount of yum—and I brushed what had to be an inch of store dust off my nose. After swallowing, I said, "You meant, let's discuss my vision, didn't you?"

Aunt Vera clucked her tongue, which sent apprehension zinging through me. A week ago, I had sent her a business plan that she had gushed over. Was she changing her mind? Granted, I was not a cook. Far from it. But I was not inept in the kitchen . . . exactly. I wasn't afraid to boil water. I knew how to make the basics: Jell-O, meatloaf, a cake from a mix. I could read a recipe, and I appreciated the nuances, but my talent ended there. On the plus side, I enjoyed an educated palate. I had tasted everything from fried alligator to raw eel, and I had savored many bottles of fine wine. Perhaps a few too many. Could my blithely carefree aunt finally see my shortcomings? Was she having doubts about me?

"Aunt Vera, speak."

She arched a dyed red eyebrow.

"What are you sensing?" I said. "Disaster?"

Aunt Vera spent her days giving psychic readings, hence the turban and caftan getup, not that she could tell people much more about their futures than I could; she didn't have a direct connect to the other world—no ghosts pals, no spirit guides. On the other hand, the way she looked at me gave me the creeps.

"Aunt Vera, c'mon. What's wrong?"

"Nothing's wrong."

"You're frowning."

"So are you. It's the dust. Be gone!" She swatted the air. To my surprise, she didn't add: *Bibbidi-bobbidi-boo,* like Cinderella's fairy godmother. I remembered prom night when she had surprised my date and me by arriving with a horse-drawn carriage. She swore she'd conjured the rig out of mice and a pumpkin.

"Truth, how do you feel about my vision for the shop?" I said.

"It's brilliant. You're a wizard. Problem solved."

Phew. Prior to returning to Crystal Cove, I had worked in advertising. Therein lay my talent. Art, conceptualizing, and glib wording. The dancing, singing popcorn campaign for Poppity Pop? Mine. Little bursts of sunshine doing cart-wheels above an orange grove to promote the citrus indus-try? Mine.

"But I didn't say, let's discuss your vision," Aunt Vera went on. "I said, let's discuss *you*. You weren't thriving in . . ." Her cherub face flushed radish-red. She wasn't the kind of person to say anything without enhancing the state-ment with optimism, but words had escaped her lips, so she finished, "In the City."

The City, San Francisco, the gem of the West. A city filled with life and laughter and high times. Super if you're single. Great if you're married. Not cool if you're a widow.

Aunt Vera petted my dusty cheek. "How are you?"

"Fine. Dandy. Ready to thrive." Choosing action over pondering life's losses, I smacked my hands together and said, "I see you have everything we need to start painting."

"I followed your list to the letter." Aunt Vera may have been the owner of Fisherman's Village, but she made me the manager of the cookbook store. Pushing sixty-five, she didn't want the added burden. "And surprise, surprise"—she twirled a finger at me—"your father is coming to help."

I gulped. *Put the past behind, behind, behind.* "How is Dad?"

Aunt Vera sidled behind the cash register, an antique National with honeysuckle inlay, and pushed the buttons like a little kid on an elevator. *Ping, ping, ping.* She slammed the drawer between each ping.

I raced to her and gripped her wrists. "Stop."

"It's sticking."

"We'll fix it." I should have purchased a new digital register, but the antique one looked handsome on the sales counter. I repeated, "How is Dad?"

"Your father? He's great. Wonderful. He's in need of a new project."

A little over two years ago—in March, to be exact—my mother and my husband died . . . within days of each other. My husband first. My mother next. She, who was never a smoker but perished from lung cancer, had been the gem and light of my youth. I attended her funeral, but I had to leave the next day to return to San Francisco so I could deal with the details of my husband's premature demise. I know, I know. I was a horrible, neglectful daughter, and I owed my father better. My pragmatic sister, who lived in Los Angeles, was a saint and stood by Dad's side. Even my hippie-dippie brother was on hand for Dad more than I was. Since the funerals, Dad and I had spoken a couple of times, but never with the same warmth. Currently, I was off all antidepressants—for three months I had taken the herbal kinds with Latin names I couldn't pronounce; I stopped when I decided life, even alone, was still worth living—but I still hadn't found my true smile. I came home to Crystal Cove to see if it was hiding there.

"You look worried, dear. Please don't be. He's not coming until the day before we're set to open. Besides, forgive and forget, that's your father's motto."

Since when? I wondered.

"He's in good shape. When he's not running his hardware store or offering his services as a handyman, he's busy with a food collection project. But he'll need a new project soon, ergo, The Cookbook Nook."

Ergo, me. Dad's career as an FBI analyst hadn't padded the coffers; his post-retirement work as an FBI consultant had. However, ten years into his retirement stint, he grew bored with consulting, and in addition to buying Nuts and Bolts, which the previous owner sold for a song, he devoted himself to all sorts of humanitarian projects. A man of his vim and vigor needed to keep busy.

"His hair isn't as black as yours any longer," my aunt went on, "but he's still got the Hart bright eyes and the Hart wit. He's standing tall, shoulders back. No osteoporosis for him, no sir." She demonstrated and saluted.

Was I slumping? Why was I reading hidden meaning into everything she said? Because I lacked vim and vigor, that's why. I straightened my spine.

"There are quite a few women in town who wish to attract my little brother's eye," Aunt Vera said, beaming like an older sister should. "But it's way too early for that. He was devoted to your mother."

Theirs had been a love that had set the standard.

"By the by, your father adores your suggestions for the shop's design."

"He does?" That surprised me. Dad always offered pointers. I had settled on a sunset-colored theme of coral and aqua. Aunt Vera suggested we add pale cream seashells. She had already sketched them on the walls. The café that connected at an angle to the shop would be painted a soft peach. I chose a border of pastel boats for the upper rim of the café; it would give just enough splash without being garish.

"Did I tell you your father walks every morning?" Aunt Vera said. "Same as you."

"I run occasionally, too. And ride the bicycle." The bike I rode, an old relic with a basket and hand bell, had belonged to my mother. In the City, I trekked from my apartment to Golden Gate Park. A challenge but worth it. "Say, you should stroll on the beach with me." The ocean was a stone's throw from Aunt Vera's back porch.

"Oh, my, no. Exercise and I don't mix." My aunt swirled her spacious caftan. "It messes up my chakras."

I grinned. "Let's get to work."

We swept and vacuumed the floors, counters, and shelves, and we dusted and stacked the old cookbooks in boxes. Many of the once-beautiful cookbooks could be salvaged, but in my business model, I planned to have lots of fresh new titles. Ours would not be a store where only your mother's *Betty Crocker Cookbook* would be sold, though we had plenty on hand. We would also sell books by Ina Garten, José Andrés, and Bobby Flay. I wanted cookbooks that featured recipes that sounded exotic or fun: grilled corn poblano salad with chipotle vinaigrette, *tournedos à la béarnaise*, beer and bison burgers with pub cheese, brandy black bottom chiffon pie. We would also stock specialty books that dealt with allergies, food restrictions, and sustainability gardening. I had picked up a few rare books, including an original copy of *The Physiology of Taste* by Brillat-Savarin, the famous cheese maker, and a first edition of *The Joy of Cooking* by Irma S. Rombauer. The bindings for both were in perfect condition. Dreaming big, bigger, biggest, I intended to feature celebrity chefs as well as local and celebrity cookbook authors. We would have food tastings in the café and perhaps throw a cookout for the town and sit-down dinners for food critics. A few weeks ago, before moving to town, I started generating buzz about The Cookbook Nook. I created a web page. I posted on social networking sites. As I had hoped, locals and tourists were chatting on blogs about The Cookbook Nook.

Aunt Vera said, "I want our little venture to be such a success."

"I know you do." I laid out tarps and opened cans of paints. "Tell me something."

"Uh-oh." She wagged a finger. "Do not glower at me like your father does. What do you want to know?"

"What's the history of this place?" Once before, I had broached the subject with my mother, but in a matter of seconds, she had snapped the lid closed on that line of query saying: *It's your aunt's private business.* "I know you purchased Fisherman's Village in the seventies." The L-shaped two-story village, with its elegant columns, white balustrades, boardwalk-style walkways, and brick parking lot had to have cost a pretty penny.

Aunt Vera pressed her lips together.

"I heard a rumor that you bought it so you could specifically own The Cookbook Nook and café. If so, why didn't you ever open the store?"

Aunt Vera looped a finger under her strands of beads. She twisted them into a fierce figure eight.

"I'll probe until I find out," I said. "I'm good at probing."

"Not now, dear." She released the beads. "Now is all about you. You are my niece. My beautiful niece. And it is your time to shine. I want to make this exactly like the store you envision, with cookbooks, gadgets, children's cooking toys, and culinary mysteries and fiction."

I planned to set up a vintage kitchen table with funky chairs where our guests could sit and pore over recipes or have fun piecing together jigsaw puzzles of delectable food. We would have a reading alcove for fiction enthusiasts, too; I was an avid reader. I adored the smell of new books; some might call it a fetish. I didn't digest as many books in a year as a librarian, but I could read a book a week. My nightstand to-be-read pile stood eight to ten books high at all times. Also, if we found the right chef for the café, we might even offer cooking classes.

So many ideas; lots of time.

"By the by," Aunt Vera said, "I expect the shop to thrive. I don't want to be giving psychic readings well into my golden years."

"Like you need to." A fact I did glean from my mother was that Aunt Vera had made a killing in the stock market way back when.

Aunt Vera didn't blink an eye. "I want to rest and relax and drink in the scent of the ocean."

"Mom said that the ocean is part of our soul." When I was young, my mother used to take me to the beach, our paint kits and canvases in hand.

"She was a special woman," Aunt Vera said as she began to color in the seashells she had drawn. "How she loved painting seascapes."

I, on the other hand, thanks to a Degas retrospective that I saw at the age of eight, liked to paint dancing girls. I enjoyed the fluidity of motion and catching girls midspin. At nine, I announced that I would become the greatest ballerina artist in the world. It didn't happen; I settled for moderate talent and huge appreciation.

"After we're done here," my aunt said, "let's get you settled into your abode. I've hung new drapes, and I updated the kitchen. The cottage has a new stove and oven."

I flashed her a wicked smile.

"You can learn to cook," she said.

"Who will have the patience to teach me?"

"If you follow a recipe to the letter, it always works."

"Ha! Tell that to someone trying to make an angel food cake. That was one of my first attempts back in high school—a disaster. Can you spell glue?"

"G-l-u-e." Aunt Vera roared. "Oh, that reminds me." She set down her paintbrush, ducked behind the counter, and popped up with a pile of cookbooks. "I've assembled a starter's set for you. A number of them are *Cook's Illustrated. The Best 30-Minute Recipe. The Best Light Recipe.* Best, best, best." She chuckled. "The smart shopping tips help make a cook's job hassle free. And I adore this one." She shook a bright pink paperback called *Cook Like a Rock Star: 125 Recipes, Lessons, and Culinary Secrets.* A picture of white-haired Chef Anne Burrell graced the cover. "You've seen her. She stars on that Food Network show."

"Personality up the wazoo."

"That's the one. Love her. In this book"—Aunt Vera opened the book to the index—"Anne offers all sorts of encouragement and professional tricks. There's a list of what to put in your basic pantry, and explanations for all sorts of scary cooking words, like *braise* and *sauté.* I'll start the collection in the storeroom."

As she carried the cookbooks out of the shop, I poured coral paint into a deep-well roller tray, soaked my paint roller in the goo, and started covering over the fleshy pink on the wall behind the sales counter.

In less than an hour, I gave the wall a single coat. I set the roller down and stretched.

Aunt Vera followed suit, groaning audibly with the effort. "You know, your father is quite a chef."

"Really?" My mother always did the cooking.

"A single man must adjust."

Yet again, I picked up her veiled meaning. A single woman must adjust, too. Not only did I need to learn to cook, but like my father, I had to move on and reconnect with the fun part of living. "Did you tell Dad our first celebrity guest is Desiree Divine?"

"I wanted to keep it hush-hush." Aunt Vera held a finger to her lips. "She's such a star."

"She was always Dad's favorite of my college roommates. They bonded at a Habitat for Humanity project."

"Her name sounds like a stripper's."

I chuckled. "Desiree is always fast to point that out."

"Really?"

I would never forget the first day of college. Desiree swept into the dorm room at Cal Poly with such confidence, plunked onto one of the tiny beds, and said, "Let's dish."

"I've read her profile on the Internet." Aunt Vera set down her paintbrush and perched on the three-step ladder by the sales counter. She crossed her legs, hoisting her caftan ever so slightly to reveal a brand-new pair of Birkenstock sandals. "She says she's a foodie fashionista who"—my aunt fanned herself—"likes to cook in stilettos and nothing else."

I rolled my eyes. "I was a party girl, but Desiree was a party expert. I attended a beer bash; she attended a champagne soiree."

"I love the fact that you keep in touch."

"We talk about once a month. She was the first person to call after David—" My mouth filled with imaginary cotton balls. I fiddled with my mother's heart-shaped locket that hung around my neck, unable to finish the sentence, but I knew my aunt understood: *After my husband died in the boating accident.*

When I regrouped, she plunged ahead. Aunt Vera was nothing if not pragmatic. "I have attempted to make Desiree's eggs and caviar recipe. I've failed miserably."

"At least you've dared." I had eaten the delicacy at a restaurant in San Francisco that mimicked the dish—a lightly poached egg, slipped into a bowl, with a dollop of caviar and two crustless toasts, drizzled with truffle butter. Melt-in-your-mouth delicious.

"When will she arrive?" Aunt Vera scooched off the ladder and picked up her paintbrush to resume her task.

"In two days. I've booked her at the Crystal Cove Inn."

Crystal Cove was a seaside community, which consisted of three crescent-shaped bays. A range of modest mountains that defined the eastern border of the town trapped ocean moisture and blessed Crystal Cove with a temperate Mediterranean climate. Stores and restaurants and quaint malls, like the Fisherman's Village, lined the roads that paralleled the ocean. Houses, hotels, and numerous bed-and-breakfast inns populated the streets that twisted up the mountains away from town. Fifty years ago, in an effort to unify Crystal Cove, the city council mandated that the buildings be whitewashed and sport red-tiled roofs. All but a few residents complied. The town was as pretty as a picture postcard. As I grew up, I didn't think there was a future for me in such a gentle town, but in the eight years since I had graduated college, Crystal Cove had burgeoned, and I was willing to give moving home a try. Anything to find that elusive smile.

"Is it true Desiree has received hate mail?" Aunt Vera said.

"If you read the gossip magazines, Desiree has stolen not only a recipe but a boyfriend and a husband. She's anorexic, bulimic, and a fraud, and she's popping pills faster than that actress . . ." I clicked my fingers trying to come up with the name and failing.

My aunt pulled a pouch from the pocket of her caftan. She brandished it and mumbled something under her breath.

"What're you doing?" I asked.

"Casting away the curse."

My pulse—which had calmed down while we painted—spiked. "Is there a curse on The Cookbook Nook?"

"Nonsense. I have a bad feeling about your friend Desiree. Such unwarranted anger and hatred can destroy a soul. She must beware."

My aunt's words sent a shiver down my spine.

Chapter 2

A T THE END of the day, my aunt and I sat in white rocking chairs on the porch of her charming Cape Cod–style beach house and chatted about the changes in Crystal Cove since I'd last visited. Waves lapped the shore. Seagulls keened overhead. In the lingering remnants of sunshine, families equipped with buckets and shovels practiced on the beach for the Labor Day Sandcastle Festival, which was set for the first weekend in September.

When the conversation with my aunt waned, we drank pinot grigio and nibbled from a plate of veggies, hummus, and pita chips purchased from The Healthy Haven's deli counter.

As the sun melted into the horizon, I yawned and said, "I'd better set up house."

I hadn't brought much with me. Clothes, a few of my paintings and sculptures and art supplies, some silk houseplants that I couldn't kill, and a red Ching two-door cabinet with brass handles—one of the gems David and I had purchased in Chinatown. In July, I'd finally divested myself of

David's Brooks Brothers clothing, giving the entire ward-
robe to his mother, who said she couldn't part with any of
it. How could I refuse her?

The cozy cottage proved to be the perfect size for me.
One expansive room with a bachelorette kitchen, a bay window facing the ocean, a redbrick fireplace, a wall of books,
and a niche for my art supplies. Aunt Vera provided all the
dishes, linens, and furniture. I nearly cried when I saw the
pretty brass bed decorated in lacy white.

After a long Epsom salts bath to relieve my painting-sore
muscles, I curled up in front of a toasty fire, a crocheted
blanket tucked around my knees—evenings in August could
be chilly on the coast—and downed Tootsie Rolls. I listened
to Judy Garland croon on a CD player about the man that
got away, and I read. In the City, after a long day at the office
when my eyes ached from reading too many proposals, I
would switch on the television and channel surf. I would
catch up on the latest Hollywood gossip, cooking shows,
and new age exercise. But in my new environment, I wanted
quiet. I wanted to hear my heart beat. I devoured the hot
new thriller by Meg Gardiner until midnight. Before nest-
ling beneath the duvet cover, I cracked open the window an
inch so I could drink in the fresh salty air. Around 1 A.M.,
I drifted into a deep sleep.

In the morning, I took a brisk barefoot walk, my toes
enjoying the grit of the sand. While living in San Francisco,
I had forgotten how much I enjoyed walking on the beach.
I wasn't a collector; I didn't pick up shells and such. I would
leave the strand as pristine as I'd found it. But I enjoyed
water lapping my ankles, the hint of mist hovering at the
edge of the horizon, and the simple beauty of sandcastles
made the day before.

For over an hour, I viewed the beach homes that lined
the ultra-expensive strand and reacquainted myself with the
familiar sights of treasure seekers scouring the sand with
diviners and families emerging from the public access paths
located between some of the houses and dashing toward the

ocean. I let the breeze kiss my face, and before long, a smile found my lips. Moving to Crystal Cove might have been the best decision I had made in months.

OVER THE NEXT two days, Aunt Vera and I set up shop. On the first day, although we had bookshelves on nearly every free inch of wall space, we aligned shorter, three-shelf cabinets at the center of the store. We filled the shelves closest to the sales counter with our previous stock, which we discounted at basement prices. One of the steals was *The Gourmet Cookbook, Volume 1,* for three dollars, with a wealth of entrees such as *escalopes de veau sautés chasseurs,* red flannel hash New England, scallops Parisian, and a treasure-load of cookies—maple black walnut kisses, brandy snaps, and cinnamon stars. However, the book had only a few pictures, which was a major drawback for present-day consumers.

In the display by the picture window, we set out seaside-related items such as seashells, sand-sculpting tools, buckets, and fishing reels, as well as food-themed novels and culinary mysteries. I had thumbed through many of the latter. Some featured stories about coffee or cheese or cookies. Many contained recipes. What fun I was going to have reading each of the books after experimenting in the kitchen. Yes, I was ready to experiment.

When we finished arranging the display, we assembled knickknacks around the shop: colorful aprons on hooks, recipe boxes serving as bookends, and items such as stackable measuring cups, quirky salt and pepper shakers, and uniquely shaped spatulas sprinkled here and there— treasures for our patrons to discover while they searched for the perfect cookbook.

On the second day, we hired the café's waitstaff and hostess and lucked into a chef, who proved to be none other than my best friend in high school, Katie Casey. We had lost touch over the years. I went to college; she stayed in Crystal Cove, and although I came to visit, I never reached out. Bad me. Katie, who reminded me of Julia Child or, rather, Dan

Aykroyd impersonating Julia Child, didn't have official restaurant credentials; yet for the past five years, she had served
as a personal chef for a wealthy widower in town. Recently
he'd passed on—not because of her cooking. She received
a tremendous letter of appreciation from his children, which
caught my aunt's attention. For her tryout, Katie didn't cook
a dish in the café. Instead, she surprised us by showing up
with a homemade meal that consisted of braised beef, cara-
melized onions, butternut squash, blackberry pie, and one
of my all-time favorites, clam chowder. The meal was to die
for. In addition, she had created a first-week's menu for the
café that knocked our sandals off.

Around noon the day before our grand opening, Aunt
Vera and I nestled at the vintage kitchen table, and we ate
lunch.

"Delicious," Aunt Vera said between bites. "Every morsel
cooked perfectly."

Not by me. Katie had thrown together a Niçoise salad of
tuna, string beans, boiled potatoes, hard-boiled eggs, olives,
green onions, and a scrumptious amount of anchovies.

"Is there garlic in the dressing?" I asked.

"*Bien sûr*, but of course." Katie hovered beside the table,
hands folded over her apron strings, her wild mass of curly
flaxen hair anchored beneath a chef's toque. She added, "I
can be heavy-handed with garlic."

"I like it," I said.

"Oh, good. I'm sorry about using canned tuna, but I think
albacore is best from May to July and yellow-fin tuna from
September to October. We're sort of in between in August."

My aunt gave the table a pat. "Good to know, so we don't
poison our guests."

"Hoo-boy." Katie's sizable chest heaved with laughter,
and her hangdog-shaped eyes sparkled with mischief.
"That's good, Vera. Poison."

Someone knocked on the doorjamb. "Is she here, Vera?"
A guy with exceptionally large forearms and a Grand Can-
yon cleft chin stopped in the arch of the door and surveyed
the store. "Is Desiree here?"

"Not yet, Tito." My aunt tapped my hand and whispered, "Tito Martinez is a local reporter." He resembled a boxer— the dog variety. Broad face, broad shoulders, short legs. Energy twitched through him. "We want him on our good side."

"I get an exclusive interview with Desiree Divine, right?" Tito beamed, his incisors razor-sharp. "You promised."

Aunt Vera nodded. "Come to the store a half hour before opening."

He flashed the thumbs-up sign and zeroed his gaze on me. "Heard you don't cook."

I glanced at my aunt.

"Small-town gossip," she muttered. "Get used to it."

"I'm on a learning curve," I said to Tito.

"Good luck. It takes years of practice, and even practice doesn't make perfect," he said, a tic grabbing his upper lip in a snarl. As he strolled away, I swear I heard him yipping.

"So tell me about Desiree Divine." Katie perched on a chair—one of the girls.

"She's a bit over the top," I said. "The woman everyone loves to hate." I added quickly, "Not *hate* hate. *Love* hate. Think Giada de Laurentiis's lusciousness and Ina Garten's talent all rolled up into one willowy glamour girl, with a smattering of Martha Stewart's uptightness, enough to make her interesting."

"Jenna met her in college," my aunt said.

"Desiree showed up to our dorm room that first day, dressed in white and looking like a goddess," I said, the memory fresh. "She wasn't haughty. She was simply perfect, with a radiant smile. Her windswept golden hair framed her face perfectly." To give an impression, I shook my shoulder-length hair and flashed my pearly whites. Katie and my aunt laughed. "A dozen freshman guys crowded in the doorway, tongues hanging out."

"Hoo-boy," Katie said.

"And yet, from the first moment, Desiree and I bonded over dating, the drudgery of classes, and helicopter parents, though hers proved worse than mine. Her mother was quite shocked and vocally disappointed when Desiree quit school to become a chef."

"Ah, a mother's dreams. Too-ra-loo," Aunt Vera said. Did I detect sadness in her tone? Hadn't my grandmother supported my aunt's dreams?

"Go on," Katie said, looking as avid as a gossip magazine reader.

"Even though Desiree didn't have her parents' support, she flew to France and learned with the best," I said. "Two years later, she returned to the States, where, thanks to the dazzling, world-renowned restaurateur Anton d'Stang, she became a sought-after chef at Chez Anton, d'Stang's New York restaurant. During her stint there, she devised her own style and wrote numerous cookbooks. A year later, she left Chez Anton to star in her own TV show."

The gold pocket watch pinned to Katie's apron chimed. "Whew," she said. "Time flies when we're yakking. I've got to get back to my duties." She needed to organize the café's kitchen and interview sous chefs. She scrambled out of the chair and shuffled away. At the entry to the café, she pivoted. "Say, Jenna, perhaps we could catch up later. There's a wine bar called Vines upstairs next to the arty movie theater."

"I can't. My dad's dropping by today."

"Oh, sure, another time." Disappointment clouded her gaze.

"How about next Tuesday when the shop is closed?"

"Super." Her eyes brightened.

Because we lived in a tourism-driven town, my aunt and I made the decision to close the shop and café on Sunday, around 6 P.M., and one full day a week—Tuesday. When working in advertising, I had been a workaholic. Seven days a week, as many hours as required. I didn't want to live that way in Crystal Cove.

As Katie walked off, Aunt Vera said, "That girl is good for gossip. She knows everyone at bookstores, shops, doctors' clinics, you name it. You ever want to know anything about anybody, ask her."

When my aunt and I finished all the displays, I said, "I'm going to pass out flyers." I planned to use my mother's old bicycle to buzz around town. Finding places to park my metallic blue VW bug, even though it was small, would be a challenge. And walking? Forget it. Crystal Cove, end-to-end, consisted of six miles of beach strand, which meant nearly four miles of brick-lined sidewalks and shops. I had stamina, but not that much stamina.

"What flyers?" Aunt Vera said.

"The ones with the coupon. If people buy one of our old cookbooks, we'll give them ten percent off a new cookbook. Haven't I shown them to you?" I fetched my briefcase from behind the sales counter and withdrew a sunset-toned flyer.

Aunt Vera beamed. "You astound me with your advertising acumen."

What might astonish her more was the campaign I'd created for Firecracker Frijoles, with animated beans strapped to rockets. My nightmares were not nearly as colorful as my ad ideas.

The front door flew open. Expecting to greet my father, who'd called and said he was on his way, I whirled around with a grin planted on my face.

A thick woman with a beaky nose, silver hair, and the glower of a rhinoceros on the warpath marched into the store. "Vera Hart, who owns those Winnebagos?"

I peeked out the picture window. Two orca-sized vehicles took up six spots in the parking lot.

"I haven't the slightest," Aunt Vera said.

"You've got to do something." Brandishing a fist, the woman charged toward my aunt.

I couldn't believe she would actually hit my aunt because of Winnebagos, but I wasn't taking chances. I cut her off near the sustainability cookbooks display, my dukes raised. I wasn't made of steel, and I had never taken karate or rammed my fist into a punching bag, but I occasionally followed a series of kickboxing workouts on television, and I was taller than the woman by a head. My tank top rose above the low-slung waistband of my shorts, but I didn't tug it down for fear of losing my intimidating demeanor.

The woman jabbed her fist at my aunt. Being forced to direct her hand around me lessened the effect.

"Now, Pepper, let's be civil," Aunt Vera said. Unflustered by the woman's behavior, she swept past me to the front door, anchored it open with a brass doorstop, and took a deep breath. "Ah, much more inviting. A fresh cool breeze soothes the soul. Lovely." She clutched the angry woman's elbow in a friendly manner. "Pepper Pritchett, say hello to my niece, Jenna Hart. Jenna, dear, this is Pepper."

What a fitting name. The woman was spicier than three-alarm chili.

"She owns the Beaders of Paradise, the store on the far corner of the mall," my aunt added.

Aha. That explained the detailed beading around the collar of her dress. I jutted out my hand to shake and said, "Jenna to my friends."

Pepper ignored my gesture. "Vera, have those trailers relocated, or I'll tell Cinnamon to tow them."

"Who's Cinnamon?" I asked.

My aunt said, "The chief of Crystal Cove's police department. Pepper's daughter. Don't you know Cinnamon? Hmm, maybe you don't. She's about five years older than you." Aunt Vera eyed Pepper. "I doubt Cinnamon will relish the job of finding someone to tow the trailers. You know how she can be, don't you?"

"Willful," Pepper muttered.

Considering the mother's temperament, I could only imagine how zesty Cinnamon Pritchett might be. Given their names, they should have opened a mother-daughter spice store.

"Don't let Pepper steer you wrong," my aunt advised me. "Cinnamon is a delight. She can sing like an angel, and she's quite a good roller skater. You taught her to skate, didn't you, Pepper?"

The woman grumbled.

"Pepper's shop is one of the main attractions in Crystal Cove," my aunt said. "She has the most unusual beads, and she is an excellent beading instructor."

The other night when we drank wine on the porch, Aunt Vera told me about the changes to Crystal Cove. In addition to being a sport lovers' haven—with a fish and bait shop at The Pier, a water ski and surf shop at the far end of the Fisherman's Village, and a kayaking and canoeing store down the street—it was now a crafters' haven, as well. The town featured a knitting, sewing, and embroidery store, as well as a chocolatier, a cupcake baker, and a gluten-free baker, all of which offered classes. Antique stores and clothing stores abounded, too. I remembered my father saying when I was young, "There's something for everyone in Crystal Cove."

As if on cue, my father—the spitting image of Cary Grant, early sixties—strutted into the shop. Invariably, because of his similarity to the movie star, people quoted the line: "Judy, Judy, Judy." It hadn't helped that my father's name was Cary and my mother's name was Judy, and it didn't matter that Cary Grant had never uttered that line. A comedian had used it in a send-up skit, my father was quick to say. He took the gibing gracefully.

"How's my Tootsie Pop?" He held out his arms to me.

At the mention of my nickname—a sobriquet my father hadn't called me since I was twelve—the months, guilt, and anguish melted away. I hurried to him and drew strength from his bear hug. As we stood there, I felt something furry brush against my bare calves.

I bolted from my father's embrace and peered down. A striped kitten tilted its head up and mewed. His tail swished into a question mark. "Yours?" I asked my father.

"Nope."

"Mrs. Pritchett?" I said.

"I hate cats."

Well, I didn't. I adored them, and this one appeared lost. I scooped him into my arms—it was a he—and nuzzled my nose against his. His purr reminded me of a motorboat revving up. "What's your name, fella?" He wasn't wearing a collar.

"The trailers, Vera," Pepper Pritchett said. "My beaders prefer to park in front of the store, and I have a class starting in an hour."

"I'm sure someone will move the Winnebagos soon," my aunt said.

I wasn't so sure. If I ventured a guess, I would bet the trailers as well as the spanking white Mercedes next to them belonged to none other than Desiree Divine, but I kept my mouth shut. When Desiree was ready to make an appearance, she would, and any amount of ordering from Pepper Pritchett or my aunt wouldn't make her budge.

Aunt Vera escorted Pepper to the exit. "Now if you don't mind, we need you to leave. We're finishing preparations for our grand opening tomorrow."

"The shop will fail," Pepper said. "Just as before."

Aunt Vera skewered Pepper with a look, which caused me to wonder whether Pepper had something to do with why my aunt had never opened the shop decades ago. Had she mounted an anticookbook campaign? I needed to know the dirt, but now wasn't the time to ask.

At the door, Pepper regarded the kitten in my arms. "Disgusting creatures."

I wished I had a masterful magic mirror like the one I had created for the Pretty Princess Doll campaign. The mirror would ricochet hateful words from Pretty's enemies back at them.

"That'll be all, thank you." Aunt Vera pushed Pepper out of the shop and smiled at me. "Put the kitten on the ground, honey. Let him walk around. You'll see by his pace what to name him."

"Name him?" I said. "I'm not keeping him."

"Nonsense," my father said. "If a kitten without a collar walks into your life, you have to keep him. Timing is everything."

I gaped. My father was advising me to keep the cat? As

a girl, I wanted a cat, but my mother was allergic, so my father adamantly refused. As an adult working twenty-four hours a day, seven days a week, I didn't feel right about having a pet. They needed attention and fresh air. On the other hand, this kitty had the cutest face. Big green eyes. A winsome mouth. And his outrageous purr stole my heart.

I said, "What if he belongs to someone in the Winnebagos?" Specifically Desiree. I hadn't dared to date any of the guys she went out with in college; I wouldn't adopt her cat.

My aunt *tsk*ed. "The very idea of letting a kitten loose in a parking lot is beyond my ken."

"Whoever let him run doesn't deserve him," Dad said.

I set the kitten on the floor. He pawed my yellow-painted toenails. I wiggled my big toe. He hunkered backward. I twitched the toe again. He did a cha-cha and bounded up to his hind legs. He twirled in the air, landing on his backside on top of my feet, then quickly flopped to his tummy and to a sit. I scooped him up again. "Okay, you've wowed me. You're as rambunctious as Tigger in *Winnie the Pooh*."

Aunt Vera clapped her hands. "Tigger, love it. We have a mascot."

I held up a finger. "Only if nobody claims him."

"Fine, we'll post signs," my aunt said.

My father slung an arm around my back. "What can I do to help?"

"Dad, I want to apologize."

"Water over the falls, sweetheart. We can't live in the past. Heartbreak affects each of us differently."

I gaped a second time. My aunt said my father had mellowed, but I hadn't expected a total overhaul.

"Now"—he brushed his hands together—"I'm here. Use me."

"Um, we're done, I think."

"I'm too late?"

"Come to think of it"—I scanned the store for a project—"I could use your handyman skills at the cash register." I scooped up the kitten—Tigger—set him into a vacant book box, and scratched his head. "You stay here until I figure out what to do with you, fella. Aunt Vera, do you have something we can put water in for the kitty?"

"Sure do." She sashayed to the back of the store, humming the popular Disney song, "The Wonderful Thing about Tiggers."

I guided my father to the sales counter. "The drawer sticks. I have WD-40 in the stockroom."

"On it." He ambled away as the front door swung open a third time.

"Yoo-hoo, Jenny," a woman called out.

I preferred being called Jenna—my given name—and I didn't mind Jen, but I hated Jenny. It sounded meek, and Desiree Divine knew it.

She posed in the doorway, bathed in the golden glow of late afternoon sunlight, her white spaghetti-strap dress clinging to her body in a way that would make any man salivate. Wiggling her fingers over her head, her signature move after she was introduced on *Cooking with Desiree*, she said, "Who's hungry?"

"I am," I responded like a trained studio audience.

"Fab." She grinned but her forehead didn't shift. I wondered if someone our age would use Botox and resolved that, yes, Desiree would. She was a star. She wanted the world to see her as youthful and hip . . . forever. And thanks to the release of her latest cookbook, *Cookies, Cakes, Sweets, and More: A Desiree Divine Dessert Extravaganza*, she had appearances scheduled up the wazoo. She strutted toward me, spiky heels clicking on the parquet floor. "What a charming place." She fondled the spines of books and swished her fire engine–red fingertips across the arty kitchen doodads. "I'm so impressed." She stopped short of me and tilted her head to one side. "You look good."

"Thanks."

She waggled a finger. "Although I see you forgot to use sun block."

Sun peeking through the clouds on my morning walk had given my pale skin a healthy glow. "Who knew I could get color at six A.M.?" I joked.

Desiree clucked her tongue with disapproval. One day during our freshman year, when I had wanted to take up ballroom dancing, I'd coated myself with bronzer. On her way to a Save the Seals rally, Desiree had caught me lathering up in the bathroom and snatched the tube out of my hand with the shouted warning that a suntan, no matter whether it was real or fake, aged a woman. She'd made me promise, cross my heart, that I would never *try* to get tan again.

I said, "I'll be more careful."

Her quasi-frown melted away and she hugged me. "I'm so glad you invited me here. This town is adorable. The little shops, the brick arcades, the hunky men."

"What hunky men?"

"There's one outside who has been ogling your shop for over an hour. I've been spying on him from inside my trailer."

"Speaking of trailers, why do you need them? I booked you a room at the nicest hotel in town."

"One is my office and my sister's hangout. The other is for my stylist and masseur. But enough about me. Back to the hunk. Do you swear you haven't seen him? Sailor's hat, fisherman's sweater, jeans that fit just right." Desiree mimed cupping a nicely shaped rear end. "Bedroom eyes for days."

Who could she have been talking about? I had taken a number of fresh air breaks on the boardwalk outside the shop. I hadn't seen a soul.

"He's there now."

My gaze swept the boardwalk and parking lot. All I saw was a buff, blond dude in a white karate outfit climbing into one of the trailers.

Desiree followed my gaze. "Not him. He's my masseur."

Another guy with a Mohawk exited the same trailer and air-punched the masseur, who responded with a fake punch.

"Not him either," Desiree said.

"The guy with the tackle box?" I gestured to a thickset man with full mustache, beard, and knit cap who was squeezing between a black minivan and truck. His right

shoulder drooped and his right foot dragged. He climbed
into the truck. The vehicle ground to a start.

"Lord, no." She frittered her fingertips. "That guy looks
like a creep. Mr. Hunk was—"

"Forget Mr. Hunk," I said. "You're here. Let's talk about
opening night."

"I'd rather dish." She offered a low, sultry cackle. "C'mon.
Local gossip. Spill. Oh, and I want you to promise to go on
a hike with all of us."

"A hike?"

"You know how I love to stretch my legs."

"Desiree?" Sabrina—darker, dourer, and five years
younger than Desiree—jogged into the shop and screeched
to a halt. Literally screeched. Her leather flats left scuff
marks on the floor. I had met Desiree's sister once before,
the day Desiree had packed up and left for Europe. She
hadn't acted happy about the prospect. Come to think of it,
she had worn all black that day, too.

"Good to see you, Jenna," Sabrina said as she righted a
gold choker so the V rested at the hollow of her throat.
"Desiree, we need to talk."

"Where's my mocha latte?" Desiree said.

"We have a problem." Sabrina patted the leather iPad in
her hand.

"My sister is a scheduling freak," Desiree said.

Sabrina flinched but quickly tamped down whatever
feathers her sister had ruffled. "We've got to handle the
problem."

"Sis, can't you see I'm chatting with Jenna? I'm convincing her to join our hiking soiree. Go get me that coffee."

"You're booked for two different appearances next
Monday," Sabrina said, intent on her mission. "How did
that happen? I know I didn't do it, but I got an e-mail that
says—"

"Repeat after me. O-o-o-om." Desiree edged behind her
sister, removed the iPad, and drew her sister's arms over her
head. "C'mon, Sabrina, o-o-o-om. Oxygenate your blood."

Sabrina obviously worked out, but she didn't seem to appreciate chanting.

"Make her do a stork pose," the man with the Mohawk said as he entered the shop. He wore a sleeveless black T-shirt and cutoff jeans, and he sported more tattoos than I had ever seen on one body. "C'mon, Sabrina, lift that knee." He sidled to Desiree's side and kissed her neck—more like sucked it—then he slung a bare arm around her shoulders. "The stork pose is good for cleansing chakras, isn't it? Or is that the one that's good for balance?" He scratched his bristly chin, a motion that made the sizable tiger tattoo on his muscular bicep writhe with delight. "Maybe it's good for sex."

Desiree slid from his grasp. "Cut it out." She handed the iPad back to her sister. "Forget the coffee, Sis. Take a look around the adorable shop. Find your center." She gave her sister a push at the small of her back.

Sabrina muttered, "Miscreant," at Tattoo Guy and meandered toward the back of the store.

Desiree whirled on Tattoo Guy. "As for you—"

"She's a piece of work," he said.

"Don't start."

"I'm not the bad guy here." He threw up his hands defensively. "I came in because I'm starving, babe."

"And we're going to eat, but first, I want to touch base with my friend, and you're being rude."

He looped a lock of her hair around his finger. "I like it when you're feisty."

Desiree smacked his hand away. "J.P., please."

His face flamed with annoyance.

I swooped into the mix and thrust my hand at him. "Hi, I'm Jenna. Nice tats," I lied. Why anyone would denigrate his body with needles and ink baffled me. On the other hand, I did appreciate art, and his artist had talent. "What's with all the lines?" The tiger nestled in the middle of a maze with no exit.

"They're jungle vines," J.P. said.

"He has a Tarzan fixation," Desiree teased.

"I do not. I'm from Florida. I wanted to honor my heritage. We've got Everglades and all sorts of wild creatures there."

Was he including himself among the wildlife? *I am man, hear me roar.* "So what's your connection with Desiree?" I asked, other than trying to suck the life out of her.

"I'm her lover." He sniggered. "And her director. Double-whammy."

I heard Sabrina snort.

Desiree shot her sister a withering glance. "Jenna, give J.P. and me a private moment, okay?"

I routed through the aisles to the back of the store and settled beside Sabrina, who was leafing through a cocktail book titled: *Name Your Poison.* "Sisters," I said, knowing how they could irritate. "My sister says I have water skis for feet." Like Desiree, I stood six inches taller than my sister, but in a wrestling match, she could take me.

"How do you do it?" Sabrina replaced the book and folded her arms across her chest, cradling the iPad like a protective breastplate.

"Deal with my sister?" I said. "Well, first—"

"No, how do you tolerate Desiree? Why would you want her within fifty miles of you?"

"I don't know what you're talking about."

"She had an affair with your husband."

My breath caught in my chest.

"C'mon, you can't be that naive," Sabrina said. "She hooked up with all your boyfriends."

"You're wrong."

"Am I?" She fiddled with a gold earring stud. "Ask her."

I cut a look toward the door, but Desiree was gone.

Chapter 3

I TORE ACROSS the parking lot and pounded on the door of the office Winnebago. "Desiree? Are you in there?" No answer. I ascended the stairs to the rightmost trailer and knocked.

The masseur opened the door. The flaps of his white karate gi hung open. He polished his glistening abs with his palm and eyed me lustfully. "What's up, gorgeous?"

I was nothing near gorgeous. I had been lucky enough to get the Hart ski-jump nose and smile, but unlucky enough to get the Hart broad shoulders and what my sister called *guy* hips. Desiree was the stunning one, and I wanted to see her. "Desiree. Where is she?"

"My name's Mackenzie Baxter, thanks for asking." He slung his thumbs under the waistband of his loosely tied pants. "What's your name?"

"Jenna Hart. Where is she?"

"Not here. What's the prob, Jenna Hart? If looks could kill."

I didn't like his laidback manner, though it was probably

a good trait for a masseur. He didn't rush. He took his time. "She was with J.P.," I said. "Have you seen him?"

Something flashed in Mackenzie's eyes. Either he wasn't fond of J.P. or he didn't appreciate Desiree hanging out with the guy.

"Did you try Desiree's cell phone?" A woman the size of an Olympic shot-putter with purple spiked hair tramped from the rear of the Winnebago and, while filing her nails, peered over Mackenzie's shoulder. "Hiya. I'm Gigi."

"I know you," I said. "You work at the Permanent Wave Salon and Spa." I had driven past the place the day I arrived in town. Gigi worked at a premium stylist spot, right by the front window. Everyone that passed by could see her wizardry.

"Yeah. That's me, all right. I'm also Desiree's hairstylist this week."

"She didn't bring someone from L.A.?"

"Her regular got sick." Gigi wore a ton of jewelry, including a combination of bracelets and watches, and at least a dozen earring studs in each ear. *Ouch.* "OTOH," she said in shorthand I could decipher: *On the other hand*, "I'll bet you can't reach Desiree by phone. She won't answer if she's, you know . . ." She pumped her hips in a lascivious way.

Mackenzie lasered her with a glare.

"So-o-orry." Gigi dragged out the word, but I could tell she wasn't sorry. Not in the least.

"If Desiree returns," I said, "please tell her I need to see her."

"You and the world." Mackenzie shut the door in my face. Nice guy.

As I headed down the stairs, I spied Pepper Pritchett glowering at me from in front of Beaders of Paradise. I ignored her.

For the next hour, I scoured the town. I raced along the brick sidewalks, past barrels of bougainvillea, ignoring tourists. J.P. had said he was starved. Maybe Desiree and he went to catch a bite to eat. There were over fifty places to

dine or snack in Crystal Cove. I stopped in Latte Luck Café,
The Pelican Brief Diner, Taste of Heaven Ice Cream Parlor,
and myriad other places. At each I introduced myself and
handed out a flyer for the opening of The Cookbook Nook.
Why not kill two birds with one stone? I didn't find Desiree
and J.P. in any of them. I called the Crystal Cove Inn, but
Desiree hadn't checked in yet.

Irritated nearly to insanity, I sped back to the shop to
rekindle my relationship with my father only to find that he
and my aunt had left, whereabouts unknown. Katie had split
for the day, as well, so I grabbed Tigger and headed home.

On the way, I stopped at the grocery store. Taking my
aunt's advice, I decided to cook. The first day in the shop,
I had landed upon a recipe for guacamole in *Bobby Flay's
Mesa Grill Cookbook: Explosive Flavors from the South-
western Kitchen*. I wasn't nearly ready to tackle all the other
items in the hot, spicy, and delectable tome, but I memorized
the few ingredients in the guacamole. How hard could mashing together a few items be? I purchased local avocados,
jalapeño peppers, limes, red onions, cumin, and fresh cilantro. Aunt Vera had stocked the cottage's kitchen with basic
spices, as well as pots and pans. Afterward, I went to Bub-
bles Pet Store and Spa and purchased kitty items, including
a pricey air-conditioned cat cage so Tigger could join me
on the beach without overheating and a darling kitty bowl
that said: *Kittens are from Heaven*. Yes, I intended to
spoil him.

Tigger took to his new environment like a champ, bound-
ing and exploring with merry abandon. I did, too. After
mashing, dicing, and squeezing—all things I could do rather
well, given my annoyed state—I mixed up the concoction
and tasted. I added an extra dash of salt and felt smugly
satisfied. I had made my first *meal* in my new place.

I carried a large glass of sauvignon blanc, the guacamole,
and a bag of tortilla chips—I didn't think I had the talent
yet to cook cumin-dusted tortillas and not burn down the
place—into the art nook that I'd fashioned by the picture
window. Whenever I suffered an emotional upset, I focused

on my art. I set a canvas on an easel and retrieved a palette of oil paints and a paintbrush from the Ching cabinet. While I drew big angry swirls, Tigger circled my ankles; he refused to get sucked into my dark hole. I wished I could face life with his panache, but I needed to know the truth. Where in the heck was Desiree?

Close to midnight, I strode outside to the porch, leaned against the railing, and listened to the roar of the ocean, which was louder at night than any other time of the day. I stood there for a long time, allowing the crash and boom to pummel my overactive brain into submission. When I returned inside, I forged a battle plan. In the morning, after my walk and breakfast, I would storm Crystal Cove Inn and demand answers from my college pal.

AROUND 6 A.M., I awoke with a start. Something clacked against the exterior of the cottage. Tigger mewled and skittered around the box sitting on the floor beside my bed. I reached over and nuzzled his neck. "Shh. You're hearing a shutter swinging in the breeze. I'll fix it later." My father had taught me a thing or two with a screwdriver and hammer, but I didn't want to deal with repairs now. I rose, checked myself in the bathroom mirror, and groaned. Puffy eyes, red nose, grim mouth. Late-night pity parties and I didn't mix.

Forbidding myself to wallow, I fed Tigger some warm milk and kitty kibble and enclosed him in a "safe" area that I created in the kitchen, after which I donned walking clothes and headed out for my stroll.

Morning sun carved a path through the gloomy clouds, giving me hope that today might go better than yesterday. I would learn that Sabrina had made a mistake, Desiree was a true friend, and the opening of The Cookbook Nook would go off without a hitch. I zipped up my navy blue hoodie and traipsed to my aunt's house. I peeked through the sheer kitchen curtains and spied Aunt Vera. Clad in robe and slippers, her hair fixed with bobby pins in tight curls to her head, she sat at the dining table reading a newspaper.

I rapped on the kitchen door and opened it.

"Good morning, dear," Aunt Vera said. "You're up early."

"Full day ahead." I didn't add that I had barely slept a wink worrying about Desiree and what I would say to her when I saw her. "Do you have any sun block?"

"What's wrong?"

"Nothing."

"You're lying."

Okay, so maybe I couldn't maintain a stoic face. Maybe it was the puffy, red-nosed look—a dead giveaway. "It's nothing, really."

Aunt Vera shuffled to a cupboard, her vintage gold genie slippers never leaving the floor, and retrieved a few items. She held up a canister of fifty-strength sun block. I allowed her to spritz me. Afterward, she offered me a bottle of water and a snack of homemade trail mix—enough for an army of squirrels. "In case," she said.

"In case I get stranded on an island?"

She tapped her head as if she knew something I didn't about my future.

I ignored the shiver that prickled my neck, thanked her for the gifts, tucked them into the deep pockets of my khaki capris, and trotted down the steps to the ocean. A glimpse back at the seaside cottage tugged at my heartstrings. David and I had exchanged our first kiss on the white lattice pergola that nestled to the right of the house. Had he and Desiree—

Stop it, Jenna!

I pressed onward. Palm trees and scrub brush jutted out of the incline that sloped from the main road to the beach. The water, which was green along the sand, grew to a deeper blue about fifteen yards out. Speed walking, with my arms pumping like train axles, I breathed through my nose and out my mouth the way I had learned on a television yoga program. From my aunt's home, the beach ran north for nearly two miles before ending in a crag of rock upon which perched a lighthouse. I was angry enough with Desiree to make the full loop.

To keep my rekindled fury in check, I opted to admire

the handiwork of yesterday's sandcastle builders. The first was a tunneled sandcastle with dozens of different-shaped turrets.

"Nice," I mumbled. "But points off for building too close to the shore." The tide had eroded much of the front wall. Next, I spotted a five-foot-square castle, complete with moat. "Simple, yet elegant." While I pondered whether I could apply for a judging position in the upcoming sandcastle competition, I heard shouts.

A man and a woman descended a set of stairs that ran from the public parking lot abutting the highway to the beach. He trailed her. Both wore floppy hats. At one point, she yelled something and pointed toward their car. She carried a diviner; the man was empty-handed. He raced back up the stairs and returned with a net bag. He reached his partner at the base of the steps, and the two moved toward the shore.

In the water, a lone surfer in a wetsuit sat on a surfboard waiting patiently for the morning's first wave. A pang of sorrow swept through me. It shouldn't have; I knew some surfers didn't need companionship when surfing. They bonded with the ocean. But seeing him floating solo, with a family of seagulls circling above, painted such a desolate picture and made me think of David. Had he drowned and died instantaneously, or had he suffered?

I stroked the locket that held his photograph and pressed on toward a third sculpture. It was longer, lower, and flatter than the others. When I neared within a few feet, I gasped. It was the figure of a naked woman—no, a mermaid—face turned sideways, a sandy hook coming out of her mouth, a clump of seaweed for her hair, and a drizzling of sand for her fingers. Care had been taken, each curve honed.

I started to giggle nervously. The mermaid reminded me of the painted woman in the movie *Goldfinger*. She looked so beautiful . . . so serene . . . so still.

I glanced around. Was the artist nearby, recording on video how people reacted as they passed? Would the treasure-seeking couple rat me out if I touched the mermaid's tail fin with my toe? Tough. I had to. Curiosity bubbled to boiling point.

I stretched out my foot and tapped the far end of the sculpture. It didn't crumble as expected. It resisted. Sand fell away and a flesh-colored toe emerged. Human.

A shriek gushed out of my mouth.

The couple down the beach swiveled. The man ran toward me shouting, "What's wrong?"

"A body," I yelled and swooped toward the mermaid's head, hoping whoever was buried was still alive. Kneeling, I swept sand away from the mouth. The nose.

A face emerged.

Desiree.

A huge fishhook punctured her lip. Her face was blue, her eyes open yet lifeless.

Stomach roiling, I leaped to a stand. Somebody had murdered Desiree. I wrapped my arms around my body. My shoulders started to shake uncontrollably. How long had she been buried here? The murderer had to have struck after nightfall; otherwise, beachgoers would have seen the attack. Who had done it? Why?

The couple reached me. The woman gagged. The man turned her so she was unable to look then dropped to his knees and started to sweep away sand where I had left off.

"She's dead." I clasped his shoulder. "Stop."

He shrugged me off, intent on his mission.

"Don't disturb the evidence," I shouted. "Stop!"

He didn't.

I punched him. "Did you kill her?"

He twisted at the waist and gawked at me. "What? No." He slumped, rump on his heels, arms limp.

I covered my mouth with the back of my hand to fight off another scream. She was dead. Desiree was dead. I hadn't made things right. I hadn't found out the truth about David and her. I hadn't—

Sobs wracked my body. Feelings that had overwhelmed me when I had learned about David's death came at me like a tidal wave. Shock, panic, despair.

"Do you have a cell phone?" I asked. During my walks, I left the danged thing behind. Whenever I cavorted with nature, I wanted the fantasy of living in the days of old, before cell phones, before faxes, before advertising and marriage and death and heartache. "We need to call 911."

"No," the man muttered.

"For heaven's sake," the woman said. "Give her your iPhone."

While casting short glances at Desiree's buried body, the man rummaged in his jeans pocket and withdrew his cell phone.

During the time I spoke to the police, a crowd amassed. The treasure-seeking man organized the throng behind a line he drew in the sand, and then he and his wife joined the assembly, wanting no part of the investigation. They had seen nothing, knew nothing. Gossip buzzed among the onlookers. Parents embraced their children, but they didn't pivot and march away from the gruesome scene.

I remained in front of the line gaping at Desiree. Shock and grief muddled my vision.

"Stand back, people." A woman in brown shorts and matching short-sleeve shirt and baseball cap, who brought to mind a well-toned camp counselor, packing a gun, moved toward us shouting through a bullhorn. Two fellows in similar uniforms trailed her. The woman—strong face, alert eyes, midthirties—pulled up alongside me. "Chief Pritchett." She flashed a badge, quickly pocketed it, and gestured to her colleagues, who immediately started unwinding yellow crime scene tape.

I gaped at the chief, surprised that she—Cinnamon Pritchett, if I recalled correctly—could be related to the bitter woman who had stormed into The Cookbook Nook.

"Are you the person that called?" she asked me.

"Yes. I'm Jenna Hart," I mumbled, my tone numb.

"Vera's niece?" The chief squinted her eyes, not to block sunlight but to evaluate me. Had her mother given her an unfavorable account? "Call me Cinnamon."

"Cinnamon," I repeated.

"Tell me what happened here." Cinnamon was nothing if not perfunctory. Her bobbed dark hair matched the serious attitude. The development girls in advertising, the young creative souls who would sit in on meetings looking hopeful that we would nurture their ideas into *the one*, hadn't looked nearly as intent, purposeful, and dedicated.

"I was taking my morning walk." I paused. Did the killer know that I walked daily? Had he . . . *she* . . . wanted me to find Desiree?

"Go on."

"I power walk. I slowed to view some sandcastles. I was going from one to the next. This one . . . It was so . . . real." My teeth started to chatter.

Cinnamon said, "Breathe."

Appreciating her show of support, I told her how I touched the toe, saw flesh, screamed, and dropped to my knees to see if the person was alive. "That's when . . . that's when"—I licked my lips—"I realized it was her."

"You know her?"

"It's Desiree Divine."

"The chef?"

"She is . . . was . . . supposed to be our celebrity at the opening of the shop." The day David died, I phoned his parents, his best friend, and his clients. Would Sabrina want me to do the same for her sister?

"Was Miss Divine an acquaintance? A friend?"

How did I answer that? I thought Desiree and I were friends, but if Sabrina was telling the truth, Desiree had duped me for years. Not knowing gnawed my insides. What else had I been blind to in my past? Had David had other affairs? *No, Jenna, stop it. He was faithful. The love of your life.*

Cinnamon studied the crowd huddling behind the yellow crime scene tape and refocused on me. "You scraped away sand from the face."

"A little, to see if"—I urged my legs to keep holding me up—"to see if she was still alive. I thought maybe someone had played a prank. Maybe she was getting air to her mouth through—"

"A straw? A tube?"

I nodded. "She wasn't breathing. That man came to help. He wanted to uncover her." I indicated the treasure hunter. The man inched behind his wife, the coward. "I told him not to disturb the evidence. We backed away. You can ask him."

"I'll get to him in a minute." Cinnamon tucked the bull-horn beneath her arm and crouched beside Desiree. Using a fingertip, she brushed away sand from Desiree's neck. "Strangled," she whispered, then mentioned something about a blow to the right side of Desiree's head. She rose and addressed a patrolman. "Get the coroner here ASAP." She trained her eyes on me. "What else did you notice?"

"There was a surfer out there when I first arrived. He's gone."

Cinnamon pulled a pad and pen from her breast pocket and jotted a note. "Can you describe him?"

"He was too far away." I reexamined the crime scene, my mind growing clear and discriminating. I pinched my leg to force myself to feel, but I couldn't. Was I separating myself from grief the way I had when I'd heard the news about David? Desiree was murdered. She did not fall off a boat and drown. She was not a mermaid that had washed up on shore. Somebody had murdered her. Sabrina? J.P.? Why? Where had the surfer gone? Why hadn't he come to shore when I screamed?

"There are no footprints," I blurted out.

"Sure there are," Cinnamon said.

"Not around the body, other than mine and the treasure seeker's prints. Look. There are none from Desiree's head to the water."

"Whoa." Cinnamon held up a hand. "Don't go all *CSI* on me."

"I'm not. All I'm saying is someone cleaned up after making a sand sculpture out of Desiree. Do you think he used a palm frond and escaped through the water?"

"Why do you think it was a he?"

Because a surfer was out in the water and he has

disappeared, I wanted to yell, but I backed off. "You said Desiree was strangled. If the killer was a she, she was a big woman. Desiree is . . . was almost six feet tall."

"Go on."

"She would have been heavy to carry." Desiree mentioned seeing a hunky fisherman outside The Cookbook Nook. What if he hadn't been looking for me? What if he had been stalking her? "What do you think about the fish-hook jabbed through her lip?"

Cinnamon took off her baseball cap, swatted it against her leg, and replaced it with a firm tug. She crouched down and reinspected the area, this time paying attention to Desiree's face and the fishhook. She didn't touch either. Over her shoulder, she said, "I'm afraid you're going to be here for quite a bit, Jenna."

I felt the bottle of water and package of trail mix that Aunt Vera had given me in my pocket, and I shuddered. Had my aunt foreseen this moment? I wasn't hungry in the least. I wasn't sure I ever would be again.

"Out of my way," a woman shrieked from the rear of the crowd.

Cinnamon stood up, leveled a hand to the bill of her cap, and peered beneath. "Mom?"

"She did it. She killed her." Pepper Pritchett pushed to the front of the crowd and aimed her finger at me. "Jenna Hart is a murderer."

Chapter 4

I GAPED AT Pepper, her daughter Cinnamon, and the swelling beach crowd. A sea of faces stared back at me. Waves of blazing August heat rose from the sand, which made all the faces wiggle. Either that, or I was getting woozy.

Pepper poked her finger as if she were trying to jump-start a jammed elevator. "They were friends." She pointed at me and at Desiree's body. "Rather, they *were* friends. They had a spat. It's the talk of the town."

"We didn't have a spat," I said.

"What was it about?" Cinnamon asked.

"She"—Pepper jutted her thumb at Desiree—"and her husband"—she stabbed an accusatory finger at me—"had an affair."

"It's a rumor," I said. "It's not true."

"Rumor, my foot. You had a bur under your saddle to track down Desiree Divine. The whole town buzzed about how you went to all the restaurants and shops under the guise of passing out flyers for your new store, but we know what really happened."

"I never talked to Desiree. We never fought."

"I saw two women walking on the beach late last night," Pepper persisted. "One was Jenna Hart."

"It couldn't have been me. I was at home."

"She's a sculptor," Pepper continued. "An artist. She would know how to create this . . . this mermaid."

"Yes, I sculpt, but I'm primarily a painter. I've never built a sandcastle in my life. I haven't even poured colored sand in a bottle." I caught sight of my friend's corpse and the hook lodged in her mouth, and another wave of horror ripped through me. Who could do such a thing? Was the hook significant?

"Jenna Hart had it in for Desiree Divine, Cinn." Pepper tapped her head. "I heard. I know."

I willed her finger to morph into a drill bit that would bore holes into her meager brain. Aeration was good for the insane, I had heard. Sadly, my wish didn't come true. I faced Cinnamon. "Crystal Cove is an artist's retreat." On my tour yesterday, I had noted over twenty private art studios. In addition, an art camp in the hills offered intensive four-week sessions, year-round.

"I'm aware," Cinnamon said.

For the first time since discovering Desiree's body, I breathed. Truly breathed. Cinnamon believed that I was innocent. The relief lasted only a nanosecond.

"Jenna Hart's husband died in a beach incident, too," Pepper said.

I gaped at the nasty woman with her beady, critical eyes. Why did she insist on calling me by my full name? How dare she bring up David's death at a time like this? "He did not die on the beach. He was on a boat." A memory of him kissing me good-bye before leaving for what was supposed to be a quick sailing tour of the bay flitted through my mind. "He drowned. The police think he fell over the side, and—"

Pepper harrumphed. "There's talk you did him in."

"Lies."

"They never found his body. Some say you carved him up and fed him to the fish."

"Only those with Mafia fixations." I addressed Cinnamon.

"No matter what the tabloid magazines published, I did not kill my husband." Following David's death, there had been talk. I was the wife. Wasn't the spouse always guilty? I was never formally accused of anything. "He was an inexperienced seaman," I said. "Midafternoon, the waves grew fierce. He must have fallen overboard. The police cleared me of all wrongdoing."

"They never found his body?" Cinnamon asked.

I shook my head. No one would ever grasp the cavity of sadness that David's death had carved in my heart. I battled fresh tears.

Cinnamon turned to the mass of people. "Has anyone seen Old Jake?"

"Old who?" I asked.

"Jake. He's the fellow who drives a tractor and rakes the sand every morning. You mentioned palm fronds. I'm thinking Old Jake cleaned up. He does his best to avoid sandcastles. He sees them as children's treasures. That might explain why there are no footprints around, other than yours and that gentleman and his wife's."

"What time does Jake hit this area?" I asked.

"Anytime after midnight."

"That sets the time of death."

Cinnamon offered an indulgent smile. "Yes, I've thought of that."

"Maybe he saw somebody with Desiree, either carrying her or dragging her or . . ." I sputtered. "Of course, you've considered that, too." I ran a hand along my collarbone. Houses upon houses stood along the strand. Someone in one of the homes must have seen something. I gazed back at Desiree. Hot emotion swam up my throat. "Her head is positioned to the left."

Cinnamon peered where I was staring.

"Doesn't it look like a left-handed person handled the hook?" I drew a hook with my finger and grabbed the imaginary grip with my left hand. "He pulled this way."

"He or she," Cinnamon corrected. "Mother, you said you saw two women on the beach. When?"

"Around one or so."

"Why did you come here?"

"Insomnia, same as always." Pepper grumbled, "Danged sleeping. Never was much good at it."

"You walk on the beach alone?" Cinnamon sounded alarmed.

"That's right."

"Why haven't you told me this until now?"

Pepper shrugged. "A woman deserves her secrets."

"It's not safe, Mother."

"Apparently. There are lots of folks who walk, but last night, only the two. Her"—Pepper pointed at me—"and her." She jabbed her index finger at Desiree.

"You're positive?" Cinnamon said.

Pepper hesitated. "Well, put that way, I can't say for sure. I don't have the best eyes, as you well know. Don't get me started on the cost of eyeglasses and contacts. But who else could it have been? Both were tall, that's for sure."

That ruled out Desiree's sister, Sabrina. Of course, Pepper Pritchett could have been fabricating the whole scenario. Who knew what she had really seen if, indeed, she'd seen anything? And why was she targeting me? I glanced back at the mermaid sculpture; it wasn't as refined as I had first gauged. Would a normal person and not an artist have been capable of creating it?

"Stand aside," a man bellowed. My father. If I didn't know better, I would have pegged him for someone on the police force. Like Cinnamon, he wore camp shorts, a camp shirt, and an outback-style hat with a broad brim. Using a carved-handle walking stick, he divined people away from his path. "Everyone, step to the right, that's it. Thank you so much."

The crowd parted as if my father were Patton ready to announce the end of the war. As he passed them, each said something to him. I heard my name bandied about. Aunt Vera traipsed behind him, gripping her caftan in folds so she wouldn't trip over the hem.

My father stopped short of the yellow police tape. "Jenna, come here."

I raced to him and grabbed his hand for courage.

"Hello, Cary," Cinnamon said. "Good morning, Vera."

"Are you arresting my daughter?" my father asked.

"Of course she is." Pepper sounded triumphant.

"Chief Pritchett," I said, choosing a more respectful address even though she had allowed me the informality of using her first name. "I didn't do this."

My father released my hand then cleared his throat. "If you ask me, burying and covering the body with sand took time and planning."

"Nobody asked you," Pepper said.

Aunt Vera huddled next to me. "How are you, dear?"

"In shock." I didn't want to ask her if she had foreseen Desiree's death. The notion gave me the heebie-jeebies.

"Arrest her," Pepper said.

"Mother, hush, please." Cinnamon addressed my father. "Cary, I'd like to know how you figure this murder was not spontaneous."

My father planted his walking stick in front of him and grasped the uppermost portion with both hands. "Most people don't walk around with oversized fishhooks and a pail."

"A pail?"

My father smiled. "A pail would be useful for carrying water from the ocean to the, um, sculpture, don't you think? And the killer would need more than his hands. Perhaps a few tools. The sand on Miss Divine is packed firmly. Given the situation, I'd say the culprit planned ahead, perhaps even had these items stowed beneath"—he pivoted and scoured the beach, pointing with his stick —"beneath that bench or that palm tree."

"For heaven's sake, Cary," Pepper said. "Who do you think you are, Hercule Poirot?"

Give the woman ten points. At least she was well-read.

Cinnamon said, "You know he's a former FBI analyst, Mother. He's seen his share of dead bodies."

"On paper." Pepper sniffed.

"Whether on paper or in person, he knows a few things."

Cinnamon instructed a deputy to search nearer the shore, then shook my father's hand. "Nice to see you again, sir, although not under these circumstances. What else do you see?"

"You've discussed the lack of footprints?"

"Noted."

I nudged my aunt. "What's up with Dad and the chief? They seem to know each other pretty well."

"Cinnamon . . ." Aunt Vera paused. "She didn't have a father. She grew up with a bit of a chip on her shoulder. She hung out with the wrong crowd, got in trouble."

"What kind of trouble?"

My aunt dismissed the question with a wave of her hand. "Your father befriended her when she was a teen. At the time, he was participating in the Big Brother program. He took her under his wing. Got her focused on the future. After college, she considered going into social service work in San Francisco to help girls like herself, but then her mother suffered an illness. Not grievous, but it scared Cinnamon. She sought your father's advice. He supported her decision to return home to Crystal Cove. The police department needed a deputy. She climbed the ranks quickly." My aunt studied her fingernails. I felt as if there were more she wanted to say, but she didn't.

I gazed at my father, in quiet consultation with Cinnamon. How could I not have known about his mentor-student relationship with her? What else didn't I know about him? I regarded Pepper Pritchett, who was staring daggers at my father. She caught me spying and snarled. I was about to tell her to back off, but the deputy returned.

"Chief. I found something beside the palm tree." He revealed an array of tools.

"Aha." Pepper pointed. "Look right there. See that trowel? I saw that trowel in Jenna Hart's display window at the shop. That proves she is the killer."

Cinnamon whirled on me. "Is that true?"

"No. It can't be the same," I said then gulped. The trowel—pie-shaped with a wood handle—did look like one of the antique tools I had used in our display. I said, "Why would the killer leave them there, in plain sight?"

The deputy said, "They were buried. I think Old Jake might have scooped them up with his machine."

"Arrest her, Cinn."

Cinnamon drew taller, shoulders back. "Miss Hart, I'd like you to come to the precinct. We'll get out of the sun, and we can chat some more."

My parched skin was thankful, but my insides twisted into a knot. Did our competent police chief think I was guilty, after all?

Chapter 5

BIDING MY TIME in the beige Crystal Cove Precinct, sitting in a hardback chair, and sipping lukewarm tea while three sergeants listened to the police chief's mother trying to convince them that I was a murderer, I pondered how I had arrived there in the first place. Not there, in the precinct, but there—*here*—this quiet, seaside town. David died and life turned sour. A job that had been riotously fun for the first five years out of college became lackluster, the rewards empty. Out of the blue, my easygoing boss became exacting, even about the most soulless campaigns. I found myself grumping about paying city parking rates with no view of the ocean. I had few real friends. My idea of an adventure was going to a new restaurant, not on a hike. And then Aunt Vera called. Cajoled. Wooed me to Crystal Cove. And my spirit had lightened . . . until now.

I pinched my thigh to end the pity party and yanked myself back to the present. To the gossip. To the lingering fingerprint ink on my fingertips. To the horror of finding my friend dead. Who did it? The killer had to be someone in her entourage. Who else in our touristy town would have a motive, unless a rabid Desiree Divine fan had come to Crystal Cove? But other than the creepy guy with the tackle box in the parking lot, I hadn't seen anyone malicious looking hanging around The Cookbook Nook awaiting Desiree's arrival. That wasn't to say that I had the best powers of observation. When I was a child, Dad, in his role of FBI analyst, challenged my siblings and me to note the particulars of a street scene: the number of people, the ratio of men to women, the primary color the people wore. My sister did the best. She also aced college, read five nonfiction books a week without fail, and had a home crafting business. Her wares were selling like hotcakes over the Internet. I came in second in what we called the lookie-loo contest only because my hippie-dippie brother could care less. He preferred to gaze at trees or buildings and to listen to ambient sounds.

I shifted in my hardback chair and urged myself to think. Did Desiree's overworked sister hate her so much she would have killed her? Was Desiree's edgy, tattooed boyfriend the jealous type? Did the local hairstylist that Desiree had hired hold a grudge against her temporary boss? Why would she?

"Miss Hart." Cinnamon beckoned me to her office. I wondered for a split second why she had called me Jenna at the crime scene and had allowed me to call her by her first name, but I put aside the notion. My bosses at Taylor & Squibb had preferred first names. Familiarity was a national trend. Befriend a person. Put her at ease . . . and possibly off her guard. Formality set the tone for the future.

Pepper tried to enter the office right behind me, but Cinnamon banished her. When she closed the office door, she grilled me. How did I know Desiree? When was the last time I talked to her? Did I suspect any personal trouble? Did I know about the affair with my husband? All standard questions I had heard on television and in movies.

I replied with pat answers and folded my arms, an act of defiance that I convinced myself was an act of strength. I asked if Old Jake had seen anything suspicious; he hadn't. I mentioned the trowel. At Taylor & Squibb, we always dealt with the snags in a campaign first. Cinnamon shared that the trowel had been wiped clean of prints. I argued that the killer must have snatched the trowel from The Cookbook Nook—*snatched* being the operative word—to frame me. Anyone in town could have stolen it. I asked if I needed an attorney. She assured me that I didn't . . . yet.

An hour later, following a discussion about Desiree's rise to fame, her family, and circle of friends, a clerk arrived to tell Cinnamon she had a phone call. The clerk also brought me a glass of water. I was so grateful for the liquid and respite. My throat felt raw, my emotions as gritty as sand.

Cinnamon returned, her mouth grim, her eyes pinpoints of intensity, and I speculated about whether she was as dogged off the job as she was on the job. According to my aunt, she could roller skate and sing like an angel. Had she appeared in any of the local theater productions? The town boasted a modest theater company that put on plays every few months. The well-known actress who had starred in my last ad campaign, the Fountain of Youth Skin Cream series, had traveled to Crystal Cove for a juicy part.

"Miss Hart, are you listening to me?" Cinnamon said with a bite.

I stiffened. She had spoken? Shoot.

"Can you think of anything else, Miss Hart? Anything at all."

"Um, no. Did you have a distressful phone call?"

"That was your father on the phone." She hitched a thumb. "Until we have more evidential proof, he suggested that I release you on your own recognizance. I've agreed. You are free to go."

Let's hear it for Dad. Whatever differences we might have had, he would always act as my advocate.

"Thank you, ma'am." I felt silly calling someone a few years older than me *ma'am*, but *miss* wasn't respectful, although I didn't see a wedding ring, and she certainly wasn't a *sir*, and I didn't think it was appropriate to call her *Cinnamon* seeing as she was calling me *Miss Hart*. I guess I could have said: *Chief*. I plucked at the wadded-up tissue that sat in my lap. Yeah, okay, the waterworks had started about midway during the questioning. How puffy did my eyes look? If only I had a jar of Fountain of Youth cream to refresh my skin.

"However, do not leave town," Cinnamon added.

"Why would I? I just relocated here." I pressed my lips together, realizing how stupid I sounded. Open mouth, insert both feet. I rose from my chair. "No, of course, I won't leave. I'll be here. At your beck and call. And I promise, if I learn anything new, you'll be the first person I dial. I'm innocent. I did not strangle Desiree."

Cinnamon eagle-eyed me. "How did you know she was strangled?"

Sheesh. Maybe I needed to wear duct tape across my mouth. "I heard you whispering when you were crouched beside the body." I tapped my head. "Good ears. My mother always told me it was rude to listen in, but I can't help myself. You said the word *strangled,* and then something about a bruise on the right side of Desiree's head."

I heard a snort and whipped around. Pepper Pritchett stood like a sentry in the doorway to her daughter's office. How had she opened it so stealthily? I wondered for a second whether she would have killed Desiree to get me in trouble but chided myself for the notion. The woman was a sourpuss; that didn't make her a murderer.

WHEN I ARRIVED at The Cookbook Nook with Tigger, I was shocked to discover that Aunt Vera had declared it Opening Day despite the morning's tragedy. Crowds of people, including sandcastle makers, complete with buckets and shovels, packed the shop. Another dozen customers clustered on the boardwalk and waited for the opportunity to enter.

I ogled my morning exercise outfit and wished I had changed it when I went to the cottage to fetch the kitten, but thought: *What the heck?* Why did I need to wear business attire? Everyone in town, locals and tourists alike, dressed down. And focusing on work would help me keep my mind off, well, everything else. I planted Tigger in the office, refreshed his water, and joined my caftan-clad aunt at the register, where a stream of buyers waited, arms filled with our bargain cookbooks, regularly priced books, utensils, aprons, and Desiree's cookbook: *Cookies, Cakes, Sweets, and More*. We had preordered fifty copies. Taking in the size of the crowd, I wasn't sure we would have enough. The closest bookseller who might have a few copies on hand was located in San Jose, a little over an hour away. On the counter beside the books stood a tier of candies. Katie must have made them with recipes gleaned from Desiree's cookbook: toffee fudge, colorful rock candy, and chocolate peanut butter crisp bonbons. In college, the two of us had downed more than our fair share of rock candy. Our teeth had ached for days and we vowed to cut out all sweets forever. *Right*. My chest tightened from the memory.

"I know we should've remained closed, in honor of your friend"—Aunt Vera flaunted a hand at the crowd—"but how could I say no? People begged me to let them inside. Death makes curious bedfellows. And you should see the café. Not a seat available."

Desiree would have been proud to see folks take such an interest in her—dead or alive. I urged the tears pooling in my eyes not to fall and pressed ahead.

"How's Katie handling the pressure?" I asked, worried that we weren't prepared in the café for such an onslaught.

"Like a pro. An Iron Chef couldn't do better. We hired a couple of very cute sous chefs. We're still looking for an assistant chef." Aunt Vera poked the keys on the ancient register to make a sale. Multitasking suited her. Her cheeks radiated with a pretty pink flush, and her eyes sparkled with energy. "By the by, Katie made some delicious fruit-filled mini-cupcakes with the most luscious whipped frosting. She decorated them with little ships. They're for the taking over there." She wiggled her bejeweled pinky in the direction of the hallway leading to the café. Cupcakes and more goodies nestled on a table laid with an aqua-checkered tablecloth. I pondered whether we might go bankrupt giving away so much food but pushed the notion aside. Good marketing required drawing in repeat customers. "She's calling them Katie's Mateys," my aunt added. "Isn't that cute, seeing as we're located in Fisherman's Village?"

So cute my head was spinning.

"Ooh, look at this, Mommy," a child screamed at the back of the store. "A bake set. Can we get it?"

"Yoo-hoo." A string-bean-shaped customer standing at the far side of the store beckoned a stouter female. "Look at this." She was holding up the *The Gourmet Cookbook, Volume I.* "The pages are gilded. No photographs, though, only drawings. But the recipes look yummy."

The other female rushed to her, waving another cookbook. "I found the *Barefoot Contessa Foolproof: Recipes You Can Trust.* I hope her fabulous chicken salad recipe is in it."

"Girls, look," a customer shouted to her cluster of pals by the bay window at the front of the store. "Culinary mysteries. Oh, get these cute titles. *To Brie or Not to Brie*, *An Appetite for Murder*, and *A Brew to a Kill*." She giggled. "Ooh, and there are recipes inside. What fun."

Why wasn't anyone using an inside voice? My head started to throb.

Aunt Vera squeezed my arm. "We're a hit."

If she was so excited, why did I feel like crawling under a log, or at the very least, a mound of quilts? Because a friend had died. Horribly. And I was the prime suspect. Except I couldn't have done it. I never could have strangled Desiree, no matter what she might have been guilty of. I wasn't nearly strong enough. Who was?

"Jenna, what's wrong?" my aunt said. "Other than the obvious, of course." Before I could lie and say, *Nothing,* she lifted my chin with her fingertip and pinned me with a concerned gaze. "I'm so sorry about Desiree. I truly am. But life continues to churn. We stop to appreciate what we lost, and we take a deep breath, and we move ahead. We will meet all those we love in the afterlife. This, I know."

How could she be so sure? "Aunt Vera, I've got to ask. What's the scoop with you and this place? Why didn't you ever open it for business?"

Aunt Vera settled into one hip. Her mouth curved up. "I loved a man, dear. A chef and my soul mate. We planned to transform this into our special place."

"Did he . . . die?" My voice caught. I felt ghastly for dredging up such a sad memory, especially today. If only I could turn back the clock a few seconds.

"Worse." Aunt Vera sniffed. "He left me at the altar."

"Why?"

"That's the awful thing. I don't have a clue. We never talked about it. A month later, he married someone else. A year later, he traveled to the netherworld, and that's when I . . ." She screwed her finger toward the ceiling.

"You pursued your psychic career."

"Multiple times I visited the cemetery where he was buried. We never connected." She fanned the air. "But enough about me." She gripped me in a hug so fierce I thought the life might be squeezed from me. In the nick of time, she released me and took my face in both of her hands. "Find a smile and your spirit will follow."

I tried. My face felt like it might crack.

Aunt Vera said, "Look around. This is life. It's here."

I found it hard not to be pleased with the activity in the shop. The design, the marketing, and the word-of-mouth had worked. The shop was going to be a success. I had carried out my aunt's vision and saved myself in the process. Well, saved, if it weren't for the fact that a local shop owner was accusing me of murder. A frown tugged at the corners of my mouth. As I worked hard to make the corners turn upward, I spied movement outside the shop, across the parking lot. The door to the Winnebago that the masseur and hairstylist shared was opening.

Sabrina, still dressed in the dark clothes I had seen her wearing yesterday, emerged. She teetered on high heels and descended the metal stairs. As she alit on the pavement, a blur of tattooed flesh rushed her—J.P., Desiree's lover-slash-director, in jeans and a Stanley Kowalski–style wife-beater T-shirt. Sabrina hitched her matching tote higher on her shoulder. J.P. flailed his arms. He was saying something. Sabrina responded and backed up a step. He spoke again. Sabrina's eyes widened. She jammed a fist into her mouth. Was she only now getting the news about Desiree? No, Chief Pritchett must have contacted her.

J.P. continued to flap his arms and move his mouth. I wished I could listen in on the conversation. Did J.P. know who killed Desiree? Did he murder her and turn her into a sand sculpture? He reached for Sabrina's purse.

Sabrina screamed and wrenched from his grasp.

People on the sidewalk in front of the store watched in horror.

J.P. lunged for Sabrina and snatched the tote. He dove his hand inside and pulled out something thin and flimsy. A photograph?

At the same time, the door to the Winnebago opened and Mackenzie, the masseur, emerged. He didn't look anything like he had when I had knocked on the door yesterday. Granted, his karate shirt was open and his bronzed chest gleamed, but his face smoldered with anger, not indifference.

Sabrina slapped J.P. As he reeled backward, she snatched what I assumed was a photograph and stomped away. Her shoulders heaved. Was she crying?

Mackenzie and J.P. exchanged hard glances before J.P. stomped off in the opposite direction.

Desperate to know what the drama was about, I told Aunt Vera I would be right back and hurried after J.P.

Halfway down the block, he barged inside Latte Luck Café. I forged in after him.

THE CAFÉ WAS an easygoing place with simple wooden tables and chairs and a few brown leather booths. Sepia pictures of what Crystal Cove looked like in the early twenties hung on the walls. The sweet aromas flooding the restaurant would make even the most devout sugar-hater dive into a sweet. I eyeballed the glass case filled with home-made goodies, and my stomach grumbled. When was the last time I had eaten? My version of Bobby Flay's guacamole the night before? I had skipped breakfast. The trail mix my aunt gave me sat unopened in the pocket of my shorts. I ordered a glass of milk and a chocolate scone drizzled with orange icing, and I headed to J.P.

Families with beach gear crowded the booths. J.P. sat at a table by himself, his bare arms and face gleaming with perspiration.

"Join you?" I said.

He took a long swig from a bottle of water. "It's cool."

I took that as a *yes* and settled into the chair opposite him. The noise in the café was much more subdued than at The Cookbook Nook. Only the folks behind the counter spoke above a whisper. I sipped my milk. "I'm sorry about Desiree."

J.P. gawked at me, his eyes red-rimmed and moist. Had he come to a popular place to flaunt how distraught he was? I scolded myself for being a cynic. Premature death of a spouse will change a person.

"You look upset," I said, stating the obvious.

"Oh, man, I adored her. She's dead. I'll"—he pushed the bottle of water to the center of the table—"never see her again." His response, even the pause, sounded rehearsed. Had he been an actor before becoming a director? A number of our commercial directors at Taylor & Squibb had acted. The director on the Daily Dose of D campaign confided that learning the craft gave him an edge up when dealing with actors' quixotic natures.

"I saw you outside my store," I said. "You manhandled Sabrina."

"No way."

"You wrestled her purse from her. You snatched some-thing from it."

"No, I didn't."

Okay, that response established that he was a liar. At least I knew the kind of person with whom I was dealing.

We sat in silence for a moment, J.P. sucking down water, me sipping milk and nibbling on my scrumptious scone, until he slammed the empty bottle of water on the table.

I snapped to attention.

"You were always jealous of her," he said.

"What? No."

"Sure you were. She told me. You said she was the pretty one, and you were the stable one. The guys always liked her best."

"Stop it. You're twisting things. Yes, I was jealous of her, but not in a bad way. I wanted to emulate her." People in the café were staring. "I loved Desiree. She was a lifelong friend."

J.P. sank into himself. After a long moment of silence, he muttered, "I heard you found her body."

"Yes." I didn't add that Pepper Pritchett had accused me of murder. I wondered if, by now, she was spewing rumors at the *Crystal Cove Crier*. Would that reporter, Tito Martinez, run with the story? Would my face be plastered on the front cover of tomorrow's paper? Headline: *Hooked on Murder: Widow Questioned in Quirky Twist of Fate*. As an ad exec, I'd had the task of coming up with catchy loglines. "Let's start over, J.P. I'm Jenna Hart." I offered a hand. He didn't shake. "What's your last name?"

"Hessman."

"You said you come from Florida."

"Yeah, that's where I started out."

"Doing what?"

"I was a cable TV director."

Not an actor.

"I had aspirations of becoming the next Martin Scorsese." He honked out a laugh and sucked in a huge gulp of air. "I had dreams. Big dreams. Making films that mattered. Films that spoke to people. Films that would stand the test of time."

"But that didn't work out."

" 'Never was so much owed by so many to so few.' "

I gaped. He was quoting Churchill. Though I was an art history major in college, I knew the phrase because we had used the quote for a Bentley commercial that starred Peter O'Toole. Had I judged J.P. by the number of tattoos and underestimated his intelligence?

"And never was so much denied to so many others," he added.

I settled back into my chair. The latter was not Churchill. J.P. wasn't bright; he was egotistical.

"To become one of the elite . . ." He waved a hand. "What does it matter, huh? I didn't succeed. To make ends meet in L.A., I took a gig at a game show. Hated that. I ended up at the Food Channel. I like to eat. That's where I met Desiree."

"And you fell in love."

"And now she's gone. Gone. It's so not cool." He rested his forehead against his fingertips.

"I'm sorry. I miss her, too." If only I could extract the insidious doubt that had wormed its way into my soul.

I glanced out the window, hoping to find my calm in the happy-faced passersby, and was startled to see Sabrina climbing out of the passenger side of a black minivan. Desiree's masseur, Mackenzie, offered a hand for support. Sabrina looked shell-shocked. Beyond them I saw Cinnamon Pritchett on roller skates. She made a figure eight, avoiding a few pedestrians, and pulled to a stop. She wasn't in uniform. Was she tailing Sabrina or simply out for a spin?

Mackenzie spotted us and guided Sabrina toward the café window. J.P. caught sight of them and snarled. Mackenzie winked then whisked Sabrina away. Cinnamon resumed skating.

"You and the masseur don't like each other," I said, stating the obvious.

"He's a jerk."

"Care to elaborate?"

"He picked apart a couple of Desiree's recipes in her current cookbook. He thinks he knows how to cook. When he said the chicken breasts in cream caper sauce lacked salt, Des got blazing mad. He made her cry."

"Are he and Sabrina an item?"

"He's into himself, the egotistical . . ." J.P. rubbed his forearm hard. "Des talked about you," he said, switching topics. "A lot."

"She did?" Did she happen to tell J.P. the truth about David and her?

Hold up, Jenna, hearsay, I could hear my father warn. As an analyst, he never let my siblings and I assume anything. Not to mention, Sabrina had started the rumor. What if Sabrina lied to me to stir the pot? What if she had some gripe with Desiree? What if Desiree told Sabrina not to date the masseur? I flashed on the confrontation between J.P. and Sabrina in the parking lot and wondered if J.P. had a thing for Sabrina and not Desiree. What if Desiree found out, accused J.P., and he lashed out?

"Um, yesterday," I said, steering the discussion in a new direction, eager to pin down J.P.'s alibi at the time of the murder. "You and Desiree went out. Did you come here to eat? See, I'm new to town. Well, not new. I grew up here. But I'd been living in San Francisco for years. So many unique places have cropped up in Crystal Cove since I left for college. This scone is fabulous. Is the regular food any good?"

"No," he said.

"No, it's not good or, no, you and Desiree didn't come here?"

"I don't know about the food. We went to the Crystal Cove Inn."

"And checked in, of course."

"Yeah."

Except I had called there before giving up my search for Desiree, and the clerk said they hadn't checked in. J.P. was lying. Again.

"Actually, we didn't register right away," he said. "We went to the courtyard restaurant, the one where you can see the ocean."

"A View with a Room?"

"That's it. Des said she needed to decompress before tomorrow's"—he coughed—"*today's* soiree."

I didn't have the courage to tell him that Desiree's fans were flocking like vultures to the store. He hadn't seemed to notice during his quarrel with Sabrina.

"Des held high hopes for this new cookbook," he went on. "The reason she wanted to launch it in August was to promote the upcoming season of our show. Our ratings fell flat last season."

I ran my finger along the rim of the coffee cup. "What did you do after you ate?"

"That's when we checked in to the hotel. Des was dog-tired. Me, I was wired. I took one of Des's sleeping pills so I could get some shut-eye, but Des got a call, and she left."

"A call from whom?"

"I don't know. I asked her, but she wouldn't say." He scraped his fingers through his Mohawk. "Man, I should've gone with her."

"Did you think she was meeting some guy?"

"Nah." He leaned back in his chair and crossed his arms. "Even if she was, it was cool. I trusted her. She loved me." His defensive pose would have made a prosecuting attorney squeal with excitement. Jealousy was a powerful motive for murder.

"When did she return?"

"I don't have a clue. I fell asleep. When I take a pill, I'm Rip Van Winkle."

Call me crazy, but I didn't believe him.

Chapter 6

A S I LEFT the coffee shop, I thought about Desiree's phone call. Truth or fiction? If it was the truth, who had called her? Did Desiree meet that person and end up walking on the beach, only to be strangled?

And buried . . .

A queasy feeling coursed through me. I tamped it down and urged myself to think logically. Desiree's purse hadn't been tucked beneath the sand with her, and the deputy hadn't discovered it with the sand tools. Where was it? Was her cell phone in the purse? Maybe the call list would reveal the killer's name.

Eager to find out, I returned to The Cookbook Nook, which was still jammed with people clamoring for Desiree's recent release, and sneaked into the office at the back. I perched on the corner of the laminate desk and telephoned the precinct. While waiting for the clerk to connect me to Chief Pritchett, I inspected cookbooks that Aunt Vera had set aside for me to take home. To the few she had selected earlier, she had added *The Best One-Dish Suppers*, *Gourmet Meals in Crappy Little Kitchens*, Betty Crocker's *Dinner for Two Cook Book*, and Mark Bittman's *How to Cook Everything: The Basics*, which was a hefty book. "Each recipe is so easy and simple," Aunt Vera said of the stack, "even a child could manage the dishes. Not that you're a child. You're an adult. A mature, responsible adult." So why didn't I feel like an adult right now? Why did I feel like stuffing myself into a file cabinet under the heading: *To be opened at a later date?* A golden oldie that used to rouse my mother to sing, full voice, played through my mind: "Don't they know it's the end of the world 'cause you don't love me anymore?"

I heard a click through the telephone receiver.

"Miss Hart," Cinnamon said. Formal. Brusque. "What's up?"

Without stuttering, which pleased me no end, I told her what J.P. had said about the late-night phone call to Desiree.

Cinnamon said, "What do you think you're doing? Why are you questioning suspects?"

"So Mr. Hessman is a suspect?"

"Right now, everyone is a suspect."

Including your mother? I wanted to snipe but kept mum. I did not need to aggravate the chief and have her lock me up simply because she could. Besides, I liked her. She seemed direct and to the point—my kind of people.

In an unthreatening, composed voice, I said, "Did you happen to find Desiree's purse?"

"We did not."

"Which means the killer might have taken it."

Silence.

I cleared my throat. "Can you look up her cell phone records?"

"I'll put it on my to-do list. I've got to go. Thanks for being a concerned citizen."

Concerned didn't do my angst justice. I wanted the chief to like me. Trust me. Believe I was innocent.

As I hung up, Tigger snuggled up to my ankles. I lifted him and pressed his face against my cheek. "Hey, sweet boy," I cooed. "What do you think of the activity in the shop?" He purred. "Yes, I agree. Pretty darned overwhelming. So many people. Desiree would have been—" A pang jabbed my heart. Proud. She would have been proud. And she would have teased me and told me none of this would have happened without her. How true. Celebrity did create a draw.

"Jenna." Katie paraded into the office, her chef's toque atilt, her white apron stained with something that I hoped was wine, catsup, or blueberry jam. "Got a sec?" She crooked a finger.

"I'd better check with Aunt Vera to see if I need to spell her at the cash register."

"I already did. And she doesn't. She's in seventh heaven."

I set Tigger on the floor and followed Katie through the shop and restaurant and outside to the patio that overlooked the ocean. The view captivated me. The roar of the waves crashing against the rocky shore beneath the patio made me catch my breath. My mother used to say that God talked to us through the waves. I never heard His voice, but I was certain she did.

Katie settled into a chair at one of the wagon-wheel-style tables, removed her hat, and set it in her lap. She folded her hands on top of the table. "I'm sorry about Desiree. You found her, huh? With that . . ." She mimed a hook.

"How did you hear?"

"People talk."

I flashed on the crime scene. Why had someone hooked Desiree like a prize catch? What was the significance?

"Finding her was a tough way to start your new life here," Katie said.

"Tell me about it."

"I heard a rumor . . ." She let the sentence hang.

I swallowed hard. Pepper said the whole town was gossiping about whether my husband had an affair with Desiree. Was I to be the laughingstock? What a cliché. *Best friend wins over roving husband.* Would a doctored picture of Desiree in David's embrace appear on the front cover of rag magazines? No matter what, I would fight the rumor tooth and nail. It wasn't true. David and I had been madly in love. I felt a thin band of perspiration forming on my upper lip.

"Someone in town said you might be interested in Desiree's boyfriend," Katie continued.

"What? J.P. No. Why?"

"Someone saw you together at Latte Luck Café."

I shook a hand. "No, no, no." Man, the rumor mill in Crystal Cove was lightning fast. "I mean, yes, I was there with J.P., but our meeting was nothing like that. Nothing. I saw . . . I followed—"

"Breathe."

In between deep calming breaths, I explained.

Katie leaned forward, her gaze keen for gossip. "You think J.P. might have killed Desiree?"

"I don't know what to think." Truly, I didn't. "I'm going to leave it to the police."

"That's all well and good, but if Pepper Pritchett has her way, she'll railroad you into jail just so she can close down this operation."

"What's her story?" I asked.

"Haven't a clue. Forget about her. Now, tell me what you saw. Why did you follow J.P.?"

I filled her in on the silent drama I'd witnessed between J.P. and Sabrina. "He denied accosting her, which means he's a liar. Mackenzie the masseur watched, too. In fact, now that I think of it, he was glowering at the two of them." I added that Mackenzie and Sabrina had appeared outside the café.

"Hoo-boy. Do you think Mackenzie has a thing for Sabrina? Maybe Desiree didn't appreciate her masseur lusting after her little sis."

I liked the fact that Katie and I had formed similar theories.

"Maybe Desiree had a chat with him and told him to back off," Katie continued, "and the guy lost it."

"Except Pepper said she saw two women, not a man and a woman, walking on the beach last night."

Katie guffawed. "Pepper Pritchett needs prescription

goggles to see the nose in front of her face. Have you seen her Beaders of Paradise shop? There are magnifying glasses everywhere. Changing the subject, I saw Desiree yesterday, when the Winnebagos took up residence in the parking lot. I was walking the staff through the table arrangements. Desiree was engaged in a heated argument with the masseur."

"Did you hear what the fight was about?"

"Desiree said she wasn't happy with his choice of hairstylist."

"Mackenzie hired the hairstylist?"

"Of his own volition. Guess he got the call that the hairstylist in L.A. wasn't going to make the grand opening—flu or some such—so he drummed up Gigi Goode." Katie fiddled with the rim of her chef's hat. "Gigi is supposed to be fabulous, by the way. At least that's the scuttlebutt, but whew, she charges an arm and another arm."

"I'll bet she doesn't ask any more than a hairstylist in Los Angeles."

"Yeah, you're right." Katie thumped the tabletop with her fingertips. She looked as if she was holding something back.

I said, "What else is bugging you?"

"Your pal Desiree was pretty darned rude. I wouldn't be surprised if a number of the people that worked for her wanted to kill her because of the way she ranted."

My first boss at Taylor & Squibb railed at everyone. One day, following a particularly brutal brainstorming session, a lot of us discussed skewering him with his laser pointer.

Katie rolled her lower lip between her teeth. "I know you were good friends with Desiree, but really, the words that came out of her mouth. No one should treat another person that way." She clucked her tongue. "She was a shrew."

Behaving like a diva was one thing, but a shrew? I stewed, wondering what had been going on in Desiree's life that might have made her act atrociously. J.P. mentioned that the show's last season ratings had been flat. Perhaps Desiree worried that her fifteen minutes of fame were nearing an end. I had chosen to terminate my career. I don't know how I would have felt if I had been forced out and forgotten.

"Is that all you wanted to discuss?" I said. "The rumor and Desiree's behavior?"

"Hoo-boy, are you kidding?" A chuckle tumbled out of Katie. She set her hat snugly back on her head and stood.

I rose, as well, and couldn't help but compare the two of us. We stood about the same height, but she had broader shoulders, a broader girth, a broader face, and a broader smile. I had to work on my smile. I considered practicing in front of a mirror.

She said, "We've got business to discuss, too. Are you up to it?"

"I have to be, don't I?"

Katie bobbed her head. Her toque flopped as if it were a marionette with its own personality. "I want to add a few items to the menu."

"So soon?"

She headed back through the restaurant. Busboys and busgirls cleared dishes from the tables by the windows. Near the entrance, a pair of waiters draped tables with white linens. A couple of college-aged waitresses followed and adorned each table with silverware, glasses, and a teensy vase filled with a white daisy.

"I can tell what tastes our patrons have," Katie said. "At lunch, we sold out of white fish with a shrimp marinara sauce and, my pasta specialty, heavy on the artichoke hearts and hearts of palm. White wine is most popular in August, so I've opted to bring in a couple of cases of Crystala from a local winery of the same name. The wine tastes like Prosecco mixed with ambrosia. Perfect for a hot summer day. Also, some folks are asking about whether we're going to have cooking classes."

"Oh, gee."

"Adult classes as well as kid-friendly classes. You might want to take a class yourself."

I pictured the stack of cookbooks Aunt Vera had set aside for me. Did I need a class? Couldn't I teach myself?

As we rounded the hallway toward the bookstore, Katie said, "Uh-oh."

"What?"

"I think we have to table this discussion." She pointed.

Out in the parking lot, Pepper Pritchett, wearing a sleeveless bejeweled sheath, was doing a chicken dance, elbows flapping, feet stomping, between a tow truck and Desiree's Winnebago.

I plowed through the dining room and outside.

Pepper screamed at the tow truck operator. "What do you mean, you can't budge the trailers?"

"Ma'am, the tires," the operator said. "Somebody's slashed them. If I can't roll 'em, I can't tow 'em."

Pepper whirled on me and poked her finger. "What are you laughing at?"

I slapped my chest with my palm. "Me? I'm not laughing. I came to help."

Gleeful snorts burst from beyond the Winnebagos.

"Who's there?" I yelled.

A handful of teens in jeans and raggedy T-shirts sprinted from behind the Winnebagos, all of them giggling so hard they had to hold their sides. One, a dystopian girl who reminded me of a fighter in *The Hunger Games*, thumbed her nose before running off.

"Why you!" Pepper dashed for the kids but didn't have a chance in heaven of catching them. Her thick, short legs held her back. Bet she wished she had donned roller skates. "My daughter will nab every one of you hooligans." She stopped short of the parking lot exit, glowered at me, and marched back to her shop. She blasted inside and slammed the door.

The weary tow truck operator gazed at me. "Who's paying my bill?"

"Don't look at me," I said.

He heaved a sigh and lumbered to his truck.

A flare caught my eye. Near the tow truck operator's vehicle, I spied another truck. In the driver's seat sat a man. Was it the creepy guy with the tackle box? He was peering through binoculars. Glimpsing me, he lowered the glasses, cranked his truck into reverse, and barreled out of the lot. I wasn't close enough to glean numbers or letters from his license plate. Drat! Who the heck was he?

At the same time, the door to the Winnebago that housed Desiree's office squeaked open. Sabrina emerged in a white sheath, sandals, a single strand of pearls, and a clutch purse. Her wavy black hair wafted behind her and shimmered in the sunlight. What happened to the dour colors she usually wore? Was wearing an angelic-looking outfit the way she intended to honor her sister's death?

I strode to her and held out my hands. "Sabrina, I am so sorry for your loss."

Out of nowhere, she threw herself into my arms. Gasping sobs heaved from her chest. When she recovered, which, yes, might have been a tad on the speedy side, she swiped the tears from her cheeks. "The police called me and then J.P. found me and . . ." She pressed her lips together then exhaled. "I can't believe Desiree's dead."

As I'd figured, the scuffle in the parking lot had been their first occasion to speak following the murder.

"Desiree was buried in the sand." Sabrina shook her head. Her curls whipped right and left. "Buried. It's so horrible."

"What else do you know?"

"What do you mean?"

"About the crime scene."

"Nothing."

"Your sister was strangled."

Sabrina's right hand flew protectively to her throat. "The police never said . . ." She gulped. "Was it symbolic?"

"What do you mean?"

"Desiree never could keep her mouth shut. She made promises she couldn't keep. She talked dirt about people. She . . . she—" Sabrina hiccupped.

Was her panic an act? Was she as cool as a cucumber inside? Perhaps she had chosen to wear white to cover a guilty conscience.

Stop it, Jenna. Not everyone is guilty.

After a moment, Sabrina lowered her arm. She pinched the edge of her Prada purse. Her knuckles grew as white as the leather. "The police want me to come to the station."

"Before you go, might I ask a question? When J.P. met you this morning, you two struggled. He wanted something from your tote bag."

"No, he didn't."

Okay, officially, I had two liars. "You argued." I remember how she had waged a stalwart defense. Though she was inches shorter than Desiree, was she strong enough to have strangled her sister? I waited for her to amend her statement.

"He asked me if I called Desiree last night," she said finally.

"Was he reaching for your cell phone?"

"He wasn't reaching for anything. Sometimes he acts like Desiree's henchman. As if he has control over me. He wanted me to join him for coffee in your café. He was going for my hand. I pulled away."

I raised a skeptical eyebrow. My father said: *Tell one lie, you can quickly amend it and offer the truth. Tell two, you're building a story. Tell three, you're digging a grave.* The thought made me shudder. J.P. had pulled something from Sabrina's purse. I could have sworn it was a photograph.

"When J.P. accosted you"—I would not back down with my choice of verbs—"you were coming out of the masseur's trailer."

Sabrina peeked over her shoulder. I don't think she meant to. But when she swiveled her head back and met my gaze, her face flushed bright pink. "Oh, all right, I'm not proud of it, but yesterday, my boyfriend in Los Angeles called and broke it off with me. Gigi, Desiree's hairstylist, mentioned this really cool place to go for drinks. The Chill Zone Bar."

The Chill Zone was a hotspot that even I, socially single and uninterested in meeting a new man, knew about.

"I went there for a drink," Sabrina said. "I'm not one to

cry into my beer, but this guy, my boyfriend—he's an actor in L.A.—I thought he was *the one*. You know?"

"Did Desiree approve of him?"

"What would I care?" Sabrina flinched. "That was cruel. Of course, I would've cared. I craved her approval. Now . . ." She fluttered a hand in front of her face. "It turned out Mackenzie was at the bar, too. He said I seemed tense. He asked me back to the trailer for a shoulder massage. One thing led to another. Like I said, I'm not proud. I . . . I passed out."

Something about the way Sabrina kept looking up and to the right bothered me. Most of my advertising staff glanced in that direction when they donned their creative hats. Was Sabrina crafting a story? Was she embarrassed that she had settled for pity sex with Mackenzie?

"Is that all?" I said.

"Isn't that enough? I was out cold while my sister was murdered. Do you know how guilty I feel?"

Actually, I didn't. I couldn't be sure.

Chapter 7

BY THE TIME I returned to the shop, the store had emptied of customers. Aunt Vera stood at the register, hand to her chest. Her face glistened with perspiration. Her eyes appeared glazed and spooky.

"Are you okay?" I said.

"Yes. All this activity is so exhilarating, I can barely stand it, but yes, yes, yes. And I have four new clients. You don't mind that I handed out my tarot reading cards, do you?"

"It's your shop."

"No, dear, it's ours. Fifty-fifty. Of course, I might sneak an occasional cookbook for my personal collection. I'll leave notes by the register when I do. Did you see *All About Braising: The Art of Uncomplicated Cooking*, by the way?" My aunt lifted a book and displayed the cover like a TV model. "Braised endive, simmering in scrumptious juices and spices, and a perfect pot roast." She kissed her fingertips. "There are sixteen color photos and fifty line drawings. Everything you need." She tapped her finger on the cover. "I'm taking it home to try out some of the recipes. I'll pass it along to you." She set the book down, shuffled away from the register, and scooped up Tigger, who had been weaving between aisles. "Hello, my little mascot," she said. "Are you being a good boy? Yes, you are. Yes, you are." She replaced him on the hardwood floor and turned back to me. "Jenna, dear, what was that *tête-à-tête* with Sabrina in the parking lot? Does the girl have an alibi for last night?"

"Why do you ask?"

"I'm picking up a vibe."

"Now, Aunt Vera . . ."

"Not that kind. I am spent. Nothing going on in this noggin right now." She tapped her temple. Her collection of silver and red bangle bracelets clattered. "But I don't like her. She's so dour and intense."

"With good reason. Sabrina played second fiddle to Desiree for forever."

"Well, no longer."

Before I could ponder that comment, Pepper barreled into the shop. "Vera!"

A trio of what I could only describe as incensed crafters followed her inside. The skinniest wore a hand-beaded summer sweater that didn't enhance her shapeless body, though the beadwork was expertly done. The spark plug–shaped woman with frowsy auburn hair sported countless strings of beads over an outfit that screamed garish. The prettiest of the crew held fast to a sizable beading kit. I actually liked the floral dress she wore. She had donned attractive beaded earrings that drew the whole ensemble together.

"We want a word with you, Vera." Pepper lasered me with an evil glare. "You, missy, can keep your distance."

Missy? My teeth clamped together. Why did this woman hate me? What had I ever done to her?

Aunt Vera clucked her tongue. "What now, Pepper?"

"We're boycotting your shop."

"Fine with me," my aunt said.

"Your niece is evil."

"Now, wait a sec." I started for the woman. Aunt Vera put a hand on my arm.

"Trouble started the moment you arrived in town." Pepper wagged a finger; her bare triceps jiggled with fury.

I gaped. "Where is all this venom coming from?"

"Betrayal is a bitter pill to swallow," the spark plug–shaped woman said.

"Henrietta Hutchinson, hush." Pepper shot the woman a hard look.

I glanced between them. Hush about what? What didn't I know? What was I supposed to know?

Pepper continued. "I overheard your chef talking about you, Jenna Hart. She said you used to be a mean girl in school."

"What?" I croaked.

"Mean girls can be killers."

"All right, Pepper." Aunt Vera stormed toward the beading shop owner and grasped her by the elbow. One thing could be said for my aunt: When she'd had all she could handle, she took action. "Leave, now. I will not have anyone accusing my niece of being a killer. Desiree Divine was one of her best friends. No way in Hades would Jenna ever put a finger on that girl."

Pepper jutted her jaw. "We'll see. I'm having my daughter do a background check on your niece."

The worst thing I had ever done was rack up a set of speeding tickets. And sneak dollar bills out of my mother's purse for the occasional bag of Tootsie Rolls. And yes, I had been a suspect in David's disappearance until the lead detective ruled his death an unfortunate accident. I had no motive; there was no life insurance policy and David's investment portfolio was drained. David hadn't written a will. I had gained nothing other than the few precious tokens we had acquired as a couple. And I hadn't been anywhere near the boat. The police found only David's fingerprints on the helm and elsewhere. He was alive one minute, gone the next.

"Let's go, beaders." Pepper trooped past her entourage. In unison, her posse did an about-face and followed. In a parting gesture, the woman in the floral ensemble, who seemed torn about being part of a gang, threw me an over-the-shoulder, perk-up smile.

As Aunt Vera closed the door, I said, "Why is Pepper set on ruining me?"

"It's nothing. Put her out of your mind."

"Aunt Vera, I'm not a child, and if I'm going to make a success of myself in Crystal Cove, I need to know everything. I have to be prepared to defend myself. That woman, Hutch-something, said, 'Betrayal is a bitter pill to swallow.' Explain."

Aunt Vera worked her tongue along her upper teeth. "Way back when, Pepper had a thing for your father."

"No."

"Yes. Your father had earned his MBA at Stanford. He wanted a summer to play in the sun. And play, he did. He swam, he hiked, he surfed. One day, he met your mother and Pepper at the beach. They were friends."

I gaped.

"They played volleyball as a group. Hitting, spiking, and whatever else they do. Pepper wanted your father in the worst way. She was a handsome woman. She had a shot."

I shook my head. No way was Pepper Pritchett ever an attractive woman. On the other hand, her daughter was pretty. Speechless, I twirled a finger indicating my aunt should continue.

"Your mother won your father's heart. Pepper never forgave your mother, but more importantly, she never forgave your father for not choosing her."

"Pepper married," I managed to say. "She had a child."

"As I told you, Cinnamon grew up without a father. He abandoned Pepper and his daughter the day Cinnamon was born. Your father, being the standup guy he is, offered financial support, but that wasn't enough for Pepper. She wanted *him*."

"Dad and Pepper never . . . I mean, Cinnamon isn't my . . ." I couldn't form the word *sister*.

"Heaven forbid." Aunt Vera waggled her head. "So now you understand why Pepper is as miserable to you as a woman can be. To this day, she feels your mother trapped your father, and if not for you and your siblings, she would have had a chance to win his affection. Mind you, I'm not asking you to cultivate civility with Pepper."

I folded my arms on the counter. "That thing the Hutch woman said. Did Dad lead Pepper on?"

"No. And your mother did not betray her either." Aunt Vera thumped her head. "Pepper is ten beads short of a full strand, if you know what I mean. Put her from your mind."

I would try, but somewhere at the back of my brain I worried that Pepper, thanks to her deep-seated feelings, would convince her daughter that I was guilty of murder. To calm myself, I reached under the counter and pulled a Tootsie Roll from my stash. The act of twisting open the little morsel soothed me. When I popped it into my mouth and chewed, I felt my emotions settle down.

"Jenna." Katie breezed into the shop carrying a stack of cookbooks. I read a couple of the spines: *Slow Cooker Revolution*, *1,001 Best Slow-Cooker Recipes*, and the *Fix-It and Forget-It Cookbook*. "I forgot that I pulled these for you. They're . . ." She swung her gaze from me, to my aunt, and back to me. "What's wrong? You're frowning."

I polished off my candy and tossed the wrapper into the trash can behind the counter. "Nothing."

Katie peeked out the window. "Did that Henrietta Hutchinson say something about the café food? She's one to talk. She burns everything she cooks. I've seen smoke more times than I can count coming from her—"

"Katie," I cut her off. "It's nothing."

"No lying, Jenna," my aunt said. "We cannot start a business on that note."

Katie set the books on the counter by the register. "Is it me? You don't like my cooking? Is that it?"

"No." I sputtered. "I mean, yes, I do. I really do. *Like* it."

Her lower lip trembled. "Did you eat the white fish tortellini today, Vera?"

"Oh, yes, dear. It was scrumptious." My aunt explained, "Katie brought me a tasting of everything on the lunch menu today. Truly divine. The pasta was so tender it melted in my mouth. I loved the rosemary sauce."

"C'mon. What is going on between you two?" Katie folded her arms.

At Taylor & Squibb, once a week, we had an *out with it* meeting. No one was allowed to sweep nasty feelings under a rug. The partners believed honesty was the best policy. Until now, I had agreed.

Katie drilled the floor with her size eleven shoe.

"Oh, all right," I said. "Pepper overheard you talking about me. You told someone I was a mean girl in high school."

"No. That's not what I . . . She . . ." Katie grew three shades of pink. Her neck splotched as if she had contracted hives. "I was talking on the telephone to my mother. I was trying to explain who you were. I didn't use the word *mean*."

"I don't understand. You needed to describe me to your mom? During high school, I spent days and nights at your house. You went on camping trips with my family. How could your mother forget me?"

"She has Alzheimer's," Katie said. "She forgets everything."

"Oh, gosh." I rushed to her and grabbed her hands. "I'm sorry. She's so young."

"She was diagnosed two years ago. Her age alters a statistic, the doctor said, but there's nothing we can do."

I frowned at my aunt, who bopped one side of her head. How could she have forgotten to notify me about Katie's mom?

"I told Mama you hung out with the popular crowd," Katie went on. "She said, 'Are you saying she was a mean girl?' and I said, 'Not mean, popular.' Pepper Pritchett has selective hearing. Forgive me?"

"Of course. How are you handling it all?"

"I'm good. My father is the one who struggles the most. He . . ." Tears pooled in Katie's eyes. "Hoo-boy, don't make me cry. We forge ahead, right?" She released my hands. "Now, about these books I set on the counter. They're all minimal ingredient books." The topmost title read: *Robin Takes 5: 500 Recipes, 5 Ingredients or Less*, by Robin Miller. Sounded easy to me. So did the second: *Six Ingredients or Less Cookbook*, by Linda Hazen. "These are all great books for a beginner cook, such as yourself. And I jotted down some of my own five-ingredient recipes, as well." She tapped cards that she had slotted into the 5-5-5 book. "I want you to try herbed chicken and soup."

"Isn't soup difficult?"

"Not all soup. There's one in here, my personal favorite. Soup marinara. Hoo-boy, it's good. With a hunk of bread and a sprinkling of Parmesan cheese. Yum. And I've been pondering some shop ideas, too. I think we should have a Share a Recipe night."

"Great idea," Aunt Vera said.

"And we should consider having a book signing with some of these culinary mystery authors. I think there are a few of them that live in the Western states. We'll make dishes that they include as recipes. We'll have a soiree. What do you think, Jenna?"

I breathed easier. Katie and I were back on solid footing. I didn't have to consider replacing a great chef and, more importantly, my "new" old friend.

"LISTEN TO THAT, Tigger." I nuzzled the kitten as we approached the front door of the cottage. "That's the sound of the sea kissing the shore." Waves rolled onto the sand and receded. The repetition relaxed me until I flashed on Desiree and David, and reality closed in. Would I ever feel at ease around the ocean again? Could I continue to live so nearby?

Yes. I had to cope. I would move on. And being near the sea brought me closer to my mother. When she died, Dad arranged for a maritime burial. A friend of my mother's sang a heartfelt song, *a capella*. At the end of the service, we all threw a long-stemmed red rose upon the water. How my mother loved red roses.

"Let's go. Inside." I set Tigger on the floor. He scampered

ahead. I kicked the door shut with my heel. "I've got homework." I slipped the reusable grocery bag off my shoulder onto the counter in the kitchenette and let the backpack filled with cookbooks slide to the Spanish tile floor.

Tigger bumped my ankle.

"Hungry?"

He cha-cha'd in a circle.

"Me, too." I pulled a can of organic cat food from the grocery bag, popped off the lid, and forked half into his bowl. As he wolfed down the food, I unpacked the rest of the groceries and opened one of the cookbooks to the recipe Katie had marked with a Post-it: herbed chicken. With only five ingredients, what could go wrong? I heated the oven, cracked open three jars of new spices—rosemary, basil, and thyme—and a bottle of olive oil. Aunt Vera swore by the clay-roaster pot she had purchased for the cottage, making me promise that I would use it as-is, adding no foil or any other kind of liner. I brushed the pot with oil, set the chicken into the pan, and obeying the recipe's directions, made a mixture of spices. I dashed them on top of the chicken— *bam!* à la Emeril—added a little water, set the top of the roaster on the lower half, and placed the roaster in the oven. In an hour and fifteen minutes, I was supposed to be eating fall-off-the-bone chicken. My taste buds moistened in anticipation.

Ready to retreat to the porch and drink in the night air, I poured myself a glass of sauvignon blanc. As I reinserted the cork, I heard a thunk. Tigger yowled. I raced to see what had happened. The kitten leaped off the Ching cabinet and skittered backward.

"It's okay, fella. Nothing's broken." I righted the gold ceramic *Maneki Neko*, literally "beckoning cat" in Japanese, that David had bought on one of our shopping outings. The sculpture, a bobtail cat holding its paw upright, was meant to bring good fortune. David had slipped a silver necklace with a key charm around the cat's neck. He said it was the *key to his heart*. Because the sculpture was popular in Chinese communities, many made the mistake thinking the

Lucky Cat was Chinese—David and myself included. We laughed over our faux pas, which of course, he kept spelling out for me: *f-o-u-r P-A-W-S*. The memory wrenched my soul. So did the sight of the golden statue on its side. My fortune was bad enough. Was its toppling an omen? If Aunt Vera were with me, she would give me her phoenix amulet and demand I wear it for eternity. She might even spin me around three times while uttering a blessing: "Rise above your misfortune. You are on a path to your perfect destiny." I had memorized a few of her inspirational sayings.

Not wishing to get sucked into bad karma thoughts, I recited my aunt's mantra in my head and returned to my glass of wine. Before I could take a sip, I heard another crash. I whirled around. Tigger, the imp, had jumped up on the oak table beside my bed and upset a silver picture frame.

I hurtled across the room and snatched the frame. The picture was of David at the bottom of Bridalveil Falls in Yosemite, his tawny hair windblown, his tanned face tilted upward as he gazed at the head of the falls. He had proposed to me that day. I clutched the frame to my chest and uttered a prayer for him and for me. Afterward, I replaced the picture and scooped up Tigger. "Bad kitty." His eyes widened. He couldn't have looked guiltier or more remorseful. A wealth of despair gushed through me. How I missed David. How I ached for Desiree. And how I longed for happiness. I thought I would find it in Crystal Cove, but perhaps I was mistaken. Maybe I was supposed to return to San Francisco and make peace with my future there. "I'm sorry I yelled, Tigger. So sorry." I hugged him with a fierceness that made him squirm.

Something bleeped. I startled. Tigger sprang from my arms. I shook a scolding finger. "Don't climb on anything else. I can't take the suspense."

He meowed. Maybe he was saying, "Try not to choke me next time," but I took his utterances for an apology and searched for the offending bleep; it came from the oven. The temperature had reached its peak. No worries.

I slumped into a chair at the tiny kitchen table, scanned the one-room cottage—really surveyed it—and suddenly felt cramped in such close quarters, but I didn't have the courage to budge, and I certainly didn't have the pluck to step outside. A murderer could be at large. I was vulnerable in my dreamy cottage by the sea.

Stop it, Jenna. Think positively. I pondered a quote I had memorized by Helen Keller: "Life is either a daring adventure or nothing."

Shaking off my anxiety, I bounded to my feet, slipped the cookbooks from the backpack, and assembled them on the coffee table by the sofa. I wasn't in the mood to browse their pages, but soon I would. As I stood, I noticed that the light on the answering machine on the table next to my bed was blinking. The machine was old; David and I had bought it when we moved in together. I couldn't bear to part with the contraption. I would never forget when we recorded the message, my only verbal reminder of David's voice: *You've reached David and Jenna. Leave a message after the bleepety-bleep-bleep*, he joked. *We'll bleepety-bleep call you back.* When David pressed End, he swooped me into a hug and we fell onto the couch laughing. Cell phones had replaced the need for a home answering machine completely—only telemarketers or politicians called on a landline telephone anymore—but Aunt Vera had installed one, so I had hooked up the answering machine.

A notion niggled at the edges of my mind. I wouldn't have paid attention to the answering machine if Tigger hadn't knocked the photograph aside. Had the kitty pawed the frame on purpose? Who had called? When? I dove for the machine and pressed Play.

The digital voice said: "You have one message."

The recording followed immediately. "Hey, Jenna, you home?" My lungs snagged in my chest. The voice was Desiree's. "We need to talk." She sounded tight and high-pitched, unusual for her. "I heard you were looking for me. I hope . . ." She sucked in a breath of air. "Let's talk tomorrow. Whatever you do, don't believe lies."

The message clicked off. The digital voice said: *Thursday, 10:01 P.M.*

My finger hovered over Erase. I didn't press the button as thoughts zipped through my mind. How had I not heard the telephone ring? I was home at the time of the call. I paused. No, actually, I wasn't home. I had gone outside for a few minutes to listen to the surf. The roar had been deafening. I would have missed hearing the ring.

A flurry of emotions cascaded through me. Desiree's message exonerated me of killing her, didn't it? Why would I kill her before learning what she had to say? If only Tigger were a reliable witness.

A whoosh of wind outside rattled the shutters. Seconds later, I heard another sound, one that sent fear spiraling down to my toes—a twist of metal. Was someone at the front door? Trying to get in? I sped to the window and pushed back the drapes an inch. I peered into the dark. No one stood on the porch. I couldn't make out a figure hovering in the shadows. I recalled one time, when I was ten and Dad went out of town and my siblings left for camp. Mom and I stayed alone in the house, and I thought I heard an intruder. Acting like a superhero, I whipped open the kitchen door and stormed outside, yelling, "You don't scare me." I swear I saw a figure run off, but my mother convinced me I had seen palm fronds waving in the dark. I didn't feel nearly so brave now. I refused to open that door.

Pulse pounding, I dialed the precinct.

Cinnamon Pritchett answered. "Hello, Jenna."

Hearing her voice surprised me. Why had she answered? How had she known it was me? And why had she called me Jenna and not Miss Hart? Had I been exonerated? I said, "Hi, um, I expected to reach the clerk."

"She needed to leave early."

"I . . . I thought you'd be on your way home by now," I stammered. I couldn't bring myself to tell her I was scared of a rattling sound.

"I should have been, however, we had a late afternoon rash of crime. Loads of paperwork. What's up?"

"Um . . ." If I told her I thought someone was trying to break into my house, would she think I was making the whole thing up to persuade her that I wasn't a killer? I hadn't heard another ping, let alone a rattle. Summoning up courage, I told her about the recording. "Desiree sounded scared. You might want to listen."

"I'll be right out."

I sat by the front door holding an umbrella as a weapon until Cinnamon arrived. Before she entered, I returned the umbrella to its proper place in the corner.

Tigger greeted Cinnamon with a samba and an excited spin on his rump. "Cute cat," she said. "How long have you had him?"

"A few days."

"Stray?"

"I didn't steal him."

"Don't act so defensive. I love strays. I have two of my own. Donner and Blitzen. I found them on Christmas day. I wasn't allowed any pets growing up."

No father and no pets, I mused, and probably not a lot of hugs and kisses from her prickly mother either. Poor, deprived kid.

Cinnamon bent down to pet Tigger and assessed my one-room cottage from that vantage point. "Nice place."

"All my Aunt Vera's doing."

"Old Jake says hello, by the way." She rose to a stand.

"Old Jake? Why would he say hello to me?"

"He's a neighbor. He lives on the strand."

"He does?"

"Raking the sand is volunteer work. He's a retired millionaire with time on his hands. Anyway, I saw him as I exited my car. He said he drove his machine by your place a bit ago. Saw your light on. You didn't hear him? Noisy machine. Clackety-clack."

Geez. Would the rumble of Old Jake's machine make the shutters and doorknob rattle? I hadn't thought to look toward the ocean when searching for what I imagined was a prowler.

Feeling as stupid as a slug, I said, "Can I pour you a glass of wine?"

"Still on the clock. Whatever you're cooking smells good."

"Roast chicken with herbs. I'd offer you some, but . . ." An hour remained on the timer.

"No, thanks. I have a leftover deli sandwich calling me." She eyed the landline telephone. "Let me hear the offending answering machine message."

"It exonerates me."

"I'll be the judge."

I replayed the message.

Cinnamon's pretty face scrunched with concentration. "Miss Divine does sound edgy," she conceded. "I'm not sure *scared* is the right word."

"Even so, doesn't this prove that I wasn't with her?"

"All it confirms is that she called you well before she was killed, and she warned you not to believe lies."

"Lies about an affair."

"That's not what she said."

"Doesn't the message substantiate that I didn't kill her?"

"Not really. The DA might argue that if Miss Divine didn't reach you, she might have come here to talk. The two of you had a heated exchange. You lost your temper."

"I didn't. *We* didn't."

"You lashed out. She ran out to the beach. You followed."

"Your mother said she saw two women *walking*, not one chasing the other."

Cinnamon shifted feet. "I forgot to tell you. My mother admitted she made that up."

"Made it up?" I said. A Kurt Cobain quote flitted through my mind: "Just because you're paranoid doesn't mean they aren't after you."

"She didn't actually say she made it up," Cinnamon back-pedaled. "She said she got her points wrong. The time. The location."

"Why was she so adamant then?" I sucked in air. "Never mind. I know why."

"Mother can be difficult."

That was an understatement, but at least Cinnamon acknowledged the problem.

"Why don't you believe me?" I said, unable to keep the piteous tone from my voice. "You know I didn't do this. You know me."

Cinnamon slid a hand into her shorts pocket. "Not true. I don't know you. At all."

"You know my father. He's been in your life for how many years?"

Cinnamon grew still. "What have you heard?"

"You were going through a rough patch in high school."

"It was worse than that. I was angry all the time. I smoked. I drank. I skipped school. I was a prankster."

I flashed on the dystopian teen that had flattened all of the Winnebago tires.

"And I did daredevil stuff. Almost killed myself taking some big air while snowboarding in Lake Tahoe. Guess I had a death wish." Cinnamon sighed. "Your father stepped in. I can remember our first talk. His finger in my face. His eyes burning holes through mine."

I knew that look.

"He was strict and curt, but I listened." She sighed again. "I had to get myself under control. Follow rules. Take responsibility. There was a difference between right and wrong. My father . . . he'd wronged me." Tigger charged her ankles. She nudged him away. "Your father talked about you guys all the time."

"Why didn't you ever visit our house?"

"I'm sure you can guess."

Her mother's decree, I imagined.

The distant wash of ocean upon the shore made its way into the silence. The flow, the ebb.

I inhaled and exhaled with its rhythm. "If my father told you about us, then you know I'm responsible. I follow rules. Doesn't that count for anything?"

"I'm sorry. Your father's opinion doesn't clear you. You came to town, and suddenly we have the first murder in a long time."

I winced. "Wow, that's exactly what your mother said. She's been bending your ear, hasn't she? Fine, haul me in." Like the dystopian teenager would have, I jutted my wrists at her. "Lock me up and throw away the key, Officer."

"Don't tempt me."

"Did it ever occur to you that I couldn't have done this crime? First of all, you're describing a crime of passion, but we know the crime was planned."

"Do we?"

"The hook, the sculpture. Granted, I'm tall, but I'm not strong enough to overpower someone Desiree's size." And yet I had pondered whether Sabrina was capable. I pushed the notion aside and continued. "And I'm not left-handed. That hook was pulled by a left-handed person."

Cinnamon regarded the carpet as if Desiree's body and all the evidence lay upon it. When she redirected her gaze to me, her face was solemn and unreadable. "I can't do this."

"Do what?"

"Discuss the case with you. I'll have to take the answering machine as evidence." She started toward the device.

"No," I cried and blocked her path then blanched, realizing how guilty I must look. What was I doing barring her from taking whatever she wanted from my cottage? Did I intend to wrestle her to the ground? She was shorter but she was sturdier. And she was a cop.

Rapid-fire, I explained the machine's importance to me. Listening to David's voice recording was like a lifeline to sanity.

Cinnamon's face softened. She pulled a business card from her pocket and handed it to me. "I promise we'll do our best to preserve your final memory. If you think of anything else, call me."

Tears flooded my eyes as she knelt and unplugged the answering machine from the wall. After she exited, Tigger's nuzzles couldn't relieve my soul.

Chapter 8

N O EERIE NOISES resonated while I downed my tender chicken dinner or through the rest of the night, and yet I woke up tense, nervous, and certain I was going to be hauled into jail for a murder I didn't commit. What could I do to resolve one or more of my issues? Get up. Be proactive. I would forge a plan in the same way I would start an ad campaign. What was the target market? What were the hurdles? Where did I begin? Face it, nobody would try to clear me of blame like I would.

A peep of sunlight shimmered through the split in the curtains and warmed my body. The cawing of birds inspired hope. Tigger, who had taken to sleeping at my feet, pounced to a sit.

I crawled to meet him nose to nose. "How about a run?" I said.

Tigger hunkered back into a tight wad of fur. He was a dancer, not a runner. I considered getting a dog as a running companion but pushed aside the thought. No use making plans if I was going to be incarcerated. Katie's words came back to me full force: *If Pepper Pritchett has her way, she'll railroad you into jail just so she can close down this operation.*

"All right, Tigger. How about, after the run, we have a tasty breakfast?" While browsing one of the culinary mysteries about a cheese shop in Ohio, I learned of a breakfast the protagonist loved—a slice of sourdough slathered with Taleggio cheese and jam—and I knew I had to have it. "Then we'll do a little sleuthing? Are you game?" That received a meow: *Yes.* What exactly we would investigate was not quite materializing in my foggy brain, but ideas would come. An ad campaign rarely started with more than a germ of an idea.

A chill hung in the air. I donned full-length leggings and a long-sleeved Under Armour shirt, slipped my bare feet into a pair of Pumas, and without applying sunscreen—it was only 6 A.M.—I set off.

With the trauma of discovering Desiree's body fresh in my mind, I ran in the opposite direction from yesterday's outing. About a half a mile south, I left the beach, crossed the main highway, and headed up a dirt road, which was kept clear for emergency vehicles in case of hillside fires.

I maintained a steady pace for a quarter of an hour. Soon, the climb intensified. About a mile along the dirt road, my legs started to cramp up. I stopped for a breather and pivoted to view the ocean. A flock of seagulls circled above the water. One seagull left the pack and plunged into the ocean. The others keened. The image brought to mind a scene in the movie *Finding Nemo,* with all the birds squawking: *Mine, mine.* When the lone seagull reappeared, would the others demand a fair share?

Not far from where the seagulls congregated, I caught sight of a couple of surfers paddling away from the beach. Male or female, I couldn't be sure. Seeing them made me reflect on the solo surfer from the day before. Could he have been the killer? Could he have planned the dastardly deed so far in advance that he had placed a surfboard at the scene, ready for his escape? Had he dumped the sculpting tools on purpose so the offending trowel would be found and implicate me? What had the killer done with his car? I assumed he met Desiree and drove her to the beach. Why else would she have gone there in the dead of night? Was he a lover, a friend? Was he the person who had telephoned her?

I wished I had asked Cinnamon last night whether she had found Desiree's cell phone or whether she had been able to review Desiree's telephone records. Thinking about Cinnamon made me itch. Did she really think I was guilty?

Eager to move ahead, in more ways than one, I pivoted and started up the hill again. I needed an endorphin rush. And I needed to stop thinking . . . dwelling. Scaling the hill made me realize how out of shape I was. I hadn't gone a quarter mile before I required another breather.

Chest heaving, I swiveled, braced my hands on my knees, and surveyed the strand below. This time I spied The Pier, which jutted near the southernmost end of town. Similar to the Santa Monica Pier, which was recognizable to theatergoers because movie companies regularly used it as a set piece, The Pier featured a carousel, some carney games, a number of shops, and restaurants. In addition, tourists could hire boats for sunset or sightseeing cruises and fishing expeditions. One of the largest shops on The Pier was Bait and Switch Fishing and Sport Supply Store. My father, a fly-fishing and deep-sea fishing aficionado, visited the store often.

I thought of Dad's personal collection of lures and hooks and flashed on the hook slung through Desiree's lip. Maybe someone at Bait and Switch had sold something like that recently.

I ZIPPED HOME, fed Tigger, downed a delectable helping of toast, cheese, and apricot jam, and I dressed. I tucked Tigger into the basket of my mom's bicycle—riding a bicycle wearing flip-flops wasn't the safest idea, but everyone in town did it—and I sped to Bait and Switch.

The barn-shaped shop regularly opened at 5 A.M.

because eager fishermen and tourists wanted to get an early start. I entered with Tigger tucked under my arm and took in the rich green leather and mahogany décor.

"Nice cat," said a man with tousled dark brown hair and a devilish grin.

I stared—no, gaped. Fisherman's sweater, jeans that fit just right, tan but not too tan. This was the hunky guy that Desiree said had lingered outside The Cookbook Nook.

"May I help you?" The man reached to nuzzle Tigger's chin. No wedding ring.

I snorted, something I hadn't done in years, and instantly felt my face flush.

"Miss?"

"I'm fine," I said, not lying. I *was* fine. I simply hadn't felt an attraction to a man in so long. I recognized my social freeze for what it was—pure, unadulterated lust—and pushed it aside, hopefully beneath the man's radar. I did not need him thinking I was a giddy schoolgirl. Not to mention, I craved information. I was on a quest. I readjusted Tigger, propping one hand under his rump. "Do you work here?"

"I own the place."

"Perfect. I'm Jenna Hart."

"Cary's daughter," the man said. "Your father talks about you all the time. He says you're a brilliant artist."

My father had never said those words to me. Ever.

"It's a pleasure to meet you," he added.

I gazed into what Desiree had called his bedroom eyes. They were the most startling ocean blue. If I were lost at sea, I might drift toward them and be swallowed whole. I pinched my forearm to make me snap out of my daze and said, "You lingered outside The Cookbook Nook the other day."

"Aha. You caught me out."

"Why didn't you come inside?"

"The shop wasn't open for business yet."

"What's your name? I told you mine."

"Forgive me." He had a gravelly voice, but it wasn't gruff. It was downright sexy. "I'm Rhett."

Uh-oh. That was exactly who he reminded me of. Rhett Butler from *Gone with the Wind*, one of my favorite teen reads. I must have devoured the story a dozen times. Rhett Butler was all swagger, the kind of man who would tease a woman for days to see if she had enough spirit to match his.

"Jenna, are you okay?" Rhett said.

I jerked out of my reverie. How long had I been off in la-la land? I moistened my mouth and said, "Last name?"

"Jackson."

Phew. Rhett Jackson. Same syllables but completely different. At least, whenever I saw him, I wouldn't feel compelled to tighten my corset, whip out a fan, and slide into a Southern accent. Putting on my serious face, I said, "Nice to meet you, Rhett." Juggling Tigger, who motored his disapproval, I extended my arm.

We shook hands. Firm, businesslike. I could offer a vise-like grip with the best of them. Rhett's grip was firm, too, but his hands were soft and recently lotioned.

"A sportsman's hands can be coarse," he explained. "I have a special line of manly lotions for that purpose." His mouth quirked up as he uttered: *manly lotions*. He was teasing. I smiled, too. He gave my hand a minor squeeze and released it. "What brings you here so early in the morning?" He guided me through the store. "We have water sports." An array of swimsuits, fins, and goggles hung on racks to the right. "And fishing to your heart's content. Do you fish?"

"As a girl, I went offshore fishing for rock cod with my father a couple of times, although my brother accompanied him more often than I did."

"There's always tomorrow." Rhett gestured to a display of kayaks, canoes, and dinghies. Beyond those were fisherman's vests, lures, rods, and reels. The aroma of canvas and fish filled the air. When Rhett reached the register, he searched my face. "But you're not here to talk about fishing, are you?"

My cheeks warmed. "I found the body . . . the victim . . .

on the beach," I said, my voice barely a whisper. "You may have heard that someone—"

"Died. Yes. Desiree Divine was to be your first celebrity at the shop."

"She was my best friend in college."

"I'm so sorry."

Me, too. Through the night, the more I rehashed my conversation with Desiree's sister, the more I believed that Sabrina had lied about Desiree having an affair with David. I was certain that Desiree had found out about the lie and wanted to clear the air. Why else would she have called me? Sometime before dawn, I determined that I would believe the best of Desiree until proven otherwise. Show me pictures— physical proof—and I would believe, but I wouldn't rely on one woman's—one bitter sister's—say-so.

I jostled Tigger, balancing him onto my left hip. Who knew the little guy could be so heavy? He squirmed. I whispered, "One more minute, buddy." I eyed Rhett. "Could I ask you a couple of questions?"

"Are they official?"

"Um, no." I gulped. I didn't want word getting around that I was misrepresenting myself. "Has someone official been to see you?"

"Nope."

I relaxed a tad. At least I wasn't stepping on Cinnamon Pritchett's toes. Or was I? Would she consider my presence at Bait and Switch intrusive? I had the right to prove myself innocent, didn't I?

Rhett rounded the register, righting business cards and a jar of pens on the desktop, before settling onto a wooden stool. He folded his arms. "I saw the article in the *Crystal Cove Crier*. It wasn't a good picture of you. It didn't do you justice."

"What picture? What article?" A chilling alliterative headline flashed in front of my eyes: *Cookbook Nook Kook Killed Celebrity Cook*. I imagined lurid pictures sprinkled throughout the article to help visualize the story. Had Pepper

Pritchett taken unfavorable candids of me setting up the shop? What if she had gotten her hands on some of the photos Desiree and I had taken during college? The toga party, the lingerie exchange, the Grateful Dead Revival.

"The article about you opening up the shop," Rhett said. "The picture made you look about seventeen, maybe eighteen. You had pigtails and braces. You appeared to be climbing a brick wall."

I exhaled. "Oh, that. It's an old high school photograph. I was dubbed: *Most persevering*." Aunt Vera must have supplied the photo.

"The article said you don't cook much. I could teach you."

"Really? What is your specialty? Beans from a can?"

He chortled. "Actually I used to be a chef."

"Where?"

"The Grotto."

A gasp slipped out of me. "That's the restaurant that burned down." I remembered hearing about the fire from my aunt. The four-star restaurant had been located on the second floor of Fisherman's Village, right above our café. The wine bistro, Vines, had taken over the refurbished space. "Why didn't you pick up a gig somewhere else?"

A cloud of sadness swept across Rhett's face and, as quickly, vanished. "A change of pace sounded good." He spanked the counter. The register ca-chinged. No pity parties for this guy. "I bought this place instead. It's a good business. Great people. An easier life."

"I'll say. Restaurant work is demanding. I know a married couple in the City who live and breathe their restaurant, twenty-four-seven."

"And yet you took on the café."

"Package deal, my aunt said." Now, of course, I understood why. My aunt's fiancé had been a chef. "Besides, Katie Casey is managing it. The café, the food, the hours. It's her baby."

"Katie?" He raised a hand in measurement. "Big girl? Ho-ho-ho laugh?"

"That's her."

"She likes to jet ski."

"Really?" I couldn't picture Katie on a small watercraft with a rooster tail of foam spraying behind her.

"And parasail."

"No way." What did her curly hair look like after those adventures?

A customer approached the counter. Rhett said, "Give me a sec," and rang up the sale of a pair of rods and lures. He knew the customer by name and gave him directions to a local fishing hole.

As the customer exited, I said, "He was gleeful."

"A happy customer is a returning customer. So what did you want to ask me?"

"I have a question about hooks."

Rhett's face grew serious. "I heard something about a hook at the crime scene."

Given that Katie and probably the rest of Crystal Cove knew the details of the crime scene, I had no reason not to elaborate. I explained how Desiree was buried, her body sculpted to look as if it were a mermaid. "I think the killer wanted it to seem like a big sea fisherman had snared Desiree."

Rhett's nose flinched. "Sick."

"My sentiments exactly. Do you sell something that looks—" I drew an imaginary hook in the air, about five inches long and three inches wide.

"A trolling hook. Sure, we sell Mustads. Let's check it out." Rhett said, "Joey." He flagged down a gawky kid who could have been Ichabod Crane's double, all Adam's apple and neck. "Man the register." Rhett ushered me to the rear of the store. His hand felt warm and firm on my elbow. The scent of him, a mixture of suntan lotion and salt, made my insides quiver.

"Sorry," Rhett said. "The stockroom is small."

He wasn't kidding. The room had no windows and a single exit door, only to be opened *in case of fire*.

Rhett crossed to shelving that held stacks of various-sized boxes, and he lifted a clipboard. He reviewed the top two sheets and shook his head. "All our hooks are accounted for. We started with fifty Mustad hooks at the beginning of the month. We still have fifty. I'll tell you, however"—he replaced the clipboard on the shelf—"that those hooks could be purchased online. The Internet is my biggest competitor. Especially with no shipping charges."

"Great," I muttered. Anybody in the world could have bought the hook. Including me.

A foghorn pealed, as if signaling my doom.

Chapter 9

AN HOUR OR so later, while I moved around The Cookbook Nook dusting shelves, my sense of doom lifted. I found myself humming, something I hadn't done in a long time. I couldn't convince myself the mood stemmed from thriving business—the shop didn't open until 9 A.M.—and I couldn't chalk up the good vibes to feeling free from persecution. Pepper Pritchett had assigned one of her pals to stand on the boardwalk with a *Don't Shop There* sign. And yet, I felt light on my feet. I took a moment to check my face in the antique mirror that Aunt Vera had hung in the teensy hall leading to the office. She'd advised me never to return to the store without a quick peek-a-boo to make sure one's makeup wasn't smudged. I was pleased to see a twinkle in my eyes and color in my cheeks. Perhaps, despite the chaotic past week, I was finding my sea legs in Crystal Cove.

I whisked back to my duty of dusting but stopped at a set of cookbooks and called out to Aunt Vera, "Get this retro title: *The Pioneer Woman Cooks: Food from My Frontier*."

She chuckled as she closed the cash register. "That woman has a wagon train of followers."

"In this day and age of women's liberation?"

"The recipes are incredible. Return-to-the-earth time."

"You mean everything is homegrown?"

"Yep. Pizza, pasta, party food, sweets. She's got it all, as well as tips on canning."

Out of my own self-preservation, I steered clear of the book. I had eons to go before I would arrive at a point where I could plant a home garden and can my own goods, but I made a mental note to promote the cookbook. Plenty of people in Crystal Cove loved their home gardens. "Hey, did I tell you about the dinner I—"

Someone knocked on the door. I peered outside. Tito Martinez, the local reporter from the *Crystal Cove Crier*, and three women I didn't recognize stood on the boardwalk. Tito tapped his watch. I must have lost track of time.

I raced to the entrance, my tank top rising up and my ruffled skirt fluting out as I ran. I tweaked my clothing back into place before unlocking the bolt. "Good morning and welcome," I said as I swung open the door and stepped back.

Tito and the new customers sauntered into the shop. I noticed that the Winnebagos still stood in the parking lot. Contrary to Pepper's claim, early bird Beaders of Paradise customers didn't seem to mind. Many had parked on the far side of the lot and were strolling the extra distance.

"If you need help finding anything, let me know," I said to our customers. "And Chef Katie has set out a tasting of four types of Danish pastry in the walkway between the store and the café. Cherry, almond, and chocolate cheesecake plus a gluten-free mixed berry selection, if you're so inclined. Help yourselves."

Katie had arrived at the café at 5 A.M. to start her preparations. I worried that she might overwork herself, but she said she had toiled hard hours for her former employer, and she was determined to create the most-talked-about café in town.

I joined my aunt behind the sales counter.

"Have you got Mexican cookbooks?" Tito said. He didn't seem to be looking for any. In fact, he paced in front of the register as if he were a feisty dog eager to bite a postman's leg. A heavy-looking leather satchel hung over his shoulder. "I have one to show you."

Aunt Vera said, "We have a terrific selection of Rick Bayless's cookbooks."

Tito snarled. What was up with that? I'm sure he didn't know Rick Bayless personally. The guy was a charming, lanky American chef who specialized in Mexican cuisine. I had seen him once on his television show, *Mexico: One Plate at a Time*. Everything he made that night looked mouthwateringly good, including the *Polvorones*, a Mexican wedding cookie, although I thought baking and pulverizing the pecans was a bit too much work. For me anyway.

"What's the problem, Tito?" my aunt said.

He patted his satchel. "I have evidence."

I gasped. Did he know who killed Desiree? Had he brought some telltale item to us so we could turn it over to the police? I held out my hand. "Let me see."

Aunt Vera clasped my arm and gave me a sidelong, rolling-eye look. Clearly she didn't give the reporter much credence. "Evidence of what?"

Tito shrugged off his satchel, pawed through it, and pulled out a floppy, tired-looking book. "*Eso es*," he said, the Spanish equivalent of *voilà*. At Taylor & Squibb, I had worked with a handful of creative Latinos who spoke in their native tongue to one another whenever they didn't want me, the *chica*, to understand. David had encouraged me to study Spanish to get a leg up. I did.

"What is it?" I asked.

"My cookbook. My authentic Mexican cookbook."

Aunt Vera said, "Re-e-e-ally."

"I am a self-published author."

"I thought you were a reporter," I said.

"A reporter with aspirations and a fine palate. My cookbook is packed with recipes from my *abuela*."

"Your grandmother," I said.

Tito bobbed his head. "And I happen to know that Desiree Divine stole a cookie recipe directly from it. Look and compare."

As he set his cookbook on the counter, more customers entered. Tito turned the cookbook so my aunt and I could read the title: *Authentic Mexican Cookbook*. Underneath was a crude drawing of a sombrero and a clay pot. Tito needed help in the creativity department, I mused.

He flipped open to a dog-eared page. The recipe was for, of all things, Mexican wedding cookies. I counted six ingredients, not nearly as many as Rick Bayless's version. I could memorize this one. Next, Tito rifled through his satchel, pulled out a copy of Desiree's cookbook, slapped the book on the counter, and twisted it so it was readable to us. He opened the cookbook to a page marked with a sticky note. "See? Her Mexican wedding cookie is the same as my grandmother's."

I compared recipe to recipe. Desiree's version had eight ingredients, including a hint of cream of tartar, and a fabulous picture of plated cookies accompanied by a *dulce de leche* coffee. My mouth started to water. "It's not the same," I said.

"I know she read it," Tito protested.

"Where?"

"Online. I watch statistics for my website. I know where Internet traffic comes from. She stole this recipe from me." He slammed his fist on the counter.

Customers in the shop gaped. Thinking quickly, I lifted Desiree's book and displayed the picture. "He's so excited," I told the astonished crowd. "He thinks these cookies look downright smashing." *Smashing,* really? When had I become British? "Do you agree?" I didn't wait for their reaction. I closed the book and lasered Tito with a glare. "You know, Mr. Martinez, given the heat of your anger, one might think you had motive to kill Desiree."

"What?" he faltered. "No, I didn't. I would never . . . not for a recipe . . . but it's the principle."

I truly didn't think Desiree had seen Tito's self-pubbed book, and even if she had, why would she have bothered to steal from it? She was schooled by the best. She had cooked for years. I would bet that she had memorized more than ten thousand recipes and more than one of them was for Mexican wedding cookies.

"Look again." Tito stabbed the counter. "The ingredients are nearly the same."

"Not exactly," I said.

"Fine, she tweaked it, that's all."

"Tweaking a recipe is perfectly legitimate," Aunt Vera said.

I gasped. "It is?" In marketing, my team and I sought ways to mimic a good campaign without outright stealing it. Advertising wasn't rocket science, though I had to admit that I wished I had developed the E-trade commercials with all the glib babies. Brilliant.

"Absolutely it's acceptable," Aunt Vera went on. "And by tweaking, I mean that you can, say, add white pepper when a recipe calls for black pepper, and you've made it yours."

Tito sneered; the cleft in his chin deepened. "He said you would say something like that."

"Who said?" I asked.

"That restaurateur who gave Desiree Divine her first gig. He said she stole recipes all the time."

"Anton d'Stang?" I asked.

"That's the one."

"You called him in Paris?"

"Didn't have to. He's here in town. I saw him at The Pelican Brief Diner. I gave him a free copy of my cookbook in thanks, although I have to say he didn't seem very appreciative."

What was Anton doing in town? He must have had a reason. I couldn't imagine his presence was coincidence. Had he come to taunt Desiree? To win her back? To kill her? I stopped myself. For all I knew, he could have arrived after her death to pay homage to her.

Aunt Vera said, "So, Tito, what did you hope to get out of proving Desiree stole a recipe from you? Fame? Fortune? A story?" She nudged me. "He's always in it for the story."

"Satisfaction." He snatched Desiree's cookbook out of

my hands, packed up his own book, and stomped from the store.

"Well, isn't he testy," Aunt Vera said as the door slammed closed.

I didn't respond, no longer focused on Tito Martinez and his claim that Desiree was a thief. Instead, I was thinking about Anton d'Stang, the man who had lost all objectivity when Desiree announced she was leaving Chez Anton to star in her own television show. The man who broke into her posh apartment and tossed all her belongings out the window and onto the sidewalk. Where was he at the time Desiree was murdered?

As if reading my mind and sensing my next plan of attack, Tigger curled around my ankles. His tail whisked my calf. "Hey, pal." I scooped him up and scratched beneath his chin. "Don't worry. I'll be careful."

"Careful about what?" Aunt Vera looked worried.

"I have to track down Anton d'Stang." I explained why. "I know we have some new hires to interview."

She took the cat from my hands. "Not until much later. Go."

I HADN'T VISITED The Pelican Brief Diner since I had returned to town. When I was a girl, our family went there all the time. My sister and I ordered the fish sticks served with tartar sauce. Our brother, who from the age of six wouldn't eat anything that had a mother or a face, stuck with the picante cole slaw and paprika fries. Dad and Mom ordered the special, no matter what it was.

The owner, Lola Bird—kid you not; pelican . . . bird—used to be a big-time lawyer in San Francisco. Although she didn't want to give up being a lawyer, she didn't want to do the seven-days-a-week, nine-to-midnight thing any longer, so she left the corporate life, returned to her hometown, and bought the diner. She named her restaurant The Pelican Brief, not because her last name was Bird, but because she adored the John Grisham novel with the same title. Like me, she was an avid reader. When I was a girl, every time our family had come into the diner, she'd recommended books to me. Because of Lola, I had read Newbery Medal winners: *A Wrinkle in Time*, *Old Yeller*, and *Charlotte's Web*. She had introduced me to classics, too: *Rebecca* and *The Secret Garden* and *The Giving Tree*. I can't remember how many times she had quoted Thornton Wilder: " 'Seek the lofty by reading, hearing, and seeing great work at some moment every day.' "

As I entered the restaurant, I inhaled the luscious aroma of fried foods. How could I learn to make this kind of meal? I wondered. The teenaged hostess, who was dressed in white short shorts, a gingham shirt tied at the waist, deck shoes, and sailor hat asked if I needed help. I shook my head and gazed past her, searching the restaurant for Anton d'Stang. Sawdust lay on the blond wood floors. Nets filled with fake fish hung on the walls. Rustic booths lined the perimeter. Wooden tables and chairs were clustered in the center of the restaurant and on the balcony that overlooked the ocean. Nearly every seat was filled. Lola, a juicy woman with super-short silver hair, a generous spirit, and a belly laugh that could carry across a football field, was talking to someone in a booth.

When she fluttered her hand flirtatiously in front of her healthy-sized chest, I knew who she was chatting up— Anton d'Stang. Even Lola, in little old Crystal Cove, would have heard of the famous entrepreneur. I weaved through the tables. She caught sight of me and met me halfway.

"Darling girl." Lola gripped my shoulders. "Look at you, all grown up. Why, you are the spitting image of your mother, rest her soul. Those gorgeous eyes and lithe body." She pulled me into a bear hug, pushed me away, and took hold of my chin. "You call me Lola now, understand? We're adults. Equals. How are you?"

"Fine. How's Bailey?" Lola's super-bright daughter still worked at Taylor & Squibb. During my stint there, Bailey had saved my rear end on many occasions, holding me back when I had wanted to voice a less-than-positive opinion.

"She's languishing. She's so underappreciated. I've told her to move home, but does she listen?" Lola sighed. "She said if I saw you, to give you her best. She's unhappy she couldn't make your opening. I meant to make it over to The Cookbook Nook for both of us. I truly did, but we have been slammed here. Don't worry. I'll visit soon enough. Bailey said I absolutely must buy a copy of Anthony Bourdain's *Medium Raw: A Bloody Valentine* yada-yada. The title has so many words that it's not very catchy. But Bailey says the book is filled with Bourdain's rise to glory and lots of insider gossip. I adore gossip." She paused. Her cheeks reddened and her eyes suddenly pooled with tears. "Oh, heavens, how horrible I am, running on so? You." She gripped me harder. "How are you holding up? It's tragic what happened. I heard you and Desiree Divine had a long history." She ushered me toward the table she had departed. "I was just telling Anton how—"

"*Mademoiselle.*" Anton d'Stang rose, coffee mug in his left hand. Remainders of a fried fish on sourdough sandwich sat on the plate in front of him. He gave me a quick once-over.

Something troubled me as I regarded him. Not the fact that he was one of the most dashing men over fifty I had ever met. I was prepared for that; I had seen photographs of him in *Bon Appetit* and similar magazines.

"Anton d'Stang," Lola said. "This is Jenna Hart."

"*Il est mon plaisir.*" Anton extended his right arm.

As we shook hands, I took note of his strong fingers. I imagined those fingers working their magic in a kitchen. That image morphed into those fingers strangling Desiree's beautiful neck. The notion made me jolt. I released Anton's hand and jerked my attention back to his face. He took a sip of his coffee and peered curiously over the rim. A shiver ran down my spine. What was it that bothered me about him, other than his surprise presence in Crystal Cove?

"Jenna's a fantastic artist," Lola continued. "And now I hear she's a wonder of a businesswoman." She shook a finger at me. "Don't look so humble. I've heard what you've got going on with that café. My, my. I might have to steal that

Katie Casey from you. She's some chef, people say." She swiveled to face Anton. "Get this. The woman's first menu included three different entrées, a whitefish tortellini dish, a seaside twist on a Caesar salad, and an open-faced cheddar melt that would knock your socks off."

If Lola hadn't visited The Cookbook Nook herself, how did she know so much about the food in our café? Maybe she had sent a spy. Restaurants, no matter what kind of food they served, had to keep current with competition.

Lola tweaked Anton's arm. "Not to mention Miss Casey offered three selections of homemade ice cream, one of which is my all-time favorite, brown sugar pecan."

"Katie makes ice cream?" I said. I was a sucker for cold desserts.

"Haven't you been tasting your own food?" Lola clucked.

When would I have had time to do that? I'd barely had a moment to breathe.

"No wonder you're stick-thin. Let's feed you." Lola beckoned a muscle-bound Nordic waiter as she confided to me, "We have a fresh influx of internationals in Crystal Cove. They enjoy the temperature . . . and the tips." The waiter pulled to a stop, arms at his side. Lola said, "What'll it be, Jenna? Your childhood favorite, fish and chips? I don't think you've ever ordered anything else, have you?"

My heart twinged. For some reason, Lola remembering what I had ordered as a child affected me in a way I couldn't understand. Suddenly I identified with Dorothy in *The Wizard of Oz:* There's no place like home. "Nothing, thanks."

As the waiter did a U-turn, I cleared my throat. "Mr. d'Stang—"

"Your store." His French accent was strong, his voice commanding. He set his coffee cup on the table. "That was where Desiree was going to sign her new cookbook, *non?*"

"Yes, she—"

"Sadly, she did not have her day in the sun."

What did he mean? Was he making an oblique reference to the fact that she had been buried in the sand, never to see the light of day again? Was he admitting to having killed her?

Lola swatted him with her fingertips. "Of course she did, Anton. Desiree Divine was a celebrity."

"That's right," I said. "Signing books at our store was not a big deal."

"But perhaps it was," Anton said. "The fate of her television show was in question, was it not?"

I tilted my head. How did he know so much about Desiree's circumstances prior to her death? "Why are you here?" I asked.

"The food is *magnifique*." He indicated his nearly finished meal.

"Not here, in The Pelican Brief Diner. Why are you in Crystal Cove?" Agatha Christie's Miss Marple, I was not. Subtlety was not my strong suit. A former boss told me that I·was a problem solver, and problem solvers had a tendency to be rudely direct. Problem solvers liked clear-cut solutions.

Anton sucked in his cheeks; his mouth puckered. He looked as if he were mulling over an answer that was distasteful. "I was in San Francisco to meet with my investors. We intend to open a sister restaurant there."

"No way," I said. "Per Desiree, you're a Francophile who deigned to go as far west as New York, but no farther."

Anton ticked a finger beneath the snug collar of his button-down shirt—perhaps his striped Armani tie was knotted too tightly—and he slumped into a teenage-type stance, one hip jutting out. I flinched as I realized what vexed me about him. His posture dipped to the right; he didn't stand tall.

"You were there," I blurted out.

"*Oui*, I was in San Francisco."

"No, you lingered outside my shop the day Desiree came to town. And I saw you yesterday, too, with binoculars."

"*Non*."

"Yes." Add more facial hair, a knit cap, and extra bulk around the waist, and Anton resembled the guy with the tackle box and the drooping right shoulder who had climbed into the truck that day. Had Desiree known the creep was

Anton? "You were in disguise. You were spying on Desiree. Don't deny it."

He sighed. "*Oui*, I wanted to see her."

"Why? There was no love lost between the two of you. You went berserk when she left you for the chance of Hollywood fame."

"*Non*." His voice was as authoritative as a chef addressing a lazy staff. "You do not understand."

"Enlighten her." Lola pointed for him to sit. When he did, she did. Then I did.

"*Très bien*. I wanted to see Desiree, for old times' sake."

"Uh-huh," Lola said in a sarcastic tone.

"Why the costume?" I asked.

"Desiree said she wished never to see me again."

"What would she have done if she'd realized it was you?" I said.

"She promised to cut me"—he glanced down at his nether region—"with a rusty razor."

I bit back a smile. That sounded like Desiree. Not that she would have carried through with the threat.

Anton avoided eye contact with me and twisted a gold ring on his right hand. "As I said, I was in San Francisco to open another Chez Anton. I thought if I could entice Desiree to appear opening night, I could lure the best critics to review the food. The world's economy demands brilliance from the first public moment. One *erreur*, and an entire venture washes away like the sand."

Again with the beach metaphor, I noted. He was guilty. If only Cinnamon Pritchett were sitting with us, listening to his confession.

"Desiree owed me," Anton continued. "I had my girl call hers."

I doubted Sabrina relished being referred to as a *girl*. "But Desiree turned you down, didn't she?"

"I never heard a word from anyone."

"So you decided to stalk her."

"*Non*."

"Anton," Lola said in a firm, lawyerly voice. "If you wore

a disguise and showed up where Desiree was, that could be perceived as stalking. Do you wish to modify your statement?"

"I was observing her," he said.

"I'll allow the distinction." Lola nodded. "Jenna, proceed."

Suddenly everything was clear to me. "You bided your time. You didn't think you could get a word in edgewise as long as J.P. Hessman was around. He spelled trouble. So you followed them when they left The Cookbook Nook. You found out where she was staying. Later that night, you called her."

"*Non.*"

"J.P. said Desiree received a telephone call."

Lola cut a sharp look at me. "How would you know that?"

"I talked to him."

"You what?"

I held up a hand. "Don't worry, I knew what I was doing." I didn't. I was way out of my league, but now, seeing as I was in a public place with a lawyer and lots of witnesses, I felt daring. "Lola, I'm the chief suspect in this murder. I need answers."

"Fine. Proceed."

I refocused on Anton d'Stang. "I assumed the telephone call came to Desiree on her cell phone. But it didn't, did it? You called Desiree in her room using one of the hotel telephones."

"*Non.*"

"Where were you at the time Desiree died?"

"On a date."

That answer surprised me. I had expected Anton to say he was with business associates. "You're a fast operator."

"I met someone special."

"Who?"

"Desiree's hairdresser."

Forgive me, but my mouth fell open.

"Explain." Lola tapped a foot.

"I needed a . . . how do you say it? A trim." Anton

fingered the nape of his neck. "I went into the Permanent Wave Salon and Spa. Gigi and I met. We made a connection. We talked about so many things. Travel. Movies. She asked if I would like to go surfing with her." His mouth curled up. "I told her *impossible*. I am from Paris. I have never surfed in my life. I barely know how to swim. But we found common ground in food. I asked her to dinner. She said yes."

No, no, no, a voice screamed in my head. I had to agree with the voice. I couldn't see the debonair Anton d'Stang dating the ginormous, purple-haired Gigi Goode. He was lying. But how could I prove it?

Chapter 10

WHEN I RETURNED to The Cookbook Nook, I stopped short inside the front door because a man—Rhett Jackson if I was sizing up his attractive backside correctly—was chatting with Katie in the hallway between the shop and the café. What was he doing there? Had he realized a Mustad hook was missing from his collection after all? If I was lucky, he had a receipt with the killer's signature on it that I could deliver to the police, and I would finally be rid of the fear of incarceration.

All of a sudden, Katie roared with laughter. Rhett followed with a deep throaty guffaw, one that, for some reason, made my insides sizzle.

Stop it, Jenna, I coaxed myself. *Be professional. Get the facts.*

Aunt Vera stood at the register, tending to a line of three customers. More patrons crowded the shop. My aunt caught sight of me and wiggled her hand with such enthusiasm that she appeared to have grown ten years younger.

I signaled *three minutes*, then strolled down the hall and

wedged into the huddle formed by Rhett, Katie, and the snack table. "What's so funny?"

"Hoo-boy, is this guy hilarious or what?" Katie slapped my arm. "Get this joke: 'Give a man a fish and you can feed him for a day. Teach a man to fish and you can get rid of him for a weekend.'"

"Cute," I said.

"I've got plenty of them." Rhett chuckled. "Every day I hear a new one."

How about that? So far, I hadn't heard one joke at The Cookbook Nook. Granted, we had only been open a few days, but perhaps cookbook buyers didn't tell jokes the same way sports fanatics did. I hoped that wasn't the case. I needed to laugh.

Katie said, "Jokes. I never could tell them, but this one, I'll remember. Thanks, Rhett."

She checked her pocket watch. "Whoa. I've got to get back to work to prep dinner. Time flies when you're having a ball." She offered a flirty wink. "Don't forget what you promised."

I made a quarter turn to Rhett. Seeing him full-face, something caught in my chest. Whereas this morning, he had been clean-shaven, now he had a fine stubble of brown hair covering the lower half of his face. I had the urge to reach up and touch. Luckily I possessed enough self-control not to. Whew. Close call. "So . . . what did you promise Katie?" I asked.

"To help her teach a cooking class or two."

"Is that why you came in to the shop?"

"Nope."

"You found out a hook was missing, after all," I said, unable to contain my glee.

"Sorry, no."

Rats.

"I came in for a self-satisfying purpose. I heard the scuttlebutt about the café's food. A man has to eat. By the way, if you haven't had the crabmeat soufflé, don't miss it. And

these"—he lifted a cookie from the two-tier Royal Albert
dessert stand—"are my new favorite." A sign beside the
stand read: *Maple Leaf Rag Cookies.*

"What's in them?" I lifted one and sniffed. If heaven had
a scent . . .

"Cinnamon, cloves, and raisins."

"And maple syrup?"

"Good guess."

We both grinned.

After a moment, Rhett said, "Katie hinted that you aren't,
um, comfortable in the kitchen."

"Comfortable. That's a kind word." I felt my cheeks
warm. In the future, I would keep my shortcomings to
myself. "Guess the secret's out. I'm a total klutz. I took
chemistry in high school, and I do know the difference
between a teaspoon and a tablespoon, but, well"—I licked
my upper lip—"my mother did all the cooking when I was
a kid, and I never got around to learning." As if I were a
little girl flirting on the playground, I folded my arms at the
arch of my back. What next? Would I rock to and fro? I
dropped my arms to my side, embarrassment brewing inside
me, not because I was acting silly, but because I felt guilty
for betraying my husband. How in the world could I possibly
have eyes for a man other than David?

Except he was dead. Gone.

"Jenna?" Rhett said.

I blinked.

"A klutz," he prompted. His gaze was tender.

"Right." My throat grew dry. I had to proceed with my
life. That was what my therapist told me. I promised her I
would. "I'm worried my customers will hold my inability
to cook, i.e. klutziness, against me."

"Not a chance."

"Are you telling me no one has ever come into Bait and
Switch and asked for fishing advice?"

"Sure they do, and yes, I can offer a few tidbits, but
that's not the crux of what I do. Folks want someone they
can talk to and confide in. They want to tell you about their

most exciting catch. They want to know the best fishing spot."

"Which is . . ."

"This fabulous little lake tucked into the hills. Prettiest site ever. Surrounded by mountain flowers. Very private." He swept his hand in front of his face to paint the picture. "The only way to get to it is on foot or on dirt bike. Have you ever ridden a dirt bike?"

"Never." A girlfriend in high school spiraled out of control on a dirt bike and shredded the side of her body. Call me chicken and possibly vain, but I wasn't up for that kind of abuse.

"You're missing out on seeing some remote areas around here and experiencing a pleasure beyond what you can dream. Not to mention taking a risk. You enjoy taking risks, don't you?"

I did. Years ago.

Rhett plucked another cookie from the display and bit into it. He hummed his pleasure. "Anyway, back to being able to cook. All I'm saying is if you learn which cookbook has what to offer, you're doing your job. Take *Bobby Flay's Throwdown!* cookbook, for example, the one based on the Food Network's show. I'm sure you have that book on the shelves, and if you don't, you should. All you need to know is that the recipes are from the television show. You've seen *Throwdown!*, right?"

"Yes." Katie would be pleased to learn that the Food Channel was a go-to TV program when I was too tired to pick up a book. I adored the colorful chef Bobby Flay. On a spur-of-the-moment weekend trip to Las Vegas, David and I had gone to Bobby Flay's Mesa Grill. The Yucatan chicken tacos with peanut-smoked barbecue sauce we devoured were piquant yet smooth. I said, "Did you see the show where Bobby faced off with national barbecue champ, Butch Lupinetti?"

"I've watched every episode." Rhett's mouth quirked up on one side. "So if you don't cook, why did you buy The Cookbook Nook?"

"I didn't. It's Aunt Vera's shop."

"Huh. I thought she sold it to you because . . ." His voice drifted to a hush.

"Because of the chef that left her at the altar?"

"You know about that?"

"Not the whole story."

Rhett tapped my forearm. "Maybe we should uncover the truth together. I love a good mystery."

Excitement sizzled through me. I tried to make light of the feeling, but I couldn't. Maybe I was too stimulated from all that I had done today. The hunt for the hook. The search for Anton d'Stang. "Are you a reader?"

"Every chance I get. You?"

"I read the gamut from cozy mysteries to thrillers. Kate Carlisle and Julie Hyzy to Jamie Freveletti and Lisa Gardner."

"Only female authors?"

I blushed. "No, I read the guys, too. Michael Connelly. Harlan Coben."

"And I read cookbooks."

"Are the plots any good?" I teased.

"It depends on who's cooking up what."

I peeked at my watch. My three-minute promise to Aunt Vera was more than up. "I should spot my aunt at the counter."

"And I should get going. See you around town." He downed the remainder of his cookie, wiped his hands on a napkin, and lobbed the napkin into the trash beneath the snack table.

As we strolled from the hall back to the bookshop, the door to the outside opened. My father entered. A warm breeze followed him inside. His eyes brightened when he spotted us. "Rhett, how are you, son?" He strode to him, hand extended. The two men matched in height and build. They shook heartily.

"Fine, sir. I was just leaving."

"Not on my account."

Rhett smiled. "No, sir. I'm in charge of closing up Bait

and Switch. By the way, you haven't stopped by the shop in a dog's age."

"I've been too busy."

"If that's the case, you have your priorities out of whack." Dad laughed. "How's the cabin? No more busted pipes?"

"No, sir, but you can bet I'll call you if another one bites the dust. Home ownership is tougher than the pundits tell you."

Rhett lived in a cabin? Wow. This guy was so different from anyone I had ever liked. I flinched as the word *liked* echoed in my mind. Did I like him? Yes. He appeared to be honest, forthright, and he had a sense of humor. Not to mention, he was respectful of my father. My mother would have said he was a keeper. She had never appreciated David. She couldn't pinpoint why. I didn't care; I was in my twenties and discarded everything she said. How I missed her and our outings to bookshops and rodeos and strawberry picking.

Dad buffed Rhett on the shoulder. "I'll stop by Bait and Switch soon."

"I'd enjoy that." Rhett gave me a wink. "See you around, Jenna," and he sauntered out of the shop.

"I like that young man." My father looped his hand around my arm and steered me toward the sales counter. "No matter what anyone says, I still think he's innocent."

Aunt Vera waltzed from behind the counter, the voluminous folds of her gold-filigreed caftan swishing as she moved. "I agree."

I gaped. "Innocent of what?"

My father scanned the shop. So did my aunt. Did they worry that someone might listen in on us? A gaggle of women, their chatter nonstop, clustered by the fiction books in the bay window. A handsome couple browsed books in the sustainable garden section. No one paid us any attention.

Aunt Vera said, sotto voce, "Innocent of starting the fire."

Of course, the fire. Why hadn't I put two and two together? "People think he started the fire at The Grotto?" I asked, matching my aunt's hushed tone.

Aunt Vera *tsk*ed. "Thanks to Pepper Pritchett, rumors spread as fast as the flames. The tenants"—my aunt flapped a hand; bangles clattered—"worried their beloved businesses might go *pffft*."

"But they didn't," my father said. "Firemen arrived quickly and doused the flames. Only the restaurant perished."

"Bait and Switch seems pretty popular," I said.

"Most locals don't think Rhett did it." My father paused. "Well, perhaps there are a few who do, but we don't." He thumbed between my aunt and himself. "Neither does Lola Bird or any of the other restaurateurs in town."

"Why not?"

"Rhett is a standup guy. And he supplies some of the fish at The Pelican Brief and other local restaurants."

I folded my arms. "So he's a necessary evil."

"He's not evil," Dad said. "He's a reliable fisherman, good businessman, and a kind man."

"But people won't hire him as a chef. Why not?"

Aunt Vera shrugged. "I don't think he ever asked."

"I'm not sure he wants to return to that life," my father offered.

I might have been bad at math, but I knew when people's accounts weren't adding up. "Okay, you two, out with it. There's something you're not telling me."

"Poor boy," Aunt Vera whispered.

Rhett was somewhere in his midthirties, older than me by at least five years. He wasn't a boy. And he owned a shop and cabin. I doubted he was poor. Images of Rhett Butler, the fictional antihero who operated outside the limits of society, popped into my mind again. "Explain," I said. "Does Rhett have a history of run-ins with the law or something?"

"A few," Aunt Vera said. "As a youth. But that's all in the past. At eighteen, he found his passion—cooking. He entered the Culinary Institute of America on a partial scholarship. He put himself through, working odd jobs. He was a wizard with sauces. The owner of The Grotto wanted to raise the restaurant's quality. She hired Rhett following graduation. And it's no wonder. Why, Rhett made this one sauce with tomatoes, capers, lemon, garlic, and white pepper that made my mouth zing. I must remind Katie of that one. And Rhett loved coming out to the folks in the restaurant and chatting up his food. He had a way with people. They adored him . . . They still do. He's a bit of a rogue and a big flirt, you've probably noticed."

Had I ever.

Aunt Vera tweaked my chin. "And he's single."

"Uh-uh." I shook my head emphatically. "Do not even think about fixing me up."

"He didn't do it," my father said.

"I don't care. I mean, I do care, but that's not the point." I threw up my hands, palms forward to caution my family backward like evil spirits. "I'm not ready for anything but managing this shop and defending myself against allegations that I might be a murderer."

"Cinnamon doesn't think you're guilty," Dad said.

"Yes, she does."

Aunt Vera sighed. "Speaking of innocent, did you track down Anton d'Stang?"

My father cocked his head. "The restaurateur? Why—"

"Hush, Cary."

"Don't tell me to hush, Vera. What's going on?"

I scanned the shop for a second time. Our customers remained enraptured with their own discussions, not ours. I filled in my family about meeting Anton at the diner. I described the vibes I received from him and how Lola came to my defense.

"Jenna, I do not want you getting involved," my father said.

"But I am involved. I'm suspected of murder."

"It's not safe."

"Relax, Dad. All I did was ask some questions." I continued my account. Anton knew about Desiree's failed TV ratings, and he showed up at The Cookbook Nook in disguise to spy on Desiree.

"He admitted that?" my aunt said.

"Vera, don't encourage her."

She waved at my father to be quiet. He grimaced.

"Anton d'Stang claimed to be in San Francisco," I said. "To start another Chez Anton. He ventured to Crystal Cove in hopes of convincing Desiree to appear at the opening of the restaurant." I shared Anton's veiled references to Desiree being buried under the sand and unable to see the sun again.

"You have to tell Cinnamon what you've learned," my father said.

The way he said her name, so informally, made me want to know more about their relationship and why he hadn't at least mentioned his role as Big Brother when I was growing up, but I didn't ask. It was none of my business. *Let the past stay in the past.*

"First things first," Aunt Vera said. "Anton claimed to be on a date with Gigi Goode at the time your friend was killed, is that right?"

I nodded. "Can you imagine? I mean, I can see Gigi dating J.P., but not Anton."

"Now, Jenna," my aunt said. "Don't judge a book by its cover. Just because a person has tattoos doesn't mean the person is a match for someone with multiple piercings. You have to analyze their inner souls."

"You're right." For years, I had offered snap judgments to the public via ten-, fifteen-, and thirty-second television ads. "I guess I'm uptight."

"Perhaps a spa day would do you good," Aunt Vera suggested.

"As if I have time for that."

"How about a teensy makeover?" She finger-combed my hair back behind my ears. "Maybe you should book an appointment with Gigi."

"Uh-uh, no." My father worked his jaw back and forth. "I'm putting my foot down. Young lady, you call Cinnamon Pritchett and tell her what you've learned."

"It will all be hearsay, Cary, and you know it," my aunt countered. "Why should your daughter give a partial accounting to the police when, and if, she can provide the whole story?"

"Yoo-hoo." I waved. "I'm right here. I can hear you."

My father and aunt regarded me.

Aunt Vera said, "All I'm suggesting is that you corroborate the facts first. If Gigi claims she was with Anton d'Stang, then he's off the suspect list. Why, you can even arrange a hair appointment today."

"It's Sunday," my father protested.

"So?" Aunt Vera folded her hands proudly over her abdomen. "The Permanent Wave is open seven days a week."

A pack of women and children entered the shop. The tallest of the women waved at Aunt Vera as she directed her group toward the children's corner at the rear of the store.

"Hello, Miss Vera. Hello, Miss Jenna," the children sang in chorus as they passed us.

Aunt Vera whispered, "Homeschoolers. The word is out about the Curious Chef products we have in stock. Those kiddie-sized chef's hats that you ordered, Jenna—the ones that can be personalized? A brilliant idea on your part. And the mothers are digging into the fiction books as frequently as the cookbooks. They adore the culinary mysteries. My faves are those Domestic Diva ones. The protagonist puts on all these fabulous events, and I think there's a ghost in her house." She clapped her hands like a mime, making no sound whatsoever. "I have to admit, this whole venture, other than losing your dear friend, has been so much fun. Now, go. Visit Gigi. And remember, a hairstylist is similar to a bartender or even a therapist. They hear all and tell all. Trust me, Gigi will spill her life story to you." She gave me a nudge.

I balked. "What about our new hire interviews?"

"Why do you think I asked your father to stop by? As a former FBI analyst, he's an expert at separating the wheat from the chaff. At the very least, he can do background checks."

"What?" my father said.

"You need a project, Cary. Leave, Jenna. Get the scoop." Aunt Vera shooed me. "We've got this."

"I promise I'll be back in time to close so you can make your Coastal Concern meeting."

Because of her deep spiritual bond with nature, Aunt Vera took an active part in ensuring our coasts remained pure and unsullied.

"However long it takes," she said. "Too-ra-loo."

Shoving my father's discontent to the back of my mind, I hurried out of the shop wondering exactly how I was going to convince Gigi Goode to confide in me, her polar opposite, and whether I would have enough time to do so before Chief Pritchett hauled me in and threw away the key.

Chapter 11

L IVING IN SAN Francisco had made me forget how much
fun Crystal Cove could be and how much people
delighted in living there. I drank in the local flavor as I
walked to the Permanent Wave Salon and Spa. Surfers with
artistically painted surfboards propped on their shoulders
paraded down the brick sidewalks. Families hoisted colorful
kites or played Frisbee in the two postage-stamp-sized parks
between shopping arcades. Tourists posed with the twin
silver statues of dancing dolphins that stood at the intersec-
tion where the egress out of town met Buena Vista Boulevard, the main drag.

When I reached my destination, I halted. Perspiration
broke out on my upper lip. I swiped it away with my pinky.
Never once had I entered a hair salon nervous. I was not
married to my hairstyle. I had worn it short, long, and in
between. Though I had never colored my hair, during one
rebellious moment in college, I had considered throwing in
a punk pink stripe. So why was I anxious? Because I was
going to outright lie.

Get a grip, I urged myself. *You can do this.* I had battled

onerous executives in sales meetings. I had gone
head-to-head with obstinate clients. I could darned well tell
a fib to a hairstylist. And truthfully, I did need a trim. I
hadn't let anyone touch my hair in over six months.

I approached a cheerful appointment clerk who sported
the pink stripe I had considered in my youth. Glittery eye-
lids, fingernail polish, and a clingy one-piece jumpsuit
matched the stripe. Beyond her, through a huge plate glass
window, I caught sight of the ocean. White caps danced
across the surface. A sailboat scudded through the water at
a tilt.

"Help you?" the clerk said.

Faking wretchedness while plucking at my stick-straight
black hair, I said, "Is Gigi Goode available for a quickie?
My aunt recommends her highly. I need a trim something
awful."

"Let's see." The young woman clacked a key on her computer keyboard. "You're in luck. She has a cancellation."
She perused the salon. "Hmm. She's not at her station. Let
me see if I can track her down and get the okay to book you.
Have a seat by the aquarium. There are magazines. Want
some cucumber water?"

I wrinkled my nose at the notion.

The clerk giggled. "It's not really cucumber water.
Cucumbers floating in the water flavor it. It's good."

"No, I'm fine. Really." Cucumbers and I weren't the best
of friends. Early in my marriage, I had attempted to make
cold cucumber soup. To my horror, David turned out to be
allergic to dill. The recipe had asked for two fresh tablespoons of the herb. David's tongue swelled up, and he was
sick all night. Needless to say, the event put me off cooking
for a long, long time. Until now, actually.

The clerk left her post and scuttled in her superhigh heels,
tight-kneed à la Bette Midler, to the right. "Gigi," she called.

As I strolled toward the large fish tank, Gigi rushed from
a room and ran headlong into the clerk. Gigi's sheer size
knocked the clerk backward into a chair on wheels.

"What?" Gigi's blue-rimmed eyes flashed with

annoyance. She jammed her hands into her apron pockets. "Well?"

The clerk regained her balance and whispered something to Gigi, who ogled me and nodded once.

Trying not to appear overly excited about scoring an appointment on such short notice, I studied the fish in the aquarium. Tetra swam in and out of a sunken ship and a grotto fit for Princess Ariel.

The clerk led me to the dressing room. "Grab a smock and come with me. We'll get you shampooed."

"No consultation first?"

"Gigi never consults until the hair is wet."

Of course she didn't. That way she ensured the client stuck around. In for a penny, in for a full haircut, I decided. I threw on a smock the color of the ocean and followed the clerk to the washbasins. She introduced me to a sweet Latina woman, who gave my hair a quick shampoo, added coconut-scented conditioner, rinsed, and led me to Gigi's station. I sank back into the soft folds of the leather chair and scrutinized myself in the seashell-bordered mirror. People on the street stopped at the window and peered in at me. The impulse to gawp at them and gurgle like a fish swelled within, but I didn't cave to the urge.

Gigi lumbered to me, pressed a pump that elevated the chair a foot, and assessed me via the mirror. "I know you. We met the other day at the trailer. You were searching for Desiree."

"That's right. I'm Jenna Hart. I own The Cookbook Nook."

"It's awful about Desiree," she said. "The whole affair made me so upset. I left my kit with my best scissors in that trailer, can you believe it?"

That didn't sound as if it were a major catastrophe. Nothing close to dying anyway.

"I've got to go back when I get a moment to breathe. And you . . ." Gigi ran her fingers through my hair. "She was a good friend, right?"

"Yes."

With tremendous vigor, Gigi rubbed my scalp and my shoulders.

"Wow," I said. "That feels great. I didn't expect a head and neck massage."

"Hair always looks better when the face is relaxed. You look tense and some of your hair is coming out in clumps. That's caused by stress."

It wasn't easy moving to a new town. Opening a store. Finding a friend dead. And being suspected of murder.

"I'd like to apply some gold oil to your hair. Are you down with that?" Gigi didn't wait for my response. She squirted liquid from a dark brown bottle into her palm and applied the oil, rubbing strands of hair between her thumb and forefinger. "You're lucky. You have thick hair. It's in pretty good condition overall."

Minus the clumps.

"Desiree's was better," I said, trying to figure out how I could turn the conversation in the direction of Anton d'Stang. So far my effort sounded ham-fisted.

"Desiree spent thousands on her hair. That doesn't mean hers was better than yours, but it was tended, shaped, and sculpted."

Signifying mine wasn't.

"Take a look at these styles." Gigi pulled a hairstyle card with famous actresses as models from her cabinet. "I like this Jennifer Garner cut with slight layering, razor cut ends, swept bangs, and a curl on the end of the hair. It will suit your face. You're pretty, and you've got her narrow chin and bright eyes."

I happened to enjoy Jennifer Garner's spunky work. Maybe I could channel her *Alias* television personae to help me find Desiree's killer. "So how did you get the gig with Desiree?"

"Her regular stylist got the flu. Desiree sent Mackenzie—you know, her masseur—up here to find a local. That way she wouldn't have to pay for another Winnebago."

"Why didn't she send Sabrina to hire you?"

"I think Sabrina was going through something at home.

Boyfriend woes. Anyway," Gigi continued, "Mackenzie passed by, saw me through the window, and appreciated my style. How could I say no to a couple of thousand, up front, for two days' work? One thousand for a test style, which was a wash and blow dry. The second thousand for the event. I planned to add a few extra highlights. Nothing too dramatic. Desiree wanted to look good. Do you know they paid me, even though . . ." Gigi screwed up her mouth.

Even though Desiree died.

"Sorry for your loss." Gigi combed out my hair, divided it into sections, and using jaw-of-death-shaped clips, secured each section to the top of my head. I stifled a laugh. I looked as if I were a warrior goddess. As Gigi smoothed out a section and snipped off the irregular ends, she said, "You're pretty compliant."

"Is that an insult?"

"No, a compliment." She cut some more. "Desiree was . . . She could be . . . exacting."

My aunt was right. Talking to a hairstylist was similar to talking to a bartender. We didn't really make eye contact. We occasionally glanced at each other via the mirror. Chatting in that manner made the conversation less intense, more aloof. And yet private. No one in the shop seemed to be listening in.

"Did Desiree come here?" I asked.

"Oh, no. I only did her hair in the trailer." Gigi released one of the sections of hair from its jaw-of-death clip. Hair tumbled to my shoulder. "She could be mean."

"Desiree?"

"She said rude things."

I flashed on Katie's comment about Desiree ranting at others on her staff.

"She told me I was heavy. I should consider losing weight."

Desiree was nothing if not direct. I recalled a time in college when she reduced a girl to tears. She told her that the outfit she bought on a trip to Germany made her look like a two-ton Heidi. I remembered another time when she told me that my art was banal and I needed to dig deeper if I wanted to wow the world. At my insistence, we didn't speak for two months. In the end, I forgave her. Everybody did.

"But the money was good," Gigi continued, "and I still have college bills to pay off. Everyone can eat humble pie to pay off a debt, right?"

"Where did you go to college?"

Gigi circled to face me and pulled on the front-most locks of hair. "I went to art school. I wanted to become a watercolor artist. I enjoy painting flowers and birds." As she continued to shape my hair, she contrasted the styles of Georgia O'Keeffe and John James Audubon. "I was all over the map with my art, never settling on one style. Do you know Andrew Wyeth's work?"

"I do."

"Have you ever seen *The Fallen Tree*?" She pressed a hand to her chest. "Every time I look at that picture, my heart breaks."

"My personal favorite of his is *Wind from the Sea*. The movement of the breeze through those sheer curtains. Exquisite realism."

Gigi's face lit up. "Are you an artist, too?"

"I am. I paint dancing girls and I do some sculpting."

"The only thing I can sculpt is hair."

Using a makeup brush, Gigi swept the snipped hair off my face, and then she hoisted a Super Solano. The drone of the hair dryer made conversation difficult, and we fell into silence. I stewed about how to raise the subject of Anton d'Stang but couldn't find an opening.

When Gigi finished drying my bangs, she said, as if we had never stopped talking, "It's hard for artists to make a buck." She swept my bangs to the side. "Doing hair feels as if I'm cheating, know what I mean? It's so easy for me."

"There are plenty of people who can't do what you do. You're well respected"—I almost cheered as I saw my opening—"not to mention popular. In fact, I heard there was a guy the other day who came in for a style and ended up asking you out for a date."

Gigi lasered a look toward the clerk at the front desk.

"She didn't blab," I said, sotto voce, girl-to-girl. "The guy told me."

"Which guy?"

"Anton d'Stang, the restaurateur."

Gigi's face soured. "We went out once." She tugged on the tips of my bangs. Hard. *Ouch*. "Just once."

"Not all dates are ideal."

"He's a lot older than me."

"But very handsome. I can see how you'd be attracted. You were, weren't you?"

"Want spray?" She lifted a metallic silver can.

"No, thanks." I licked my lips. "Um, Anton said you spent time together the night Desiree died."

If eyes could shoot flames, Gigi would have ignited my hair with her fiery glance. "I think we're done. Take a peek." She shoved a hand mirror at me and spun the chair so fast my head flopped. "Happy?"

What could I say, that I wanted her to redo my hair? I might end up with a mullet. I wasn't willing to risk it.

GIVEN MY NEW hairstyle, I had to admit that when I headed back to The Cookbook Nook, I clipped along the sidewalk with a different attitude, sort of cocky and ready to take on any adversary. In my mind, I did a couple of boxing motions. Right uppercut, left hook, one-two-jab-jab-jab. My imaginary foe plunged to the mat.

As I reached the Fisherman's Village parking lot, I drew up short and stared at Sabrina, who stood with J.P. by the entrance to the office Winnebago. Sabrina was clad in her typical black sheath, her dark hair tied in a severe knot. The two faced each other, his hands holding her upper arms, her head tilted forward. The pose looked supportive, not threatening. How I wished I had learned more about yesterday's argument.

"Hey, you two." I strolled toward them.

J.P. locked eyes with me. He did not look happy at my arrival. A second later, he gave Sabrina a peck on the cheek, rubbed her upper arm once in a comforting way, and hurried into a Chevy Camaro. To say he peeled out of the parking lot was an understatement.

"He sure was in a hurry," I said.

Sabrina wrung the sheer black shawl she held in her hands and watched the Camaro as it swung onto Buena Vista Boulevard. "J.P. is hurting. He wants to get this over with."

I bet he did. Especially if he killed Desiree.

"At least you weren't arguing today," I said.

"We were discussing burial arrangements," Sabrina said. "J.P. wants to take the hike Desiree planned so we can strew Desiree's ashes."

"I'm not sure that's legal in California." As far as I knew, a person's ashes could only be disposed of in a maritime burial. "You might need a license of some sort."

"I don't care. We're going up there." She pointed to the crest of mountains beyond the Artiste Arcade, a cluster of high-end jewelry and fashion shops across the street from Fisherman's Village.

"Have the police released her body?"

"Not yet. I don't know when they will either."

"Would you like me to ask Chief Pritchett?"

"That woman." Sabrina slung the shawl around her shoulders and looped it into a knot at the front. "She's asking so many questions."

I was pleased to hear that. Maybe Cinnamon Pritchett didn't think I was guilty, or at the very least, she wanted to consider the possibility of my innocence. "That's her job. You want to see your sister's murder solved, don't you?"

"Chief Pritchett asked me about that thing I told you. You know, that Desiree was having an affair with your husband." Sabrina chewed her lower lip. "I told her I wasn't sure if it was true."

I felt as if someone had released the cinch around my ribs and lungs.

"She was sort of curt," Sabrina continued. "She said that kind of lie made me look suspicious and suggested I was spreading rumors to set you up."

"Were you?"

"I was so angry that day." Sabrina toyed with the tails of her shawl. "I hadn't heard from my boyfriend, and Desiree said I should give him the boot. She said he wasn't good enough."

"She thought a lot of you."

"No, she didn't. Desiree said I wasn't merely short, I was short on brains. I wasn't a good judge of men." Sabrina sucked back a sob. "She always said things to hurt me. If she wasn't happy, she didn't want me to be happy."

"Desiree wasn't happy?"

"Not really. I mean, she was in lust with J.P., but he's not the end-all-be-all. She wanted love. Real love. And the show? I'm sure you heard. It wasn't doing all that hot in the ratings. These past couple of months, she was getting meaner by the minute. Spiteful. I wanted a week off, but 'No go,' she said. Mackenzie wanted a chance at being more than a masseur. Desiree said, 'No go,' and called him a hack. J.P. wanted to introduce another cooking show to the network and guess what my cheery sister said?"

No go had been one of Desiree's catchphrases in college, too. Decisions weren't always her way or the highway, but close. Her friends—I, included—went along. Her energy was captivating.

"Don't get me wrong," Sabrina said. "I wasn't angry enough to kill my sister. None of us were. We understood Desiree and sort of went with her ebb and flow, but at times . . ." She sighed. "Chief Pritchett is hounding every one of us for info. I wish . . ." Sabrina checked her watch. "Oh, my, I have a hair appointment with Gigi. I had to cancel earlier because that cop summoned me."

"I just came from the Permanent Wave. I guess I nabbed your appointment."

"I thought something was different about you." Sabrina twirled a finger in the direction of my head. "My roots . . .

I can't go to a funeral with . . ." She toyed again with the ends of her shawl, drawing the tips into knots. "Listen, what I was talking about, that was normal, everyday kind of stuff for me and Desiree. I loved her. I miss her. I don't want you to get the wrong idea. And I'm sorry about telling you that she and your husband—"

"Forget it. Bygones." I patted her forearm.

She fetched a business card from her purse and handed it to me. "Call me if you learn anything, okay? And I'll let you know about the funeral hike."

"Please do." I tucked her card into the pocket of my ruffled skirt.

As she headed off, I felt something was off about our exchange, but I couldn't dwell on it because, when I entered The Cookbook Nook, I found my Aunt Vera chatting with none other than my good friend Bailey. As eclectic as always, Bailey wore a colorful sarong, exotic Egyptian goddesslike earrings, and strappy, four-inch wedged sandals to boost her to nearly five-feet-two. Sunlight streaming in the window highlighted Bailey's prominent cheekbones and made her copper hair, which was the same supershort style as her mother Lola's, glisten like rare metal. Typical Bailey, she was talking with her hands as well as her mouth.

Upon seeing me, she shrieked with glee. I echoed the scream and raced to her. We embraced as though we hadn't seen each other in years, when in reality we had gone to lunch in the City less than three weeks before.

"I'm so sorry I missed the opening of your shop," she said. "And I'm even sorrier to hear the news about the murder. How horrible."

We chatted briefly about the unfolding drama. She assured me the police would find the real killer. I hoped she was right.

"How long are you staying in town?" I said.

"Forever." A big-belly rumble rolled out of itty-bitty Bailey.

"Very funny."

"Truth." She held up three fingers like a Girl Scout.

"Taylor & Squibb isn't the same without you there, and, well, I quit. I couldn't take it any longer. I craved the ocean. I need a tan." Her skin was creamy white. "When I heard about a job opp, I motored down."

"What job opp?"

"I'm your new cookbook maven."

"Really? What do you know about cookbooks?"

"Other than the ones I have on my shelves, not a thing, but you know me." She tapped her head. Bailey had a razor-sharp memory; she was a walking card catalog. At Taylor & Squibb, she had been in charge of monitoring all the campaigns—on air, in magazines, and on the Internet. She didn't need a computer for any of her work. Information planted in her brain. In a matter of hours, she would have every product at The Cookbook Nook memorized, down to the color of the item and its location. I wouldn't be surprised if she could load all the cookbooks' indexes in her brain, as well. "I'll be a good employee," Bailey went on. "Loyal and dedicated."

"The salary isn't enough."

"Sure, it is. Mom is letting me live, rent free, above The Pelican Brief. I have a view and meals."

Aunt Vera said, "Don't be mad."

"Never," I said. "Um . . . Did Dad vet her?"

Aunt Vera nodded. "He did, but first he ran a background check."

Bailey said, "He did not . . . Did he?"

Aunt Vera chuckled.

I echoed her then said, "Aunt Vera, there's no need to stick around here. I'll bring Bailey up to speed. Go to your Coastal Concern meeting."

"I don't have to go. It was rescheduled to Wednesday."

Tigger moseyed out of the back room. Yawning, he brushed my ankles and eyed the newcomer. I scooped him up and said, "Tigger, this is Bailey. Bailey, this is our mascot."

"Ooh, I love kitties." She knuckled his chin. From the euphoric look on his face, I worried he might throw me over for her.

Aunt Vera said, "By the by, Jenna, dear, what did you learn from the hairstylist?"

"She wasn't forthcoming."

"What a shame."

"Speaking of forthcoming," Bailey said, "what was going on out there between you and that gal in black? She was acting very buddy-buddy."

"Sabrina"—I thumbed toward the parking lot—"is Desiree's sister."

"Bet she'll be coming into a bundle," Bailey observed.

The comment caught me up short.

"What's with the frown?" Bailey raised her hands in defense. "A gallows joke isn't PG around here?"

"No, that's not it." I glanced outside. Desiree had to have been worth millions. Did she have a will? Did she die intestate? She didn't have a husband or children. What if Sabrina stood to inherit Desiree's fortune?

Chapter 12

I PACED IN front of the sales counter, energy chug-a-
lugging through me.

"Jenna Starrett Hart, your aura is as dark as ink." Aunt
Vera gripped my arm. "What is going on?"

I told her my theory.

"Oh, my. This is my fault," she said. "Your father is right.
This has to stop." She fluttered her fingers and uttered some
mumbo-jumbo about scattering my bad juju to the four corners of the earth. "No more talking about murder, do you
hear me?" She corralled me toward the front door. "Your
father has asked us to dinner, and since my meeting was
canceled, I said yes. It's Sunday. The shop and café are
closed for the evening. Katie's cooking. Let's go. Bailey,
you're invited, too."

My aunt's quasi-magic spell must have worked because
I didn't protest. An hour later, we arrived in caravan at my
father's.

"Bailey, what a pleasant surprise," Dad crooned. He took
my friend by the hand and escorted her through the house—
a beauty of a Mediterranean villa set way up in the

hills—and out to the porch, which boasted a spectacular view of the ocean. My mother's taste for an unpretentious color scheme—white furniture, blue and green throw pillows, sleek silver accents—encouraged guests to pay attention to the environment. Even at this elevation, we could hear the ocean's steady flow.

"Jenna, guide Katie into the kitchen," Aunt Vera said as she closed the front door. "Show her where to set the grocery bags."

"What a gal to offer to cook on her night off," my father said.

Katie hooted. "Offer? Vera coerced me, but don't fret. Cooking makes me happy."

"I hear you're terrific," Bailey said. Though Bailey had grown up with us, she had hung out with a different crowd through elementary and high school. Bailey and I bonded at work; she didn't know Katie well at all. The two hit it off, however, as we drove Tigger back to the cottage and made a grocery run. Katie told jokes; Bailey responded as heartily as a comedy club audience.

I ushered Katie to the kitchen and set down the bag of cheese and *accoutrements* I was carrying. Katie wanted to start the evening with a goat cheese platter. Even I, she teased, couldn't mess that up. At the darling Say Cheese Shoppe located near the center of town, we picked up River's Edge Up in Smoke, a tiny ball of chèvre that was wrapped in a maple leaf and spritzed with bourbon; Cypress Grove's Purple Haze, which was goat cheese flavored with lavender and fennel; and Cowgirl Creamery's Pierce Point, a beautiful morsel of lusciousness rolled in dried herbs.

I pulled a rectangular platter from my father's cabinet, set the cheeses in the center, added dollops of apricot and fig jam, and clustered crostini crackers circuitously throughout. Feeling rather proud of myself, I took the artistic platter to the living room and said, "*Voilà.*" No one applauded—spoilsports—but as I returned to the kitchen, I heard Aunt Vera, Bailey, and Dad singing my praises.

"Sounds like success," Katie said as she rinsed lettuce at the sink.

"Yay me." I fetched the rest of the items from grocery bags and set them on the granite counter. "By the way, I've been thinking that I want music playing in the café on cool days." On warm days, we kept the sliding doors open and allowed the outside in, but on foggy or wintry days, we needed to keep the doors shut.

"What kind of music?"

"Judy Garland's greatest hits."

"Judy, in honor of your mother?"

"No. Because I adore Judy Garland. She had the most incredible talent."

"And the most tragic life. Maybe, instead, we should consider something more upbeat. Perhaps rock and roll music with food themes to keep people in the mood for dining."

"You mean songs like 'Cheeseburger in Paradise'?"

"Or 'Blueberry Hill.' "

I grabbed a spatula from a stainless steel utensil holder and sang into it. *"Bye, bye, Miss American Pie."*

Katie plucked a wooden spoon and crooned, *"Brown Sugar."*

"On the go-o-o-d ship lollipop."

"Lollipop, lollipop, oh-lolli-lolli-lolli."

"By the Chordettes," I shouted. "My mother loved that song."

"My mother, too. Oldies but goodies."

We laughed so hard we sounded as if we were monkeys gone wild.

When we settled down, I began to open the containers and packages we had purchased, "You know, I must have watched *The Wizard of Oz* over fifty times."

"Perhaps you should take that fandom and transfer it to some cooking stars like Paula Deene or Jamie Oliver."

"Jamie who?"

"You don't know him? He's the British chef that made goose fat popular and promotes the Food Revolution."

I shook my head. I didn't have a clue.

"Mr. Gorgeous. Tawny hair, dimples. Looks like your Dav—" Katie flushed rhubarb pink. She shook her wet hands over the sink. "I'm so sorry."

"You can say my husband's name. I won't crumple into a mass of tears." At least, I hoped I wouldn't. Honestly, I couldn't fall into a funk whenever someone mentioned David's name. I forged a smile. "What can I do to assist with the meal?"

"Everything."

"Ha-ha. Something easy. Not the chicken thighs. I'm afraid I'll char them."

"Which reminds me." Katie reached into her huge brown tote and removed a copy of *Mastering the Art of French Cooking*, by Julia Child. "For you."

"Katie, I can't accept this." It wasn't an expensive book— it was still available for sale, in its umpteenth printing—but the book looked used; it had to have sentimental value.

"Nonsense. I have three more copies. Take it. What always impresses me about Julia Child's recipes is that they work. They're simple, clear instructions, for even the most elaborate of dishes. They all taste good. I've tucked a few of my own recipes, on three-by-five cards, at the back of the book." In addition, she pulled out a red spiral notepad with my name artistically crafted on the cover and handed it to me. "And I want you to have this, too. Flip it open."

I obeyed. On the first page Katie had written a list of television shows, complete with airing times and celebrity chef stars' names.

"You should watch all of these shows and the reruns," she said.

"I've seen a couple." *Kelsey's Essentials* and *Rachael Ray's Week in a Day*. Both female chefs were perky and inspiring. Desiree's *Cooking with Des* show was partway down the list. *Throwdown!* was directly beneath. I pointed. "Rhett and I talked about Bobby Flay."

"You'll learn a lot from all of these chefs. Their techniques. Their tips. Take notes. And watch some of the specialty shows, you know, *Cupcake Wars* and *Radical Cake Battle*."

"I've actually seen that show. It had a water theme. Desiree was a judge on it."

"Therefore, you know what not to do . . . like act too cocky. Hoo-boy, some of the contestants are full of themselves."

"One of the bakers used a chainsaw. Another wielded an axe."

"Wicked."

"Not my cuppa."

"Mine either." Katie chortled. "Now, find a cookie sheet in the cupboards. I'm sure your father owns one. You're going to make baking powder biscuits. Simple. Five ingredients or less."

I was game. I adored biscuits lathered with butter.

When I finished whipping together the flour, baking powder, milk, and butter and I formed the concoction into reasonable-looking mounds of dough, I followed Katie's direction and prepared the chicken. I liberally coated the chicken thighs with paprika, olive oil, garlic salt, rosemary, and basil—an activity that I found very therapeutic. Afterward, my father lit the wood briquettes and showed me how to oil the grill. A short while later, I set the chicken to roast. Katie cautioned that chicken needed to cook slowly to stay tender. I kept watch like a hawk and flipped the chicken every five minutes. When it was cooked through, I set the pieces on a carving board and covered them with foil—to make them supertender, as Katie had coached.

In the meantime, Aunt Vera and Bailey prepared the table in the dining room. In keeping with my mother's décor, they placed blue and green swirled mats on the whitewashed farmhouse table and lit blue tapers.

Our first course—avocado and marinated artichokes on top of mache lettuce with a citrus dressing, created by Katie and assembled by me—was to everyone's liking. I forked a bite of everything into my mouth and savored the blend of flavors. Perfect, if I did say so myself.

"Katie," Bailey said, "where do you get your recipes?"

"Some from my mother. Some from my grandmother. Both excelled in the kitchen. I have over a thousand three-by-five cards."

My mouth dropped open. "A thousand, really?"

"I'll bet your father appreciates your talent," Dad said.

Katie frowned. "Not really, Cary. He doesn't have much of an appetite."

"Because of your mom's condition?" I asked.

"No." Katie tapped the tines of her fork on her plate. "I mean, yes, mom's illness has hit him hard, but he's a bit of a stickler. I never quite measure up. I'm bright but I'm homely."

"Katie Casey." Aunt Vera reproved my friend with a shake of her finger.

"Oh, don't bother trying to tell me otherwise, Vera. I'm plain. I don't mind. But my father? *Perfect is as perfect does.* That's his favorite saying. He doesn't care much about talent or a sense of humor. Beauty matters."

I felt sick to my core. As many hours as we had spent together back in high school, how had I not noticed that Katie had suffered emotional abuse?

Katie downed a bite of her salad and gave me a wink. "Enough about me. Bring me up to snuff. I want the scoop."

"There's more scoop?" Bailey leaned back in her chair and folded her hands over her stomach.

"Jenna," my father warned.

"Hush, Cary." Aunt Vera twisted in her chair to face me. "Do tell us, Jenna."

"Uh-uh. My house, my rules," Dad countered.

Without looking at him, Aunt Vera batted the air. "Stop being such a fuddy-duddy. Jenna, dear, what did you find out?"

Bailey nailed me with a shrewd gaze. "Are you doing what you do best?"

"What does she do best?" Katie said.

"Not cook," I joshed, trying to dispel the tension in the room as I threw Bailey an *ix-nay* on the *oop-scay* look.

Either Bailey didn't pick up on my overt gesture or she chose to ignore it. "Jenna was a prodigy at Taylor & Squibb," she went on. "Not only did she come up with the Whirling Dervish Hot Dogs campaign, which was brilliant in its effortlessness . . ."

A people-sized hot dog break dancing with a rock star on a barbecue grill. Big whoop. And yet the ad had earned me a CLIO Award—an award that honored inventive excellence in advertising and communication.

"She also knew how to get the goods on what other ad companies had in the works," Bailey continued. "She sized up the competition as if she were a professional sleuth. She knew who was developing this, that, and the other, and she also knew who was sleeping with whom. Most of the time."

"Jenna, is this true?" Aunt Vera said.

I shrugged a shoulder. "People blabbed on social networking sites. I paid attention."

"And did I mention," Bailey said, "that Jenna was our ace problem solver? If someone had a hitch in a campaign, they called her."

My aunt beamed. "She gets her smarts from our side of the family."

Dad grunted.

"Hoo-boy." Katie spanked the table. "So back to the investigation."

"Please don't call it that," my father ordered.

"What should we call it?" Aunt Vera said. "Jenna is tracking down suspects and questioning them. Is Cinnamon Pritchett doing that?"

"I'm sure she is," I rushed to say, not wanting to enrage my father further. I added, "Dad, don't worry. I'm being careful."

He leaned forward on his elbows. "Jenna, I told you earlier that I want you to steer clear of this."

"And do what? Let the police arrest me? Convict me? Would an FBI agent sit idly by if someone accused him of a crime he didn't commit?"

"You're not trained."

"Train me."

Dad's eyes narrowed. "You're sounding defensive."

"Like Cinnamon was in her teens?"

"No." He cut a quick glance at my aunt, who shrugged. "Like your sister, Whitney."

"Good. You've always said that Whitney is the brains in the family."

"I've never said—"

"Yes, you have."

Dad rolled his lip under his teeth, and I glowered at him, even though I was angry with myself. Why couldn't I bite my tongue? Why was I inciting him to battle with me the way we had when my mother and David died?

Following a long standoff, Aunt Vera said, "Too-ra-loo, Jenna. You don't need training. Bailey said you were the problem solver at your former job, and that's exactly why I made you my partner at The Cookbook Nook."

My father thwacked the table with his palm. "This is nonsense."

"Now, you listen to me, little brother," Aunt Vera started.

"Forget it, Aunt Vera. He's never going to bend." I shoveled another bite of avocado and mache into my mouth. Not nearly as tasty as the first bite. Perhaps the bitterness creeping up my esophagus wasn't such a good addition to the dish. I tucked my chin into my chest, unwilling to make direct eye contact with my father.

After a long tense moment, Dad said, "Jenna, your mother—"

"Leave her out of this."

"Let me finish." My father snapped his napkin on the table. "I know I will never compare to your mother. I'll never understand you the way she did. I'll never find the right words to say."

"'I support what you're doing,' would be a good start," I muttered. "Or 'I believe you're innocent.'"

Aunt Vera tittered. So did Bailey and Katie.

"How about, 'You're smart and you've got a good head on your shoulders'?" Dad said.

I peeked at him from beneath my lashes. His amused expression relieved me.

"You are," he said. "And you know it and I know it. Truce?"

I reached for his hand. He squeezed mine and didn't release it. "I do expect you to train me," I said.

"What do you think I've been doing all your life, Tootsie Pop? I worry. That's all. A father's prerogative. Now, because your aunt won't have it any other way, tell us everything."

Aunt Vera, Bailey, and Katie gawked at me. Waiting.

I licked my lips. "Fine, but let's serve up dinner first. The chicken's done, right, Katie?"

With everyone pitching in, minutes later we settled at the table with plates of crispy herbed chicken, fresh green beans dredged in melted butter, and flaky, light biscuits.

Bailey took a bite of the chicken. Her eyes widened. "You made this, Jenna? It's so moist."

I worked hard not to pat myself on the back for a job well done. "I had a good teacher."

Katie beamed.

"Maybe you should author a cookbook, Katie," Bailey said. "I know a literary agent in San Francisco who might help you. I know lots of people in San Francisco."

A wistful look passed across my friend's face. Was Bailey ruing her decision to leave the City? Had she left a loved one behind? I couldn't remember her ever having a long-term relationship. She was, as she preferred to call herself, the one-night-stand queen. She didn't know why. Maybe because her very first boyfriend had been a *punk-jerk-loser*—her words. Her father, an eminent legal mind and Lola's ex, was still in Bailey's life.

Bailey forced a grin. "Back to the matter at hand. Your investigation. Details, please."

As I broke into my second biscuit, I said, "I think Sabrina Divine killed her sister. She might be in line to inherit Desiree's millions."

Dad said, "You should ask—"

"Cinnamon? I don't think I'll get an answer. Our

illustrious chief doesn't appreciate that I'm sticking my nose into things." I told them about the message that Desiree had left on my answering machine and Cinnamon's response.

Dad grumbled. Aunt Vera wagged a finger to zip it.

"Sabrina lied about Desiree and David having an affair," I added.

"She did?" Katie hooted.

"She rescinded the rumor," I said, "which means she could also be lying about her alibi. Supposedly she spent the night with the masseur Mackenzie."

Katie said, "Mr. Tan and Muscular? The fellow I saw arguing with Desiree? He's a tad on the egotistical side, don't you think?"

"A tad?" I snorted.

"Okay, a ton. You know, he took a part-time job at the Permanent Wave Salon and Spa."

"He did? Why?"

Dad cleared his throat. "I would imagine Desiree's assets have been frozen. To make ends meet, the man might need a paycheck."

Aunt Vera plucked a biscuit from the basket. "Have you asked this Mackenzie whether Sabrina's alibi holds up?"

I shook my head. "I haven't had the chance. He emerged from the Winnebago once, when Sabrina exited, scowled at J.P., and retreated."

"J.P.?" Bailey said. "Who's he? What's he look like?"

"Mohawk and tattoos," I said, resorting to verbal shorthand. "J.P. was not only Desiree's director but her lover. Jealousy could be his motive for murder, if he felt Desiree was cheating on him. But he also seems torn up about her death. Then there's Anton d'Stang, Desiree's first sponsor, a well-known restaurateur."

"Mother mentioned him," Bailey said. "She told me you figured out that he was stalking Desiree."

"Stalking?" Katie, Aunt Vera, and Dad said in unison.

I met everyone's stare. "The day Desiree arrived, Anton was loitering in disguise outside The Cookbook Nook."

"Mother said he seemed strapped for money, by the way. Digging in his pockets for change to pay for lunch."

That fostered a variety of opinions. Aunt Vera believed a man that would dress in costume was capable of all sorts of deceit. Katie said she thought Anton might have hounded Desiree for a loan. Bailey suggested he was seeking vengeance.

"But"—I held up my hand—"Anton claims he was with Gigi Goode the night Desiree was murdered, and when Gigi cut my hair, she didn't deny it."

"You asked her outright?" my father said.

"I tried. She skirted the conversation and ended our appointment."

"Guilty guilty guilty," Bailey chimed.

"On the other hand," Katie said, "I think the boyfriend-slash-director with the Mohawk might be the killer."

"J.P." Bailey beamed as if she had just keyed in the winning answer on a game show.

"Right." Katie eyed me. "Didn't he tell you that Desiree received a phone call the night she died, and he went to sleep?" She slapped her thigh. "Hoo-boy, that's about as nebulous an alibi as saying he was watching TV. Did anyone at the hotel see him? Can anyone corroborate his whereabouts?"

"Vera, what do you think?" Bailey said. "I hear you get vibes."

My father wiggled his fingers overhead. "O-o-ooh. Vera gets vibes."

"Don't make fun, Cary," Aunt Vera said. "I *do* get vibes. ESP, if you will."

"Hot flashes," Dad joked.

Aunt Vera folded her arms on the table and glowered at him. "There have been government studies done on mind control."

"Mind control is one thing. ESP is entirely another."

"Is it?" Aunt Vera taunted. "How can you be so sure, Cary? What exactly did you do for the FBI? Will you ever reveal your secret? How do I know you weren't involved in some *Manchurian Candidate* experiment yourself?" The FBI had given my father the job description *analyst*, but there were times when he left home for weeks. Afterward my mother would press him for details. He would claim what he did was hush-hush.

"All right, all right, Vera." My father held up his hands and laughed. "I concede. You have ESP."

"Sadly, however, I have no vibes about this murder," Aunt Vera said.

"Hey, everyone." Bailey clapped her hands. "I've got an idea. I think Jenna should get a massage with the new guy so she can do some reconnaissance. All in favor?"

Katie, Bailey, and my aunt said, "Aye." Dad grunted.

"What?" I yelped. "No, uh-uh, no way." Getting a haircut to learn the truth was one thing, but going for a massage? I hadn't felt a man's hands on my body since David died. I couldn't, could I?

Chapter 13

A DENSE WALL of fog packed the seashore Monday morning. Luckily the gloom didn't translate into lack of sales. In fact, the weather might have encouraged the passel of families and children to shop rather than head for the beaches to practice their sandcastle skills. Katie's tasty cranberry chocolate muffins might have had something to do with the size of the swelling crowd, as well.

"Mmmm." Bailey took a second bite-sized muffin from the tier of goodies, peeled off the wrapper, and popped it into her mouth. "The flavor is divine," she mumbled between bites. "If I keep eating like this, I'm going to grow into the size of that blueberry girl in *Willy Wonka and the Chocolate Factory.*" One thing Bailey and I shared in common was our love of books. One day over lunch while at Taylor & Squibb, we realized we had read not only the complete collection of Nancy Drew books but the entire set of Agatha Christie Hercule Poirot mysteries, as well. "Remember the blueberry girl?" Bailey puffed out her cheeks. I laughed.

A few customers who were inspecting the aprons display stopped and gawked at us. Bailey, a bit of an exhibitionist, waved and yelled, "Hi, folks. Once you're done buying a couple of knickknacks and cookbooks, make your way into the café for a midmorning coffee and pastry. You won't be disappointed." She bumped my hip with hers. "By the way, did you see the recent order catalog from Ingram's?"

Ingram's was the major book distributor in the world, with over two million titles. We ordered books from other distributors, but Ingram's supplied our mainstay.

"I found some top-selling cookbooks that we don't have on the shelves. *The Cook's Illustrated Cookbook: 2,000 Recipes from 20 Years of America's Most Trusted Cooking Magazine* and *Guy Fieri Food: Cookin' It, Livin' It, Lovin' It.* You know about Guy Fieri, right?"

"I saw him on the Food Network. He visits diners around America? I love his spiky hair and his *joie de vivre.*"

"He's a cutie. Also, I noticed *Everyday Food: Great Food Fast*, by Martha Stewart, was on the Ingram's list. We don't have any of her cookbooks, and though she's not my cup of tea, I'm sure she'll appeal to many of our moms on the go."

"Does her cookbook have lots of photographs?"

"Plenty."

Our customers preferred cookbooks with eye-catching pictures. "Write the titles on the order sheet, and we'll get them."

The front door opened and a pair of bronzed surfer girls shuffled in and made a beeline to the natural foods cookbook section. Right behind them, a swarm of preschool girls buzzed in, followed by what I assumed were their mothers.

One girl shrieked, "Oh, look, a kitty." The rest echoed her, and they darted to the children's corner and pounced on Tigger. Luckily the little guy loved affection. Soon I heard the girls singing, *"But the cat came back, she wouldn't stay away, she was sitting on the porch the very next day"*— lyrics I had heard the Muppets sing years ago. Too sweet.

"Jenna, you have a phone call." Aunt Vera, wearing an ocean-patterned caftan, stood at the sales counter and brandished the telephone receiver.

"Who is it?"

"Chief Pritchett."

A sinking feeling gripped my insides. Cinnamon must have decided that the answering machine message from Desiree, along with the suspicious trowel and my history, gave her enough evidence to haul me in and book me. I was doomed. Perhaps I should ask her who stood to inherit Desiree's estate. *A good offense was the best defense*, my father would say.

Anxiety Poppity Pop popping inside me, I hurried to the telephone. Using a steady voice, I said, "Hi, there." Too casual? Too bad.

"I have the answering machine to return to you," Cinnamon said. I heard pages moving in the background. Was she leafing through my future arrest record?

"And . . ."

"And I've decided there's nothing I can prove with Miss Divine's message."

My shoulders loosened. Another day of freedom. "Do you know that the famous restaurateur Anton d'Stang is in town?"

"I do."

I was pleased to hear that she was on top of things. "Are you going to question him?"

"Perhaps."

"Might I ask who stands to inherit Desiree's money?"

"You may."

Wow, she was being cryptic. I said, "You won't tell me?"

"I'm waiting for a call from Miss Divine's attorney. Good day, Miss Hart."

I hung up, my stomach snarling into a knot again. No news was typically good news, but in this case, no news stirred my overactive imagination to send me to jail. *Do not pass Go*.

Bailey hurried toward me wearing a bright turquoise, supertight Cookbook Nook T-shirt. What had she done with her other chic top? "What do you think?" She paraded in a circle, arms out. "We have a pile in the storeroom. Your Aunt Vera ordered them."

"Let's lose it," I said. "Matching T-shirts are too theme park for me."

Bailey folded her hands in prayer. "Praise the pope. I was hoping you'd say that. Will you tell your aunt?"

"Absolutely. Go change."

As she clip-clopped in her wedge heels toward the back room—the girl had more shoes than Saks Fifth Avenue's shoe salon—she said over her shoulder, "By the way, I made an eleven o'clock massage appointment for you at the Permanent Wave Salon and Spa today with Desiree's former masseur. You're looking tense." She hiccupped with laughter as she exited.

At the same time, Katie ran in, her face white with fear. "It's gone."

"What's gone?"

"My heirloom watch." She tapped the front of her white jacket where she normally pinned the pocket watch.

"Haven't you switched out jackets since yesterday?"

"No. I mean, yes, of course. I can't seem to make a meal without making a mess." She was kidding. We had done a smack-down job of leaving my father's kitchen spic and span last night, and I hadn't gotten a splatter of food on me. "But I always unhook the watch," she went on. "And I methodically pin it to my next uniform. I hung the jacket in the closet in the kitchen." She pointed toward the café. "Someone stole it."

"Do you think it was one of the staff?"

"I don't know. It could have been, I guess. I can't imagine . . ." She covered her mouth with the back of her hand then lowered it as tears pooled in her eyes. "It was my grandpa's, on my mother's side. It means everything to Mama. If she finds out . . ."

I didn't want to point out that her mother had Alzheimer's and wouldn't likely remember tomorrow what someone told her today.

"You've got to help me find it," Katie wailed.

"Find what?" Bailey returned, wearing the silky summer sweater that matched her capris. Much better.

I filled her in.

My aunt moseyed to us. "Is it possible . . ." She left the sentence hanging.

"Is what possible?"

Aunt Vera flapped her hand. "I hate to speak ill, but I saw . . ."

Again with the dangling.

"Saw what?" I prompted.

"The first day Desiree was here, Gigi came into The Cookbook Nook before everyone else. She said she needed to use the bathroom. The one in the Winnebago wasn't working." My aunt pointed at the hallway connecting the shop to the café. "She had time to . . . you know . . ."

"But it only went missing now," Katie said.

"Maybe she came back," Aunt Vera replied. "Maybe that day she was casing the joint, as they say."

I thought of the first time I met Gigi in the Winnebago, when I was on the hunt for Desiree and J.P. She wore so much jewelry—beads, bracelets, earrings. And the other day, when I saw her tiptoeing out of the dressing room at the salon. At first, she had acted peeved at the appointment clerk, but in review, Gigi had looked mortified. She shoved her hands into her apron pockets. Had we interrupted her while she was filching someone's stuff?

The door to the shop opened and Tito Martinez hustled inside, an iPad tucked under his arm, a cell phone in his hand. "Morning, everyone." He seemed chipper for someone who, the day before, had accused a dead woman of pilfering his ideas. "Thought I'd browse."

To swipe some recipes for his e-book cookbook? I mused. *Be nice, Jenna.* Everyone in town was free to peruse the shelves, and if someone picked up a tip for a recipe, so be it. The thing that made cookbooks unique was the personality behind the book. The cook, the chef, the voice in the dialogue about each recipe. A recipe box filled with recipes had a story to tell. *The French Laundry Cookbook*, written by the famous chef Thomas Keller, didn't sell simply because of the recipes; it sold because of the saga. Keller related how he started the famous French Laundry restaurant in Yountville, California, and the pictures he included, starting with the beautifully lit table settings and the pastoral garden photographs, were phenomenal.

Katie plucked my sleeve. "What do you think about Gigi being the culprit?"

"She did your hair, Jenna," Aunt Vera said. "Did you get a vibe?" Her eyes widened. "Ahh. You did. Speak up." So much for me having a poker face. My aunt shook her fingers as if summoning otherworldly spirits. "Trust your instincts."

I told them about Gigi's guilty reaction as she exited the dressing room at the salon.

Bailey said, "Remember the gal at Taylor & Squibb who kept stealing pens from the stock room? They caught her on a security camera. Does the Permanent Wave have one of those?"

"Who are you talking about?" Tito said, homing in on our private conversation.

"Nobody," the group responded.

"Don't kid a kidder. I have supersonic hearing." Tito drew his fingers up to a point at the tops of his ears. If only I had a dog whistle.

"Who are you?" Bailey cut a look from Tito to me.

"This is Tito Martinez," I said. "Local reporter for the *Crystal Cove Crier* and wannabe cookbook author."

"Not wannabe," Tito said. "I write cookbooks on the side."

"One," my aunt said. "You've written one. And the recipes are your grandmother's."

Katie elbowed Bailey and twirled her finger by her head, signifying the man was loco.

"Fine. Whatever," Tito said. "You're talking about Gigi Goode, aren't you?"

I stepped toward him. "You know Gigi?"

"I know everyone in town. Ev-er-y-one." Tito carved the air with a finger. "And I've thought she was a thief for ages. Want to know why? Because at night, I'd see her cruising the streets, window-shopping supposedly."

I shifted feet. "We all window-shop."

"Late at night. *Real* late. And then, get this, the other night, I caught her sizing up a place. It was that Art from the Heart jewelry store. Gigi went inside and she started pawing everything."

I liked to touch when I shopped, too. That didn't make me a thief. "Did you see her take anything?"

"Well, no."

"When was this?"

"Friday at midnight."

"You're lying. No stores are open at midnight."

"The whole arcade was. They were having an all-night supersale. Some stupid promotional thing."

"Are you sure of the day?" I said. "That was the night Desiree was killed."

Tito rubbed his formidable chin. "Yep. Gigi was in there for at least a half hour. I was just hanging around, waiting for her to pinch something so I could get the goods on her."

"Anton d'Stang said he and Gigi spent the evening together. When I asked Gigi—" I halted, peeked around. "Where's Katie?" Her toque sat on the vintage kitchen table alongside jigsaw puzzle pieces of a fruit basket. Bailey gestured toward the door. "She said she had an errand."

"At a time like this?" I squawked. Losing her heirloom watch must have really upset her.

"Continue, dear." Aunt Vera revved her hand at me. "You were saying when you asked Gigi . . ."

"She didn't corroborate Anton's story," I went on. "She kept mute. I understand that a pickpocket might want an alibi, but the only reason Anton would need an alibi was if he killed Desiree himself, right? What did Gigi take?" I turned to Tito for his answer, but he was rushing out of the store as if he were a bloodhound following a scent.

I sank into the chair by the kitchen table and gazed at the puzzle pieces, a mishmash of color, sort of like the array of suspects in Desiree's murder. Why couldn't I see the big picture? Last night I believed Sabrina Divine was the culprit, and now I was aiming my sights on Anton d'Stang. Had

Anton killed Desiree and used Gigi as his alibi? Gigi wouldn't come forward if telling the truth would nail her as a thief. On the other hand, Tito hadn't validated that he had caught Gigi doing anything wrong. Maybe Gigi could deny Tito's claim while at the same time refute Anton's alibi.

A little voice in my mind reminded me not to forget about J.P. Hessman. He had no verifiable alibi. And how did Mackenzie whatever-his-last-name-was fit in? Why had Desiree brought him on this particular road trip?

Bailey and Aunt Vera joined me at the table.

"This is good news," Bailey said as she fitted puzzle pieces together. "You have other suspects. It's time to go to the police."

"But I don't want to get Gigi in trouble. I mean, what if she isn't a thief?"

"But she is." Katie burst into the shop and skidded to a halt.

The customers at the back of the store straightened to attention, even the children, which gave Tigger a chance to escape. He dashed to me and leaped into my arms.

"No worries, folks," I said above their concerns. "Katie bought a lottery ticket." I cooed to Tigger to calm him. "She gets excited over the simplest things." I begged my aunt and Bailey to tend to our patrons and herded Katie into the hall-way between the shop and the café. "What are you saying?"

"I tiptoed into the masseur's Winnebago."

"It was open?"

"Not really. I know how to pick locks."

Oh, boy. Trouble with a capital T.

Katie hastened to explain. "My former employer was notorious for bolting himself in his bedroom. He couldn't be left alone. We had a locksmith over nearly every week. I paid attention." She petted Tigger's ears. He chugged his appreciation. "Anyway, I found the hairdresser's kit sitting on top of an autograph book and a couple of Desiree's cookbooks."

The kit that Gigi mentioned she had left behind.

"And inside was my grandfather's watch. Want to know what else I found?"

I did. Every fiber inside me vibrated with curiosity.

"There was an empty billfold and this really fancy-schmancy silver pill box, as well as a diamond-studded tennis bracelet, and a heart-shaped necklace."

Instinctively, my hand reached for the locket around my neck.

"How could Gigi afford those things on a hairdresser's salary?" Katie said. "She's a thief. Just like Tito said. I knew she was guilty. I felt it. In here." She tapped her chest. "You have to tell Chief Pritchett."

"And get you arrested for breaking and entering?"

Katie blushed the color of a tasty rosé. "But what if Desiree found out Gigi was a thief and threatened to turn her in? Maybe Gigi killed Desiree to shut her up."

I hadn't considered that.

"You need to find out more about Gigi."

"How would you suggest I do that?"

Chapter 14

꧁✕✕꧂

THE PERMANENT WAVE Salon and Spa buzzed with chatter. Customers filled the hairstylists' chairs and the chairs at the washbasins. An older woman perched on a stool at the makeup counter while an exotic younger woman applied chartreuse eye shadow—not a color I would ever allow near my face. Two women and a man huddled by the appointment desk.

As I stood behind them waiting to check in—to coerce me to keep the massage appointment Bailey set up, Katie had bribed me with dark chocolate cupcake pops—I caught sight of the aquarium, and something prickled the edges of my mind. I stared harder. I wasn't interested in the tetra that swam in figure eights. I fixated on the grotto beneath the water and, more specifically, on the mermaid anchored inside the grotto. The killer had enshrined Desiree's body within a mermaid sculpture. Was it significant that the salon featured an aquarium with a mermaid? Had the miniature mermaid ignited a salon employee's deadly imagination?

I cut a look at Gigi, who was working on a client. As if sensing my appraisal, she glanced at me and then the aquarium. Her mouth quirked up at the edges. A cat holding a bird in its mouth couldn't have looked more culpable.

Before I could march to her and say point-blank, "You killed Desiree," the appointment clerk with the pink hair said, "Miss Hart, Mackenzie is ready for your massage."

Mackenzie strolled toward me, arms hanging loosely by his sides. Gone was the antagonism of our first meeting. Gone was the angry scowl he had thrown at J.P. the other day. Clad in a white pajama-style outfit, with sunlight streaming through the picture window and highlighting his blond hair, he struck me as handsome and vibrant. The flock of good-looking surfers in town had nothing on him. "Welcome, my friend." He clasped my hand and smiled.

I bit back a laugh. If I were looking to cast Prince Charming in a Stay Bright toothpaste commercial, this would be the guy. I'd even make a single tooth sparkle.

"Right this way," he said. "I'll show you to the therapy room."

Keeping hold of my hand—so much for me getting a shot at confronting Gigi—Mackenzie opened a solid oak door and ushered me along a hall. A waterfall burbled at the far end. Soothing music played through speakers. The scent of lavender filled the air. Mackenzie directed me into a dark massage room, told me to undress to my comfort level, and slip between the sheets with my face nestled in the massage cradle. He would return in a couple of minutes.

In the semidark, I started to perspire. To say I was nervous was an understatement. Not because I hadn't experienced a man's touch for some time, but because I was anxious as all get-out about questioning someone while I was bare naked. What had my pals talked me into?

When Mackenzie's hands first touched my neck, I flinched.

"Relax. I promise I won't hurt you," he said. "But, my friend, I've got to tell you, you have knots. I need your muscles to obey. Breathe."

I tried. I really tried. Mackenzie told me to envision the lull of a mountain lake rippling on the shore and to imagine a breeze whistling through palm fronds, but I knew, and so did Mackenzie, that his words were useless. I was wound tighter than a spring.

He rolled his knuckles down my back and dragged his palms upward to my neck. "So, tell me where you're from originally."

"Here. Crystal Cove."

"Family?"

"Dad, sister in L.A., brother in Napa. You?"

"Los Angeles. Born and raised. No siblings. Breathe . . . hold it . . ." He worked his fingers into the hollow of my neck. "Release. Good, my friend."

I wondered if massage school had taught him to repeat *my friend* every few sentences to engage a client. It wasn't working, but I wasn't a typical client.

"Married?" he asked. "I don't see a ring on your left hand."

"My husband died."

"Wow. Sorry. I . . ." More knuckles. More dragging. Back and forth. "That's a tragedy."

Understatement of the decade. But enough about me. "You?" I said. "Married?"

"Nah. I let one get away. Now there's too much going on in my career."

A point Sabrina had mentioned came to me. I said, "Did you ever want to do something other than massage?"

"Yeah, sure. Doctor, baker, Indian chief," he said, quoting the *Tinker Tailor* nursery rhyme.

I reflected on the word *chief*. Did Mackenzie have aspirations of running a company? He came from Los Angeles. Had he, like J.P., dreamed of becoming a famous director? Wasn't that the goal of everyone who lived in L.A.? Had he asked Desiree for the chance? Was that why she had said, *No go,* because she held fast to the rule that he had to pay his dues? Instead, she gave him the chore of securing a replacement hairstylist, and he resented being her lackey. He lashed out because . . .

No. I was grasping at straws. When I was a child, Dad warned my siblings and me not to pluck an idea out of thin air. We needed facts for any conclusion. That was the FBI way. The truth and nothing but the truth. Black and white. Had he taught Cinnamon the same thing?

I said, "I heard you hired Gigi Goode."

"Yep." Mackenzie bent my left arm at the elbow and wedged my wrist against by back. He kneaded my shoulder so hard that I moaned. "Good, my friend. Let it out."

"Why Gigi?" I bit back another groan.

"I contacted the Better Business Bureau, learned about this salon, and asked who was their best, and then I observed her."

I recalled Gigi saying he had watched her from the street. "Why didn't Sabrina handle the problem?"

"I offered. You see, I was pals with Desiree's regular stylist. A real talent. It was a shame she got sick, but at least she's not part of the spectacle up here."

"Spectacle?"

"With the police. Chief Pritchett has this chart going at the precinct. You must have seen it. You've been called in, if rumors are true. Push pins, yarn, red flags."

"I haven't seen it," I said, though I was glad to hear Cinnamon was doing her job, even if her chart was a tad colorful. I considered dropping by the precinct to view what she had written on the chart. Perhaps I wasn't her number one suspect any longer. A girl could dream.

"How's the pressure, my friend?" Mackenzie asked as he walked around the top of the massage table.

"Good."

He started in on my other arm. "Massage is so important for a person's body. Say, you own The Cookbook Nook. You must be a great cook. Think of me as the chef and you're the meal. I stir up the ingredients, add TLC, set the timer, and in less than an hour, *voilà*, you're done."

"Sounds like a perfect recipe for relaxation."

"That's the ticket. Now, shh."

"In a sec. You've got me intrigued. Tell me more about Chief Pritchett."

Mackenzie kneaded my hand and forearm. "She's a piece of work. She nearly tackled me, push pins in hand, when I told her I saw Desiree with Anton d'Stang at the Chill Zone Bar."

"You know who Anton is?" I twisted my head so I could peer at him.

"Everybody does. He's world famous."

"Did you see Anton leave the bar with Gigi?"

"Nope. Can't say I saw Gigi there. But I didn't stick around for long. I . . ." He hesitated. "I hooked up with someone."

How gallant of him not to reveal Sabrina's name.

"My friend, we have to stop talking. You're not getting the full benefit of your massage." Mackenzie guided my face back into the cradle, then worked his thumbs up my triceps. "Also, remember to drink lots of water following this session."

"Will do. But one more thing. Back to you seeing Anton with Desiree."

"Me, J.P., and everyone else."

"J.P.?" My voice escalated to way above a tone appropriate for the massage room.

"Shh," Mackenzie cautioned.

"J.P. said he fell asleep in his hotel room."

"He may have gone nighty-night at some point, but he was at the Chill Zone, sitting at the bar by himself, giving Desiree and Anton evil glares while making repeated calls on his cell phone. When that didn't work, he used the pay phone down the hall by the restrooms."

Was J.P. dialing Desiree, waiting for her to pick up so he could chew her out? Why did he sit on the sidelines? Why didn't he confront her face-to-face? I said, "Did Desiree see J.P.?"

"Don't think so. She was pretty into Anton. Now, no more questions."

* * *

I DIDN'T RELAX through the rest of the massage. How could
I? I mean, yes, the deep tissue work Mackenzie did on my
legs and feet was incredible; he had great hands. But I kept
cycling the conflicting stories through my mind. What if
Gigi was a petty thief? Did she kill Desiree to keep her
penchant for stealing a secret? Had she convinced Anton
d'Stang to lie for her, or vice versa? Anton said he was with
Gigi at the time of Desiree's murder. Did he leave Desiree
and go out with Gigi? He didn't mention having seen Desiree
that night. Did he honestly believe no one had noticed them
at the Chill Zone? And I couldn't forget about J.P. He showed
up at the bar, too. Did he believe he was invisible? To my
surprise, Sabrina's whereabouts appeared to be solid.
Though Mackenzie didn't mention Sabrina's name outright,
he claimed to have hooked up with a woman. I had seen
Sabrina emerging from his Winnebago the next morning. I
could do the math.

As I checked out at the reception desk, I scanned the
place for Gigi. She wasn't at her station. When I asked to
speak with her, the appointment clerk said Gigi went
window-shopping. She loved to do that, the clerk added.

I'll bet. I whisked my signature on the credit card receipt,
added a hefty tip for Mackenzie, and hurried outside. I
caught sight of Gigi veering into the Artiste Arcade across
the street from Fisherman's Village.

Eager to follow but knowing I had responsibilities to
attend to first, I made a quick call to The Cookbook Nook.
Even from a distance, I saw a trail of people lined up across
the Fisherman's Village parking lot. Bailey answered the
telephone and assured me all was in order.

I asked what was up with the stream of customers. Bailey
said Katie had made some extraordinarily delicious fish
chowder laced with white wine. In addition, numerous mem-
bers of a women's book club had dropped in to survey the
culinary mysteries. According to one, the group had grown

tired of reading nationally bestselling *yawn* books. They wanted books with flavor.

"How was your massage?" Bailey added.

"Informative."

"Really?"

"I'll explain when I return." I ended the conversation and scurried after Gigi.

The Artiste Arcade featured a brick archway adorned with purple morning glory vines. The vines' scent wasn't as strong at midday as in the morning, but the fragrance was still enchanting. I strode beneath the arch and halted when I spied Gigi peering into the Adorn Yourself accessory shop. The display window featured floral scarves, dangly earrings, jewelry, and glitzy hair clips. Gigi clung to the strap of her tote bag with both hands as if to keep herself from reaching out. Inside the shop, a customer haggled with a salesclerk.

Taking the direct approach, I strode to Gigi and said, "Hi. Fancy seeing you here."

She whipped toward me and again reminded me of an intensely focused Olympic shot-putter. We had never stood face-to-face. As tall as I was, she bested me by at least three inches and outweighed me by thirty pounds. One good shove of her palm to my face would send me reeling.

"Are you okay?" I said.

"Um, yes, fine." Gigi's pupils narrowed; her mouth ticked up on one side; her foot began to tap. All classic signs of lying. "What do you want?"

"The truth."

"About?"

"Anton d'Stang."

She drew her large tote bag closer to her abdomen.

"Anton said you and he spent the evening together the night Desiree was killed."

"Sure."

Sure wasn't really *yes*.

"Are you in a relationship with him?"

"We had one date." Her tapping foot picked up speed.

"Are you using him as your alibi to keep your own secret?"

"What do you mean?"

I nodded toward the display window. "Adorn Yourself sells pretty things. I see a couple of handsome watches. Do you need a new watch?"

She seared me with a glare and primed her claws.

I edged away, but I didn't stop my interrogation. "Desiree found out that you were a thief, didn't she? You took something of hers. Something that meant a lot to her, like that necklace her parents gave her or perhaps her prized autograph book." Desiree had been collecting famous chefs' signatures for years. "She accused you, and you got angry."

"You've got it all wrong."

"Do I? You stole my chef's heirloom pocket watch."

"How do you know—"

"We found it," I said, taking the blame as much as Katie.

Gigi exhaled. "What a dolt I am. I let slip that I left my hairstylist kit in the Winnebago. Dang. I knew I should have retrieved it by now." She jutted a hip. "Listen, I didn't take anything of Desiree's. Ever."

"Not a silver pill box. No jewelry?"

"No way, and I promise she had no clue I have a weakness for . . ." She made a pinching gesture. "But you're right. Anton figured it out. He followed me. He saw me take a wallet. And a bracelet. He took pictures. He blackmailed me and said I had to agree that I was with him that night, or he would let everyone in town know what I do."

"So you didn't go on a date with Anton?"

She lengthened her spine. "You already know the answer, don't you? I mean, I assumed he told you the truth, didn't he? Isn't he the one who ratted me out?"

"No."

"Who then?"

"Tito Martinez, the reporter."

"How did he know?"

"He saw you at Art from the Heart the night Desiree died."

"Hey, that's good news for me, right? That means you know where I was. I've got an alibi."

"Not for the whole time."

"I didn't kill Desiree," she said, her voice taut. "I'll bet Anton d'Stang did. That's why he wanted me to lie about us having a date, don't you think?"

"Is he an artist?"

"What does that have to do with the price of rice in China?"

"You're an artist."

"So?"

"The aquarium in the salon."

Gigi huffed. "Are we playing *Jeopardy* or something? What's your question?"

"There's a mermaid in the grotto."

"Big fat deal."

"Desiree's body was enshrined in a mermaid sand sculpture. It wasn't a gorgeous work of art, but it took talent."

Gigi's eyes widened with realization. "Uh-uh. No, ma'am. You will not use the fact that I went to an art college to frame me. I did not kill Desiree. I did not create that mermaid sculpture. Heck, almost every place in Crystal Cove has an ocean theme going. I'm telling you Anton d'Stang killed her. Why else would he need me to corroborate his alibi? And FYI, he became famous by sculpting gigantic cakes for royalty."

Chapter 15

"ARE YOU KIDDING me?" I clutched Gigi's shoulders. "You've got to tell Chief Pritchett."

"Let me go." Gigi shuddered beneath my grasp.

I scanned the Artiste Arcade. I didn't see a soul. Where had all the shoppers gone? Maybe to the beach to check out the sandcastles. The customers and saleslady in the accessories shop, still haggling, paid no attention to us.

Though Gigi wriggled to free herself, I continued to cling to her and said, "Anton d'Stang doesn't have an alibi."

"Mine isn't so hot."

"But you don't have motive."

Gigi rolled her lip between her teeth. "Please, let me go."

I released her but kept my gaze firm. "The police think I killed Desiree. I didn't. I need them to know there's another suspect. You've got to tell them."

A long moment passed before she gave a jerk of her head signifying okay.

I clapped her on the shoulder. "You're doing the right thing. I—"

"Jenna," my father called from behind me.

As I swiveled, Gigi rushed away. Given her long stride, she was gone from view in a nanosecond. Would she talk to the police? Should I follow her to the precinct or give her the benefit of the doubt? I didn't get a choice. My father embraced me.

"Sweetheart."

"Hey, Dad."

"I was just at The Cookbook Nook." He released me. "Actually, I was at the café having lunch. The place is packed. Katie is serving—"

"Chowder."

"Did you taste it?"

"Not yet." My stomach grumbled with discontent.

"It's delicious."

"Is everything else okay at the store?"

"Absolutely. Your aunt is in her element, giving a tarot reading to one of the customers, and Bailey was holding court with a party of women. That girl"—he tapped his head—"is a brain. Do you think she'll stick around Crystal Cove?"

"For now." But the job at The Cookbook Nook wouldn't captivate her for long.

Dad slung an arm around me. "Walk with me to the hardware store."

"Can't. I've got boxes upon boxes of new cookbooks to put on shelves." And hopefully I would receive a phone call from Cinnamon Pritchett, who would tell me her sights were set on Anton d'Stang because Gigi had cleared me of all wrongdoing.

A horn honked. Another horn blared. I swung around and caught sight of a cavalcade of antique cars motoring along Buena Vista. Vehicle occupants hung out the windows and flashed pedestrians the Hawaiian *Shaka* sign, thumbs and pinkies extended. Many sang, "*Don't worry, be happy.*"

My father mirrored the gesture and chimed, "*Don't worry, be happy.*" He pulled me close and gave me a squeeze.

"Dad." I wriggled free wondering who this cuddly alien

was beside me, and what had he done with my typically judgmental father?

He slipped his arm through mine. "C'mon. Let's spend some time together. I'm only going to open the shop for a couple of hours." One of the benefits of being retired and financially well off was that my father didn't care if his business made money or not. "You haven't seen the place since I spruced it up. How can you say no?"

"That's heading in the opposite direction."

"It's located in the next complex."

Seagulls squawked overhead, chiding me I was pretty sure. At Taylor & Squibb, I'd lived by schedules. Now I really didn't have a strict schedule, and I had hired capable people at The Cookbook Nook. I needed to learn to relax and drink in the fresh sea air.

"Okay, but just for a brief look-see."

As we strolled along, my father said, "What was going on back there between you and the hairstylist?"

"Nothing."

"Don't kid a kidder."

"Really. Nothing."

When we arrived at Nuts and Bolts, my father said, "Here we are. Do you like the new sign above the door?" The sign was made of rough-hewn wood with the store's name carved in bold block letters and hammer and nail icons burnished into the wood on either end. "I framed it."

I hesitated. I couldn't see any difference from the old sign.

"It's a good four inches wider and taller."

"Nice," I lied.

Dad opened the door and switched on lights. "I cleared out excess junk and added a skylight. Sunshine makes everything look better."

The place, similar to the neighboring shops, was long and narrow. Streamlined shelves, each categorized with labels made from one of those label machines, held multiple boxes of screws, nails, and whatnot. Dad was superorganized. A plaque with a quote that Dad had drilled into our brains at a young age hung on the wall behind the checkout counter: *The primary sign of a well-ordered mind is a man's ability to remain in one place and linger in his own company*—Seneca.

Dozens of pictures commemorating family adventures lined the wall above the quotation plaque: seashell collecting, offshore fishing, skiing. I especially loved the one of my sister, brother, and me nestled on a cascade of rocks, our faces dirty as all get-out, thanks to a long day of hiking. My siblings and I didn't have much in common, but we loved to hit the trails.

I settled onto a stool behind one of the counters, rested my feet on a rung, and knitted my hands around my knees thinking, despite the tragic turn of events in the past week, how much I enjoyed being back in Crystal Cove. Being *home*. I reread the plaque with the Seneca quote. The words held a whole new meaning for me.

"Now are you going to talk to me or not?" Dad said.

"About?"

He twirled a finger. "That thing back at the Artiste Arcade between you and the hairstylist."

I inhaled and released a long breath. "Is Aunt Vera correct? Was interrogation part of your secret FBI life?"

"Don't sidetrack." He tapped two fingers on the counter.

"You know what we were discussing at dinner last night? Well, today things turned topsy-turvy." I explained how Katie figured out Gigi was a thief. I followed up with the points Mackenzie revealed to me during my massage session.

"Just because Desiree and Anton met that night before the murder doesn't prove Anton killed her." My father opened the register and counted the cash. "What about the J.P. guy? You said he was at the bar phoning her repeatedly."

"But Anton blackmailed Gigi, and get this, he was a baker before he owned all his restaurants. A baker of massive cakes. That takes skill. He is talented enough to create the mermaid sculpture."

Dad slammed the drawer. "Okay, now you've got me hooked."

Hooked? A frisson of fear raced from my fingertips to my skull. I twisted on the stool and gawked at the family photos.

"What are you staring at?" my father asked.

I stabbed a finger at a photograph of him and me fishing offshore. We had caught a huge rock cod. The hook we used was at least five inches long. "What if . . . what if . . . someone saw that picture of us snaring the rock cod. Like Anton d'Stang. What if he came in here and spied that photo?"

"He's never been in here."

"He was in disguise the first day I set eyes on him. Maybe he came here dressed up, too. What if he saw the photograph and got an idea to frame me, so he stole the trowel from the shop, and he . . . he . . ." I flapped my arms. "What if Cinnamon Pritchett sees the photo? She'll think I was inspired to sculpt Desiree into a fish—"

"A mermaid."

"And I sank a hook into her mouth because . . . because . . ." I stopped myself. The words coming out of me were saturated with paranoia. I knew in the *sane* part of my brain that no one was going to think I murdered Desiree based on an ages-old photo and a fingerprint-less trowel, but if more evidence mounted up . . .

My father steadied me. "Breathe, Tootsie Pop. Stick to the facts."

"Cinnamon Pritchett thinks I killed Desiree, Dad."

"She does not."

"It's just like with David, all over again. Water cooler gossip. Town gossip. It's the same thing. I don't have an alibi for the night Desiree died."

"You also don't have a motive."

"There's the rumor about David and Desiree."

"Which Sabrina rescinded."

I snapped my fingers. "I know what I'll do. I'll take the photo to Cinnamon myself. That'll prove it means nothing. You're the one who says, 'The best defense is a good offense.'" I rushed toward the photograph.

My father tore after me and gripped my shoulders. "Leave it."

"Dad."

"Get hold of yourself. Cinnamon will not leap to conclusions."

There it was again. The tender tone in his voice when he said her name. Curiosity got the better of me. I wrested free of his hold. "Why didn't you ever tell me you were her mentor?"

"It was on a need-to-know basis."

"I need to know. Why did you do it? Why her? I get that she had a tough life. Fine. But why you?"

He rubbed his chin, deliberating. "Your mother asked me to."

"Mom? Why?"

"Your mother was such a special woman." He smiled. His eyes grew moist. "She couldn't sit by and watch Cinnamon go down the tubes. She felt, in some screwy way, that Cinnamon's existence was her fault. She said Cinnamon shouldn't suffer because of the foibles of the parents. She said Cinnamon's father, the cad, had done wrong, and I, Mr. Do It by the Book—that's what your mother called me—should teach the girl otherwise."

"Didn't Pepper object?"

"At first. But once she realized there weren't a lot of people willing to step in . . ." My father moved behind the sales counter and opened and closed a drawer. For no reason. "Pepper loved Cinnamon. She realized something had to be done. Cinnamon and I met once a week, on Saturdays. Over the course of time, I taught her that doing the right thing was what would make her different from her father."

"Why didn't you introduce us? Why didn't you bring her over to our house?" I held up a hand. "Don't answer. I know why. Pepper wouldn't allow it. She didn't want her precious daughter anywhere near Mom, the woman who stole you away."

My father reached across the counter and grabbed my hand. "Cinnamon will do right by you. I promise."

IN THE END. my father convinced me. I left the photograph on the wall of his hardware store. By the time I returned to The Cookbook Nook, I was calm but thirsty. Mackenzie had advised me to hydrate. Maybe that was my problem; I was parched. I hustled into the store and found Bailey perched on a chair beside the vintage kitchen table. She sat with her arm extended, palm up, to my aunt.

Aunt Vera traced a finger along Bailey's hand and blinked repeatedly. "You will meet a man in the village," she intoned as if in a trance—all part of her act. "He will be very tall."

Bailey snickered. "To me that could be anyone over five feet."

Aunt Vera gave Bailey a scathing look.

"Sorry, Vera, I know I'm supposed to be serious. Go on." Bailey caught sight of me and said, "Hey, stranger, welcome back. How was the massage?"

"Shh," Aunt Vera said. "I need to concentrate."

Bailey mimed for me to talk anyway.

"Informative." I kept my paranoid overreaction at the hardware shop to myself. I saw no reason to foster rumors about my mental status.

Bailey tried to withdraw her hand from my aunt's, but Aunt Vera held on tightly.

Aunt Vera gasped. "This man will hurt you."

"Hurt her?" I said.

Bailey frowned. "She means he'll break my heart. Tell him to get in line." She freed herself, hobbled to a stand, and brushed off her stylish capris and silky peasant blouse. "Every man I've ever known has broken my heart, including a brat in kindergarten that trapped me behind the tree in the schoolyard to give me a smooch. Did anybody ever break your heart, Vera?"

It was my turn to say, "Shh."

Aunt Vera's face paled. She stood up and tucked a stray hair behind an ear. "Yes, dear, a man broke my heart into a million pieces." Without another word, she strode to the rear of the shop and disappeared into the office.

"Gee, I'm sorry," Bailey said. "What happened?"

I explained.

Bailey shook her head. "He left her at the altar and married somebody else? Wow. And then he died. Why?"

"I don't know."

"Nothing's worse than not knowing why."

Actually, nothing was worse than not knowing where the body of the man you loved ended up. Closure was highly underrated. But I wasn't about to argue the point. The past was the past. *Movin' on.* "Where are all the customers?" I said. "Did you scare them away?"

"Haven't you noticed? Our customer traffic seems to ebb and flow with the café traffic. They come in midmorning and at lunch and dinnertime. Speaking of which, did you eat?"

"Not yet."

As if on cue, Katie strolled into the shop carrying a tray filled with soup bowls and a basket of aromatic bread. "Hungry?" she asked.

"Famished." I grasped a spoon and one of the bowls from the tray and nestled at the table. How I relished our midafternoon tastings. "Is this the soup I heard people stood in line for?" I took a bite.

"Nope. It's a new one I concocted for dinner. Bacon leek with melted Brie."

"Scrumptious. What's the spice?"

"Who needs spice when there's bacon?" Katie chortled. "Glad you like it. When you're done with that, I set a few lemon cookies in the hallway."

"Which reminds me," Bailey said. "We got a stack of new cookie cookbooks today. One is titled *Chewy Gooey Crispy Crunchy Melt-in-Your-Mouth Cookies.* Doesn't that sound sinful? I especially loved the pictures of the meringues. And *Sticky, Chewy, Messy, Gooey: Desserts for the Serious Sweet Tooth* has a recipe for chocolate chip cookie pizza."

"Wow," I said. "To die for."

"And last but not least, *Sweet Designs: Bake It, Craft It, Style It*, by Amy Atlas."

"Craft it?"

"Atlas is a home baker and party planner. According to online reviews, she transforms a sugar cookie into something extraordinary."

I slurped down more of the tasty soup and sighed. "Eating soup and hearing about sweets is way better than a massage."

"Hoo-boy. I almost forgot. Tell us what you found out from the masseur." Katie set the tray on the table and settled on a chair opposite me. Tigger bolted into the room and nudged Katie's ankles. She ripped off a bite of bread and set it on the floor by his nose. He downed it in one bite and begged for more.

Playing bad guy, I said, "Uh-uh, kitty." Tigger mewled and opened his eyes wide. I stifled a grin. "Nice try."

"Oh, no!" Katie cried. "No, no, no." She pointed toward the parking lot.

I swiveled in my seat. *Oh, no!* was an understatement. Pepper, dressed in yet another unflattering gray outfit that made her look like a prison warden ready to lock me up in solitary confinement, pushed her daughter toward the entrance of The Cookbook Nook. Cinnamon appeared resistant but not nearly enough for my liking. Hadn't Gigi Goode contacted her? Ooh, why had I listened to my father? I should have been proactive. I should have gone to the precinct with the incriminating—albeit ancient—photograph. Dang.

"There you are." Pepper prodded Cinnamon into the shop and blocked the doorway with her broad frame. Did she think I would try to bolt? How could I hide, in this day and age, without someone locating me by a superultra satellite gizmo?

I stood up and did my best to look innocent yet powerful. If only I didn't detect the scent of massage oil at the roots of my hair and feel oil clinging to my arms and legs. "Hi, Pepper," I said. "Don't you look lovely today? I like the chic silver beading."

"Don't mollycoddle me," Pepper said. "I have conducted a personal investigation into your past." She plucked a ream of papers from her steel gray tote. "I have dirt."

"What are you talking about?" I took a step forward. Katie and Bailey flanked me as if they were stalwart troops. Tigger crouched in front of me as if ready to attack Pepper at my command.

"You, missy, demonstrated in San Francisco."

Again with the *missy?* What was up with that? My insides simmered.

Pepper brandished the papers. "You hit a cop. You're violent." She eyeballed her daughter. "I told you she's capable of murder."

Quickly I described the demonstration, one that concerned unfair pay for women. The cop—a female—grabbed my *Equal Pay Every Day* sign. I reached for the sign. My purse swung ahead of me and whacked the cop on the hip. I apologized, but she wrote up a report. I paid a modest fine. "I'm not capable of murder."

"Yes, you are," Pepper said.

"I am not, you wicked—" I stopped short and regarded Cinnamon. Was it really possible that she shared the same DNA with the despicable woman beside her? "Didn't Gigi Goode come to the station and file a report, Chief?"

"No."

Swell. As fast as I could, I explained how Anton d'Stang, a former king-sized cake maker, had blackmailed Gigi.

"Cinnamon, you can't believe what she's saying," Pepper said. "This is biased information."

"It is not," I said. "Anton lied, don't you see? He created an alibi for himself, and he—"

"That doesn't make him guilty," Pepper cut me off.

"But one minor infraction, years ago in my past, and I *am* guilty?"

"Not one," Pepper countered. "Many."

I opened my arms. "C'mon, Chief Pritchett. Find Gigi. She works at the Permanent Wave Salon and Spa. Call her."

Cinnamon held up a finger as she pulled her cell phone off her utility belt. She dialed and told the person she reached to link her to the salon. Soon after, Cinnamon identified herself and asked for Gigi. She listened and offered cryptic responses: "She hasn't? When was the last time? Yes, please, and her address." Cinnamon disconnected and stood zombie-like for a moment.

"What?" My stomach knotted up.

"Gigi Goode has disappeared. Her coworker thinks she split town."

Chapter 16

I LOOKED TO Katie and Bailey for support. They stood beside the vintage kitchen table, their mouths agape. I whipped my focus to Cinnamon and her miserable mother. "But Gigi can't have split," I said. "She's . . . she's . . ." The cogs in my brain kicked into high gear. "Wait. What if Gigi hasn't left town? What if something horrible happened to her? What if the person who killed Desiree murdered Gigi?"

"Oh, no, you don't." Pepper shook her fist. "You can't wangle out of this with *that*."

"Huh?" I said. Even an English teacher would have a tough time diagramming Pepper's sentence.

"You have an overly active imagination," Pepper said.

No, I had a deep-seated desire for everyone to believe I was innocent.

"Mother, please, be quiet." Cinnamon zeroed in on me. "I will look into this, but for now . . ." She let the sentence hang. She didn't have to say what I knew was on the tip of her tongue: *Don't leave town.*

I didn't tell Katie, Bailey, or my aunt about the massage or tracking down Gigi or anything else, for that matter. I could hardly form thoughts. An hour later, when I couldn't concentrate on work any longer, I gathered Tigger and left for home. Katie, who was as worried as a mother hen, scuttled from the café and shoved a recipe and a grocery bag of ingredients for homemade chocolate chip cookies into my arms. "Baking will make you feel better," she said. "Promise. Let it take your mind off things. Turn on the TV. Relax."

Relax? I could barely breathe. What had happened to Gigi? Had the killer seen me questioning her? Had she run? Had she come to harm? Was I in danger, too?

I RUSHED INTO the cottage and locked the door. Fear morphing into anger, I dumped the grocery bag of goodies noisily on the counter and cursed. How dare Pepper Pritchett invade my shop. How dare she accuse me of murder . . . again. Why were bitter people allowed to exist in this world? I stormed around the place, kicking the feet of chairs and spanking the tops of tables. Tigger followed in my wake, meowing and chuffing. Poor little guy couldn't ask what was wrong, and I wasn't in the mood to provide an answer to a cat.

Five minutes into my rant, I found myself back in the kitchen facing the recipe and the bag of ingredients. Would baking truly help me calm down?

Following Katie's suggestion, I switched on the television and located the Food Network. I couldn't believe it. Though I rarely watched TV, I had landed on a repeat of the *Radical Cake Battle* show that Desiree had judged. Contestants and their assistants raced around their individual kitchens. Dora the Lady in Red, wielded a chainsaw; Leo the Latin Lover brandished a blowtorch; Macbeth the Gay Blade hacked with an axe. Like I told Katie, not quite my cup of tea, even with Desiree's appearance. I clicked the dial until I found the Travel Channel and Anthony Bourdain's *No Reservations*. Bourdain was on a food tour of Greece. While he educated his audience about the wild foods found on the islands, I fetched a mixing bowl, measuring cup, and spoon. Next, I pulled a cube of butter from the refrigerator. Katie had reminded me not to cheat on the recipe; I had to use butter, not oil or lard. As the oven preheated, I measured oats and flour, sugar and butter. I cracked eggs. I added vanilla, chocolate chips, and nuts. By the time I had put all the ingredients into the bowl, I was salivating but my palms were clammy. Not from fear. I had put the killer from my mind. No, I was worried that my cookies would stink. I questioned whether I had added baking soda or baking powder. I tasted the raw batter. Not bad. Memories of myself, as a kid, sneaking table-spoons of batter and my mother rapping my knuckles play-fully with a wooden spoon, rushed through me.

Fifteen minutes later, I pulled my first batch of chocolate chip cookies from the oven. Obeying the recipe's directions to the letter, I let them rest on the cookie sheet for two minutes. Next, I transferred them, using a spatula, to paper towels to cool. Unable to restrain myself, I snatched two. *Hot, hot, hot.* I juggled them between hands, fetched some kibble for Tigger, and retreated to the comfort of my sofa. The kitty sprang into my lap and snuggled into a ball. By this time, Bourdain—Tony to his friends—was sipping ouzo, a licorice-tasting liqueur David used to enjoy. As the show shifted to commercial, I heard a thud.

A shiver skittered along my skin. I seized the television remote, hit the mute button, and listened. The thud hadn't come from shutters banging; it hadn't been wood on wood. And it hadn't sounded like clackety-clack. Old Jake hadn't just passed by.

I plunked Tigger on the floor and darted to the window. I pushed back the drape. My breath caught in my throat. White powder dusted the pane. *What the heck?* Off in the distance, I spied movement. A tall figure stood on the beach. Man, woman, or dystopian teen, I couldn't tell. I released the drape and stumbled back a step. Was the lurker a killer, prepared to dispatch me now that Gigi was gone? What had he or she thrown at the cottage? Should I call Aunt Vera and ask her to save me? Was she even home?

Taking charge, I galloped toward the landline telephone.

At the same time, my cell phone jangled. I swept it up and stared at the readout: *Whitney*, my sister. Wonderful, winsome Whitney. I stabbed Enter and said, "Hi. I'm so glad you called. There's a—"

I hurried back to the window and peeked out. Whoever had been standing on the beach was gone. Maybe the figure had been Old Jake, after all, except I couldn't make out a sand raking machine anywhere. A vehicle that large would be hard to miss, wouldn't it? And why would he have hurled white powder at my window? I weighed whether to tell Whitney; if I was wrong and the intruder was nothing more than a kid carrying out a prank, she would lord my fear over me for years. "What's up?" I crooned like a phony.

"Have you heard from Mitchell?"

"Why would I have?" When our mother died, our brother turned to Whitney for solace. It didn't matter that, growing up, he and I had spent hours going on hikes and exploring creeks or that I had helped him TP the house of the boy that had shoved his head into a toilet. Mitchell had beaten the kid, fair and square, at the science expo. I didn't blame my brother for throwing me over for Whitney. I had been in a state of disconnect.

"He's missing." Whitney sounded panicked. She *never* panicked.

"Maybe he's doing a supersecret house design. Remember that millionaire he worked for? The guy required that Mitchell live in the house and never make a phone call. He was incommunicado for how long?"

"I'm telling you he's missing. We've been in touch every day for the past month."

"Why?"

"We're planning a surprise party for Dad."

Oh, really? Without including me? Wicked, waspish Whitney. My worry over her panic vanished. A pang of rejection cut through me. "I'm sure—"

The doorbell rang. I nearly leaped out of my skin.

"Is someone at your door?" Whitney shouted. "Maybe it's Mitchell."

Or a killer. But would a killer ring the bell? Would my brother visit me out of the blue? "Calm down," I said, though I was far from composed.

The visitor pounded on the door. "Jenna?" The voice belonged to my father.

"It's Dad," I said into the phone and sped to the entrance. Tigger scampered behind me. After peering through the peephole to make sure whoever was on the other side hadn't duped me by imitating my father's voice, I whipped open the door. I glanced past my father to see if anyone was lurking beyond him. No one. My fear of immediate danger lessened.

"Where's Mitchell?" My father pushed past me. "Your sister called."

"I'm on the phone with her now." I pointed at the receiver. "Whitney—"

"Don't spoil the surprise," she said.

Oh, yeah, like I would. "Why did you call Dad before me?" I asked her.

"Jenna . . ."

I made a face. How I despised my sister's condescending tone. "Don't worry. If I have to drive to Napa myself, I'll find our brother." First, of course, I would explain to Chief Pritchett where I was going.

My cell phone bleeped. A second call was coming in: *Mitchell*. I felt a momentary elation. He had dialed me before our sister.

I said, "Wait. Mitchell is on the other line."

"Thank heavens."

I pressed the Hold then Answer buttons. "Hey, little bro, where are you?"

"In hiding. I couldn't take any more surprise party calls. You know about that, right?" He didn't wait for my response. "I needed air. I went to an ashram. You get it, right? Our sister likes to plan ad infinitum."

I laughed. We chatted for a second, got caught up on his latest house design—a ten-thousand-square-foot ranch house with an overlook of Napa—and blew kisses good-bye.

I returned to my sister, assured her that our brother was okay, and promised to call her soon with an update. She didn't mention Desiree's murder. I was glad.

Upon ending the call, I found my father pacing the kitchen. "Are you okay?" I asked.

"Wound up." He ogled the cookies.

"Hungry?"

"Are they any good?"

I nodded with confidence. They weren't Famous Amos or Mrs. Fields, and they were a tad crispy, but they tasted delicious. I filled a plate with cookies, strode to the couch, and patted the seat beside me. My father sat down, took a treat, and then reached for my hand.

"What are we watching?" he asked.

"Cooking shows." I cranked up the volume.

Dad bit into a cookie and hummed his appreciation. When the next commercial appeared, he said, "I miss your mother."

"I'm sure you do."

"She wouldn't have overreacted to your sister calling."

"David wouldn't have either. He would have said Whitney was the one acting dramatic."

My father smiled. "How are you doing?"

"Every time I see a ship on the ocean, a piece of me dies." Raw emotions stuck in my chest. I ordered them to crawl back into their hiding place. "And now, with this whole murder thing and being a suspect? David would have told me to remain aloof, but how can I, huh? Pepper continues to harass me."

"I'm sorry."

"After I saw you at the hardware shop, she brought Cinnamon to The Cookbook Nook. Pepper brought up that rally arrest years ago. She vilified me, and now"—I jumped to my feet and jerked a thumb at the rear window—"I'm acting all scared and girlie because I hear creepy noises outside the house, and I see figures on the beach that freak me out, and—"

"Where? When?"

"Right before you showed up. Someone threw something at the window. White powder."

My father dashed outside. James Bond couldn't have acted more courageous. He returned seconds later with an empty bag. "Flour," he said.

"Flour?"

"Baker's Mix."

"I'll bet those hooligans who let out the air of the Winnebago tires did this."

"The who?"

"Forget it. The wind will clean it off."

He tossed the empty Baker's Mix bag into the garbage can by the sink. Remnants of flour billowed upward. Out of nowhere, I envisioned an ominous spirit bursting from the white cloud and scavenging the cottage. The lid closed. The vision vanished.

My father strode back to me. "If it's any consolation, your sister says that you're one of the strongest people she has ever met."

"No way."

"Way."

MY FATHER SPENT the night on my couch. He claimed he was so tired that he couldn't drive home, but I knew better. The call from Whitney and my overwrought state had rattled him. On Tuesday morning, as the sun rose and warmed the cottage, I made my father coffee. We nibbled cookies and drank in silence. When he left and I realized the shop was closed, I decided to take our official day off and address my fears.

I secured Tigger in his air-conditioned beach cage and, barefoot, with an easel, canvas, and charcoal pencil in hand, traipsed to the beach—my intent, to sketch the images that plagued me: a raging ocean, a teetering sailboat, and a mermaid-shaped sandcastle. When I finished, I planned to hurl the painting into the water and beg the tide to lure my two-dimensional ship of sadness to another place.

The beach was deserted. Offshore breezes blew horizontally across the ocean. Seagulls greeted me with their shrieks. I placed Tigger's cage on the sand, erected my easel, and set to work.

The first stroke of black charcoal on white canvas infused me with energy and, with the vitality, came inspiration. I thought of David and how, whenever he caught me painting, he would tiptoe behind me and trace a finger down my spine. It was his way of saying he loved me without interrupting my alpha state of heightened creativity.

As a picture took shape on the page, an image formed in my mind—a memory of the morning Desiree died. The temperature hovered in the sixties. A breeze wafted through the fronds of the palms. I spied the treasure hunters and the lone surfer. Seconds later, I spotted the sand sculpture with Desiree's body buried beneath.

A fleeting notion made me shift to an earlier moment in my timeline. To the surfer. How long had he been floating, waiting to catch a wave? Some surfers went on what they liked to call dawn patrol, taking to the water before the sun rose. Had he? I had told Cinnamon about the surfer. Had she discovered his identity?

I scanned the ocean. To my surprise, I glimpsed a solitary surfer straddling a surfboard on the water to the north. Where had he come from? He acknowledged me with a gesture akin to saluting. Was it a signal that he saw me . . . he knew me . . . he killed Desiree and Gigi . . . and he was coming after me? Fear jagged my insides. I staggered backward; my heel rammed against Tigger's cage.

A wave swelled behind the surfer. He leaped to a stand on his board.

I sprang to action.

Chapter 17

WITH MY PULSE pounding so hard it throbbed in my ears, I shoved my pencils into my satchel, snatched the easel, canvas, and Tigger in his cage, and bolted from the ocean. Sand etched the bottoms of my feet. Seagulls scudded ahead of me as if leading a brigade. Did the surfer know where I lived? Was he the stranger who had hurled a bag of flour at my window? Did I dare go home? *Halt, Jenna*, I chided myself. *Slow down. Rethink this.* But I couldn't stop fleeing. The guy was racing toward the shore as fast as a cigarette speedboat.

I glanced at my aunt's house. Her car was gone. Yesterday she mentioned that she had an early morning meeting with fellow psychics; she must have left. I didn't know any of the neighbors. How would they react if I landed on their doorstep and begged to come inside?

Down the strand, I spied The Pier. People milled about on the boardwalk. I caught sight of the silver Pier flag glimmering on a pole near Bait and Switch and thought of clear-headed Rhett Jackson. Maybe he could reel me back to earth.

Minutes later, I charged into the huge warehouse out of breath. Customers stopped browsing the sales racks and gawked at me. I skidded to a stop. Carrying Tigger in his cage and all my other gear, I must have looked like I intended to move in. Tough. I scanned the aisles for Rhett, but I didn't see any sign of him.

The gangly clerk with the prominent Adam's apple approached me. "Help you?" His voice had a natural crack to it, as if he hadn't quite cleared puberty.

"Rhett," I gasped out of breath.

The clerk hitched a thumb. I didn't see Rhett in the direction he indicated, but I figured he wouldn't steer me wrong. Dodging bargain-hungry customers, I hustled toward the rear of the store. I stopped short, right before slamming into Rhett, who was scooping up scattered kayak paddles.

"What happened?" I said.

"Some teen playing hide-and-seek with a buddy knocked over the entire display." He struggled to a stand. "What's up?"

I felt like a dolt, panting as if I had just seen the scariest movie ever.

"Jenna." He searched my face. "Did someone accost you? Are you okay?"

"It's . . . It's nothing."

"Bullpuckey." He relieved me of my bag, the easel, and Tigger's cage and ushered me to a green leather chair that stood beside a full-length mirror. "Sit down and tell me what happened."

"Really, it's—"

"Jenna, sit."

"I feel silly bothering you."

Rhett forced me into the chair and rested the easel and bag beside the mirror. He released Tigger from his confinement. The poor cat lurched into Rhett's arms. He scruffed Tigger's chin and said to me, "Talk."

"A surfer—"

"There are a bunch out today. Surf's great."

I explained that there weren't many surfers in my neck of the beach. "In fact, there was only one."

"The guy must be a novice. The surf's rarely good north of The Pier. What about him?"

"He—" I halted. Was I putting together a scenario that didn't add up? Was the lone surfer who had floated on the water the day Desiree died a novice and harmless? How I wished I could rewind the past moment of my life and reenter Bait and Switch as a composed, semisane woman.

"What about the surfer?" Rhett said.

"I was worried . . . that he was . . ." I batted the air. "It doesn't matter. I'm going to leave now." I tucked a loose strand of hair behind my ear and rose from the chair. I reached for Tigger.

Rhett handed him over. "Actually, I'm glad you stopped by. I've been meaning to call you. Joey—"

"The young man that greeted me."

"That's the one. Joey Pritchett."

"Pritchett?" I cut a look in the kid's direction. "Is he related to Pepper?"

"He's her nephew. Her deceased brother's kid. He's a sweet guy."

I couldn't help frowning.

"Really." Rhett bobbed his head with understanding. "I know, Pepper's an acerbic woman. She's got issues. But Joey's different. He's not as bright as his cousin, Cinnamon, but not many kids are. Anyway, Joey discovered that a Mustad hook had been stolen from the shop, after all."

"What?" I jostled Tigger. He yowled his displeasure. I calmed him. "Go on."

"When you came in the other day, remember how we surveyed the inventory and it appeared intact? Well, a customer came in to buy a hook last night, and Joey discovered an empty box."

"You don't have a record of anyone buying the hook?"

"Nope. I'm thinking someone filched it."

"Gigi," I muttered.

"Who?"

I described Gigi Goode with her purple hair and multiple-studded ears. "She's a hairstylist in town and a thief. She must have sneaked in here." I took two paces to the right, pivoted, and returned. "That must be why she split town."

"What are you talking about?"

I told Rhett how Gigi claimed Anton had blackmailed her into corroborating his alibi. "What if that was a ruse? What if Desiree knew about Gigi's bent for stealing? What if she threatened to turn her in? Gigi is a big gal. She could have overpowered Desiree, and she's an artist. She could have created the mermaid sand sculpture."

"I don't think I've ever seen the woman you're describing. Hey, Joey." Rhett beckoned his clerk. To me, he said, "The kid's got a great memory for faces. He's a budding photographer."

My ears perked up. If Joey had a camera with a telephoto lens, maybe I could take a long-range photo of the surfer and ID him.

Joey loped to us, a hank of hair covering one eye. "What's up?"

"Rhett tells me you're a pretty good photographer," I said. "What do you like to take pictures of?"

"Birds."

"Do you have your camera with you?"

Rhett shot me a questioning look.

"Nope." Joey shifted feet. "It's locked in a safe at home. It cost me the last four summer's earnings. I only take it out when I've got the day off. Why?"

"Oh, gee, um, because I . . . I love cameras." I was way past the point of admitting my fear of the lone surfer. "I used to work at an advertising company. Photographers ruled the roost."

The kid preened.

Rhett said, "I think we're getting off track. Joey, did you see a woman named Gigi Goode come in the shop?" He reiterated my description of Gigi.

Joey raked the hair off his forehead. "Yeah, I remember her. She and this muscular blond dude came in together. Don't know their names, but the two of them laughed like goofs. She kept saying she hated being a gofer, and he said he did, too. Guess they were on some kind of errand."

"Was it Mackenzie Baxter?" I asked. He had hired Gigi. Maybe they hung out together when he wasn't with Sabrina.

Joey bobbed his head. "Could've been. She called him Mac. They asked about our guided hikes. I guess their boss—the *dictator* as the chick, I mean, lady called her—thought a hiking trip would be a good bonding event for her crew."

I gazed at Rhett. "Gigi had opportunity to steal the hook." Which meant that she also might have stolen the trowel from my store window, perhaps on the morning she had pinched Katie's pocket watch. "We need to call Chief Pritchett right now."

Joey said, "Hold up. If you're talking about that Mustad hook, I was mistaken. It turns out someone stuffed two hooks into one box. I think I got confused when I put things back. You know, we've got so much junk, I mean, quality items in the display case." He jerked his thumb. In the center of the fishing section stood a beautiful hand-carved case with a glass top. On my previous visit, I had noticed the array of shiny hooks inside. "I meant to tell you, Mr. Jackson."

Great. Another dead end.

TOTING MY CAT and paraphernalia, I tramped out of Bait and Switch and headed for home. Along the way, my cell phone rang. I answered.

"Jenna," my aunt said. "Let's go to brunch."

"Can't." Although Tuesday was my only day off, I had housekeeping and laundry to do, as well as figuring out where Gigi had gone. Her disappearance gnawed at me, not to mention that I wanted to finish my painting, toss the canvas out to sea, and be done with the angst, the musing, and the past.

Aunt Vera said, "Whatever you have to do can wait."

"I've got Tigger with me."

"Drop the kitten at home and meet us at The Pelican Brief Diner."

"Us, as in you and—"

"Your father."

Uh-oh. Why did her request sound like an invitation to an intervention? Mine. Had Dad's concern fueled hers? I was fine. I was coping. I was a suspect in a friend's murder investigation. No big deal. Ri-i-ight.

"Thirty minutes," she said. "Don't stall."

"How can I say no to such a charming summons?"

She clucked and disconnected.

As I drew nearer to home, I spied Bailey jogging along the beach. In orange harem pants and matching halter top and carrying a pair of strappy sandals slung over an index finger, she didn't look like she had started the day prepared to go for a run. If I were a betting woman, I would say my aunt had sent her in search of me. Swell.

When I reached her, she bent over and rested her hands on her thighs. "Whew. Am I ever out of shape." She wasn't. She relished exercise. She studied Tigger in his air-conditioned tote. "Run out of room at the cottage?"

"He prefers a morning stroll."

"Shouldn't you let him walk, in that case?"

"He's not leash-trained." I cocked a hip. "Have you been hired to wrangle me?"

"*Wrangle* you?"

"Round me up in case I decide to make a run for it."

"Why would you think—"

"My aunt can be pretty persuasive. Or my father appointed you."

Bailey stood upright. "They're worried, and Katie, too."

Double-swell. It wasn't enough that my kin fretted. Now I had extended family to please. I strolled ahead.

Bailey did a U-turn and kept pace on my right. "Mind if I join you? I've been meaning to see your new place. Now is a good time. Hint-hint."

We entered the cottage, and I said, "Make yourself at home." I set the easel and canvas against the far wall and released Tigger. "I've got to shower."

As I let water rinse off sand and salty grit, I heard Bailey puttering around the cottage. Curiosity getting the better of me, I slipped out of the shower, slung a towel around my damp body, and opened the door an inch. Bailey, nibbling on a cookie, stood beside the Ching cabinet, its pocket doors wide open.

I cleared my throat. "What're you doing?"

She jerked upright and did a double take on the cookie. "Hope you don't mind."

"*Mi casa es su casa*. I baked them."

"Really? Not bad."

"But I wasn't talking about your snack." I gathered a skirt and tank top from the closet. "Are you spying on me?"

"What? No."

"What's so interesting in the cabinet?"

"Uh, the porcelain cat," she stammered.

I coughed and muttered an under-my-breath, skeptical curse. "That's *on,* not *in.* Truth. What are you really doing, judging the state of everything in my place so you can report back to my aunt and father? 'Jenna's paints in the cabinet are all messed up; she's a slob; she didn't make her bed. All signs of a distracted mind. It's definitely time for you to send her to the loony bin.' Enter guys in white coats."

"Whoa." Bailey held up the universal halt sign. "You're sounding paranoid. Get a grip."

"I've got one, but it's choking the life out of me."

"Remember our motto at the office? *We will find the humor in every situation.*"

"I'm a suspect in a murder."

"That's downright hysterical."

"You're a sadist."

"At times." She pointed. "Finish getting dressed. I'm starved."

I retreated to the bathroom and put on my clothes. Afterward, I twisted my hair and secured it with a tortoiseshell clip, then daubed my cheeks with blush. I added extra moisture to the skin beneath my eyes, but I still looked tired. Short of taking a vacation or getting seventy-two hours of straight, uninterrupted sleep, I couldn't fix that.

"By the way, I like the artwork," Bailey said as I emerged from the bathroom. "You're maturing. This one"—she indicated the canvas from this morning—"is very raw. If Old Man Taylor knew you could do this kind of work, T&S would be hiring you back as one of their premier artists."

I laughed. "Okay, that's enough. You don't have to bolster my ego."

"Find the humor."

"Ha-ha."

"So what was going on in your brain when you started painting this one?" She tapped the corner of the canvas.

"I . . ." Words caught in my chest. Tears formed in the corners of my eyes. Uh-oh.

"What?" Bailey hustled to me.

All of sudden, everything that I couldn't tell Rhett gushed out in one long stream—the need to paint, the memory of finding Desiree, the fear of the surfer.

Bailey flew to the window and peeped through a crack in the drapes. "I don't see any surfers on the beach or the ocean."

"Of course not. It was over an hour ago. Besides, I'm probably, as you said, paranoid."

"Stop that." She returned to me and gripped me by the shoulders.

"It's true. I'm imagining things. Seeing shadows. Hearing creaks."

"Repeat after me. I'm in a new place, a new town, with a new career, and new hope. C'mon."

I echoed the quasi-mantra.

"What other people think doesn't matter," Bailey added. "Say it."

I groaned but followed her lead.

"Creative visualization." She poked my forehead with her fingertip. "Repeat."

"Creative visualization."

Weekly at Taylor & Squibb, a trainer taught positive thinking techniques. At one point, the company forced every employee to read *Who Moved My Cheese?* subtitled: *An*

Amazing Way to Deal with Change in Your Work and in Your Life. Literally, the book was about mice navigating a maze. Team cooperation, the instructor said, worked.

"Deep breath." Bailey inhaled. I copied. She released her breath; so did I. "Great. Now let's go to lunch. We'll hash this over with your dad and your aunt. We'll solve this, okay?"

Chapter 18

ON TUESDAY MORNING at 10 A.M., The Pelican Brief Diner was hopping. A splashy array of surfboards and bicycles and a baker's rack, which held beachgoers' sand toys and tools, flanked the entryway. In the foyer by the hostess's stand, over twenty customers waited for tables.

Bailey dragged me past them and scanned the restaurant. "I see my mom." She waved.

Lola, her silver hair matching her silver drape-shouldered blouse, air-kissed us. Typical mother, she made a quick fuss over her daughter's hair, plucking pieces forward. "There," she muttered as if she had fixed Bailey for life. "Now, follow me. Jenna, I'll never get over how tall you are."

I had been five-foot-eight since I turned twelve. Kids used to tease me and call me Gigrantress. My sister, Whitney, who wished she were my height, often instigated the taunts. I flashed on the people in Desiree's life, all as tall as she was except for her sister. I wondered whether I should rule out Sabrina as a murderer because of her size.

As if conjuring her with my thoughts, I caught sight of Sabrina sitting at a booth by the window. Sunlight streamed through the window and dappled the hair of her tablemate. It wasn't J.P.; he had dark hair. I diverged from the path Lola cut through the tables to get a better look and spied Mackenzie. Sabrina and he sat tilted forward in their chairs, their hands extended on the table. Their fingertips almost touched. They seemed deep in conversation. Intimate. Had the one-night stand that Sabrina confessed to blossomed into something more?

"Jenna," Bailey said.

I scurried to catch up. Seconds later, we arrived at the table where my father and aunt were seated.

"You look lovely, dear," Aunt Vera said.

My father agreed. "Rested."

After my morning panic, I was far from rested, but I wasn't about to admit that. Bailey and I scooted onto the booth bench opposite them.

"Everybody, listen up." Lola thumped the tabletop then recited the specials: jumbo crab cakes with a red pepper sauce, salmon with brown sugar and mustard glaze, Baja fish tacos, heavy on cilantro and red onions, and a California omelet.

I was so hungry I considered asking for one of everything.

"I'll send a waiter over," Lola said.

Aunt Vera gripped Lola's wrist. "Don't go. Join us."

"I can't, thanks."

"Your staff has the place well in hand. C'mon. Say yes." Aunt Vera fondled the phoenix amulet she wore. "We have lots to discuss with Jenna. Your opinion would be much appreciated."

"Well . . . okay." Moving as if she were under a spell, Lola sidled into the booth beside me.

"Sure, what's one more opinion?" I groused.

"Don't be a grump." Bailey beckoned a waiter.

After we gave the waiter our orders and he poured coffee for all of us, Lola said, "What does Jenna need an opinion on?"

"She had an incident, didn't you, dear?" Aunt Vera said.

"Incident?"

"Your father told me all about it. Why don't you share with the rest of us?" My aunt caressed her amulet again.

Suddenly I felt the urge to blab. Did the amulet really possess mystical powers? If I tore the necklace from my aunt's neck, could I stifle the impulse? What would be the use? Everyone was staring at me . . . waiting.

"Fine." In a flurry, I filled them in about last night's flour attack, my brother and sister's drama, my father's heroic act, this morning's surfer sighting, and the Mustad hook that Joey thought had gone missing but hadn't.

Aunt Vera eyeballed my father. "Did Jenna tell you last night that Gigi Goode has run away?"

My father cut me a look.

"Don't glower at me," I said. "The point might have slipped my mind with everything going on. And we aren't totally sure she fled, but she didn't show up for work."

My father and Lola said, "Oh, my," in unison.

"And I can't remember if I mentioned this to any of you," I continued, "but Mackenzie, Desiree's masseur, saw Anton d'Stang with Desiree at the Chill Zone Bar the night she died."

"You did tell me that," my father said. "Anton saw J.P. there, too."

Aunt Vera pressed her hand to her chest. "Correct me if I'm wrong, but didn't J.P. say he took a sleeping pill and went out like a light?"

I nodded. "Except he lied. He was spying on Desiree and Anton."

"How did they look?" Bailey asked.

I tilted my head. "What do you mean?"

"Anton and Desiree. The last time he saw her was the day he turned her apartment upside down. How did they act with one another? Civil? Were they friendly? Angry?"

"Mackenzie didn't say. He was busy hooking up with Sabrina."

"She was there, too?" Bailey said.

"Sabrina spent the night with Mackenzie in the Winnebago."

Aunt Vera clucked her tongue. "Sounds like we live in Peyton Place."

I peeked around the edge of our booth and glimpsed Sabrina and Mackenzie. He was checking out a sparkling gold bangle on Sabrina's arm. The bracelet looked expensive. Was Sabrina spending money she didn't yet have?

Bailey craned to see what I was fixated on. "The masseur," she said. "Does he have a motive to want Desiree dead?"

"None that I can figure."

"Maybe he and Desiree were having an affair, but then he took a liking to the sister," Bailey said. "What if he convinced Sabrina she was better off if Desiree were dead?"

I gaped. "And they conspired to kill Desiree?"

Bailey nodded. "Did you ever find out if Sabrina stands to inherit her sister's estate?"

"Cinnamon never got back to me on that." Not that she ever would.

Our waiter arrived with our meals, which stalled the conversation. If hums of appreciation could be counted as restaurant ratings, The Pelican Brief earned ten stars all around. Ending my tradition of only ordering fish sticks, I had requested a California omelet, which was filled with avocado, bacon, and cheddar cheese, and topped with a mound of sour cream and green onions. The dish was delectable and decidedly healthier than the cookies I had eaten for dinner and breakfast.

As the waiter refreshed coffee mugs and water glasses, Lola said, "Let's not forget Anton d'Stang. He blackmailed Gigi to establish an alibi, and yet we have an eyewitness, your masseur"—she aimed her fork at me—"who saw Anton meet with Desiree the night she was killed. If I were you, I'd have a chat with Anton. You'll find him at the Nature's Retreat Hotel."

"How would you know that, Mother?" Bailey said.

"Because I was handing out business cards at the local hotels to drum up business less than a half hour ago, and I saw him in deep conversation with a couple of shady-looking characters."

"Shady?" My father scoffed.

Aunt Vera drummed the table. "Don't make fun, Cary."

"I wasn't—"

"Have you forgotten what Lola's legal practice entails?"

"I know exactly what kind of practice she has. In fact, I know a lot more about her than you think I know."

Oh, really? A few minutes before, when my father and Lola had chimed, "Oh, my," in unison, they had looked at each other and reddened. Was there something going on between the two of them?

"Do not assume, Vera, that I am an idiot," my father said.

"I never implied—"

"C'mon, you two." Lola set down her fork. "Cool your jets."

"You stay out of it," my father barked. Lola bridled. Without breaking eye contact with my aunt, my father pressed ahead. "Vera, we shouldn't encourage Jenna to go off half-cocked."

"Who said anything about sending her off half-cocked?" Aunt Vera squawked.

"Lola did."

"I did no such thing." Lola spanked the table.

Like kids caught in a family squabble, Bailey and I excused ourselves to the ladies' room and scooched out of the booth. However, instead of heading down the rustic hallway, I gripped Bailey's elbow and steered her toward the front door.

Bailey dug in her heels. "Whoa. I'm not fond of that look on your face."

"What look?"

"This look." She squinched her mouth and wrinkled her nose. "Whenever you do that, you're up to something."

"That's right. We're going to track down Anton d'Stang."

"We? No, ma'am. I can't. I've got a doctor's appointment."

"For what?"

"Girl stuff."

"Well, I'm going to find him."

"No, come with me first. Afterwards, we'll track him down together."

"Finding Anton can't wait. You heard your mom. He's at the hotel now. He could be long gone if I wait. What if he killed Desiree and, because Gigi wouldn't confirm his alibi, killed her, too?"

"Did you hear yourself?" Bailey bleated. "He could be a killer. A double murderer. You can't face him alone."

"But I won't be alone with him. He's staying in a public place."

I gazed at her mother, my aunt, and my father, each pointing fingers and arguing the finer points of my future. Yes, we could hear them clear across the restaurant. *My future.* I had to be the one in control of it. *Me.*

I said, "I promise I'll be careful. What could possibly go wrong?"

Chapter 19

HE NATURE'S RETREAT Hotel was tucked into a hill above Crystal Cove. Hundreds of California oak trees provided shade. In the foyer and adjacent *chat room*, as the hotel liked to call its lobby, natural wood set the tone. The designer, a local architect with a big ego, had employed fine wood for all the cabinetry and tables. He had even trimmed the gigantic fireplace in wood, and a waterfall cascaded down slats of teak and pooled into a rock quarry below. Dozens of backpack-toting tourists as well as families with sizable luggage and beach gear milled by the reception desk.

I spotted Anton d'Stang conversing with two swarthy-skinned men—one skinny, one ponderously obese —near a grouping of green brocade chairs. A roller suitcase stood by Anton's side. A travel coat was draped over his left forearm. Had he hoped to get out of town before these goons showed up? Mr. Big demanded something. Anton fished in his pocket and withdrew a wad of money. He handed it over and stabbed his finger at his adversary. Mr. Big batted Anton's hand aside.

Eager to know what was going on, I raced toward Anton,

waving my hand like an enthusiastic foodie fan. "Mr. d'Stang. Mr. d'Stang." People in the lobby craned their heads to get a look. Perfect. I was making a mini-scene. No way would the goons harm me. To keep my performance strong, I pulled a pad and pen from my tote and flailed them. "May I have your autograph?"

Anton squinted at his buddies. The skinny one, not nearly as ominous as Mr. Big, elbowed Anton and offered a you-could-get-lucky wink.

Not a chance, I thought, but I wasn't going to ruin the charade. "Ple-e-ease?" I shouted.

"We're done here, Tony," Mr. Big said with a New Jersey accent John Travolta would be proud of. "Catch you in Frisco."

Frisco? Honestly? Nobody but people from the turn of the twentieth century referred to San Francisco as Frisco. Who were these guys?

Mr. Big swatted his cohort on the back and pushed him out of the hotel.

I continued toward Anton. When I reached him, I stowed the pad and pen and said, "We need to talk."

"Sorry, *chérie*. I do not have the time. I have a bus to catch."

The sophisticated Anton d'Stang traveled via bus? No way. And his pals called him Tony. Maybe he lived a double life. Charming restaurateur by night, low-life by day. I clasped his arm. "Halt," I ordered. He pulled to free himself. If my father had taught me one thing, it was how FBI guys could be assertive with attitude, so I pretended I was him— without the age, without the silver hair, a young *Dad* in summer wear and flip-flops. "Don't move," I repeated, my voice low and intimidating. This time he obeyed. "Do you know where Gigi Goode is?"

"It is Tuesday. I assume she is at work."

"She's not. She's been missing since yesterday."

"*Pourquoi voulez-vous*—" He swiped his hand across his forehead as if to clear his mind of French. "Why ask me?"

He shook free of me and backed away; his calves bumped the suitcase. He looked left and right as if he wanted to bolt, but he had no exit. Chairs and I trapped him.

I took a step toward him. "Gigi disagreed with your version of what happened the night Desiree was killed. Actually, she didn't disagree. She flat-out refuted it."

"She lies."

"She said you blackmailed her. She was on her way to the police to give a statement, but she didn't make it there."

"That is not a surprise. The girl is a thief. She fled."

"Or somebody wanted her out of the way."

Anton blinked. "Not I."

I had no way of proving my theory, not without a body. I opted for another approach. "You met Desiree on the night of the murder."

"*Non*."

"*Oui*," I said like a smart aleck. "You met at the Chill Zone Bar."

"*Merde*." He slumped forward as if someone had punctured his lungs with a needle and all the air escaped. He wasn't going to collapse, but he appeared beaten.

"You were the last person seen with Desiree."

"*Impossible*."

I counted points on my fingertips. "You held a grudge against Desiree. You stalked her, wearing a fisherman's costume. You lied about your alibi. And Gigi recently reminded me, you began your career as a cake artist. You have the skill to shape a mermaid in the sand."

"I did not do this," Anton roared, catching the attention of guests and staff. He lowered his voice. "You must believe me. Desiree and I met that night, it is true. I tried to convince her to . . ," He hesitated.

"To what?"

"I want my restaurants to go global. I asked Desiree to lend me money. She owed me. I gave her a start. She would be nothing without me."

I flinched. Desiree *was* nothing; she was dead.

Anton must have realized what he had said. He blanched and rushed to continue. "Desiree said no. She said I did not have the business"—he searched for a word—"acumen."

"Enough reason to kill her."

"*Non.* I did not do it. We parted, and she retreated to her room to talk to that *imbécile.*"

I flashed on J.P., who had lied about his whereabouts. Had Desiree gone to confront him? Had he lured her to the beach with a promise of reconciliation before killing her?

I eyed Anton. He looked cagey, as if he was hiding something. During our conversation at The Pelican Brief Diner, he had told Lola and me about the opening of his San Francisco restaurant. Why hadn't he mentioned greater expansion at that time?

I said, "You're full of it. Try again."

He spread his arms. "*Il est vrai.* The truth. Desiree said no. I accepted her response."

"I'm not buying it. Those guys you were just talking to . . ." I gestured toward the hotel's entrance.

"Thugs," Anton muttered.

"You gave them money. Why?" Lola told Bailey that she thought Anton might be hard up for cash. He had dug in his pockets for loose change to pay for his meal at the diner. "Did they expect Desiree's presence on opening night and, now that she's dead, pull out of the venture?"

"*Exactement.*"

Something still didn't ring true. What was I missing? "How did you hook up with Gigi Goode?"

"May I sit?" Anton asked. "My legs. It is why I limp. The circulation."

He didn't look fit enough to escape. I stepped aside and followed him to a pair of chairs. A bevy of mocha-skinned beauties in skimpy swimsuits shuffled in behind us and nestled in a nearby grouping. One young woman ogled Anton and whispered, "*Hermoso.*" Handsome. The others agreed with enthusiasm.

Anton's mouth curved up as he sat down.

I perched at the front of my chair. "Gigi," I repeated.

"Why did you choose her? There are dozens of other hair-stylists in Crystal Cove."

"The day I arrived, when I was in *costume*, I spied on Desiree. She left your store, and I followed her to the inn. I waited, deliberating. What would I say? How would she react? There was no love between us." He wove his fingers together. "When I found the *courage*, I headed for her room."

"How did you know which one was hers?"

"I charmed a maid." He leered at the beauties; they tittered. "When I reached the room, the door was ajar. I heard two women arguing. I peered inside. Gigi was with her. Desiree maligned Gigi about her hairstyle. It was too frou-frou on top and the ends needed a trim. Gigi offered to take care of it immediately, but Desiree, who did not know the word *modeste*, flew into a rage. Gigi glared at Desiree, and I felt an instant *rapport*. When she left, rather than approach Desiree, I followed Gigi to see if I could enlist her services."

"To do what?"

A beach ball bounced between us. A scraggly youth in cutoffs and Croc clogs sprinted to recover the ball. His mortified mother chased after him. "Sorry," she said as she bounded over my feet.

Anton stood. "Perhaps we should take this conversation outside." Without waiting for my approval, he rose and sauntered out the gigantic double French doors to a stone terrace.

"What about your suitcase?"

"There is nothing of value inside." He stopped at the cement balustrade and propped his back against it. Sun baked his cheeks. A gentle breeze ruffled his salt-and-pepper hair.

To avoid direct sunlight, I remained in the shadow of the overhang; Desiree would have been proud. "Go on. You and Gigi. You wanted to enlist her services for what?"

"I craved insider information on Desiree."

"You decided blackmailing her would be easier than asking for a loan."

He shrugged. "I wanted options. Desiree could be heartless. I needed dirt to coerce her to invest."

Dirt. Secrets. Items he could threaten to release to scandal magazines.

Anton pivoted and bent forward with his elbows on the balustrade.

I needed to watch his eyes. How else could I know if he was lying? I moved into the sunlight. "Go on. Gigi."

"Ahh, yes. I followed her. However, before I could approach, she stopped at a grocery store, and *voilà*, before I knew it, she stole a wallet from a woman's purse. And then another and another." He cast a triumphant look at me. "As she crept from cart to cart à la the Pink Panther, I knew I could have her in my pocket, as you say. I approached her. Her face became *rouge*, such shame. She agreed to do my bidding and drum up dirt. However, when I heard that Desiree had died"—he licked his lips—"when I learned she was *assassiné*, I assumed I would be a suspect. Why else would I have come to Crystal Cove, *non*? I needed an alibi. I pursued Gigi. She obliged."

"What's your real alibi?"

He didn't answer.

I said, "Perhaps talking with the police will get you to open up."

"I have spoken to them."

"I'll bet you didn't tell them about needing a loan. You were desperate."

"*Non.*"

I pulled my cell phone from my tote.

"Wait." Anton faced me. "You do not understand."

"Enlighten me."

"*Oui,* I am short on cash."

"You needed Desiree's money. Got it."

"*Non.* It is worse. I have a habit."

"Drugs?"

"*Mon Dieu,* no. Gambling. I am a gambler." Words gushed out of him. "I cannot control myself. I have wagered my life's savings. I lost all the money my investors loaned me to expand Chez Anton."

"Did those thugs loan you money? Did they come to collect?"

He gave a curt nod.

"Maybe they killed Desiree," I said.

Anton shook his head. "They would not. They hoped I could convince her to invest."

"You planned to rob Peter to pay Paul." The guy was shrewd. "So if you weren't with Gigi the night Desiree died, where were you?"

Anton pressed his lips together.

I grumbled. Getting complete answers from him was taking longer than it took me to make my disastrous angel food cake back in high school. I aimed a finger at the numbers on my cell phone. "I'm dialing . . ."

He growled. "I was on the telephone with my *thérapeute* . . . therapist . . . from midnight until four A.M."

"What therapist in his right mind would take a call that late at night?"

"My doctor is a she, and she lives in France. It is a nine-hour difference."

A flock of seagulls cruised over the Nature's Retreat terrace. Their squawks mimicked the shock I felt. "You want me to believe that you spoke to your therapist for four hours?"

"We talk that long every day," he said. "That is how bad I am."

And expensive. I did a quick calculation in my head. Maybe he paid her using a barter system. "Did you tell this to the police?"

"I cannot. If my investors find out I have gambled away their money, they will kill me."

"Not a good enough excuse." I stabbed in the precinct number and held out the cell phone to him. "Ask for Chief Pritchett."

Begrudgingly Anton took the phone. As he set an

appointment to come in and I contemplated visiting the Chill Zone Bar for corroboration of Anton's account, my aunt breezed through the terrace archway.

"Jenna, dear, too-ra-loo," she warbled. She may have sounded cheery, but I could tell she was stressed to the point of cracking. Her forehead was as wrinkled as a relief map. "Thank the spirits." She tugged me into a fierce hug. "How thoughtless of us, arguing and leaving you to take matters into your own hands. Bailey told her mother. I worried that you were—"

"Aunt Vera, let me go. I'm fine." I twisted free and glanced around. "Oh, no."

During the few seconds Aunt Vera had taken hold of me, Anton had fled. He was gone, as in G-O-N-E. My cell phone rested on the balustrade. I scooped it up. The display read: *Searching for signal.* Anton had pulled a fast one; he hadn't connected with the precinct at all.

I tore into the lobby of the hotel. Anton's suitcase and overcoat were nowhere to be seen. Shoot, shoot, shoot! He didn't have complications with his legs. He had faked it, exactly as he had faked his fisherman disguise. Had he lied about his gambling problem, too? Was he the killer, after all?

Chapter 20

FROM THE HOTEL lobby, I dialed the precinct. The clerk assured me that after she handled the handful of drunk-and disorderly calls pertaining to the upcoming Sandcastle Festival, she would put me through. I started to explain that a killer might be on the loose, but she clicked Hold too fast.

"Jenna Starrett Hart, hang up."

"But —"

"No buts," Aunt Vera said. "You're coming with me. You need focus."

Honestly, I thought I was pretty darned focused when I had tracked down Anton and even more focused now that he was on the run, but my aunt wouldn't concede.

She swished her hand over my head and intoned, "Negativity, disperse with the wind," then practically dragged me to The Cookbook Nook.

I protested that it was our day off, but Aunt Vera claimed she wanted to go over the shop's inventory. The first week's sales had astonished her. She intended to review all the books we had in stock and order more. A store like ours had to keep up to date to lure repeat customers. She reminded me that every week publishers put out new books—cookbooks, non-fiction, women's fiction, and mysteries. As an aside, she told me she had just finished the entire cupcake bakery mysteries featuring adorable bakers living in Scottsdale. Until last week, she hadn't known the series existed.

When we arrived at the shop, I was surprised to catch a whiff of sugar and spice and everything nice. I followed the scent to the café to find Katie, looking like Betty Crocker herself, in a gingham dress and matching apron. "M-m-mm," I murmured. "What are you cooking?"

Katie held out a platter filled with Hawaiian-style appe-tizers, or as she called them, puu puus. "Chicken and Maui onions," she said of the first. "A kabob of moist chicken marinated in island flavors."

Given that I hadn't eaten more than half of my omelet before darting from The Pelican Brief Diner, I dug in. The pineapple-based morsel made my mouth ping with pleasure. "Yum," I said.

"The other choice is a meatball, similar in flavor. Lots of brown sugar and soy sauce."

I popped one into my mouth and wished I could consume all of them. "What are these for?"

"I was thinking we should do themed nights at the res-taurant. You know, French, Greek, Hawaiian. You name it."

"Great idea," I said. "For Italian night, we could feature recipes from cookbooks by, say, Mario Batali. Did you see the one entitled *Cooking with Italian Grandmothers*? It's luscious. There are stories from Tuscany to Sicily, and the photographs are stupendous."

Katie grinned. "Aren't you becoming the cookbook gourmet."

"Yeah, well, a reading and visual gourmet, perhaps." I had years of learning before I would become a cooking gourmet . . . if ever. "Why aren't you taking the day off?"

"Hoo-boy." She swatted the air. "There's no rest for me. No, ma'am. Not until we bring on another full-time chef."

"Don't the sous chefs help out?"

"Sure, but a restaurant is a twenty-four-seven operation,

even if it's not open twenty-four-seven. I have to do the ordering, the taste tests, and whatnot. Don't worry. I still plan to take the evening off for a glass of wine with my pal." She knuckled my upper arm.

Wine . . . Tuesday. I had forgotten. Oops. Luckily I hadn't made other plans.

"I've got my taste buds set on a crisp pinot grigio," Katie said.

"Sounds delicious."

"Now, let's take this platter to the shop, so I can badger your aunt for info." Katie led the way and added over her shoulder, "There's a reason she brought you here, and I want to know what it is."

"Why would you think—"

"I'm as woo-woo connected as she is."

Aunt Vera caught up with us in the hall between the café and the shop. "I heard that, Miss Casey."

Katie plowed past her, holding the platter as if it were a peace offering. "Puu puu?"

"Do not make fun of my powers." Aunt Vera selected a meatball.

"I would never make fun. I'm in total awe."

My aunt brandished the meatball on its skewer. "I'll have you know I've been much more spiritually attuned ever since we opened the shop."

I gawked. "Aunt Vera, you're not telling me that we have ghosts, are you? If Dad finds out, he will cart you off to an asylum so fast your head will spin."

Katie guffawed. "I get it. That's an *Exorcist* reference."

"No, it wasn't. Not intentionally." I hadn't read the book nor seen the movie. Never would. Reading about some topics, such as body snatchers and freaky possessed kids, didn't sit well with me. "Aunt Vera?"

"Too-ra-loo. I haven't communed with any ghosts . . . yet." She downed the meatball and hummed her approval. "I simply feel I have something to live for. Busy ness is good for the soul."

"I wholeheartedly agree." Katie set the platter on the

vintage kitchen table and folded her large frame into one of the chairs. "Now fill me in on the reason you're both at the shop."

"Our darling Jenna has been snooping again," Aunt Vera said.

"Clearing my name," I argued.

"Putting herself in harm's way."

Katie folded her arms in judgment. "So, what you're saying, Vera, is you brought her here so you could keep an eye on her."

"I never said . . ." Aunt Vera fanned the air. "Okay. Yes. Whatever. I'm worried and so is her father and Lola."

"I'm fine," I assured them.

Katie thumped the table. "I'm on pins and needles. Spill."

I told her about the brunch and Lola's intel that led me to track down Anton at his hotel and how he revealed he was a gambler, but afterward, he bolted. "If he was innocent, why would he run off, right?" My cell phone rang. The display read: *Private caller.* I usually didn't answer those calls—most of them political robo-calls—but something in my gut told me to respond.

"Miss Hart," Cinnamon Pritchett said through the receiver.

"Oh, phew, Anton d'Stang contacted you."

"No. Why would he?"

"Because . . ." I paused. "Why are you calling me then?"

Cinnamon cleared her throat. "A witness implicating you in Miss Divine's murder has come forward."

I gaped. Please tell me this wasn't about the idiotic photograph in my father's hardware store. I had pushed that notion from my mind.

"You were overheard talking to Mr. Hessman in a café."

I started to vibrate, head to toe. My conversation with J. P. was days ago. What had I said? What had been misconstrued? "Who is the witness? What did she say?"

"My mother heard from a third party that you told Mr. Hessman you were so jealous of Desiree that you wanted to kill her."

"Are you kidding me? Yes, I said I was jealous, but I didn't say—" I blew out a burst of air. My life was turning into a bad game of *Telephone*. "You do realize your mother has it in for me, don't you? Way back when, she had a crush on my father. She thinks my mother stole him away from her. She hates both of my siblings and me. You can't possibly believe her."

"I have to follow every clue. That's my job. My duty."

"You follow the rules. I got it. My father set you on the straight and narrow. But this time—"

Before I could say more, my aunt wrestled the phone from my grasp and said, "Cinnamon Pritchett, this is Vera Hart. You know perfectly well what's going on. Your mother is muckraking." I heard Cinnamon respond but couldn't make out the words. "Listen to me, young lady. If you want to arrest my niece, then arrest her; otherwise, stop harassing her. There's no way in heaven she killed her friend, and the sooner you get that into your pretty head, the sooner you'll find the real killer. That is, if Jenna doesn't beat you to it." Aunt Vera puffed with pride. "You heard me right. Jenna is an ace problem solver."

Katie thwacked my aunt on the arm in support.

"If you want her, come and get her." Aunt Vera stabbed the End button and handed the cell phone to me.

"Aunt Vera—"

"Don't thank me, dear. It had to be said."

I wasn't about to thank her. I was pretty sure that, push come to shove, Cinnamon Pritchett wouldn't allow herself to be browbeaten. In fact, I would bet she was on her way to the shop with handcuffs at the ready. I stared out the window and breathed shallowly in my chest while downing another meatball. I would need sustenance in jail.

"Let's go over this one more time," Aunt Vera said, cutting into my nightmare about a future behind bars. "What do we really know about suspects other than Anton d'Stang?"

"Gigi Goode." I ticked my finger. "Motive: to keep Desiree from revealing her proclivity for theft."

"J.P. Hessman," Aunt Vera coached.

"Motive: jealousy." I pictured J.P.'s bulging biceps with the writhing tattoos. He was definitely strong enough to kill Desiree and lug her to the beach, but did he have the artistic ability to create a mermaid sculpture? Maybe I was making too much of that skill. Perhaps a hack could have pulled it off.

"Let's pin down his alibi." Aunt Vera shuffled to the cashier's counter, picked up the telephone, and whistled as she dialed.

"Who are you calling?" I said.

"The Crystal Cove Inn." Aunt Vera asked for the manager. While waiting, she twirled a tendril of red hair. A moment later, someone came on the line and my aunt said she needed information on J.P. Hessman's comings and goings. "Uh-huh," she muttered repeatedly. A short while later, she giggled like a schoolgirl and hung up. "Well, the manager—you know him, with the big handlebar mustache? The man is crazy about mc." Judging by her flirty demeanor, she was crazy about him, too. "He tells me that one of his Russian housekeepers—those girls have relocated here in droves, you know. They share a room and expenses. Anyway, one of the girls saw a man with big muscular arms, tattoos, and funky hair"—Aunt Vera used both hands to outline an imaginary Mohawk—"sneaking around the hotel on the night of the murder."

Which further corroborated Anton's story, establishing that J.P. was not in bed, as he claimed.

"The Russian added that she saw Desiree arguing with a young dark-haired woman."

"Sabrina," Katie said.

I rose to my feet. "I should go to the inn and talk to the housekeeper. Maybe she—"

A whoop of laughter coming from across the parking lot drew me up short. A pack of teens flew out the front door of Beaders of Paradise. Right behind them charged Pepper wielding a broom.

I dashed outside to help.

"How dare you, you urchins," Pepper screeched.

The teens, led by the dystopian girl, juggled spools of thread and bags of loose beads as they fled between the Winnebagos and disappeared from sight.

Pepper whirled on me. "What are you staring at?" she sniped and stomped into her store.

I would have felt sympathetic and excused her for her rudeness, except that I was still angry at her for reigniting her daughter's suspicions about me, and a sudden urge to have it out with her overtook me. I hurried to Beaders of Paradise and plowed inside. I let the front door slam shut. The strands of seashell-shaped beads that served as a window shade clacked with riotous scorn. No customers populated the shop. All the better.

I darted between racks of sparkling beads toward Pepper, who was heading toward the stockroom behind the sales counter. "Who told you that I said I wanted to kill Desiree?" I demanded.

Pepper wheeled around; her nose flared. "Joey."

Her nephew, the kid who clerked for Rhett. The traitor. And here I thought the kid liked me. "Bullpuckey." I borrowed Rhett's semi–curse word, liking the way it tripped off my tongue.

"He was there. He heard you."

"He's lying."

"If he were, you wouldn't be so upset."

"Stop. This. Now." I shook a fist at her.

Pepper gasped. The space went deadly silent.

Heat flooded my cheeks. I lowered my fist and clutched my hands in front of me. "Look, Pepper, I'm sorry it didn't work out between you and my father. I'm sorry your husband left you and your daughter. I'm sorry for everything. But please, can't you put the past behind you? You are harassing me out of spite. Can't you forgive and forget?"

"No. Never." Pepper jammed the butt end of the broom on the floor. "Leave."

As I fled, I heard her weeping.

Chapter 21

I TRUDGED INTO The Cookbook Nook. Katie was nowhere to be seen. Aunt Vera fiddled with the new display of foodie bookmarks, all hanging by their cute tassels. She glanced at me, her face pinched with apprehension. "What happened?"

"I ran into Pepper's shop, and I . . . I . . ." I pulled free and flung myself into a chair by the vintage kitchen table. "I wish . . . No, I regret my behavior just now. I wanted to sock her in the nose."

"But you didn't."

"No."

Aunt Vera inhaled and petted the amulet around her neck. "Not to worry then. I'll patch things up."

"How can you?"

"That's not your concern. It's mine. Pepper is my tenant. My contemporary. I'll think of something." Aunt Vera sat in a chair opposite me. "Now, you said you wanted to go to the Crystal Cove Inn and talk to the housekeeper. Might I recommend against that? You don't want the woman to lose her work visa, do you?"

"Why would she lose . . ." I paused. "Oh, I get it. She doesn't have a visa at all. She's an illegal."

"My manager friend didn't suggest she come forth as a witness because the murder happened elsewhere."

"Do you know if the housekeeper can pinpoint what time she saw J.P.?"

"She wasn't sure. The next morning, she knocked on his door. No answer. She entered and was shocked to find him passed out on top of the bed, bare naked."

"Didn't he have a *Do Not Disturb* sign on his door?"

"Guess not."

Unless I could confirm that J.P. met with Desiree after she left the Chill Zone Bar, I had nothing. "I'll find other witnesses. I'll question the bartender and the waitresses."

"Don't you think Chief Pritchett has done that?"

"Even if she has, it never hurts to have a second opinion." At Taylor & Squibb, my superior demanded a comparative analysis. A client couldn't be expected to sink millions into a campaign without one. "I was planning on going out for drinks with Katie. Instead of Vines, we'll go to the Chill Zone Bar."

"Great idea, and ask Bailey to join you."

"Bailey?"

Aunt Vera bobbed her chin toward the stockroom. "She came in while you visited Pepper."

Visited. Ha!

"She looks a little blue."

Earlier at the diner, Bailey had mentioned a doctor's appointment. Was something wrong? Was she sick?

Aunt Vera tapped her heart with her fingertips. "My sixth sense tells me she might be suffering man trouble."

I LED THE charge into the Chill Zone Bar. Bailey and Katie followed.

"Hoo-boy, get a load of this place." Katie twirled in a circle, the skirt of her gingham dress fluting out. "How hip."

Rays of blue and purple light filtered through a heavy

gauze ceiling. Gray leather barrel-style chairs clustered around dark granite tables. Every few feet stood plastic ice sculptures shaped like stacks of two-foot-square ice cubes. Water cascaded out of the tops of the sculptures and down the sides.

"I've always wanted to come here," Katie went on, "but I never had the courage."

"Why not?" Bailey said. On the way to the bar, I hadn't found the opportunity to ask her whether anything was bothering her. She didn't look sad. In fact, she looked radiant, her skin tone rosy, enhanced by the summery orange halter and harem pants she had worn to brunch.

Katie said, "You know, single women, out on the town. Not what Mama expects of me. Or Papa." Her eyes widened. "Wow. Take a look at the bar."

A stream of men chatted up women. No families. No children.

"All those selections of rum," Katie went on. "So much for a glass of wine. I want the jellyfish mojito. According to the description in the cocktail list that the bar posts online, it's got a real sting to it." She wended through the chairs and tables to one of the booths along the perimeter of the room.

Bailey and I followed. We ordered from a waitress in a low-cut, electric blue spandex dress—Katie and I opting for the mojitos and Bailey selecting San Pellegrino water, claiming she was the designated driver. Loud instrumental Caribbean music, heavy on the steel drums and maracas, made it nearly impossible to talk.

"Hey." Bailey pointed at the dance floor. "Isn't that Desiree's sister?"

Sabrina swayed with Mackenzie, her head planted on the masseur's chest, her palms resting on his shoulders.

"They look pretty intimate, if you ask me," Katie said.

She wasn't kidding. Mackenzie's right hand massaged Sabrina's back. At the same time, his left hand cupped her firm rear end. I speculated about the extent of their relationship. Only days before, Sabrina had seemed distraught that her boyfriend had broken up with her. Had Mackenzie made a play for Sabrina, hoping she might inherit her sister's estate? Had he, as Bailey had suggested earlier, conspired with Sabrina to kill Desiree?

I scanned the place and spotted the bartender, a woman with Cleopatra's luscious eyes and asp-like black tendrils trailing down her cheeks. She shimmied a martini shaker with the gusto of a Mix Master. Up for an impromptu interrogation, I excused myself from my friends and made a beeline for the woman. I settled onto a seat between two empty stools and slipped a twenty-dollar bill onto the counter. Rays from the blue lights overhead gave the bartender's unblemished skin an otherworldly glow.

"What'll it be?" she asked.

"What's good?"

"The margarita. It's my mother's recipe."

"Perfect." As she twisted to get the fixings, I said, "Before you go, could I ask you a couple of questions?"

She eyed the twenty-dollar bill. "Friend or foe?"

"Curious local."

"A local gets three questions, but make them good."

Three limited my options, so I started with a couple of statements. "Desiree Divine died last week. She was my friend. She was seen talking with a man for quite a long time." I described Anton. "Did you catch any of their conversation?"

"No. Next question." She put a pinky on the twenty and drew the bill toward her.

"Did you see Desiree argue with anyone that night and, if so, with whom?"

"That's two questions."

"It's one, all phrased within one parenthetical."

Cleopatra wrinkled her nose. "What are you, an English teacher?"

"A recovering advertising exec."

Without letting go of the twenty, Cleopatra polished the bar with a dry towel. "Yes, she argued with a couple of people."

A couple? I was thinking that if Desiree had left Anton

to have it out with J.P., maybe she had caught him before he left the bar. Who was the other? "Can you describe them?"

"Yes." She didn't offer more.

I glowered at her. "C'mon, not fair. I'm not an attorney."

"Maybe you need one."

"Very funny. Please describe them."

Cleopatra leaned forward and rested her elbows on the bar, a move that emphasized her ample cleavage. "One was a pretty thing, dark and short with eyes as black as arrowheads." I peeked at Sabrina. The bartender winked, indicating I had hit the mark. "Your friend was ticked off to the max. She met Short Stuff at the door. They wrestled. Your pal pulled something out of Short Stuff's purse. A bottle of pills, I think. Shortie snatched it back. When your pal was done ranting, she tried to make a call on her cell phone, but apparently it wasn't charged, so she made a beeline for the telephone down the hall." Cleopatra tilted her head in that direction. "Later, she met up with that guy with the Mohawk."

A chiseled guy farther down the bar said, "Hey, babe, getting thirsty here."

Cleopatra tucked the twenty-dollar bill into her bra and mouthed, "Be right back." She sambaed to the far end of the bar to pour a martini for the customer.

I blotted the bar in front of me with a cocktail napkin and studied the other customers. A couple of casually dressed men down the bar ogled me. I offered a blasé smile—not interested.

A flash of light caught my eye. A door in the hall beyond the bar opened. Even from a distance, I made out the figure of a man with a Mohawk exiting the restroom. J.P. In a flash, I realized that the bartender had tried to alert me to his presence. What would J.P. do if he found me nosing around? I hunched forward over the bar and, out of the corner of my eye, glimpsed him heading straight for me. A queasy feeling flooded through me as I spied a tumbler with an inch of weak brown liquid and melted ice on a cardboard Chill Zone coaster to my right. Was it J.P.'s? Shoot.

Chill out, I urged myself and suddenly erupted in giggles.

Chill out. At the Chill Zone Bar. More giggles. J.P. drew nearer. I could make a run for it, but why should I? All I had to do was play innocent. I was a single girl out for a night on the town with her friends.

Trying to act natural, I slung one leg over the other and gave my hair a shake. Oh, yeah, real natural.

As J.P. settled into his stool, Cleopatra returned. I ordered a margarita with salt, and overemoting like a ham actor, I did a double take at J.P. "Hey, fancy seeing you here. How are you doing?"

"I'm cool."

Cool. In the Chill Zone Bar. More giggles. Silently, I threatened my lungs with brute force. The giggles subsided. "Buy you another drink?" I pointed at the nearly empty tumbler in front of J.P.

His world-weary gaze took me in head to toe. He didn't seem impressed with my performance. If only I had thought to wear an electric blue spandex dress . . . which I did not own and never would.

"Another Black on the rocks?" the bartender said and winked at J.P. flirtatiously. She offered me a wry glance.

"Sure." J.P. said.

"This is my first time here," I said like an awestruck tourist. "It's some place."

"It's okay if you enjoy the dark."

"Is this your first time, too?"

"Nah. I've been here a couple of times. The concierge at the inn recommended it."

"I've wanted to check it out, but I hadn't found the time until now. Day off," I added, as if that explained my sudden presence.

"Cool."

The bartender set down our drinks. I pulled a second twenty from my purse and pushed it toward her. She didn't make change.

"How are you holding up?" I asked J.P.

"I'm cool." He ran his finger around the lip of his tumbler. "Real cool."

So much for an extensive vocabulary.

"Sabrina and Mackenzie are here," I said. "Did you come with them?"

"Yeah. We're the Three Musketeers." J.P. squinted toward the dance floor. "They're into each other."

"Seems so. I hear they hooked up the night Desiree died. You must have seen them."

"Where?"

"Here." I licked the rim of my margarita glass and took a sip. The concoction was good. Nice and tart.

J.P. flinched. "Why would you think—" He glowered at the bartender.

"She didn't tell me," I said, not lying. She and I hadn't finished our conversation. "Anton d'Stang did."

J.P. cut a hard look at me. "That buffoon."

"You came here," I continued.

"Yeah, so what?"

"You lied to me about hanging out in your room that night. You said you took one of Desiree's sleeping pills. But you didn't, did you?" I stabbed my finger on the bar. "Did you think no one would notice you? If not Anton, then Sabrina or Mackenzie or any number of regulars? Have the police asked you about this?"

"You're the first to mention it."

"You were jealous."

"Dang right I was." He growled. "Jealous as all get-out. Wouldn't you have been? Desiree took a phone call and she nearly ran out of the room. Did she think I wouldn't find out that she was meeting her former lover? The man jump-started her career. Des was feeling insecure with the ratings. Anton's timing . . ." J.P. lifted his beverage, almost jabbing me with his left elbow, and slugged back the entire drink in one gulp. He slammed the glass on the bar and pushed it away. "Suffice it to say, Des was primed to repeat bad habits. D'Stang was a Svengali. He could mesmerize her. What was I? A two-bit director. I had nothing on him."

"You sat at the bar and dialed her repeatedly. She didn't answer. Why didn't you confront her?"

"I wanted to see if she'd text me a lie. That way I'd have proof. Physical proof."

"Jealousy is a powerful motive for murder," I said. "You were drinking. Alcohol can—"

"I was downing club soda that night. Ask her." J.P. tilted his head at the bartender. "Five bucks for a lousy club soda. Highway robbery. Anyway, I gave up. I needed to ponder my options."

"What options?"

"If Desiree was going to quit and go back to Anton, I needed to get my résumé in order. Pronto."

"Anton didn't ask Desiree to come back to him. He asked her for a loan."

"No lie?"

"He said when Desiree left him, she was headed back to the room to talk with you."

"I . . ." He worked his tongue inside his cheek. "I never saw her. Look, I'm not proud of it, but after I left here, I hit the mini-bar in the room."

"So you did drink."

"Yeah, I drowned my sorrows, and I passed out."

"In the nude."

"How do you know that? Ah, who cares? I paid for my sins the next day. Ask Sabrina. She said I smelled like a still."

I flashed on J.P. and Sabrina meeting in the parking lot outside The Cookbook Nook. He had yanked something from her purse. Perhaps Sabrina had taunted him with a less-than-flattering snapshot of him drunk that he wouldn't have wanted made public.

J.P. rubbed a hand along the top of his Mohawk. "You have no idea how guilty I feel. If I'd stayed sober, if I hadn't left the bar, maybe Desiree . . ." He twirled his tumbler, which spun out of control and careened over the bar. The glass shattered in a metal sink. The bartender raced toward our end of the bar. J.P. raised his hands in apology. "Eighty six me. I'll pay for the glass." As Cleopatra cleaned up the mess, J.P. continued. "If you ask me, Anton's lying. He killed her. I mean, c'mon, why was he in Crystal Cove? For a loan? Give me a break."

"He's a gambler. He claims he's in debt up to his eyeballs."

"Cock-and-bull story."

"You think he's making it all up?" This from a guy who had bald-faced lied to me about where he was the night Desiree was murdered.

"Anton had issues with Desiree. He couldn't let her go. He wrote her love letters. When Desiree continued to snub him, he wrote her hate mail."

"Do you have any of those?"

J.P. shook his head. "Desiree burned them."

Chapter 22

WHEN I RETURNED to the booth, the music at the Chill Zone Bar was blasting so loudly I could barely think. Bailey and Katie leaned forward in their seats. "Well?"

Raising my voice, I told them what J.P. had said about Anton sending hate mail to Desiree.

Bailey patted the table. "You're not safe with Anton on the loose."

I disagreed. "I think he's long gone." In fact, I felt so sure about that, I fetched my cell phone and dialed the precinct. I asked to be put through to Chief Pritchett. I reached her voice mail. Quickly I reiterated that I believed Anton d'Stang was the killer. "Not only did Anton lie about his alibi and blackmail Gigi Goode to corroborate that lie, and not only did he start his career as a baker of large-sized cakes, as I stated in our previous conversation at my shop"— I flashed on my initial meeting with Anton at the diner and added—"a left-handed baker, by the way."

Katie whispered, "How can you be so sure?"

"He held his coffee cup in his left hand."

"Circumstantial," Bailey said.

I waved them off and continued my message. "But if Anton is to be believed, he dunned Desiree for money because he's a gambler. In addition, I just learned from J.P. Hessman that Anton sent Desiree hate mail, but she destroyed it. You might wonder how I know all this? I tracked down Anton d'Stang at his hotel. There were some thugs with him." I described Mr. Big and his cohort in brief detail and recapped my conversation with Anton. "While he and I were talking, he ran off. I think you should—" I paused. I wasn't sure what I thought Cinnamon should do. Find Anton. Book him. Solve the puzzle. She knew what she had to do; she didn't need a directive from me. "I think you should call me if you need anything further."

As I aimed my finger at the cell phone's End button, I heard a click, and then Cinnamon said, "Miss Hart, why do you continue to act as if I don't know what I'm doing?"

I blanched. The sneak had been listening in. Bailey and Katie mouthed, *What?* I said, "Hi, Chief Pritchett."

"I've got this handled," Cinnamon said. "I need you to take a backseat."

"You've got to bring in Anton d'Stang."

"And I will."

"For all we know, he's going to flee to France, where he'll find—"

"Stop this. You're going to make yourself sick. Investigations take time. We don't solve crimes in a matter of days. That only happens on TV. Why, last month, there was a Southern California woman who was arrested following a five-year investigation. She swore she accidentally shot her husband with his pistol. It took the police all that time to prove it was murder. People have to go on with their lives. Stop nosing around in this case and get on with your own."

"How am I supposed to do that? You think I'm guilty."

"I've never said that."

"Not directly, but you've found planted evidence and you've received erroneous witness statements, and on a daily basis, your mother is trolling for more of my so-called shady past. How could you not?"

"I am pursuing other leads."

"Like what?"

Cinnamon inhaled then exhaled as if she were trying to rein in a retort.

I said, "Don't you see this whole affair has changed my life? Not only have I lost a good friend, and not only am I trying to prove myself innocent, but I've become jumpy. I'm scared to enter my cottage without a full perimeter check. I'm afraid to make eye contact with surfers and sandcastle builders."

"Because you're making yourself a target," Cinnamon cut in. "Which is why I'm asking you nicely, for the last time, to back off. I am doing my job. Do you understand me?"

"Yes." I bit my lip and drew blood to keep myself from saying another word. As I hung up, however, I realized she hadn't said categorically that she thought I was innocent.

I APOLOGIZED TO my friends for being a lousy date, and I drove to my cottage, fingers drumming the steering wheel. Nervous energy writhed beneath my skin. As I pulled past my aunt's house, I flared the headlights at the front of the cottage and examined the azaleas and hydrangeas for interlopers. No sign of anything out of the ordinary. I yanked a flashlight—the hefty kind, nearly two feet long and as heavy as a sledgehammer—from beneath the front seat of my VW bug and made a tour of the cottage. I didn't see a soul. No one on the beach, not even Old Jake driving his tractor.

Feeling a little bit safer, I slipped into the cottage. Tigger scampered to me and danced around my feet. He pawed my bare toes. I scooped him up and tucked him into my neck. "Missed you, too, handsome." Tears pressed at the corners of my eyes and I moaned. One margarita and I was a weepy mess. Swell. I swiped the waterworks off my face and traipsed to the window. I scanned the beach and wished I felt confident enough to take a late evening stroll. The moon hung high in the sky. A long strand of light cut a path to the window. I couldn't see anyone roaming the beach, and yet a ripple of panic shimmied down my spine. I checked the window locks and prepared a snack of sliced cheddar cheese. I took the plate and a bottle of sparkling water to the kitchen table, then I fetched a sketch pad and piece of charcoal and I settled into a chair.

Tucking one foot under my rump, I closed my eyes and began an old relaxation technique that my mother taught me. She said free-form sketching was a way to open one's mind to a deeper creative trove. I drew big swirling lines, letting my hand roam the page with unbridled urges. Five minutes later, I opened my eyes and glimpsed my work. A small squeal escaped my lips. The image I had sketched was a mermaid. I tossed the charcoal on the table and jammed my hand in my mouth. *Please, Jenna, move on*, I coaxed the way my therapist would. I couldn't relive finding Desiree, day in and day out. I couldn't continue, over and over, to imagine her blue face and the hook or I would go insane.

Grabbing the plate of cheese and bottle of water, I scuttled to the sofa, seized the television remote controller, and switched on the TV. I thought of Katie and Bailey, both demanding that they come home with me. I had held them at bay. *I'm fine*, I had lied. If only I had said yes to one or both. Why was I so danged independent?

I advanced channels and paused on a repeat of the *Radical Cake Battle* show that Desiree had judged. Was the network replaying it frequently because she had been murdered? Egad. I flipped to another cooking channel and saw chefs arguing about original recipes. I thought briefly of Tito Martinez's complaint that Desiree had stolen his recipe. Her murder couldn't be about something so simple, could it? No, Tito was quirky, but he wasn't a murderer. I switched to another channel and landed on a forensic mystery. The morgue assistant was dissecting a brain. Yuck. No, no, no.

As I searched for a comedy—any comedy—the landline telephone rang. I nearly jumped out of my skin. Who was calling? Was it Anton d'Stang prepared to tell me he was right outside my door? Cue scary music . . . *Here's Anton!*

Refusing to cave to fear, I seized the receiver and yelled, "Hello!"

My aunt said, "Jenna, dear? Are you all right?"

"I . . . I . . . My kitten tackled my leg and—" I eyed Tigger, who was sitting on the floor by the Ching cabinet craning to stare down the ceramic Lucky Cat above, and I felt a twinge in my heart. Bad me. How dare I implicate my innocent cat? A teeny inner voice screamed to admit my distress to my aunt, but I couldn't. I was fine. Dandy. "What's up?"

"I have a guest at the house."

I hadn't noticed a second car in her driveway, but I hadn't been looking for one.

"He brought a picnic," my aunt went on.

"Who was crazy enough to bring you food this late? Don't tell me you conjured up a magic spell to lure that mustachioed manager of the bed-and-breakfast to your doorstep."

My aunt tittered. "Heavens, no. I have powers, but I would never—" She laughed again. "It's Rhett Jackson. Looking for you."

A flush like the rush from a delicious champagne bubbled up inside me. "Really?"

"He said he was thinking about you all day. This morning, you acted upset when you went to visit him. When Rhett ponders a problem, he cooks. Whatever he brought smells divine. Hungry?"

Rhett said something in the background, and before I knew it, he was on the line. "I'm an after-hours eater. A chef's habit, I'm afraid."

"You made a picnic?"

"Most restaurants in town aren't open past nine P.M. on Tuesdays. I had a craving for ribs and all the fixings. I've brought a bottle of pinot noir. Say yes."

I cradled the phone against my cheek, liking the sound of his voice, treasuring having a man to talk to. Two years had passed since David died. Was it time for me to open my heart to someone new? I didn't know anything about Rhett, but my father, my aunt, and Katie liked him. Even Tigger had taken to him. Cats were perceptive, right?

"C'mon," Rhett coaxed. "Be spontaneous. I have a blanket to throw on the floor. I came prepared."

"Wow, a regular Boy Scout." I winked at Tigger. "Think he's a safe bet?" Tigger flicked his tail and meowed. I whispered, "Yeah, me, too." To Rhett, I said, "Sold."

In less than sixty seconds, I made my bed, swooped scattered clothing into the laundry bin or closet, dumped my cheese and sparkling water, wiped down the counters in the kitchen, and fluffed the pillows on the sofa. I spritzed a mist of Shalimar over my head. Next, using the remote controller, I flipped the television back to the Food Channel because I had promised Katie I would watch more episodes, except I caught sight of the *Radical Cake Battle*, still in progress with the shaggy blond guy wielding the axe, and I knew I couldn't bear seeing Desiree again. I hit End, zipped to the stereo system that was perched on the Ching cabinet, slung my iPhone into it, and clicked on an album of Judy Garland's Greatest Hits. "I Feel a Song Coming On" started playing. I sang along: *"I feel a song coming on, and I'm warning you, it's a victorious, happy, and glorious new strain."* Positive feedback. That was exactly what I needed.

Something fluttered at my core when I heard Rhett's knock on the door. Butterflies, I was pretty sure—totally unfitting for a woman nearing thirty. I peered through the peephole. Rhett gazed back at me with a rakish, disarming grin.

I unbolted the lock and opened the door. Rhett stood there, basket in one hand, wine in the other, a folded blanket draped over his shoulder. I glanced beyond him, at my aunt's house, and imagined her rubbing that phoenix amulet and uttering an incantation for me to open my mind to new things. *Bibbidi-bobbidi-boo.* I would do my best.

The aroma of spicy ribs and something sweet and savory

preceded Rhett into the cottage. He unfurled the blanket and laid it on the floor by the sofa.

"We can put the food here." I shoved the cookbooks that I had stacked on the coffee table to one side.

Rhett opened the basket and removed glass containers filled with his creations. He set them on the coffee table and popped the lids. The delicious aromas magnified. As he laid out paper plates, napkins, and utensils, Tigger pranced in a circle as if scoping out what morsel he might score from our new visitor. Red pepper ribs? Bacon and cheddar cornbread? Salad with feta cheese, kalamata olives, and onions?

I scuttled to the kitchen and fetched a handful of kibble, set it on a paper plate beside the blanket, and said, "Feast, cat." Tigger grumbled. I muttered, "Get used to it." I tapped Rhett's shoulder. "Thank you."

"For . . ."

For caring. For watching over me. For somehow sensing that I was shaky and in need of company.

"For bringing food. I'm starved."

Rhett took in the cottage. "Nice place. You've settled in quickly."

"My aunt's doing."

I fetched a pair of bowl-shaped wineglasses. Rhett opened the wine, a pinot noir from the Storrs Winery in the nearby Santa Cruz Mountains, and poured us each a healthy portion.

I sat Indian-style on the blanket. So did Rhett. I tapped the rim of my glass to his. "Cheers." I inhaled the aroma, then took a sip and swirled the liquid around my tongue as I had learned at wine-tasting classes. "Hints of strawberry and cherry and . . . mint?"

Rhett grinned. "Show-off."

During dinner, we started out like people who barely knew each other, talking about the basics: what movies we enjoyed—typical man, Rhett was a *Godfather* aficionado; where we had traveled; what music we had listened to growing up—he boasted that he knew the lyrics to every Stones' song. He knew more than that, I realized, when I caught him mouthing the words to "Zing! Went the Strings of My Heart."

I finished a rib and tossed it onto the pile of discarded bones forming on a separate paper plate. Rhett laughed.

"What?" My cheeks warmed.

"You can tell a lot about people by the way they eat ribs."

"How's that?"

"Do they hold both ends or only one end? Do they grip tightly or extend a pinky?" He demonstrated.

I giggled. "I'm a one-end holder. What does that say about me?"

"You're neat, but you're not a control freak and you're not obsessive."

"Good to know."

"You prefer loose ends sewn up."

"Now you're putting me on." I dabbed my mouth with a napkin. "How can you tell that?"

"You finish every bit of meat on the bone. You don't leave any for someone else to pick over."

"Not true." I intentionally ignored a piece of meat on my current bone and tossed the bone onto the pile.

"Cheater," he said. "You're trying to deceive me, but you can't."

"Oh, really? Are you a modern-day Sherlock Holmes?"

"Aha. The game is afoot. Let's see." He surveyed the cottage. "Take your art, for instance. It's mature and thoughtful. You don't slap it together. Your oils are akin to Degas or Cézanne, but your pen and charcoal work is similar to Rembrandt's. It's feral yet within reason. There might be some anger behind it."

I cocked my head. "Aunt Vera's been bending your ear."

"Nope. I'm an art fiend. Have you been to the Palace of Fine Arts in the City? We should go sometime."

Was he asking me on a date? The flutter I felt when I opened the door kicked into a flurry. Tornado warnings on the horizon.

I snatched another rib and chewed with vigor. "How do

you know so much?" I said between nibbles. "Did you study psychology in college?"

"Never went to college."

I recalled Aunt Vera's account. At eighteen, Rhett had gone straight to culinary school. David said a man's degree established his pedigree. Had I bought into his snobbery? Rhett appeared educated, smart, and worldly. His vocabulary was top-notch. He used what my mother called fifty-cent words— *acerbic* and *feral*. And he was romantic as well as kind. I liked him, a lot, so I made a silent pact to adjust my thinking.

"Aunt Vera told me you grew up in Northern California. Do you have family? Brothers, sisters?"

"Both. They live near my folks." He didn't elaborate.

"Why did you take up cooking?"

"I always enjoyed it. I learned from my mother."

Using one of the wet wipes that Rhett considerately thought to bring, I cleaned my fingers. "Jackson is an interesting last name. Stately. Son of Jack."

"That's right. My grandmother tells me we are linked to the Knights of the Round Table. Sir Galahad, to be specific."

"Does that make you honorable and true?"

"Indeed, milady."

I winked. "You're a renaissance man."

"In all senses of the word. Get this? I even journal."

I slapped my chest in mock shock.

"A therapist talked me into it." Rhett's mouth screwed up at the mention of a therapist. "The fire . . . You heard about the fire?"

I nodded. "Were you there when it started?"

"Your aunt hasn't told you?"

"Broad strokes."

"That night, I closed up the kitchen. I rang up the receipts. I locked everything in the safe. Around three A.M. I got a call. Fire."

"Arson."

He nodded. "I raced to the restaurant. Despite warnings, I rushed inside."

"Why?"

"To save my mother's recipe box. Stupid, I know. The ceiling was beamed. One burst in two. It fell and knocked me down. I was pinned. A firefighter saved my life. Luckily, the blaze shot upward and didn't melt through the floor. Only the corner unit was destroyed. I can't tell you how badly I would have felt if Fisherman's Village had burned down."

"You didn't set the blaze."

His face darkened. "No. All the artwork—"

"What artwork?"

"The Grotto proudly displayed fine art."

"It was destroyed?"

"That's the thing. I'm not sure it was. The owner swears every last piece perished, but when I hobbled through the remains with the fire chief, I noted a few frames were different. You know, in size, shape, and general makeup."

"You think the owner filched the art and set the fire?"

Rhett ground his teeth. "I couldn't prove a thing."

"But you mentioned your theory to the police."

"I did, but the owner was out of town, nowhere near the scene. I was their fall guy, but they never charged me."

"How do you handle the rumors?"

He shrugged. "You make do."

Would I get through this latest mess with the same *esprit de corps*?

"Did you rescue the recipe box?" I asked.

"I did. It was singed but the recipes were safe." Rhett glanced at my fireplace, which would go unused until late fall. "I still have issues with fire. I can handle a campfire, and I cook over a hot flame, but sitting by a fire inside a house? Not my thing. Ergo, the therapist." He waved a hand, dismissing the conversation. "Want to hear a chef's joke?"

"Is it better than the fishing one you told Katie the other day?" I teased.

"You decide. Long ago, a baker called Richard the Pourer, whose job it was to pour the dough mixture in the making of sausage rolls, noted that he was running low on one of the necessary spices. He sent his apprentice to the store to buy more. Upon arriving at the shop, however, the apprentice forgot the name of the ingredient. So he said to the shopkeeper that it was: *"For Richard the Pourer, for batter for wurst."*

I groaned. "I get it. Wurst . . . sausage. For better or worse, like in marriage vows. Ho-ho." I slapped my knee with exaggeration. "Okay, we've established that you're not destined to become a stand-up comedian."

He chuckled. "I've got a million of 'em. Chefs are funny."

"Funny . . . odd, you mean."

A quiet calm settled between us.

I took a bite of my salad. The dressing was tongue-tingling good. "What do you like to do on your days off?"

"Not question suspects like you."

I shook a finger. "Okay, Aunt Vera has been blabbing."

"She's worried. She said she was getting vibes that you're in danger."

"What's new? She picks up vibes at the shop, too."

"So do I."

I groaned. "Uh-uh, we're not going there. No hoodoo nonsense out of you."

"You think the spiritual world is hoodoo?"

"I didn't say—"

Tigger leaped onto the Ching table and batted the necklace around the Lucky Cat's neck.

Spooked, I scrambled to my feet and charged him. "Okay, that's it, mister." When I snared him, I surprised myself by saying, "Rhett, let's take a walk."

After we cleaned up the remains of dinner, I grabbed a shawl from the closet, and we headed outside. In the time it took us to eat dinner, people had populated the beach. A couple, linked arm-in-arm, strolled barefoot in the opposite direction. A half-dozen teens played Frisbee with a glow-in-the-dark disk. A family with flashlights wandered the shore gazing at the multiple sandcastles. In two days, the official Sandcastle Festival competition would begin. Hopefully Desiree's murder would be solved, despite Cinnamon's warning that the investigation could go on for years, and the people of Crystal Cove would be able to put the horror of the murder behind them and enjoy the festivities.

Rhett found a seashell and tossed it repeatedly into the air as we ambled side by side. "I love the sea," he said.

The moon, which hovered close to the horizon, cast a long swath of light across the water and straight to our feet.

"I used to love it," I said. "When I was little, I would play at the beach every day. I thought the moon's rays followed me wherever I went until . . ." I gazed out at the ocean, the waves gentler at night than at any other time of the day. "After my husband died, spending time on the beach didn't seem so important. Tragedy always felt a breath away. I came back to Crystal Cove and thought I might discover the joy I used to know, but when I found Desiree—"

Rhett slung an arm around my shoulder and drew me closer. "Shh." He kissed the side of my head. "No more negative thoughts tonight. It's time to concentrate on your future."

"My aunt coached you."

"She means well, Jenna. She loves you. And I—" He stopped walking and gripped my shoulders. He looked as if he wanted to kiss me but wasn't sure what my response would be.

Heck, I wasn't sure what my reaction would be either.

Rhett tucked the tip of his finger beneath my chin. "You're safe with me. I won't do a thing until you're ready. Do you understand? Nod if you do."

I obeyed.

Later that night, shards of images peppered my dreams. Desiree, David, surfers, sandcastles. A hook tore a giant mermaid to shreds. A chainsaw, axe, and sledgehammer found their way into the mix. Cash swirled in a frenzy around everything. I woke in a sweat and vowed never to eat spare ribs again. I was lying, of course. The wine was probably the culprit.

The next morning, as I downed a breakfast of granola and fresh fruit, one question about my nightmare plagued me. Did the images in my nightmare, if pieced together like a jigsaw puzzle, actually paint the answer to murder?

Chapter 23

THAT AFTERNOON, WHEN store traffic was at a lull, I nestled into one of the overstuffed chairs with a couple of cookbooks. No one needed me. My aunt was busy at the vintage table giving a zaftig woman a tarot card reading; a woman and her towheaded twins played hide-and-seek with Tigger; and Bailey stood with a younger customer, touting *The Food Allergy Mama's Baking Book,* a terrific cookbook with commonplace recipes made with foods every cook ought to have in her cupboard.

With the memory of last night's picnic still fresh in my mind, I opened my two books, *Bobby Flay's Grill It!* and Steve Raichlen's *Barbecue! Bible: Sauces, Rubs, and Marinades, Bastes, Butters, and Glazes,* and compared dry rub recipes. As I read, I caught myself humming "Zing! Went the Strings of My Heart." I glanced around to see if anyone else had heard me. No one seemed to have. I returned to my humming.

Minutes later, the front door opened and a man said, "Hey, all."

Recognizing Rhett's voice, I snapped to attention. Had

my musings lured him here? Despite my disavowal of the supernatural, my stomach did a delightful somersault at the prospect. I eyed the cookbooks in my lap, and worried that Rhett might get the wrong idea—so what if I was interested in dry rubs all of a sudden?—I clambered out of the chair and deposited the cookbooks by the register. Trying to act nonchalant, I swirled around and rested an elbow on the counter. Corners of the cookbooks poked through my lacy summer sweater. *Yow.* "Hello, Rhett."

"Hi, yourself." He sauntered toward me carrying a bouquet of daisies.

"Yoo-hoo." Katie breezed down the hallway with a plateful of what smelled like snickerdoodle cookies, rich with cinnamon. "Sweets for the sweets," she announced but stopped when she spied Rhett. Her gaze hopscotched from his face, to the flowers, to me.

Rhett thrust the daisies at me. "These are for you."

When I had awakened this morning, I could still feel the hint of last night's parting kiss on my forehead. Now, for some crazy reason, I wanted him to grab me in his arms and kiss me full on. Where was a cold shower when I needed one? "Nice," I said, my tone reserved and ultra-proper.

Katie whistled under her breath.

I threw her a snarky look. "The store can always use a bit of sunshine."

"No, I meant . . ." Rhett tilted his head and appraised me, a twinkle in his eyes. "Yes, they're for the store. They need water."

"They're beautiful." I took the bouquet from him, filled a pitcher from the stockroom with water—making a mental note to have a supply of pretty crystal vases for future bouquets— and I set the flowers on the counter beside the cookbooks. "What brings you here?"

Rhett jammed his hands into his jeans pockets. "It's my day off. I was hoping you might go on another date with me."

"*Another*," Katie said. "Hoo-boy. I knew it. I'm picking up vibes like Vera now."

"You are not," I said.

"When was your first date?"

"We haven't had—"

"Last night," my aunt said as she cruised to the counter, her tarot reading complete.

Bailey left her customer and crowded Aunt Vera. "Which is it?" She eyed my aunt and me.

Rhett stood so close I detected his tropical suntan lotion scent, the same that lingered in my cottage. Delicious.

"We had a picnic last night," I said.

"A picnic?" Katie teased. "Ooh."

"Ooh, yourself."

"But you spent the evening with *us*," Bailey argued.

"Yes . . ." I snatched a cookie from Katie's offering and popped it into my mouth. Soft, buttery, and perfect.

"Fess up," Bailey demanded.

I explained how Rhett had come to check up on me and saved me from having to watch a repeat of *Radical Cake Battle*.

Katie snapped her fingers. "I saw that show finally. Mama was viewing it when I got home."

Whew. At least the topic had steered away from Rhett and me and, well, *us*.

"That was a years-old repeat," Katie went on. "What a mishmash all of those wannabe chefs made of the water theme. Did you see the lighthouse that the pint-sized woman made? It was tilting as badly as the Tower of Pisa. And the Triton King of the Sea one? Or the underwater volcano? I know *Radical Cake Battle* is an art form, but c'mon. One show does not a chef make. Why do so many of these shows allow complete hacks to compete? They aren't all tried-and-tested chefs." She thumped her chest. "Though I should talk. I only had one employer before you gave me my break."

"And luckily she did," Rhett said. "That fish cassoulet with the piping of mustard-laced mashed potatoes that you made for lunch today was downright orgasmic."

I gaped.

"What?" he said. "A man's got to eat. I . . ." His eyebrow

rose as dawning struck. "Oh, that's not what I meant to say. What I—"

"It's okay," I said, enjoying his stammering. "Everyone who came into the shop around lunchtime said the same thing. Now where are we going on that date?"

"Well, Katie didn't make any ice cream today."

"Bad Katie," I joshed. "Bad, bad Katie."

Our jolly chef threw her hands up in defense. "Key lime drizzle cake or chocolate truffle deluxe weren't enough dessert choices, Rhett? You ate both."

He grinned a devilish grin that made my knees threaten to give way. "Not when a man has a hankering for freshly made ice cream."

ENTERING TASTE OF Heaven Ice Cream Parlor always buoyed my spirit. The establishment, adorned with royal-blue-and-white-checkered floors, white counters, and arty canvases of ice cream cones and sundaes hanging on the walls, was downright fun. Loud Beach Boys' music played nonstop. The owner, a chunky woman with an angelic face, claimed to have dated one of the Beach Boys and nearly made it to the altar with him, but she would never reveal the singer's name. A jar in the shape of a Little Red Coupe stood on the counter. Each day, the owner encouraged people to entertain a guess as to which singer had been her lover. At five she would pick an entry, say, "Close but no cigar," and would award a free ice cream cone to whomever's name she had drawn. The winner need not be present.

Rhett and I ordered bowls of Chocoholic's Delight—a combination of chocolate ice cream, chocolate chips, and chunks of chocolate cookies—and we settled at the one remaining French café–style table.

"So tell me about Tigger," Rhett said. "When did you get him?"

"He wandered into the shop the day we started redecorating."

"You've got a real love affair going."

"He's cute, all right. Do you have pets?"

"I had a dog. Rufus. A Great Dane. He passed away last year."

What could I say? *Sorry* never quite covered the loss of a furry friend.

"He was a good companion. Liked to take walks." Rhett's eyes grew moist, but he forced a smile. "Never could get him to go kayaking with me."

"Gee, big surprise, although I bet you could have enticed him onto a sailboat."

"Speaking of sailboats."

"You want to know about my husband and how he died," I blurted out.

"No." Rhett shook his head. "It's none of my business. I was going to ask if you wanted to go sailing sometime."

"Shoot," I muttered.

"Does that mean no?"

"No." I set my spoon down with a clank. "I apologize. Everyone in the world has asked me the same question about David over the past two years. If he was so inexperienced, why did he go out alone?"

"You don't have to talk about it unless you feel the need to."

My mouth had turned as dry as sandpaper and yet I did want to talk about David. I didn't want secrets with Rhett. I wanted him to know everything about me, down to my odd fetish for the smell of a new book. "What have you heard so far?"

"*Nada*. Not a word."

"Not from my Aunt Vera?"

"She's as quiet as a clam." Rhett held up his hand, swearing to his statement.

"David had taken a few sailing lessons," I began. "He wanted to try a solo run. He said it was a rite of passage. He needed to prove himself. Jumping out of a perfectly good airplane wasn't enough."

"He did that?"

"We both did. With instructors strapped to our backs." I

would never forget the blast of air and the gut-gasping thrill of seeing land over thirteen thousand feet below. "But David wanted more thrills. He was a risk taker. He wanted to face swells on the high seas. He had all the right equipment. He was a good swimmer." Something twinged in my chest. "All I can think is the boat must have rocked hard and he hit his head before falling overboard. I'll never know what happened."

Cascades of female laughter filled the air. I cut a look at the pair of women by the register. Cinnamon tried to steady her companion's tilting double-decker ice cream cone. "Help," she cried and laughed harder. Her friend, who was wearing an outfit similar to a policeman's uniform but clearly unofficial, propped the ice cream up with her fingers.

The owner skirted around the counter wielding a Tupperware garbage bin. "Let's dump that one, ladies, and start over."

With Cinnamon in such a cheerful mood, an idea came to me. I didn't want to continue discussing the end of David's life. Maybe now was as good a time as any to clear the air with our police chief. Without asking Rhett's permission, I rose from my chair and hailed Cinnamon.

She signaled to give her a second.

As I hunkered down in my chair, Rhett stood up, his eyes as hard as rock candy.

"What's wrong?" I reached for his hand.

He stuffed it into his pocket. "I can't stay."

"Why not?"

He hitched his head toward Cinnamon. "She and I don't see eye to eye. I keep my distance."

"Why?" I was baffled. Just yesterday, when discussing his clerk, Joey, he had paid Cinnamon a compliment.

A long moment passed. Finally Rhett said, "We were dating when The Grotto burned down."

My heart snagged. He and Cinnamon had dated? For how long?

"She suspected me of the deed."

"Didn't you tell her what you've told me?"

"Sure I did. She could never convince herself I didn't do it. Let's just say it put a crimp in our relationship."

"But the evidence. The missing art."

"Wasn't enough for her. So much for love and trust." He pinched his lips together as if deciding whether to say more. He didn't. He left his ice cream and strode out of the shop. As the door closed, a chime played the first seven notes of "Good Vibrations."

The irony was not lost on me. I leaned back in my chair, upset with myself for not knowing more of Rhett's story before I'd asked Cinnamon to join us. How insensitive could I be? Luckily ice cream was good for two things: to celebrate a joyous occasion or to drown one's sorrows. I finished mine and his.

A minute later, Cinnamon and her colleague, whom she introduced as a college intern helping out for the summer, joined me at the table. "Thanks for the invite since there's no room elsewhere," Cinnamon said. "Where did Rhett go?"

I cocked my head. She wasn't stupid. I could tell by her gaze that she knew she had scared him away. In fact, she looked exultant. "He's innocent."

"Here we go." Cinnamon sighed. "Now you're going to fight his battles, too? He's free. Isn't that enough?"

"Freedom from suspicion matters, too."

Cinnamon inhaled sharply; her nose thinned.

"Did you track down Anton d'Stang?" I asked, gearing the topic back to my personal problem. "I told you, I think he killed Desiree. He might have killed Gigi Goode."

"He didn't kill her."

"How can you be so sure?"

"Because Gigi Goode has returned."

I gaped. "She's not dead?"

"She's alive and well." Cinnamon licked the lemon sorbet that dribbled down the sides of her cone. "She admitted that living in hiding doesn't suit her. She brought back everything she stole, and she entered a rehab program at the Y in Santa Cruz. In addition, I've given her community service, working with some of the local kids."

"Then back to Anton. Did you locate him?"

Cinnamon stood and laid the rest of her cone in Rhett's empty bowl.

I rose, as well. "Without a confirmed suspect, suspicions linger."

"Yes, they do."

There it was, her true opinion, out in the open. She believed I was guilty until proven innocent. Well, I wasn't going to remain her number one suspect, not as long as I had eyes, ears, and a brain.

Chapter 24

FUELED BY ANGER and a chocolate-sugar rush, I jogged back to The Cookbook Nook. Someone had moved the furniture and relocated the bookshelves to the far side of the space. In their place stood tables and chairs from the café and a portable cooking station preset with food and cooking utensils. Judy Garland, singing "Get Happy," blasted from a CD player. Had someone put that particular song on for my benefit? What had happened to the mix of food-themed songs Katie had created?

"What's going on?" I said.

"Have you forgotten?" Aunt Vera waltzed from chair to chair setting out recipe cards. "At five P.M., less than ten minutes away, we have our first cooking class. Well, our guests won't actually be cooking yet. We're waiting for our license. But too-ra-loo, we're having a tasting."

"Katie's made some deliriously good food." Bailey followed in my aunt's wake and placed teensy measuring cups on the chairs. "Each participant will receive a recipe card for deviled eggs with shrimp and dill and a cute measuring cup." She jiggled one. "We have twenty participants signed up."

"And I'm one of them," a man said.

I swiveled toward the door. Rhett entered, hair tousled, hands jammed into his jeans pockets. He didn't scowl at me, which I took as a good sign. Maybe he didn't hold me accountable for Cinnamon's presence at the ice cream store. He came over to me and whispered, "I'm sorry about earlier."

"Me, too. I had no idea. If it makes you feel better, I defended you."

"You didn't have to do that."

"I wanted to. I don't believe in bullying. Cinnamon's mother might have raised her, but my father was her mentor. She knows to get the facts before rushing to judgment."

"She didn't rush—"

I put my finger to his lips.

He kissed my finger, and a delicious shiver ran through me to my toes.

"Places, everyone." Aunt Vera clapped her hands. "Our students are arriving."

I was surprised to see two of the three women who had accompanied Pepper into the shop the other day—the pretty one who preferred floral patterns, telling by the sundress she wore, and the skinny one who had donned yet another shapeless beaded sweater with capris that made her calves look as thin as pencils. Did they come to make trouble? The nuisance with the frowsy hair was nowhere to be seen, thank heavens. A pair of moms that I recognized, sans children, sat down at one of the tables and praised the recipe card and mini–measuring cup, which they called party favors. I liked that. I wanted our customers to think of our shop as a fun destination. A dozen more people, including my father and the reporter, Tito Martinez, wandered in and took seats. What was Tito doing here? Had he come to give us a nasty write-up?

Bad, Jenna. Do not always think the worst.

Katie rushed in with preparations and took her place behind the portable cooking station. "Welcome, everyone." She introduced herself and held up a cluster of beautiful appetizer cookbooks, including *Small Bites* and *Bite for Bite,* tasty little books filled with hundreds of recipes. "Let's start with something easy tonight. We'll give you a sampling of what fabulous things you can do with a few simple ingredients. For example, these crispy chorizo quesadillas and serrano-rolled asparagus, or this mini-plate of pasta with melted Brie, onion, and spinach." She held up display plates. "And we'll also make my grandmother's version of deviled eggs. You will find that recipe on your chairs."

The crowd *oohed.*

"Boring," Tito said.

"Shush." Aunt Vera thwacked him on the shoulder.

A flash of red in the parking lot caught my eye. Sabrina, wearing a halter dress and clutching a number of shopping bags, ascended the stairs to her trailer.

"Psst. Come with me." Bailey grasped my elbow and dragged me outside. "We've got to talk." She shepherded me out of sight from our customers.

"What's with all the secrecy? Are you sick? Yesterday you carried a load on your shoulders. I meant to ask you last night when we went out. Does it have to do with the doctor's appointment?"

"Forget that. My mother has been investigating on your behalf."

"Oh, no. I can't pay her."

"She doesn't want payment. She loves you like a daughter. More than she loves me."

"Whoa. Why the pity party?"

"I'm not—" Bailey coughed. "It's nothing."

I didn't believe her. Her eyes looked puffy and swollen. Had she been crying?

"Back to Mom," Bailey said. "She did some searching into Sabrina Divine's life after we trash-talked her at brunch. Love and intrigue always pique my mother's interest. Anyway, remember how the bartender at the Chill Zone told you Desiree and Sabrina argued, and Desiree waggled a bottle of pills at Sabrina? Turns out, good old Sabrina did a couple of stints in drug rehab, but her visits were kept hush-hush."

When I ran into Sabrina the morning I found Desiree dead, she admitted to having passed out the night before. A friend in college had a drug problem. She hadn't been able to keep current with her classes. She had battled anorexia. In the end, she had given up her career plans to become a lawyer and took a job slinging hash. Had Sabrina settled for being Desiree's assistant because she couldn't manage a career of her own?

"What if Sabrina was relapsing?" Bailey said. "What if Desiree told her to get clean or she'd fire her?"

A trailer door slammed.

Sabrina jogged down the stairs, bouncing car keys in her hand. She headed toward Desiree's white Mercedes and executed a happier-than-happy twirl. I squeezed Bailey's arm, signaled I would learn the truth, and hurried across the parking lot.

"Hey, Sabrina, hold up," I said. "Why the big grin?"

"My boyfriend in L.A. contacted me." She tweeted the unlock car door button. "He never wanted to break up with me. The call I received the night . . ." She hesitated, swallowed hard. "*That* night." The night her sister died. "It must have been a prank call. He has all sorts of friends—jerks—who don't like me."

"Because of your drug problem?"

Sabrina jolted to a stop. "Well, aren't you a primo snoop." I waited.

"Fine, yes, I used to do drugs. But I gave them up. I've been clean for six months. Everybody knows that."

"And yet the night your sister was murdered, you went back to the trailer with Mackenzie, and soon after, you *passed out*. Your words."

"I had a drink. I was upset with my boyfriend. I needed to take the edge off."

"Desiree saw you at the bar. You argued."

"How do you know that?" Sabrina worked her lip between her teeth. "That wicked bartender must have seen us near the ladies' room." She slumped into a hip. "Desiree was missing a bottle of sleeping pills. She thought I took them. As if they would give me a high. I told her to stop hounding me."

"Did she threaten to fire you?"

"No."

"Maybe she warned you that she would cut you out of her will."

Sabrina choked out a laugh. "What will? She gave all her money to charity, didn't you hear?"

"Which charity?"

"Homeless women. Desiree was all about causes."

During college Desiree had participated in walks to fight cancer, diabetes, and all sorts of other diseases. "Retrace your steps the night Desiree died."

"Why should I? You're not the police."

"Call me a concerned citizen."

Sabrina huffed. "I got the phone call from a guy I thought was my boyfriend—the prank phone call—and he dumped me. I felt so betrayed. I loved him so much. I went to the bar for one drink. Gigi claimed the Chill Zone had the best Hurricanes. I felt as if I were caught in one."

"You ran into your sister."

"Uh-uh, she ran into me. Literally. Bam!" Sabrina smacked her hand against the car. "Desiree's face went livid when she realized I was there. She accused me of stealing her pills. For your information, I have never stolen a thing in my life. Not one thing." Tears brimmed in Sabrina's eyes. "I muscled her down the hall. We exchanged words. I said everybody knew I used to do drugs. Anybody could have stolen that stupid Tiffany's pill case of hers. Just to make me look bad in her eyes."

I thought of Katie and the treasure trove she had found hidden in Gigi Goode's hairstyling kit: her grandfather's watch, a *fancy-schmancy* pill case, and more. Gigi had denied taking anything of Desiree's. She was a liar.

"Then Desiree saw Anton," Sabrina continued. "Talk about a blast from the past. She went off with him to a booth." She hooked a finger over her shoulder, as if the booth were right behind her. "They acted real cozy. That's when

I saw J.P. stalking her. He sidled up to me at the bar, all angry and bitter. I told him to grow up. Desiree loved him, not Anton, but he didn't believe me. He settled onto a stool and started calling her on his cell phone. Over and over. A while later, Mackenzie joined me. He said he'd hoped to find Gigi there, but he didn't. 'Any port in the storm,' I joshed. When the drink hit me and I started to feel sleepy, Mac offered to drive me back to the trailer. I said, 'Sure.' One thing led to another. I ended up in his trailer, not mine." She shook her head. "I'm not sure what we did. He must have been good, right? I mean, he's a hunk. And . . . And . . ." She raised her hand to her mouth and bit into her forefinger as if she wanted to keep herself from screaming. "The next day, when J.P. told me what had happened—"

"He accosted you in the parking lot. He tried to take something from your purse. Did he think you had the sleeping pills? Was he accusing you of drugging Desiree so you could lure her to the beach?"

"What? No." She choked out a laugh. "J.P. What a joke. I've got the goods on him."

"What do you mean?"

"From the get-go, I didn't trust him. He breezed into my sister's life a few months ago claiming to be this *fabuloso* director. I knew a phony when I met one, but I didn't do anything about it until he started to weasel his way into Des's life. A work friend was one thing. A brother-in-law would be another."

"Brother-in-law?"

"Yeah, they recently got engaged. Desiree told me the day we arrived in Crystal Cove. No engagement ring. J.P. can be cheap." Sabrina brandished her hand. "I was worried that she'd go through with it, so I hired a detective via the Internet, and guess what I found out the morning Desiree was killed? J.P., big surprise, is not who he claims to be."

"He's not?"

"He's one of those identity thief guys. Well, not the way you understand it. He doesn't steal credit cards and charge up a storm, but he's not from Florida."

"Where's he from?"

"California. See, he worked up a bogus résumé and said he directed all these defunct shows in Florida that some deceased guy named John Paul Hessman did, and he cobbled together a reel. It's easy to do nowadays with all the film footage on the Web. My boyfriend did it. His actor's demo reel looks totally legit, but it's pieced together with bits he did at regional theater."

"Stay on target . . . J.P."

"I have proof." Sabrina rummaged in her purse and withdrew a photograph. "You were right the other day. J.P. tried to get his hands on this. I texted him that I had it. I wasn't ready to show you because . . . Because I thought I might need something to—"

"Blackmail him with?"

"Look at this dude." In the snapshot, J.P., teenaged, tanned and half-naked, clad in low-slung denim shorts and flip-flops, posed with a fiery-themed surfboard. "His real name is Jake. He participated in a local surfing competition. To become J.P., he changed his hair and added the tiger and vine tattoos. The whole ball of wax. Downright creepy, if you ask me."

"He surfs?"

"What California boy doesn't?"

Was he the surfer that was floating on the ocean when I found Desiree's body? Was he the surfer that had ogled me the other morning?

I said, "Did you tell Desiree you were investigating J.P.?"

Sabrina shook her head.

"Did you dun him for money? Is that how you have extra cash for all your shopping sprees?"

"How dare you. I earn a salary. I told J.P. I had proof, hoping he would bolt. Get out of our lives. Leave Desiree alone. I was a day late."

My core vibrated with tension. What if Desiree had found out about J.P.'s ruse on her own? What if she had threatened to expose him? What if J.P. had stopped her before she could?

Chapter 25

THOUGHTS WHIZZED THROUGH my mind as I entered The Cookbook Nook. If I called Cinnamon, would she take me seriously? Would she arrest J.P.? On what charge, impersonation?

Katie beckoned Rhett to the portable cooking station. "And now," she said in midspeech, while raising her arms overhead, "I'm thrilled to announce that next week, we'll have our first guest chef. The one, the incomparable, Rhett Jackson."

All of the guests applauded, except Tito, who stood off by himself snapping quick photographs of pages in a cookbook. Telling by the size of the book and its location, Tito had snagged a copy of *Fiesta at Rick's: Fabulous Food for Great Times with Friends*. I couldn't see the feisty reporter having enough friends for a classic Mexican mole fiesta for twenty-four. Was he trying to scale down the enchilada Suizas recipe, a creamy yet spicy chicken combination, so he could palm it off as his own? I'd have to keep my eye on him, the sneak.

Trying not to draw attention to myself, I tiptoed behind the audience.

"Psst." Bailey signaled me from her spot by the stockroom

door. I scurried to her. "Take these." She offered me her plate of appetizers. "I can't finish the quesadillas, but they're delicious. The chorizo makes them zing."

"Not now." I skirted around her, hurried into the stockroom to my purse, and fished out my cell phone.

Bailey pivoted and propped her back against the archway. "You found out something. Spill."

I dialed the precinct and asked for Cinnamon. The clerk informed me she was indisposed.

"Why are you calling her?" Bailey demanded.

I retrieved the business card Cinnamon had given me, stabbed in her mobile number, and reached a recording. Frustrated but not defeated, in a last-ditch effort, I sent her a text message: *Must talk. Urgent.*

My aunt entered the stockroom. "Jenna, is everything all right?"

My father arrived on her heels. "What's gotten into you?"

"She just faced off with Sabrina Divine in the parking lot," Bailey said. "Is she the killer?"

"No." I told them about J.P. being an impostor. "That gives him motive. His career would be over if Desiree revealed his secret."

Aunt Vera clucked. "Would that really matter in Hollywood?"

"A lie is a lie."

"But Sabrina found out about him, not Desiree," Bailey argued.

"Call Cinnamon," my father ordered.

"I already did. I left her a message and texted her."

"Good girl."

"But she's not responding."

Aunt Vera said, "I know where to find her. Come with me."

"Vera," my father cautioned.

"Cary, it's our civic duty."

My father protested that telephone and text messages were enough, but my aunt prodded me out of the stockroom.

"Don't worry about anything here," Bailey said. "I'll close up."

"I'm driving." I hurried ahead of my aunt across the parking lot. She was a notoriously bad driver. She tended to drift into a meditative state when she got behind the wheel. "Where are we going?"

"The aquarium."

"Isn't that where the Coastal Concern is having its meeting?"

"Cinnamon is a strong advocate."

As I climbed into my VW bug, I spied Sabrina standing at the top of the stairs facing Mackenzie's trailer door. The door opened. Mackenzie, still wearing his white spa uniform, grinned. Sabrina palmed his chest and pushed past him.

"What's wrong, dear?" Aunt Vera said as she buckled her seat belt. "Why aren't you starting the car?"

"Did you see that?" I ground the key in the ignition. The car spluttered to life.

"See what?"

"Sabrina and Mackenzie," I said, my curiosity revving like the VW's engine. "Seconds ago, she told me how excited she was to be reuniting with her boyfriend in L.A., but she just plowed into the trailer with Mackenzie."

"Perhaps she wants to share the good news."

I drummed the steering wheel. "Am I being stupid? Did Sabrina lie about J.P. to mess with my head? The other day, I wondered whether she and Mackenzie had joined forces."

"Why would they?"

"Sabrina claimed her sister donated her estate to a homeless women's charity. What if that was a lie, too?"

THE CRYSTAL COVE Coastal Concern, or the Four C's as the locals dubbed it, met regularly in the Aquarium by the Sea, a beautiful building with floor-to-ceiling windows and a wave-shaped roof. An artist had carved images of seahorses, manta rays, sharks, and more into the stone sections of the edifice. A moat of steadily flowing water and exotic gardens surrounded the site. The widow who had donated the money for the aquarium took great pride in offering exhibits that expanded the mind. Above the front entrance, she had posted her favorite quote by Plutarch: "The mind is not a vessel to be filled but a fire to be kindled."

Even at dusk, the aquarium teemed with visitors. My aunt clutched my elbow and guided me past the crowd to the cream-and-aqua-colored auditorium at the rear of the building. At least fifty people occupied the theater's loge seats. On the raised stage, a man I dubbed Nature Guy—tanned, lean, and brimming with passion for the cause—pounded a gavel on the podium. On the giant-sized movie screen behind him blazed the logo for the Four C's, a quadruplet of dolphins arcing through gold hoops. If I had been in charge of the ad campaign, I would have added a series of waves below the hoops. Icons of water invariably inspired people.

I spotted Cinnamon Pritchett sitting by herself and started for her, but my aunt tugged my elbow and forced me to settle onto a chair.

"Cinnamon will not take kindly to you foisting your opinion on her before the meeting," my aunt whispered. "Be patient. No one's going anywhere. Besides, it'll do your soul good to know what is going on around our community."

Our community. The words brought a smile to my lips. Until now, I hadn't fully appreciated the fact that I was, indeed, a Crystal Cove resident. If only I could put the horror of Desiree's death behind me.

Nature Guy started the meeting by saying, "The job of environmental stewardship of the coast is never done."

For a half hour, he presented slides showing the positive changes to our coastline—the cleanup of the beaches made possible through grants and the growth in some species of fish, thanks to policies that fined polluters. When Nature Guy concluded and opened the floor to questions, I was surprised to find myself applauding louder than most. I couldn't believe how stirred I was to become part of the

solution to preserve the area. A few heated discussions followed, most dealing with a proposed housing development
that might erode shores south of Crystal Cove. Nothing was
resolved, but Nature Guy promised, with fervor, that the
committee would be looking into everything.

"And now," he said, flashing his pearly whites, "bever-
ages and all-natural cookies will be served on the courtyard
abutting the auditorium. Meeting adjourned."

I hurried from the room, dashed across the patio, past
the glorious fountain with streams of water shooting straight
into the air, and caught up to Cinnamon by a buffet stocked
with sweets, coffee, tea, and water. Not wanting to act as if
I were hounding her, I seized a nubby cookie and bit into it.
Heavy with honey and quite chewy. A recipe card was available for a dollar donation. I paid the buck and stowed the
card in my purse. Between bites, I said, "Fancy meeting you
here, Chief Pritchett."

She offered a wry smile. "Well, well."

"Say, did you get my text message?" I sounded casual
and breezy. If I were in a commercial, a wisp of wind would
blow through my hair and prisms of light would gleam in
my eyes.

"Sorry, can't say I did." Cinnamon retrieved her cell
phone from her pocket and glanced at the readout. My message fell at the bottom of a long list of texts. "*Must talk.
Urgent,*" she recited. "That's certainly cryptic. Does this
have anything to do with your interrogating the bartender
at the Chill Zone?"

I felt my face flush.

The corners of her mouth curved up. "On one of our
previous telephone calls and again at Taste of Heaven, you
neglected to mention your *tête-à-tête* with the enchanting
Cleopatra."

I scoffed. "That can't be her real name."

"No, it's Brandy, but she looks like—"

"Cleopatra," we said together.

A pregnant pause occurred. I tried to assess the impact

of my transgression. Cinnamon didn't seem mad. Heck, I had told her everything I had learned to date, hadn't I? Perhaps with our in-sync Cleopatra moment, we had connected on a sisters-of-the-world level.

"I'm sorry. I meant to tell you."

"But we locked horns earlier, so you didn't. Actually, I'm sort of pleased. You got the bartender thinking. She remembered things she hadn't thought to tell me before. Her account stirred something in my mind, so I reviewed Desiree Divine's phone records."

"You hadn't done that y—" I stopped short of saying *yet* and sealed my lips. I did not . . . NOT . . . need to aggravate our chief of police. "What did you find out?"

"The phone call that Desiree received the night she died originated from the bar's pay phone."

"Aha. J.P. called her and lied about it."

"Why would you suspect that?"

"He's a phony." I told her everything that Sabrina had shared about J.P. Hessman. The fake résumé. The surfer photograph. The engagement to Desiree, *sans* ring. I didn't add that I thought J.P. might have been the surfer on the ocean the morning I discovered Desiree's body. Cinnamon could make her own assumption. "If Desiree learned the truth and confronted him—"

"But Desiree isn't the one who figured out the ruse. Sabrina did and she kept it to herself," Cinnamon said, reiterating the argument Bailey had made earlier. "No, I am not convinced the killer is J.P. Hessman. However, I am convinced that the mermaid theme matters. And the hook. Why the hook? Speaking of which, I believe you're off the hook."

"Truly?" My heart inflated with hope.

"Everything we have is circumstantial, and honestly, I don't believe you would be going to all this trouble to prove a case otherwise."

I whipped out my iPhone and held it up. "May I memorialize this moment?"

"Sure." Cinnamon grinned.

I snapped a picture of her with the fountain and building in the background. "What about your mother and her quest to convict me?"

"I know my mother can be a bulldozer, but she means well."

I did my best not to snort. Pepper Pritchett did not mean well. She would *never* mean well, because she was downright, well, *mean*. "So we're back to square one."

"Not we."

"You." I polished off my cookie and brushed crumbs off my hands. "One question."

"Shoot."

"Sabrina Divine mentioned that Desiree donated her estate to a homeless women's shelter. Is that true?"

"Yes."

"Wow." Score one for Sabrina. Or lose one. What if she actually knew about Desiree's bequest before Desiree died? How mad would that have made her? "One more question. Any word from Anton d'Stang?"

Cinnamon frowned.

Oops. I had overstepped. Without another word, I bade her good night.

WHEN I ARRIVED home, I realized I was too keyed up to sleep. A bath, a glass of wine, and a book sounded heavenly, but when I was soaking in the tub, I couldn't relax; I couldn't read. What I really needed was a project. I didn't have the concentration to paint, but I was hungry, having passed on the chorizo quesadillas at The Cookbook Nook. And though I had indulged in a cookie at the Four C's meeting, I craved sweets.

I climbed out of the tub, dried off and applied a vanilla-scented lotion, and threw on an old college T-shirt and cutoff jeans. In the kitchen, I poured myself a glass of pinot grigio and whipped open *The Joy of Cooking*. I withdrew the three-by-five cards Katie had stowed at the back and spied one with the title: *Savory Cheese Cookies*. Beside the title,

Katie had written: *Zesty*. Magically my sweet tooth disappeared. I gauged whether my cupboards and refrigerator held the seven ingredients. They did. Could I swing it? Was making a seven-ingredient recipe that much harder than a five-ingredient recipe?

Tigger, who was delighted that I was roused to do something other than leave my little one-room flat and, thus, ignore him, bolted around the cottage, leaping from the floor to the tops of furniture.

"Cool it, wild thing," I said, but he didn't listen. "Fine. You break something, you own it. Your fanny is on the line, you hear me?" I switched on Judy Garland's *Over the Rainbow: 24 Greatest Hits*, took a sip of my wine, and set to work. I pulled a bowl and measuring cup from the cabinet, retrieved a set of decorative measuring spoons—the same that we sold at the store—and fetched the ingredients: Cheddar cheese, flour, butter, sugar, baking powder, cayenne pepper, and salt. I set the heat on the oven and began mixing, grating, and whisking.

While listening to "Over the Rainbow," a notion niggled the edges of my mind. Not about lullabies or blue skies or dreams. About murder. Why? Had something Cinnamon said at the meeting or something Aunt Vera mentioned on the drive home triggered the notion? *Think, Jenna, think. Create a mental storyboard.* Except how could I? My mind was cluttered.

Forcing my mind to go blank, I followed baking instructions to the letter. I rolled out the dough, cut it into squares, and placed them inches apart on the cookie sheet.

As I slid the sheet into the oven, a new thought zinged into my mind. Cinnamon said, "*Why* the hook?" but that wasn't what was important. The real question was *what* was the hook? What was the motive? What had incited the murderer on that day, at that hour, in that way, to kill Desiree?

The word *hook* had so many meanings. A hook was a snare to catch someone. A hook, in advertising and publishing, was something to attract someone or lure them. A hook in music was a pleasing refrain, one that could be easily remembered. And at sea, a hook was the crest of a wave that was about to break.

Why the hook?

As I waited for the cookies to bake, I decided to address Desiree's murder suspect list as I would start a day at Taylor & Squibb, by writing down random thoughts about projects. Three to five words each, to stir my imagination. But this time, I would turn that concept on its ear.

I pulled a sketch pad and sharp pencil from the Ching cabinet, sat at the kitchen table, and began in alphabetical order.

> *Anton d'Stang—talented, powerful, gambler, Svengali, blackmailer. Motive: vengeance?*
> *Gigi Goode—stylist, artist, cagey, strong, big woman. Motive: to keep her penchant for stealing a secret?*
> *J.P. Hessman—phony, director, lover, liar, surfer. Motive: jealousy or self-preservation?*
> *Mackenzie Baxter—handsome, cocky, manipulative, beleaguered employee. Motive: wanted Desiree or Sabrina for himself?*
> *Sabrina Divine—sister, spirited, druggie, needy, second fiddle. Motive: money, spite, or a conspiracy with Mackenzie?*

I reviewed the motives while drawing a simplistic storyboard with stick figure characters. One by one the figures met Desiree. At the Winnebagos. At my shop. At the inn. At the Chill Zone Bar, Desiree argued with J.P., fought with Sabrina, and toyed with Anton while Mackenzie and possibly Gigi looked on. One led her to her death. I sketched the beach and stiffened when I realized the last stick figure I had drawn was me, standing over Desiree's body. I drew a small cartoon bubble and filled in the blank with the words: *I didn't do it.*

I wadded the paper and tossed it on the floor and started a fresh sketch of a mermaid. And then another. And another. I fashioned a hook in each beautiful mouth.

The timer dinged, saving me from myself. Using potholders, I pulled the cheese cookies from the oven.

"Oh, my," I said.

Tigger cha-cha'd around my feet as if to ask: *What's up?*

"They're so deliciously golden, I have to text a picture of them to Katie. She'll be proud."

Tigger meowed.

"Uh-uh. No cookies. Sorry, pal." I raised my cell phone and took a couple of photographs at a distance and close up. As I reviewed the photos, gliding my finger across the screen, I bypassed the first snapshot and landed on the picture that I had taken of Cinnamon at the aquarium. Shimmering light behind her highlighted the fountain and edifice.

"What the heck?" I gazed harder. On the aquarium walls, etchings of mermaids, which I hadn't noticed earlier, swam among the manta rays, sharks, and dolphins. Was that what had stirred me to draw mermaids over and over tonight? I thought of the hook. A mermaid was a type of hook; she was a siren, a lure. Had the killer buried Desiree beneath a mermaid sculpture because she had lured him? Had she hooked him with a promise of devotion? Had she then reneged? J.P., Anton, Mackenzie. Had one of the men been so in love with her that he couldn't let her live if she didn't choose him?

I raced to retrieve my wadded up storyboard.

Crash!

I whipped around. Tigger jumped off the table beside my bed, peeked at the fallen frame of David, and sprang across the floor. He leaped on top of the Ching cabinet.

"Don't!" I screamed.

But my wound-up kitten couldn't stop. He ran headlong into the Lucky Cat. The statue teetered. The necklace swung to and fro. I sprinted. Caught the statue before it toppled. Set it right.

Tigger hurtled to the floor, across the kitchen, and onto the table. He batted the sketches of mermaids.

"Bad kitty," I said, trying to snatch him. He dodged me

and darted beneath the sofa. I crouched to get eye level with him. "What is up with you? Are you mad I won't spoil you with human food? Are you jealous of the fake cat, or are you trying to tell me something?"

Really, Jenna? The cat is communicating? Get real.

I viewed the mermaid sketches on the table. "Wait a sec," I whispered. Maybe the cat *was* trying to tell me something. Maybe he thought I wasn't on the right track and I needed a jolt to my system to wake up. Was the killer a woman instead of a man? Did Sabrina kill her sister? The mermaid was a fantasy creature. Did the mermaid represent the fantastical life that Desiree had created for herself? Had Sabrina been jealous that her sister had won the limelight or had won a man Sabrina loved?

I went one step further. Yesterday, Katie asked if I remembered the pint-sized woman who had crafted a lighthouse cake on the rerun of *Radical Cake Battle*. Could the woman have been Sabrina, perpetuating the seaside theme? I squeezed my eyes together, trying to remember her features. The chef brought to mind a minisized version of Nicole Kidman, complete with red hair and freckles. The total opposite of Sabrina. Not even a talented makeup artist could have changed Sabrina's look that much, not to mention Sabrina had never given the impression that she'd wanted to become a chef. I was on the wrong track.

Tigger poked his face from beneath the sofa.

"It's okay," I said. "Come out. I'm not mad." I crooked a finger. He tiptoed toward me. I gathered him into my arms and stroked his chin and ears. Tears formed in my eyes. How David would have loved the little guy. Maybe that was what Tigger was doing, trying to commune with my sweet, departed husband. Not wanting to plummet into self-pity, I carried the kitten to the stove. I plucked a cookie from the cookie sheet and took a bite. Surprisingly good and salty. I broke a teensy nibble from the edge and offered it to Tigger. He lapped it up. As he licked my thumb and I finger-combed his fur, something new hit me. Something vital.

Hair.

One of the hacks, as Katie had referred to the cooks on *Radical Cake Battle*—a fellow that the show had dubbed Macbeth the Gay Blade—had constructed a Triton King of the Sea cake. Triton was a merman, wasn't he? The Gay Blade had long, oily blond hair. He had wielded an axe in his left hand. The killer was left-handed. So was Anton. Had he changed his look—gone from dark to light, short to long—so he could compete on the show? Anton had fooled me the day Desiree had come to town. I hadn't recognized him; neither had she. Had he entered the *Radical Cake Battle* as a contestant to prove a point? To show her up or embarrass her? The other day, I was wrong when I'd thought a hack could construct the mermaid sculpture that had surrounded Desiree's body; the creation had taken skill.

Adrenaline zipping through me, I flipped on the television, brought up the guide, and searched the Food Network channel for the TV show. A series of them would start at 8 P.M.; none aired now. I switched off the television and ripped out a new sheet of paper from the sketch pad.

I drew an oval and added long, stringy hair, an unkempt beard, and intense eyes. The resulting image looked like a character out of an Elizabethan play. Dirty, feral. *Macbeth* was a play about ambition run amok. How did that fit the scenario with Anton?

I paced the floor, returned to the table, peered again at my drawing, and a flurry of exhilaration rushed through me as I recalled more of the television show. The Gay Blade started out in the same manner as the other contestants, answering questions about himself, talking about the benefactor who was going to make his dreams come true. His career had nowhere to go but up, he said. He didn't have an accent, but Anton, a refined world traveler, could have managed that. Then the contestants hoisted their tools. The camera focused on each one; the microphone picked up their chatter. As the Gay Blade made violent swipes at his cake, he said, *Fantasy was for children. Promises were the lure of a siren. Broken promises demanded retribution.* The audience applauded and hooted their support. Soon the Gay

Blade set aside his axe and worked with his hands to mold the face, eyes, and mouth of the mermaid. As he did, he said: *I need you to obey me.*

I stopped pacing the cottage. I had heard those commanding words. Mackenzie, Desiree's masseur, had said the same thing to me when he had kneaded my back into submission.

What was his last name? Baxter. Mackenzie Baxter. Macbeth. Or *Mac B* as the announcer had dubbed him. He was the Gay Blade, not Anton. I flashed on a conversation with Sabrina. She had said Mackenzie asked Desiree for a chance to be more than a masseur, but Desiree had said, *No go.* At the time, I had imagined Mackenzie wanted to become a producer or director. When I met with J.P. at Latte Luck Café, Mackenzie showed up outside and taunted J.P., who snarled and muttered that Mackenzie thought he knew how to cook. He said Mackenzie had picked apart a couple of Desiree's recipes in her current cookbook, and she got blazing mad.

I pivoted and caught sight of the cookbooks that Aunt Vera had given me stacked on my coffee table. Katie had seen cookbooks in the Winnebago when she went searching for her missing pocket watch. Was Mackenzie's appearance on *Radical Cake Battle* a step toward a career as a chef? Did he pore over Desiree's recipes? Maybe he approached her, the celebrity judge, with a concept. Perhaps she made promises to help him advance his career and then reneged. Was his story, like Macbeth's, about ambition run amok?

I flashed on something else. At the spa, Mackenzie said he aspired to become a *doctor, baker, Indian chief.* At the time, I hadn't thought twice about his phrasing, but in review, I realized those weren't the correct words to the *Tinker Tailor* rhyme. Doctor, *lawyer,* Indian chief were. Was *baker* a slipup, or had Mackenzie said the words on purpose to toy with me? He had fed me information about the police investigation. Had he known I was snooping around? Had he thrown the bag of Baker's Mix at my cottage window as a dare to see if I could figure out his identity?

Had he watched my place to intimidate me, hoping I would cease my personal investigation, or had he stood there trying to screw up his courage to kill me, too?

I backed up a few steps in my thought process. On *Radical Cake Battle* the announcer had referred to Mackenzie as the Gay Blade. Was he gay? If so, why had he hit on Sabrina? Or had he? Sabrina couldn't remember anything from that night. She didn't remember whether they had sex. What if he had drugged her to make her his alibi? That would establish premeditation.

Chapter 26

I PLOPPED ONTO the sofa, scooped Tigger into my arms, and constructed a scenario for the night Desiree died. Mackenzie—Macbeth, Mac B, the Gay Blade—with malice aforethought, went to the Chill Zone Bar. He, not J.P., used the pay phone to call Desiree. He said he needed to talk to her, maybe even threatened her. Desiree told J.P. she had a meeting and raced out of the hotel room. She entered the Chill Zone Bar, but she got sidetracked when she saw Sabrina and then Anton.

Not one to lose momentum, Mackenzie came up with an idea for his alibi. He homed in on Sabrina. Maybe he always carried the date rape drug—what was it called? Rohypnol. I remembered a report that said Rohypnol worked its toxic magic in about fifteen minutes. Could the drug knock a girl out faster if added to alcohol? I pictured Mackenzie sidling up to Sabrina at the bar. He slipped the drug into her drink. In seconds, she grew groggy. Many knew Sabrina had a drug problem. If she remembered anything about that night or if the police detected evidence of drugs in her system later, Mackenzie could claim total innocence. Mackenzie marshaled Sabrina to his black minivan and dumped her inside.

He went back for Desiree, who had finished with Anton and was going in search of J.P., but Mackenzie cut her off. He isolated her in the parking lot. They struggled. Maybe he hit her. Her head could have slammed against the passenger window. At the crime scene, Cinnamon said Desiree had received a blow to the right side of her head. Next, Mackenzie hauled Desiree to the beach and strangled her. The sculpting came easily to him. How many times had he practiced making his Triton merman cake sculpture? In a matter of minutes, he finished the job.

He didn't worry about signs of his having been there. I would bet, if he had preplanned everything, that he knew Old Jake would wipe out evidence. He returned to his van, drove Sabrina to the Winnebago, and woke up beside her in the morning. He pretended that they had screwed their brains out. She was none the wiser and too embarrassed to say anything.

I wanted to telephone Cinnamon and share my theory, but first I needed to corroborate it. Sabrina might not remember everything, but she might recall snippets. I set Tigger on the floor and strode to the laundry basket. I found the skirt I had worn the day Sabrina and I chatted in the parking lot, and I retrieved the business card she had given me. I dialed her number.

Sabrina answered on the first ring. "I can't talk."

Then why the heck did she answer the phone? I hated when people did that. Let the call go to voice mail, for heaven's sake. I heard a male whispering in the background. Maybe her boyfriend had flown up from Los Angeles to make up after their faux dissolution. Did I care if I was interrupting? Not in the least.

I said, "This is important."

Sabrina groaned. "Okay, go ahead. What?"

I told her my theory that Mackenzie Baxter was the Gay Blade. He killed Desiree because she had reneged on a promise to boost his career. He plotted out Desiree's murder and drugged Sabrina to use her as his alibi. "That's why you passed out that night."

She mumbled, "Uh-huh," throughout my spiel, totally disinterested.

"You need to go to the police and tell them anything you can remember. Please say you'll do that, sooner rather than later."

She grunted and said, "Promise."

I disconnected and dialed Cinnamon's cell phone.

"Chief Pritchett," she answered.

"It's Jenna Hart."

"What do you want?" she said, sounding as testy as Sabrina.

"Did I catch you at a bad time?"

"Hang up," a woman shrieked in the background.

"Mother, please, police business comes first, and you—"

"That's not police business. I saw the display. I know who it is. Hang up."

Cinnamon muttered, "Can I call you back, Jenna?"

I told her not to bother. The information I had wouldn't translate well over the phone anyway. I was heading for the precinct. I added that Sabrina Divine was on her way, too. "She has news you'll want to hear."

Cinnamon promised to be on the lookout. I hung up wondering about her family dispute. At least my father and I were getting along. No blowups. No drama. In fact, I saw blue skies ahead for us.

Tigger circled my feet, tail twitching. I checked his water, nuzzled his ears, and said, "Back soon." I grabbed my purse and raced to the front door.

When I opened it, Mackenzie barged inside with Sabrina in tow. Her hands were tied in front of her. Without losing his grip on Sabrina's upper arm, Mackenzie shoved me in the chest. I careened to the floor. Scrambling like a crab, I fumbled to find my footing. I bumped into the sofa.

Using the back of the couch for support, I thrust myself up. "How . . . why . . ."

"You know why, my friend. I heard everything you said to Sabrina."

Shoot. Mackenzie was the man who had been whispering in the background when I'd phoned Sabrina. She had wanted to cut me off at the beginning. Mackenzie must have prodded her to respond, hence her groans and moans.

"Sweet Sabrina and I were on a date," he continued. "I was taking her for a midnight swim, but you interrupted."

A midnight swim that she was not meant to survive, I realized.

"I'm sorry," Sabrina said, rapid-fire. "After we talked in the parking lot, I thought about the night Desiree died. Mackenzie was so friendly. Why? He was never into me. That's when I remembered he had cozied up to my drink at the Chill Zone Bar, and I knew what he'd done. He had dropped in a pill. After talking to you, I went to his Winnebago to confront him—"

"Shut up," Mackenzie ordered.

I didn't need to hear more. I knew what had gone down. Fearing exposure, Mackenzie took Sabrina hostage. While I attended the Four C's meeting to track down Cinnamon, he must have deliberated about what to do with Sabrina. I called as he was carrying out his plan. I dug into my purse for my cell phone.

Mackenzie knocked the phone out of my hand. "Not a chance." He took hold of the front of my lacy sweater and tugged me around the end of the couch. He propelled Sabrina into the sofa. "Stay." She slumped back, her head against the cushion. At the same time, Mackenzie pulled me close. "Now the question is, what to do with you?" His breath reeked of sour food and fury.

"First, you might consider mouthwash and deodorant."

He backhanded me.

My cheek smarted something fierce, but I refused to surrender. "Can't take criticism, huh?"

"Quiet, woman."

"Need me to obey? Need silence to think? Maybe you'd like to go outside? It's real quiet out there."

He growled.

What in the heck was I doing? Why was I provoking him? Because I was downright scared. I needed a weapon. I scrutinized the area beyond Mackenzie. All I saw was a tray of freshly baked cookies. Could I feed him into submission?

Focus, Jenna.

A recipe box. Utensils. Knives. How could I reach a really sharp one of those?

"The police know everything," I lied, wishing Cinnamon would come looking for me when I didn't show up at the precinct but knowing she wouldn't. Her mother would convince her I was a sheep that was crying wolf.

"Sit." Mackenzie heaved me onto the sofa beside Sabrina.

She groped for my hand; I gripped hers as I scanned the room for an item closer than knives to subdue the maniac who paced between the coffee table and us. To my right: the picture frame, a lamp, and the answering machine. To my left: the art easel, paintbrushes, and items on the Ching cabinet. The fire poker wasn't close enough. I would never get that far before Mackenzie attacked.

"Desiree upset you," I said, channeling my therapist's calm tone. If only I could recall the words she had used to hypnotize me.

"What Desiree did was inexcusable," Mackenzie said. "She made a promise. I was supposed to become her partner."

"Partner?"

"We were soul mates."

"No way. You weren't her lover."

"At first, I was."

"But you're gay," I said. "You're nickname was the Gay Blade."

Realization dawned in his eyes. "So that's how you figured out who I was. You saw *Radical Cake Battle.* Well, get this, I'm not gay."

"You're not?"

"The producers wanted different, unusual. They wanted flair. I wanted a chance."

I released Sabrina's hand. "I get it now. You met Desiree on the set. You made a play for her so she would feature you on her show."

"Women, such as Desiree, go for a sex machine." He smirked. His nasty grin turned into a grimace. "But she led me on. First, she hired me as her errand boy. She told me where to go and what to say. To her, I was no more than a puppet. When she discovered I was a licensed masseur—"

"Why are you a masseur?" I asked. That detail had perplexed me.

"An up-and-comer still needs a day job. Desiree added that task to her to-do list. I didn't mind. I enjoy touching a beautiful woman's body."

My skin crawled.

Mackenzie bent forward, hands on his knees, and breathed into our faces with acidic venom. "However, when Desiree withdrew the promise, claiming she couldn't risk putting an unknown like me on her show or her audience might think less of her, she said it all with a smile, and I thought too bad for her. She didn't have a clue what I would do if crossed." He reached forward and stroked Sabrina's left breast. "Same as you, I imagine."

Sabrina mewled. Tigger leaped onto the couch, hissed at Mackenzie, and jumped into Sabrina's lap. Though her hands were bound, she clutched Tigger fiercely.

"Desiree didn't think once about me," Mackenzie continued. "She didn't consider what an appearance could do for my career. Her heart was ice. That night—"

"The night she died," I inserted.

"I saw her sweet-talking Anton. She flirted. She touched his hand and ran her fingers up his arm. Man, you should have seen him. The dolt was bug-eyed in love." Mackenzie snorted. "J.P. was the same way. Desiree devoured men as easily as if they were road kill. But not me."

"Stop it," Sabrina cried. "Desiree was a good person."

Mackenzie shot a finger at her. "Open your eyes, little sister. She squashed you as if you were a gnat. Day in, day out."

"No."

"Go ahead. Lie to yourself."

Tears welled up in Sabrina's eyes.

"I called Desiree," Mackenzie went on, "and asked her to come to the bar so we could talk. I was giving her a second chance—more than she gave me. When she arrived, she had it out with you and then she caught sight of Anton, so she snubbed me. I knew what I had to do. What I had planned all along. I had to kill her. Seeing you made it that much easier. I had roofies in my pocket."

As I had guessed. "Why would you carry those with you?" I asked.

"I told you. I enjoy sex. I'm always prepared."

"To dominate."

"If that's what it takes." Mackenzie grinned. "Sabrina had problems. Everyone knew it. I slipped her a roofie. She was slurring her words in minutes."

"You stowed her in your van and returned to the bar."

Mackenzie stopped in front of me and planted his fists on his hips. "You're a smart one."

"I do my best."

"Typical Desiree, she forgot all about me. I followed her out."

"And nabbed her in the parking lot. You hurled her into the van."

"She fought, you'll be glad to know. She came at me fast."

"You shoved her into the passenger window, which knocked her out."

"I drove to the beach, carried her to the shore, strangled her, and molded her into one of my beautiful creations."

I could hear him talking to her throughout: *I need you to obey, my friend. Obey, obey, obey.* "Wait, you had sand-sculpting tools. You stole the trowel from my store. You preplanned everything."

Mackenzie leered. "It was a stroke of luck having the

sand-sculpting contest in town. I thought making a mermaid was a nice touch. The woman no man can have. An ice princess, like Desiree. The hook was a stroke of genius, don't you think?"

"About the hook. Where did you get it?"

"Desiree sent Gigi and I to Bait and Switch to do some recon about taking a hike. Turns out, Gigi has an itchy finger. She pinched the hook as well as a few shiny lures."

"You're lying. The clerk that works there said all hooks were accounted for."

"You went looking?" His gaze sharpened. "Clever. But the kid was wrong. Good guy that I am, I slipped into the stockroom and messed up all the hooks to cover for Gigi."

"You stowed two hooks in one box."

"Others had three. Some had none. If you were the clerk, wouldn't you have given up trying to make it right?" He shrugged. "What can I say? I had that job at one time. Doing inventory sucks."

"Big risk."

"The risk was worth the reward. That night—that fateful night—I remembered Gigi had hidden the hook in the base of the stylist kit she left in the Winnebago. Adding the hook to my creation, well, it was an innovative idea, don't you think? I drove back to the trailer with Sabrina, tucked her in for the night, swiped the hook, and returned to the beach. I added the hook and waited beneath a palm tree until I was certain Old Jake had swept up my footprints. The guy was ponderous but a perfectionist, I'll give him that. Now, enough talking." Mackenzie began pacing again. Four steps left, four steps right, back and forth, as if he was trying to make a decision. He halted. "It's time." He fished in his pocket and retrieved a bottle of pills. "You two are going to take a tandem swim, Jenna." He aimed a finger at me. "Fetch a glass of water. Be quick about it."

Was that how he intended to handle us both, by drugging and then drowning us? No way.

Mackenzie resumed pacing. As he passed by, I glimpsed the stack of cookbooks on the coffee table. I dove for them and snatched the top two, a *Cook's Illustrated* and Mark Bittman's hefty hardcover, *How to Cook Everything: The Basics*. I swung at Mackenzie's head. Not an ace in the softball batting department, I connected with his shoulders. He stumbled forward. I flogged him again, attacking his spine, his shoulder, his arm. *Whack, whack, whack*. Beating an old mattress couldn't have sounded duller.

He scrabbled on hands and knees toward the Ching cabinet. He clawed to a stand and got hold of the Lucky Cat. He hurled it at me. My insides clenched as a memory of David presenting me with the statue flashed before me. In the nick of time, I caught the statue—I wasn't so bad as an outfielder. I set it aside, and refocused on Mackenzie, aka Macbeth, the messenger of death.

He leered and headed for the redbrick fireplace. I couldn't let him reach the poker. I snared Chef Anne Burrell's cookbook and hurled it. The book clocked Mackenzie in the kidneys. He pitched forward. His head slammed into the mantle. He slumped to the ground.

Sabrina didn't miss a beat. She lunged from the sofa and threw herself on top of him. "Call the police," she yelled as she pounded him, double-fisted, and uttered curse words I hadn't heard in years.

Chapter 27

CINNAMON PRITCHETT RESPONDED in lickety-split time. She marched in, as crisp as her uniform, her mouth grim, her gaze searing. I was relieved to see that her cranky mother was nowhere in site. On Cinnamon's heels followed paramedics and deputies. Cinnamon ordered them to tend to Mackenzie and mark the crime scene, then she herded Sabrina and me to the kitchen table.

I related the evening's events.

"How did he get on the *Radical Cake Battle* show?" Cinnamon asked.

"He was raised in a small town on the coast of Oregon," Sabrina said. Apparently as Mackenzie drove her to the beach, he had regaled her—his captive audience—with his history. "Baking ran in his family. His parents expected the same career path from him. But he wanted something more than running a two-bit, small-town bakery. He was good with tools, so he auditioned for the show and wowed them with his axe work."

Cinnamon said, "When Desiree reneged, why didn't he seek out another opportunity?"

"Because Desiree promised him stardom. And . . ." Sabrina licked her lips.

I leaped to my feet and filled a glass with water from the tap. I handed the glass to Sabrina. She drank in gulps.

"And . . ." Cinnamon prompted.

"Because he was in love with her. He wanted her approval." Sabrina shook her head. Moisture glistened in her eyes. "If only I had caught on. I hate men. All men. My boyfriend, his wicked friends. Mackenzie." Sabrina ground her teeth. "Poor Desiree. Yes, she was imperious and domineering and she could anger the most patient of people, but she didn't deserve to die. She could be very loving and generous. She gave money to a women's shelter, of all things."

"And not you." Cinnamon drummed her fingers on the table. Didn't she believe Sabrina?

"What do I care? The shelter needs the money more than I do. I can get another job, another boyfriend. I can start over." Sabrina sucked back a sob. "Des . . . can't . . . ever." She slurped down the rest of her water and slammed the glass on the table. "I'm pitiful. I should've seen . . . I should've—"

I petted her shoulder. "You couldn't have prevented this. Mackenzie Baxter was demented."

"I know," she whispered.

I scowled at Cinnamon.

She offered a *just doing her duty* shrug then said, "Read Mackenzie Baxter his rights."

"I'm free to go?" I said, before realizing I had nowhere to go. I was home.

"You're innocent. I already told you that."

"Please alert your mother."

"No need. My mother has no say over anything in this town ever again."

Cinnamon's terse words had to have something to do with the fight I had interrupted earlier when I'd called, but I didn't have the guts to ask details. Had the argument been about me? Did it matter? Another time, another day.

"Jenna," my aunt yelled from outside. "What are all the police cars . . ." Aunt Vera skidded to a halt in the doorway and raised a hand to her chest. "Oh, dear. I knew it. I sensed it."

Chapter 28

A S SABRINA DEPARTED with a deputy, she vowed to inform me when J.P. and she set the burial date for Desiree. She still wanted to take a memorial hike. I promised I would do my best to attend.

The next morning, while sitting on the porch eating my breakfast of toast with Taleggio cheese and jam, the realization hit me that I had stopped enjoying life two years ago. With David gone, I had believed there was nothing left to live for, but I was wrong. I was not yet thirty. I could be happy, right here in Crystal Cove, spending time with family and friends and breathing in the salt air. As I lifted a glass of fresh-squeezed orange juice, I remembered a celebratory date with David at the Fairmont Hotel. We clinked glasses of champagne to commemorate my new job at Taylor & Squibb, and he said: *To your wonderful new life. May it be everything you ever wanted.*

I raised my juice glass higher and said, "To my wonderful *new* life."

After I rinsed my breakfast dishes, I found the courage to call David's mother and ask how she was doing. Fine, she said. She hoped I liked Crystal Cove. David often told her that I might return to my roots. How had he known?

Around 9 A.M., I dressed in the cheeriest outfit I owned and, with Tigger for company, drove to work. Although the Winnebagos had been towed from the parking lot, Pepper Pritchett didn't look very pleased. She paced in front of Beaders of Paradise, arms locked across her chest, and glared at the string of people—more than one hundred—streaming out of The Cookbook Nook.

I exited my VW bug and searched for a route where I could avoid her detection. I didn't want her to spoil my upbeat mood. I stopped when I spied my father hustling along the boardwalk toward Pepper. He said something as he moved near. She scowled and shook a fist. He spoke again. She mouthed a few words. Dad responded. How I wished I could be a fly on one of the nearby columns so I could listen in. Dad reached for her. Pepper backed up and lowered her chin. She scuffed the boardwalk with the toe of her sandal. My father uttered what seemed to be a speech. He reached out, and this time, Pepper didn't resist. He squeezed her arm. She looked up, offered a weak smile, then turned on her heel and marched into her shop. *Too-ra-loo*, as my aunt would say.

I entered The Cookbook Nook, and as I passed the throng of customers, I heard chatter about Aunt Vera having foreseen something terrible happening at my cottage. Had all the people come to have their fortunes read? I spied my aunt at the vintage kitchen table predicting a curly-haired woman's future, but the queue didn't lead to her. The line snaked to the back of the store.

Katie swooped toward me with a platter of mini cinnamon rolls. "Coming through."

I stopped her. "What's going on?"

"Hoo-boy, do we have a surprise. Your pal Rhett invited Chef Tory Fellows—you know, of Liaison fame—to make an appearance."

Liaison, a fabulous San Francisco restaurant, had become the training ground for many celebrated chefs. How did Rhett know such a famous guy?

"He's so handsome," Katie went on. "Look at me. I'm swooning." She freed a hand from the platter and fanned herself. "Can you tell I'm swooning? I'm his biggest admirer."

I couldn't catch a glimpse of the chef through the throng, but I had seen his photograph in the *Liaison: An Intimate Look* cookbook. He was handsome with an engaging smile.

"If I had only known he was coming," Katie gushed. "I would have made sure I had the ingredients for cracked pepper crab soup. Did you know that's what Liaison is known for?"

I didn't.

"How do I look?" Her toque was atilt, but her face was flushed with sheer bliss.

"Radiant."

"Yeah, right, if I lost thirty pounds, shrank six inches, and straightened my hair."

"He's married, isn't he?"

"I don't know. Is he?" Giggling like a schoolgirl, she joined the line of customers.

I scooted around them and caught sight of Chef Tory, who sat behind a table at the rear of the store. A rebellious thatch of blond hair fell across his forehead, making him look like a *bad boy,* the kind mothers warned you about. A stack of *Liaison: An Intimate Look* sat on the floor as well as the tabletop. Rhett, who was standing to the chef's right and looked equally *bad boy* with that rakish grin of his, chatted up the patrons in line.

"Hey, you." Bailey approached and bucked me on the shoulder. "Your aunt told us what went down last night. I'm so proud of you."

I cleared my throat, the fear of last night's encounter not quite quelled. "Where did we get all of the chef's books?" Last I counted, we'd only had a couple in the stockroom.

"Chef Tory brought them with him. We're selling on consignment. Isn't that great? Ca-ching." Bailey drew me into a hug and whispered, "At some point, after the furor dies down, we need to talk."

"What's up? This time, tell me everything. Are you sick, or is my aunt right? It's man trouble."

Bailey cut a quick look at Aunt Vera.

"Blab now," I ordered.

"I thought I was pregnant."

"Preg—" I felt like an idiot. Why hadn't I picked up the signs? She had clutched her stomach; she had passed on an alcoholic beverage; she had grown testy when she mentioned people she had left behind in San Francisco; she had given up a lucrative career to move in with her mother.

"But I'm not, thank heavens." Bailey flicked a shoulder-length earring without conviction. "Not that I don't want to be at some time in the future, but not now. Not from *him*."

"Him who?"

"*H-I-M.*"

I mouthed: *Your boss?*

"What a cliché, right? Married. Twice my age. Ugh. Anyway, the doctor said it was just a false positive caused by stress and—" Bailey gasped. "Shh."

I gazed where she was looking. Her mother, in a turquoise outfit complemented by oversized turquoise jewelry, came into the shop.

"Mom doesn't have a clue," Bailey said.

"You've got to tell her."

"I will." Bailey pinched my arm then moved to Lola and air-kissed her. "Hi, Mom, isn't this place great?"

My father entered seconds behind Lola and made a bee-line for me. His face was etched with concern and something more—despair. "Jenna, what did you think you were doing, battling a madman?"

"Dad, stop. I couldn't have prevented what happened. I didn't lure the killer to my place."

"If you hadn't snooped around—"

"You know why I snooped, and if I hadn't, the case might have gone unsolved."

He started to speak, but I pressed my finger to his lips and said, "I love you, too. Now tell me what you and Pepper were talking about."

"You don't have to worry about her maligning you in the future. All she wanted was a real apology from me. I never gave her that courtesy."

"I'm proud of you."

"And I'm proud of you."

Recipes

From Jenna:

I adore cookies. This recipe (from my pal Desiree) requires that you form the dough into crescent shapes. Whoopee! Now we're talking. I loved Play-Doh as a kid, and I loved to sculpt when I was in college. Making these cookies is all about having fun. Let the child in you party.

Mexican Wedding Cookies

(makes 30–36 cookies)

1 cup unsalted butter, at room temperature
½ cup confectioners' sugar, plus more for coating baked cookies
1 teaspoon vanilla extract
1¾ cups all-purpose flour
1 cup almonds (or pecans), chopped into very small pieces
water, if needed

Preheat the oven to 275 degrees.
Line cookie sheets with parchment paper.

Using an electric mixer, cream the butter and sugar at low speed until it is smooth. Beat in the vanilla.

At low speed, gradually add in the flour.

To chop the nuts, I used my food processer. You can also use a manual food chopper—what I like to call a *whackah-whackah*—or you can also put them in a baggie and smash them with a meat tenderizer hammer.

Mix the nuts into the butter mixture with a spatula.

For each cookie, take out about 1 tablespoon of dough and shape into a crescent. Dust hands with flour, if necessary, as you make more cookies.

Place the cookies onto prepared cookie sheets. Bake for 40 minutes. When the cookies are cool enough to handle, but still warm, roll the cookies in additional confectioners' sugar to coat.

Cool entirely before eating. Store in an airtight container.

From Katie:

Hoo-boy, do I love these cookies. They are not crisp, so don't expect that. They are chewy, moist, and filled with good things. I'm a major fan of dolled-up pancakes. That's what inspired me to make these cookies. Syrup. To shake up the flavor or give the cookies the "Ragtime" feel of fun, I added the chocolate and raisins. You can even add in chopped dates. Enjoy.

Maple Leaf Rag Cookies

à la Katie

(makes 3–4 dozen cookies)

For Cookie:

- ½ cup butter
- ½ cup brown sugar
- 2 eggs
- ¼ cup maple syrup
- ½ cup sour cream
- ¼ cup water
- 3 cups flour (If using gluten-free flour, add ½ teaspoon xanthan gum.)
- ½ teaspoon baking soda
- ½ teaspoon salt
- 1 cup chocolate chips or raisins (or mixture)

For Glaze:

- ½ cup butter
- 2 cups confectioners' sugar
- 2 teaspoons maple syrup
- 2–4 tablespoons milk (I use 2.)

Heat the oven to 375 degrees.

Cream together the butter, sugar, and eggs.

Add in the maple syrup, sour cream, and water, and blend well.

In a separate bowl combine the flour, soda, and salt; then gradually add the dry ingredients to the wet ingredients, stirring until well combined.

Gently stir in the chocolate chips and/or raisins and/or dates.

Drop the dough by rounded tablespoons onto ungreased cookie sheet, leaving about 2 inches between cookies. Press with fingers or the back of a spoon to flatten the dough.

Bake 8–10 minutes, until light brown.

Remove to a cooling rack (or paper towels) and allow cookies to cool completely.

Meanwhile, make the glaze. Heat the butter until it begins to change color (light caramel); then remove from heat and allow to cool completely.

Using a whisk, stir in the confectioners' sugar and maple syrup. Gradually add the milk until the glaze is the desired consistency.

Spread the glaze over the cooled cookies.

Note: If you want to do something fun and wind up with a delicious toffee candy, make the icing all by itself. Same ingredients. Cook on medium heat to a full boil. Stir constantly for 8–10 minutes. It will bubble and froth. Pour the candy onto a sheet of wax paper (laid on top of a cookie tray). Let stand until completely cool. Break into pieces.

From Aunt Vera:

Oh, how I adore making cookies. I love time-intensive cookies, the kind I can sink my hands into. Hands, as you might have figured out, have great meaning to me. They are the symbolic equivalent of power and balance. With your hands, you can make delicious foods as well as bring comfort. These biscotti, which I have chosen to make gluten-free because one of my dearest friends cannot eat wheat, are a wonderful combination of textures and the perfect accompaniment to a good cup of coffee or tea. (I have made these same cookies using regular flour. Just substitute regular flour for the sweet rice flour and tapioca starch. You won't need the xanthan gum, a magical ingredient for gluten-free bakers.)

Gluten-Free Orange Chocolate Biscotti

(makes 30–36 biscotti)

1 cup sweet rice flour
¾ cup tapioca starch
½ teaspoon xanthan gum
¼ teaspoon salt
½ teaspoon baking soda
2 eggs
¾ cup granulated sugar
1 teaspoon vanilla extract
¼ teaspoon orange extract
½ of an orange, grated zest
2 tablespoons fresh orange juice
1 cup semisweet chocolate chips

Preheat the oven to 300 degrees. Put the racks in the upper and lower thirds of the oven.

Note: This recipe takes no time to put together, but the dough takes a long time to bake.

Line a cookie sheet with foil or parchment paper, or you can grease the cookie sheet.

In a small bowl, mix the gluten-free flours (do not tamp down), xanthan gum, salt, and baking soda. Set aside.

In another bowl, mix the eggs, sugar, vanilla, and orange extract. Over the top of the bowl, grate the orange zest. Add the orange juice. Mix in the gluten-free flour mixture. Then stir in the chocolate chips. The mixture will be cookie-dough consistency—gooey.

Scrape the batter, in 2 skinny lines, the full length of the cookie sheet, leaving 3 inches between lines. Use a spatula to clean up the strips. If necessary, rinse the spatula with hot water.

Put the cookie sheet on the lower rack and bake for 15 minutes. Turn the pan front to back and bake another 20 minutes until golden brown. Remove the pan and cool on a rack for 15 minutes. LEAVE THE OVEN ON.

Using a spatula, transfer the baked strips to a cutting board. Using a serrated knife, slice the loaves on a diagonal—about ½-inch wide slices. Place the cookies on their narrow sides to "stand," this time on an unlined cookie sheet, at least ½-inch apart. Bake for 20–25 minutes, until golden brown. If necessary, rotate the pans halfway through the baking process so the cookies are evenly baked.

Cool the biscotti completely before storing. These may be kept in an airtight container for a few weeks. They are fabulous dipped into a cup of coffee.

From Jenna:

*This is the recipe I found in my stash of recipes from
Katie. Oh, yum! It requires seven ingredients but it's
not difficult at all, other than I had to be careful
when I was grating the cheese (knuckles are precious).
When it came to the part about cutting with cookie
cutters, I thought, Yeah, right. I went with Katie's
easy suggestion (see below) and rolled and cut. I don't
need pretty; I need tasty.*

Savory Cheese Cookies

(makes 30–36 cookies)

**4 ounces butter, softened
1 cup flour
1 teaspoon baking powder
½ teaspoon salt
1 tablespoon sugar
1 teaspoon cayenne pepper
1 cup shredded Cheddar cheese (4 ounces), at room
   temperature
1 teaspoon water, if needed**

Preheat the oven to 400 degrees.

Cut the butter into the flour, baking powder, salt, sugar,
and cayenne pepper. Mix in the cheese.

Chill. Roll onto a board using a rolling pin (and a dusting
of extra flour to keep the mixture from sticking).

Cut with cookie cutters. (Note from Katie: To make this
easier, roll out the dough and cut into a checkerboard. This
makes square cookies.)

Place the cookies on an ungreased cookie sheet.

Bake the cookies for 8–9 minutes, until lightly browned.
Serve with jam, if desired. The jam cuts the spiciness.

From Jenna:

*One of Katie's favorite serving tips is to put candies
alongside cookies on a cookie platter. She says the eye
is drawn to the variety of shapes. These little beauties
(another from my friend Desiree's cookbook) are the
easiest things in the world to make. I like Tootsie Rolls,
but I also adore chocolate and peanut butter. Especially
the chunky kind. And when I need a quick pick-me-up,
one will do. Peanut butter has lots of protein, right?
That makes me feel like this is almost a "healthy"
snack. I have to admit that I wasn't so sure about
paraffin. I mean, I've used that to make candles. But
in Desiree's book, she assures the reader that paraffin is
used in all sorts of things, like canning and such. You
sure can't taste it.*

Chocolate Peanut Butter
Crisp Bonbons

à la Desiree

(makes 24–30 candies)

   1 cup peanut butter
   2 cups powdered sugar
   ½ cup butter, softened
   1 teaspoon vanilla
   1 cup chopped Rice Krispies

1 (12-ounce) package dark chocolate chips
2 tablespoons paraffin

Beat together the peanut butter, powdered sugar, butter, vanilla, and Rice Krispies (gluten-free, if needed).

Form into small balls, smaller than walnuts, and place on a tray lined with waxed paper.

Set the tray of balls in the refrigerator while preparing the chocolate chips.

Melt the chocolate and paraffin in the top of a double boiler, or in a saucepan set over another larger saucepan, the bottom pan half-filled with hot water (not boiling).

Remove the balls from the refrigerator. Reshape them so they are smooth and round, which is much easier to do now that they are cold. Dip the bonbons in chocolate mixture. (Super tip: Use 2 forks to handle the balls. This makes them easy to turn when coating. Even I could do it.) Return the bonbons to the waxed paper. Cool completely.

Store in an airtight container.

TURN THE PAGE FOR A PREVIEW OF
DARYL WOOD GERBER'S NEXT
COOKBOOK NOOK MYSTERY . . .

Inherit the Word

COMING SOON FROM BERKLEY PRIME CRIME!

I CLAMBERED DOWN the ladder in the storeroom of The Cookbook Nook, carrying a stack of cookie cookbooks in my arms. My foot hit something soft. I shrieked. Tigger, a kitten that had scampered into my life and won my heart a month ago, yowled. His claws skittered beneath him as he dashed from my path.

"Shh, Tigger. Hush, baby." I had barely touched him with my toe. I knew he wasn't hurt. "C'mere, little guy." I arrived at the floor, knelt down, and spied him hunkering beneath the ladder, staring at me with his wide eyes. "It's okay," I cooed. As I scooped him up, one-armed, and nuzzled his neck, I felt a cool stream of the unknowable course its way up my spine. Tigger was a ginger-striped tabby, not a black cat, so passing beneath a ladder wasn't a bad omen, was it? Why did I suddenly feel like seven years of bad luck was lurking in the shadows?

"Miss Jenna, yoo-hoo," a girl squealed. "Miss Jenna, come quick!"

Fear ticked inside me. We had invited children to The Cookbook Nook for a cookie-decorating event—my Aunt

Vera's idea. She was a master cookie baker herself, with an extensive personal collection of cookie cookbooks. Had one of the children gotten hurt? Was that the dark cloud I'd sensed in the storeroom? I raced into the shop and skidded to a slippery halt in my flip-flops.

"Look at my killer shark." The girl with frothy orange hair was standing beside a tot-height table in the children's corner, brandishing a deep blue, shark-shaped cookie.

Nothing amiss. Kids being kids. No one hurt. *Thank the breezes*, as my mother used to say.

I steadied my racing heart and said, "Cool!" I set the cookbooks on the sales counter, then put Tigger on the floor and gave his bottom a push. Brave feline, he meandered beneath the children's table, probably hoping to score a crumb. "But please, kids, call me Jenna. Not Miss. I'm not a teacher."

The girl's father frowned. Guess he preferred decorum. I wasn't so hot on it. I liked to live fast and loose . . . sort of.

"But you're so tall," the girl said.

I grinned. I wasn't an Amazon, but at five-eight, I was slightly taller than her doughy father. "Teachers can be short, too."

"If you say so."

The first Friday of September was a perfect time in Crystal Cove to invite children to a cookie-decorating class. The weather hovered in the low seventies. Nearly every day by midmorning, the sun shone brightly. And school and homework hadn't taken over the kids' total concentration, quite yet. For the class, in addition to ordering a fresh batch of cookie cookbooks like *The All-American Cookie Book*, *Betty Crocker The Big Book of Cookies*, and *Simply Sensational Cookies*, we had stocked up on fun cookie-decorating sets complete with squeezable icing bottles and interchangeable design tips. Our theme for today's class was creatures of the deep.

"Did you bake the cookies, Jenna?" one of the parents asked.

"Me? What a laugh." I still wasn't adept at making cookie

batter—my limit of ingredients for recipes was a *daring* total of seven—but as an occasional artist, I totally embraced piping icing out of a squeeze bottle.

"Miss Jenna, look at my octopus." A little boy with gigantic freckles wiggled his green, gooey octopus cookie in the air, and then shoved his gruesome creation toward the face of the frothy-haired girl. She squealed.

Aunt Vera, a flamboyant sixty-something and co-owner of The Cookbook Nook, moved to my side, the fabric of her exotic caftan billowing and falling. "Don't you love kids?"

Me? I adored them. Except for the time I did an ad campaign at Taylor & Squibb, my previous employer, for Dipsy Doodles. A few prankster boys squeezed the contents of their glue and glitter pens onto the girls' clothing and—*gag me*—hair. Parents were livid.

"Yoo-hoo, Jenna. Kids?" my aunt repeated.

"Uh, sure. Love 'em." I didn't want any of my own. Not yet. I wasn't quite thirty. And a widow. Timing was everything. I said, "Absolutely. How about you?"

She adjusted the silver bejeweled turban on her head—my aunt would prefer to give tarot card readings than figure out how to market our joint enterprise—and chuckled. "I would have loved to have a dozen. Just like you."

"Aw. I love you, too." My aunt, on my father's side, had doted on me from the day I was born. When I moved back to Crystal Cove to help her open the cookbook shop, she offered me the cottage beside her beach house. I felt blessed to have her in my life, especially with my mother gone.

"While the kiddies finish up," Aunt Vera said, "let's discuss the town's other ventures for this week."

"As far as I know, the mayor has planned a dozen new events for the month of September, including a Frisbee contest, a paddleboarding race, and Movie Night on the Strand." Crystal Cove was a lovely seaside town on the coast of California with beautiful rolling hills to the east and a glorious stretch of ocean running the length of the town to the west. The mayor of our fair city was always on the lookout for events that would lure tourists. "To pay tribute to the events the mayor has fashioned, I've ordered dozens of new cookbooks with beach and/or movie themes."

"Good idea. You've included *The Beach House Cookbook*, I assume?"

"I have." *The Beach House Cookbook* had beautiful photographs of food and the seaside. Cookbooks with enticing pictures, in our business, were guaranteed sales. I still couldn't believe it, but some people bought cookbooks merely to peruse. Prior to my new enterprise, I was a function and use person. If it didn't have a function, I didn't use it. "I've also brought in *At Blanchard's Table: A Trip to the Beach Cookbook*." This particular cookbook included recipes that were as delicious as they were simple. Prosciutto bundles? Balsamic goat cheese? They sounded easy enough that even I could make them. "Also, I ordered *Good Fish: Sustainable Seafood Recipes from the Pacific Coast*." The Seattle-based author of *Good Fish* was a seafood advocate who really educated her readers. I especially loved that she had brought in another knowledgeable source to pair the fish with wine.

"That title's a mouthful."

"Between you, me, and the lamppost," I said, "some titles on cookbooks go on forever."

"They do, but competition is fierce and specificity matters. An unpretentious title like *Good Food* won't light a fire under the audience intended."

My aunt was right. She was always right. She knew cookbooks backward and forward. Me? I was just getting the hang of how popular they were. At my aunt's behest, I had returned to Crystal Cove to run The Cookbook Nook and café because, well, my life in San Francisco, as I'd dreamed it, was over. I needed a new beginning. My aunt needed a marketing whiz.

"I love what you've done in the bay window," Aunt Vera said.

Our store was one of many in Crystal Cove Fisherman's Village. The bay window faced the parking lot and was our first calling card to passersby. In keeping with the town's monthly events, I had set out a seaside–themed display, complete with bright yellow oars, aqua blue Frisbees, and coral and white sand toys. On a table by the decorative kitchen items that we carried, I had set up our movie-themed table, which included the women's fiction books *Chocolat* and *Like Water for Chocolate,* both of which had been made into movies, and a mystery series about a cheese shop, which I heard might become a television show à la *Murder, She Wrote.*

"Jenna." My best friend and new assistant in the store, Bailey Bird—Minnie Mouse in size and Mighty Mouse in energy—hurried into the shop. "Whee. You'll never guess." She gripped my hands and spun me around. The skirt of her silky halter dress fluted around her well-formed calves. Sun streaming in the big plate glass windows highlighted her short copper hair. "I just spoke with the mayor, and she wants us."

"For what?"

"To hold the Grill Fest."

"But Brick's always hosts the Grill Fest." Brick's was a barbecue restaurant about a half mile from Fisherman's Village.

"Brick's is going under. It just declared bankruptcy."

"Oh, no. That's horrible."

"It is, isn't it? Tragic. However, the mayor doesn't want to delay the fest. She's afraid that could hurt the town's economy," Bailey rushed on. "Tourism—"

"Can't afford any setbacks," I finished, quoting the mayor.

"It takes money to run this place, she says. The squeaky wheel gets the biggest piece of the pie."

"Now you're mixing metaphors."

"The mayor said it."

Our mayor, a frizzy bundle of raw energy, was nothing if not Crystal Cove proactive. Without tourists and the taxes they paid, how else could we finance our infrastructure? Only ten thousand people, including part-timers, lived here. Though many residents had incomes well above normal, the town still couldn't manage to maintain the elaborate maze of windy roads, the parks, the aquarium, the city college that specialized in the study of grapes—truly—and The Pier, which was a major go-to spot, complete with a boardwalk, restaurants, stores, and more.

"I suggested we have the fest here," Bailey said, polishing her fingernails on her silky bodice. "I said, 'Jenna will think it's a fabulous idea.' You do, don't you? Think it's a good idea?" She slurped in an excited breath. "We can set up portable cooking stations, like we do for our cooking classes. We can have the kitchen shop down the way provide the tools and grills or sauté pans, depending on a contestant's preference. Think of the traffic. The cross-promotion. The conflict. The press."

Last year's fest had garnered all sorts of media coverage thanks to one contestant—the winner for eight straight years—who had lambasted the runner-up for her grill steak recipe. They had ended up in a spatula fight. Someone had filmed the spectacle, which went viral on *YouTube*.

"And think of all the grilling cookbooks we can stock, like *Simply Grilling: 105 Recipes for Quick and Casual Grilling*," Bailey said, the title tripping easily off her tongue.

I was familiar with this particular cookbook.

"The author not only gives a clear account of the types of grilling and the utensils needed," Bailey continued, "but she also includes a recipe for one of my all-time favorite foods, Buffalo Sliders with Blue Cheese Slaw. And the pictures? Family-style adorable." Bailey had a mind like a steel trap. If I let her, she could probably recite the contents of every book in the shop.

See what I mean about long titles? "What's this year's challenge?" I asked.

"Grilled cheese."

Aunt Vera applauded. "Oh, yum. We'll serve delectable sandwiches at the Nook Café." The café was an adjunct to The Cookbook Nook. During the opening month, we hadn't landed on a name for the café, and then we settled on the obvious. "Folks will flock to us for lunch and dinner.

Ca-ching." My aunt was not interested in money. She had plenty because, years ago, she had invested wisely in the stock market. But she was all about bragging rights. She took great pride in our tasty enterprise.

My friend Bailey on the other hand, was all about dollar signs. "You're right, Vera." Back at Taylor & Squibb, Bailey, who had been in charge of monitoring on-air, magazine, and Internet campaigns, would visit my office daily and give me a rundown of our earnings. Not *our*, as in Taylor & Squibb, but *our*, as in ours. Hers and mine. She knew, down to the penny, what we were earning for our holiday bonuses. She needed to know because most of her monthly paycheck went to clothes.

"Meow!" Tigger raced from beneath the cookie preparation table and leaped onto the counter by the register.

"I didn't do it." The freckle-faced boy threw his hands in the air, which of course meant he had . . . whatever *it* was.

I hurried to the counter and scooped up Tigger, a new wave of anxiety gushing through me. "Shh, fella. You're okay. Why are you so jumpy today?" I checked him out, making sure he didn't have icing in his eyes or ears—he didn't—and breathed a sigh of relief. I frowned at the boy, whose mother was giving him a quiet talking-to. I imagined pulling a cat's tail had been one of his crimes. He nodded to her, but I could see he was holding back giggles.

As I set Tigger on the ground and encouraged him to be brave and mingle with the public again, I heard a jangle.

"Phone's ringing," Bailey said as she rounded the counter and set down her things.

I rummaged through my purse, which I had stowed on a shelf beneath the antique National cash register, and retrieved my cell phone. The readout said: *Whitney.* Wholesome, wondrous Whitney. My sister was brilliant at most things, but being a home business entrepreneur, she was a little dim when it came to knowing the hours other people kept at work. I asked Bailey to mind the shop, then sneaked to the storage room with my cell phone and pressed Send. "Hey, Sis."

"Sit down."

"I can't. We have a kids' soiree going on." Not to mention a café to run and more cookbooks to inventory.

"Jenna Starrett Hart.

Because I had established myself in my previous career as Jenna Hart, I had used my maiden name, even after David and I got married. I decided not to change it. Harris . . . Hart. Too close to mess with.

"Jenna," my sister barked. She rarely barked.

I settled onto the old hardback chair at the desk. "What's up?"

"You know I'm here in Crystal Cove."

"No." If she was checking up on me after my encounter with a murderer last month, I was going to clock her. I didn't need a reminder. I had put the past behind me. And I could clock her. I had six inches on her and a lot more hard-earned muscle, especially since I'd returned to a daily routine of running on the beach.

"Yes. I'm at the Seaside Bakery on The Pier getting the cake for Dad's surprise party tonight. You know it's tonight, right?"

I would if she would clue me in. To anything. Ever. Luckily I didn't have plans.

"Anyway, you will never guess who I am looking at right now."

I groaned. My sister could be such a celebrity hound. "Brad Pitt? George Clooney?" I asked, playing along. Lots of famous people vacationed in Crystal Cove.

"He's got a surfboard. He's tan. And he's dyed his hair, but it's him. It's David."

My breath snagged in my chest. "What?"

"He's not dead, Jenna. David is alive."

"He can't be . . . He isn't . . ." My husband died in a boating accident. Two years ago.

"I'm going to follow him. I'll call you back." The call ended.

The air around me turned to ice. I leaped to my feet and hurried from the stockroom to the sale counter. "Bailey." I clutched my friend's wrists. "He's . . . He's . . ." I couldn't catch my breath.

"Spit it out."

I did. In one quick stream.

"He can't be. Whitney was wrong," Bailey assured me. "She didn't see correctly."

"Whitney . . ." Well-meaning, warped Whitney. I inhaled. "My sister has supersonic vision. She's like a hawk. As a kid, I could never win at hide-and-seek. She always knew where I was."

"She didn't see him. David is—"

"I have to go. I have to find out for sure."

*Greenwich Village coffeehouse manager Clare Cosi
is rolling with a popular new trend,
until someone close to her is driven to kill . . .*

From National Bestselling Author
CLEO COYLE

A Brew to a Kill
A Coffeehouse Mystery

The Village Blend's *Muffin Muse* coffee truck is all the
rage. But a fatal hit-and-run followed by a mysterious
death at a food truck–catered wedding give Clare a clue
that something bitter is brewing.

Then she opens a bag of imported coffee beans and
finds ten pounds of rocks—the kind that will earn you
a twenty-year jail sentence. Is her ex-husband and business partner smuggling Brazilian crack? Is her staff
now in danger?

To clear up this murky brew, Clare must sweet-talk
two federal agents, dupe a drug kingpin, stake out a
Dragon Boat festival, and teach a cocky young under-
cover cop how to pull the perfect espresso—all while
keeping herself and her baristas out of hot water.

Coffee. It can get a girl killed.

Includes coffee cake and muffin recipes!

facebook.com/TheCrimeSceneBooks
penguin.com